D1005048

"Hale's first foray into the realm of fantasy
pleases on many levels, and her voice and characterization
stand out and immediately pull readers into this fantastical
tale…. Fans of Deborah Hale are sure to enjoy
The Wizard's Ward, and I have no doubt
that lovers of fantasy romance will eagerly
accept Ms. Hale into their fold!"
—*Romance Reviews Today*

"In her first crossover foray into fantasy,
romance writer Hale *(Beauty and the Baron)*
nicely blends the two genres in an upbeat, feel-good story."
—*Publishers Weekly*

"Although Hale is renowned for her works of historical
romance, she has succeeded in writing a very readable high
fantasy with powerful romantic undercurrents.
Fast-paced and emotionally riveting, *The Wizard's Ward*
will appeal not only to Hale's throngs of romance followers
but also to fans of Patricia A. McKillip's and Juliet Marillier's
folklore-powered fantasy novels."
—Paul Goat Allen, *Barnes & Noble*

"Another wonderful fantasy has hit the shelf from LUNA.
Deborah Hale has already proven that she can write great
historical stories. Now, she amazes us with her ability
to touch our hearts in the realm of fantasy as well.
The Wizard's Ward is an incredible journey of faith and love."
—*ARomanceReview.com*

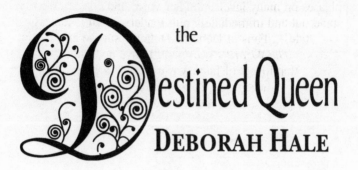

the **Destined Queen**

DEBORAH HALE

www.LUNA-Books.com

LUNA™

First edition August 2005

THE DESTINED QUEEN

ISBN 0-373-80243-9

www.LUNA-Books.com

Printed in U.S.A.

To my mother, Marion MacDonald, with gratitude and love. I never could have finished this book without you.

CAST OF CHARACTERS

Maura Woodbury—a young enchantress

Rath Talward—her outlaw escort

Langbard of Westborne—Maura's wizard guardian

King Elzaban—the Waiting King; legendary warrior of old

Abrielle—Elzaban's beloved; a powerful enchantress who put a spell of immortal sleep upon the Waiting King

Captain Gull—a pirate of the Dusk Coast

Lord Idrygon—member of the Vestan Council of Sages

Delyon—Idrygon's brother; a scholar of the Elderways

Dame Diotta—a Vestan enchantress

Madame Verise—member of the Vestan Council of Sages

Trochard—member of the Vestan Council of Sages

The Oracle of Margyle—a famous Vestan seer, said to be centuries old

Brandel Woodbury—late patriarch of a noble Vestan family

Bran
Jophie
Quilla } children from the island of Galene
Gath

Jule
Lib } Vestan kinswomen of Maura's

Sorsha Swinley—Maura's best friend

Newlyn Swinley—Sorsha's husband; an escaped prisoner from the Blood Moon mines

Bard
Lael } Sorsha and Newlyn's children
Orna

Vaylen—Prince of Tarsha; once betrothed to Maura's mother

Songrid—a Hanish woman

Kez—a Hanish sentry

Vang Spear of Heaven—an outlaw chief

Boyd Tanner—a citizen of Prum

Snake—a young orphan thief befriended by Maura

Master Starbow—a shopkeeper in Windleford

Anulf
Odger
Theto } escaped Blood Moon miners led by Rath
Tobryn

THE KINGDOM OF UMBRIA

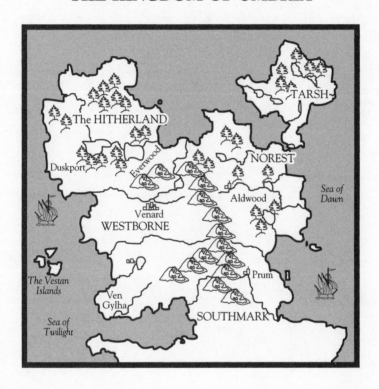

1

Stirring in her sleep, Maura Woodbury felt her lover's strong arms about her. Snuggling deeper into his embrace, she had never felt happier…or more frightened.

Her movement startled Rath Talward awake, his big, hard body gripped with a taut wariness. His right hand groped for a weapon. When it found only the soft flesh of his beloved, the tension bled out of him and he pressed his lips to her forehead.

"Can this be real?" he whispered, tightening his hold on her. "Or did I dream it all?"

Maura gave a husky chuckle. "This place does seem too wonderful to be true, doesn't it?"

For some hours they had slept on the grass in the Secret Glade. Over the tops of the trees, the rising sun now kissed the first blush of dawn into the eastern face of the sky. The luminous midsummer moon was fading, having revealed to the lovers a sweet and terrible marvel.

"For most of my life I've slept on the ground." Rath flexed his lean, muscular frame. "But it never felt like this before."

Maura nodded, her tumble of curls rubbing against his

shoulder in a caress. Since beginning the quest that had led them here, she, too, had passed many a restless night on the cold, hard ground. The thick grass beneath them now felt more comfortable than any proper bed she'd ever slept in. The soft, warm earth yielded to the shapes of their bodies, cradling them in perfect repose.

Not even the faintest chill of night had nipped their bare skin while they slept. Instead, the darkness had wrapped around them, warm yet weightless. No queen and king could have asked for a more luxurious resting place…or trysting place.

That thought sent a muted shiver up Maura's back, making the fine hairs on her nape prickle. Many weeks ago, she had set out on her quest to find and waken the Waiting King—a legendary warrior destined to liberate her people…and be her husband. The murder of her wizard guardian had forced her to rely on Rath for protection.

At first she had been as suspicious of the ruthless outlaw as he was of her modest magical powers. But each day of their journey, each new challenge or peril overcome, had forged a stronger bond of trust and respect between them. And fueled their forbidden desire for one another.

"Are you cold, love?" Rath pressed his cheek to the crown of Maura's head and passed his large, warm hand down her arm to rest over her hip. "Shall I pull my cloak over us?"

Maura shook her head, wishing it had been nothing more than a cool breeze that made her shiver. "Just hold me closer."

"I'm not sure I can without hurting you."

"You did last night." Maura slid her hand down to graze his thigh. "Though you warned me it might hurt, it brought me a great deal of pleasure."

They had entered the Secret Glade at sunset, resolved to rouse the Waiting King, even though it would doom their unspoken love. Instead, the kind moon had revealed that Rath *was* the Waiting King, whose true nobility Maura had wakened during their journey. In a daze of delight, they had lost no time consummating their love.

Now Maura wondered if part of their haste had not been a bid to evade a host of troubling questions about their future. It had worked, though, and worked well. As doubts threatened to ambush her again, she sought assurance and happiness, however fleeting, in the one place she knew she would always find it.

"Again?" Rath's dusky eyes shimmered with desire. "So soon?"

She wriggled against him, lofting a teasing glance through her lashes. "Too soon for you, is it?"

Rath threw back his head and his whole powerful body quaked with laughter. "If you cannot feel the truth of that, with all your wanton squirming, then you are not half as clever as I gave you credit for!"

So they made love again, of a different kind than they had the night before. This time the soft glow of daybreak let them see one another as they touched and kissed and explored. The hushed, earnest endearments of the night gave way to lusty banter. Soon their love play took fire and consumed them both.

In the drowsy warmth that followed, Maura's mind wandered, then shrank from what it encountered. She could not stifle an anxious sigh.

"I do not know," Rath murmured his answer to the question she had dreaded asking aloud—*"What do we do now?"*

She had come to love him with all her heart and she could not have asked for a more precious gift than this sign that destiny had meant them for one another. Yet for all he had proven himself clever and brave and resourceful...even grudgingly compassionate, Rath Talward was not the superhuman warrior she had expected the Waiting King to be. He had no powerful magical weapons with which to fight the Han. No enchanted army to oust those cruel conquerors from the shores of Umbria.

"Where do we even begin?" Maura whispered, scarcely aware she was giving voice to her thoughts. "You liberated one of those horrible mines, which was an amazing feat for a single man and his prisoner comrades. But to free the whole kingdom..."

"We had help, don't forget." Gratitude for that aid and admiration for her courage warmed Rath's words. Then his arms tightened around her once again, and his voice took on a harsh edge. "And you barely escaped with your life."

How Maura wished she *could* forget. Forget the seductive poison with which the death-mage had enticed her. Forget the suffocating darkness into which she'd descended after defying him. One victory had not tempered her fear of the Echtroi, and their death magic.

With gentle restraint, Rath disengaged himself from her embrace and sat up. He nodded toward the giant wooden font that stood in the middle of the glade. "Are you certain of what you thought you saw in there last night?"

Gathering up his discarded clothing, he began to dress.

With his arms no longer about her, Maura felt truly naked for the first time since she'd woken. "As certain as I have been about anything in this whole baffling business."

She plucked up her shift from the grass and pulled it over her head. "And yet, now that I think back on last night, it *all* seems like a dream."

"Perhaps that's what it was." Rath reached for her hand. "A dream, a trick of the moonlight."

How much easier her life would be if she could believe that!

"I am no king." With his other hand, Rath pointed to the pale scars that laced the tanned flesh of his body. "Though I once bore his high-flown name, I did not reign over Umbria a thousand years ago. I did not lie in an enchanted sleep after I took my death blow. I did not do any of the brave deeds you told me of King Elzaban. I am just an ignorant outlaw who has done a great many things he is not proud of to keep himself alive."

When he tried to let go of Maura's hand, she clung to it. "You have also done a great many things you should be proud of to keep others alive, or help them in some way."

Rath's full brow creased into a scowl that could not conceal the flicker of satisfaction in his deep-set dark eyes. "And thought myself a daft fool for doing them. I cannot pretend it comes natural to me looking out for other folks."

"No one could have done better looking out for me these past weeks." Maura's gaze ranged over his rugged features as she relished the freedom to indulge in such loving looks.

Rath's mock scowl deepened, but the twinkle in his eyes glinted brighter. "You did not make it easy—always trying to help everyone who crossed your path, no matter how much trouble it might land you in."

He brushed his knuckles against her chin. "I would defend you to my last drop of blood. But to look out for the welfare of a whole kingdom, and one in such deep trouble, it is beyond me."

Scooping up his shirt from the grass, Rath pulled it on.

"I know how you feel," said Maura.

When he cast her a dubious glance, she insisted, "I do! The day Langbard told me it was my destiny to seek out the Waiting King, I could not believe it—did not want to believe it. How could a simple country girl who'd never stepped five miles from home search the breadth of the kingdom to find…a legend?"

As Rath donned his vest of black padded leather, he pulled a wry face, perhaps at the thought of himself as a "legend."

"I did it, just the same." A sweeping motion of Maura's arm took in the whole enchanted glade, ringed with slender white-bark trees, straight and regular as the columns of any palace. "I reached here in time for the full moon of Solsticetide, in spite of a good many obstacles, too."

"Obstacles?" Rath gave a snort of laughter as he shoved his feet into his boots. "I would call Vang Spear of Heaven, the lank-wolves in the Waste, Raynor's Rift and all the rest more than *obstacles.*"

Just thinking back on them made Maura shudder. She pulled on her gown, but no amount of clothing could warm her against the chill of fear. "Whatever you call them, if I'd had any notion such dangers awaited me on my quest, I would have hidden under my bed and never come out again. But I have learned to trust in the Giver's providence. And I have come to believe in my destiny."

"I don't want a destiny!" Rath leaped to his feet. "Not this one, at any rate!"

Maura shrank back. It seemed like a long time since Rath had spoken to her in such a hostile tone. Back then, she'd scarcely cared, for she had feared him almost as much as any of the unknown dangers she'd faced.

As quickly as he'd lashed out, Rath repented and gathered her into his arms, "Your pardon! I am not angry with you, I swear. Last night, I was the happiest fellow in the world to find that I need not yield you to another man. I could think of nothing beyond that. This morning…"

"I know." Maura passed her hand over his shaggy mane of tawny brown hair in a reassuring caress, as she might have done to a troubled child.

This morning Rath had woken to discover the vast bride price he must pay to claim her. Did he regret having given in last night to their long-suppressed desire? She could hardly blame him if he did.

"Poor lass!" Rath held her close, still not trusting his right to do it. "You left behind everything you ever knew or cared for to travel all this way, facing dangers that would make a hardened outlaw flinch. All to find the mighty hero who would deliver your people. Look what you found instead."

Him. A man who, until a few days ago, had despised the whole legend of the Waiting King. A man who'd just begun to have faith in the Giver. A man who had only lately come to care for anyone or anything beyond his own survival. She must wonder if the Giver had played some kind of cruel trick on her. If only he could be certain she had given herself to him, body and heart, because of who he was…not what he was destined to become.

"Look what I found!" Maura tilted her head to gaze at him with her luminous green eyes and perhaps to invite his kiss. "That the man I have come to love and admire was meant to be my partner in the greatest adventure of Umbrian history."

The fond tone of her voice and the hopeful springtime glow in her eyes might convince Rath, if he let them. But the life he'd lived had cultivated a bone-deep wariness of anything that seemed too good—like the possibility of happiness with Maura. With a great effort, he willed himself to put those doubts aside, and to kiss her the way he'd so often longed to during their journey.

A few moments later, the flutter of wings and an insistent squawk stirred them from their kiss.

Rath glanced back to see a large brown and white bird perched on the lip of the carved wooden font into which he and Maura had gazed last night.

"Go find your own nestmate, noisy one!" he called. "Leave us to kiss in peace."

But when his lips sought Maura's again, she squirmed out of his embrace and moved toward the font. "This is a messenger bird. It looks just like the one that brought Langbard word it was time for me to begin my quest."

"What word?" He hung back as she approached the bird with steady, deliberate steps so as not to frighten it. "From where?"

"The Vestan Islands, Langbard said." Maura brought her hand to rest upon the bird's back in a touch that might have been meant to reassure it, or to grab the creature if it tried to fly away. "He told me scholars there had studied the writings of the Elderways and reckoned the time was right."

The bird seemed accustomed to being handled by people, for it made no effort to fly away. Not even when Maura peeled a strip of parchment from around its leg.

Rath's curiosity battled his apprehension and won…but just

barely. He moved toward Maura, peering over her shoulder. "What does this message say?"

She unrolled the slender strip of parchment. An anxious frown creased her features as she deciphered the words written there. "It says, 'Come at once.'"

"Come?" Rath stared hard at the message, as if willing the strange letters to have some meaning different than the one Maura had gleaned. "Come where? And how?"

"To the Vestan Islands, I suppose. And there's more. It says, 'Captain Gull of Duskport will convey you.'"

"Duskport." Rath seized on the one part he understood. "I've been there. It's a fishing town on the Dusk Coast. A rough place."

Perhaps satisfied that it had fulfilled its task, the bird gave another raucous cry. Then it launched itself from the lip of the font, its wings moving in strong, rapid strokes to bear it skyward. As Rath and Maura watched, it circled the glade, then headed off in the opposite direction from the rising sun.

Maura glanced down at the message again, then lifted her gaze to meet Rath's with a look of apology. "I reckon this answers our question, doesn't it?"

"What question?" asked Rath, his tone gruffer than he meant it to sound.

"The one you read in my thoughts when we woke. The one about what we should do next."

"Oh, that." The question he'd been eager to delay answering for as long as possible. "I reckon so. Does the message say anything else? Anything to prove it was meant for you and me?"

Maura shook her head. "Who else could it be meant for?"

"How should I know?" Rath half wished some hunter's arrow had struck down that cursed bird before it reached here. "Not a fancy scholar of the Elderways, am I—living free and easy on their safe island paradise?"

The few tales he'd heard of the Vestan Islands had long made him burn with resentment. Why had *they* never come to Umbria's aid during the long, bleak years the mainland had suffered under Hanish tyranny?

"Rath…"

"Does it not gall you that they summon us like this? Taking for granted you'll have reached here and done what needed doing—as if it was some dance through a garden, rather than a near-impossible trek that might have killed you a dozen times over?"

"I'm sure they did not mean it to sound that way." Maura entreated him with her soft, green gaze that might have moved the heart of a death mage…if such creatures had hearts.

There'd been times Rath wished he had no heart. The cursed thing was a weakness he could ill afford.

"I know it sounded rather…curt." Maura held out the strip of parchment to him. "There is hardly room to write a long, courteous letter on something small enough to wrap around a bird's leg."

Rath gave a grunt of grudging agreement. For all he loved Maura, he hated it when she was right.

"I doubt the Vestan wizards take it for granted I have accomplished my task. This message is a sign of their faith that I would prevail. Now they will be waiting and watching for us to come, perhaps fearing we will not."

Rath pointed skyward, to where the messenger bird had disappeared from sight. "When that fellow returns with his leg band removed, it should give them reason to hope."

"True." Maura reached for his hand with the air of a weary laborer once again shouldering a burden from which she had hoped to rest. "All the more reason we must not tarry."

"Why should we not?" Rath demanded. "You were all but dead a few days ago, and I am not long out of the mines. Who has the right to deny us a little well-earned rest and a chance for some quiet time together? Umbria has waited a thousand years for its Waiting King. Can it not wait a few days more?"

An even more defiant notion followed on the heels of that

one. "Why must we do this at all, Maura? Any half-wit would know better than to think the two of us can liberate an entire kingdom. If those oracles and wizards on the islands have done nothing about it in all these years, who are they to lay an impossible burden upon *our* shoulders. Slag them all, I say!"

When he would not let her lead him away quietly to do the wizards' bidding, like some tame dog, Maura headed off on her own. "You do not mean that."

"I do mean it." Rath had little choice but to follow her. "What makes you think I don't?"

Maura whirled about to face him. That soft green gaze had turned as hard and fierce as glittering poison gems. Rath had not seen that look since the day he'd taunted her into crossing Raynor's Rift. He had missed it—daft as that seemed.

"Where is the man who brought me to this glade last night?" She peered around Rath, pretending to look for someone else. "The man who offered himself as my champion? The man who promised to go wherever I bid him and do anything in my service?"

Rath growled. The only thing he hated worse than Maura being right was when she managed to turn his own words back against him. "That was different!"

"How? Was your pledge of homage just empty talk?" Beneath the scornful challenge of her questions, Rath heard a bitter edge of disappointment.

"I did mean it—every word!" Could he put into words all that had changed between then and now, in a way that would make sense to himself, let alone her? "Like you, I expected to find some powerful warrior king of legend. I would gladly have served him, and you, playing my small part in the certain success of his battle against the Han."

A sigh welled up from the depths of his bowels. "But there is no magical warrior king. There is only me and you. Whether something went amiss, or this whole Waiting King business is only an ancient joke, there is no way I can do what people expect of King Elzaban."

The sharp angle of Maura's brows slackened and a flicker of doubt muted the righteous anger of her gaze. Perhaps she was remembering the dread of certain failure with which she'd first faced her own impossible quest.

Rath had done enough dirty fighting in his life to know he must strike hard while her resolve was weakened.

"What good will our deaths do anyone? A failed uprising will only make the Han clamp down harder and serve to discourage more able rebels who might come after us."

Maura caught her full lower lip between her teeth and a troubled look crept into her eyes, like an ominous shadow. Rath knew how she would shrink from the prospect of bringing harm to others. Part of him felt ashamed to exploit such a noble vulnerability, but he told himself it was for her own good.

If it were only his life at stake, he might have risked it. But he had felt the helpless, gnawing torment of seeing Maura in peril. It weakened him in a way he could not abide. Let the rest of Umbria perish—he must keep her safe at any cost.

"We will do a sight more good going back to Windleford, once all this fuss has settled down." His tone mellowed as he spoke of his modest dreams. "Rebuild Langbard's cottage, make a peaceful living, raise a family in the Elderways."

That kind of life would be enough of a challenge for a man who'd lived as he had, but Rath felt confident he could succeed, with Maura's love and support to anchor him.

A smile tugged at the corner of his mouth as he pictured the two of them sitting at a cozy supper table surrounded by several ruddy-haired, merry-eyed younglings.

He could tell Maura was imagining it, too, for a brooding look softened her features and her arms angled, as if cradling a phantom child. He prepared to take her in his arms again and kiss away any dangerous ideas of Vestan wizards or Waiting Kings.

But before he could enfold her, a tremor vibrated through Maura's slender body. Her eyes misted with tears, even as they flashed with indignant fury.

"Damn you, Rath Talward!" she cried, shattering his fragile fancy of a safe, peaceful future. "Damn you!"

Then she turned and fled from the pristine enchantment of the Secret Glade into the tangled peril of the ancient forest that surrounded it.

There was nothing Rath could do but mutter a curse…and go after her.

As she fled toward the soothing sound of the waterfall they had passed the previous night on their search for the Secret Glade, Maura heard the pounding of Rath's footfall behind her.

Contrary urges battled within her. A powerful one tempted her back to the seductive haven of his arms, and his dreams for their future. Another, less strong but all the more desperate, made her run from him as if a pack of Hanish hounds were baying for her blood.

"Maura, stop!" he gasped, catching her by the full sleeve of her tunic. "How can we…decide anything…if you will not…stay and listen to me?"

"I dare not listen!" She twisted the cloth out of his grip and ran on.

It would be as foolhardy as stopping to face a Hanish warrior in armed combat. Rath had shown he was armed with potent weapons of persuasion—weapons she had forged for him.

"I mean you no harm!" His breathless words held a plaintive plea. One she was powerless to ignore.

"That is what—" she stumbled to a halt, wilting onto a fallen tree trunk "—makes you so…dangerous."

"Me, dangerous to you?" Rath dropped to the ground at her feet, his chest heaving beneath his padded leather vest. "What daft talk is that?"

He reached for her hand, raising it to graze the backs of her fingers against his stubbled cheek. "I want nothing more in the world than to keep you safe."

She had no doubt of that. He had proven it again and again on their journey. Should she not feel the same way about him?

"Dangerous," she repeated, "because you tempt me worse than that Echtroi with his nightmare wand."

During the few days they'd spent recovering their strength for the last leg of their journey, she and Rath had avoided speaking of their terrifying battles with the death mage.

"He made the mistake of offering me the last thing in the world I desire—power. But you lure me with visions of something I want with all my heart—peace."

Rath clasped her hand tighter. "If it is what you want, why should you not have it, love? After all you have done and all you have risked, you deserve every scrap of peace and happiness I can wrest from life for you!"

"But don't you see, Rath, my task is only half done. What does anything I have ventured thus far matter if I cannot persuade the Waiting King to fight for the freedom of his people? I want what you offer me, so badly my bones ache for it and my heart feels like it will tear itself in two. But I know it is an illusion."

"You doubt I could protect you and provide for you?"

Maura shook her head. "I believe you could give me everything you promise. But how could I breathe fresh air and savor the sunshine on my face when I know there are men forced to labor in the stifling darkness of the mines, breathing that foul slag? How could I watch my children play in the yard or eat their supper, knowing hordes of young beggars run the countryside, one step ahead of the Hanish soldiers, with no one to care for them?"

Rath flinched from the harsh truth—something Maura had never seen him do before. "You are a dreamer if you think all Umbria's problems will be solved by ousting the Han from our shores!"

"Dreamer? Is that another way of saying *fool*?" Perhaps she was both, for believing she would find a long-dead hero sleeping in this forest, waiting to be wakened by her.

"No!" Rath dragged a hand down his face. "I told you of my dreams. They may not be as grand and noble as yours, but they are good and they are *possible*."

His arguments were sensible and sincere…and too convincing by half! Part of her wanted to forget about the mine slaves, the bedgirls and slaggies and think only of herself and her beloved. But another part clung to the beliefs in which her wise guardian Langbard had raised her. Somehow, it felt as if she was fighting for her very soul…and for Rath's.

"Can you be so certain my dreams are not?" Her voice fell to a whisper. "That night at the inn in Prum, when I first told you of my quest to find the Secret Glade and the Waiting King, you thought *that* would be impossible. Yet here we are."

Rath made a sudden movement toward her, his mouth opened, as if pouncing to contradict her. But his words seemed to stick in his throat. He looked around at the swaths of lacy fern, the ancient, towering trees and the misty beauty of the waterfall, as though seeing it all for the first time.

"Yet here we are," he murmured.

"How many times did my quest appear doomed, only to be saved at the last moment? Little by little I began to believe this was my destiny." She held out her hand to him. "*Our* destiny. If we have faith in it, I trust that whatever we risk to fulfill it may be difficult, but not impossible. I must answer this summons. Will you go with me?"

Rath stared at her hand for a long, anxious moment. What would she do, Maura wondered, if he refused? Did she truly have the resolve to go on without him?

At last a sigh shuddered through his powerful frame and he reached for her hand with a shrug of surrender. "Stubborn wench. If I could not let you go back in Prum, do you reckon I can now?"

The force of her relief sapped every ounce of strength from Maura's body. She pitched toward Rath, throwing her arms around his neck. "It will be well, *aira*." She used the ancient Umbrian word for dearest or beloved. "I know it will! Think how we dreaded coming here last night and the parting it would mean for us. Instead, the Giver blessed our union."

At length Rath drew back. "If the Giver had offered me a choice last night, between following the Waiting King to certain victory with you lost to me as his queen, or risking almost certain defeat with you by my side—this would have been my choice. Do not expect me always to behave in noble ways, just because you saw a crown of stars on my head. I am still an outlaw at heart, whose first instinct is to save his own hide and fill his own belly."

She would hear no ill of him, not even from his own lips. "Even when you were an outlaw, there was more of a king in your heart than you ever guessed, Rath Talward. The first time I saw you, you were rallying others to escape a Hanish ambush. If they had trusted in you and held together, instead of scattering…"

Rath leaped to his feet, brushing away some bits of bracken that clung to his breeches. "Let us go, before my doubts get the better of me. Perhaps if we travel fast enough, we may outstrip them."

Before he had a change of heart—or she did—Maura rose and took his arm to begin their new journey. She only hoped they would not be rushing into an ambush of fate.

As Rath and Maura picked their way down the narrow stone step beside the waterfall, he strove to quench the memory her words had kindled in his mind. Of that day in Betchwood when he had failed to keep his outlaw band together long enough to gain the relative safety of the forest.

He told himself he had done all he could. Those men had each thought and acted for themselves. When a few had taken fright and bolted, splintering the strength of their cluster, it had doomed the rest. That was why he preferred to act alone. He could always count on himself.

But one man alone could not hope to defeat the Hanish army that occupied Umbria, any more than a single drop of rain could quench a wildfire.

Spying a hollowed stone filled with water at the base of the rock staircase, he asked Maura, "May we stop long enough for a drink, at least?"

She nodded, then stooped and gathered the clear water into her cupped palms. "A wise outlaw once taught me I should always eat, drink and rest when I have the chance. Otherwise I might find myself hungry, thirsty and tired at a time when I dare not stop."

In spite of all the worries that weighed on him, Rath could feel an impudent grin rippling across his lips. "If you want good advice about staying alive, ask an outlaw."

A musical chuckle bubbled from the depths of Maura's throat, in perfect harmony with the splash of the waterfall. "So I shall, outlaw."

As she sipped the water from her hands, Rath bent to drink.

He had never tasted anything like this! If Maura's life magic had a flavor, it would taste just so—clean and wholesome, with a wild, vital tang that quenched more than thirst. For a moment at least, it seemed to ease his foreboding and self-doubt, nourishing fragile seedlings of hope and confidence.

"This is better than ale!" He drank until he could hold no more, then he filled his drink skin and bid Maura do likewise.

Then he jerked his thumb toward the waterfall and the pool at its base. "Do you reckon we have time for a washup before we head off to Duskport?"

"The message said 'Come at once,'" Maura reminded him with an air of apology. "Besides, I fear the longer we tarry here, the harder it will be to make ourselves go. Who knows but we may already have been here longer than we think. Did you not tell me the local folk claim time runs slow in Everwood, and what feels like only a few hours may be months or years in the outside world?"

"Aye." Rath forced himself to turn his back on the inviting pool and walk in the direction of a giant hitherpine some distance away. "I always reckoned such tales were only fanciful nonsense. Now that I have been here, I am not so sure."

"A pity it could not have been the other way around." Maura hurried to catch up with him. "Then we might have dallied here a long while with only an hour or two passing in the outside world."

"That would have been fine indeed." Rath reached for her hand.

Together, they followed the trail of six tall hitherpines until it brought them to the path they had traveled the night before. Now and then, Maura paused long enough to gather a sample of flowers or leaves from some unusual plant they passed.

"Perhaps one of the Vestan wizards can tell me what magical or healing properties these may possess." She tucked a cluster of tiny, red, bell-shaped flowerlets into one of the many pockets in the sash she wore over her tunic.

Rath also wondered what those innocent-looking little blossoms might do—make his mouth lock shut or knock him into a dead swoon? Since meeting Maura, he had learned the difference between the gentle vitcraft she practiced, using plant and animal matter, and the lethal mortcraft wielded by the Echtroi with their wands of metal and gemstones. Though he had come to respect the capricious power of her life-magic, he still had trouble trusting it.

When he spotted a familiar-looking boulder, draped with moss, Rath beckoned Maura off the path, though part of him wondered where it might lead them if they continued to follow it.

"Where next?" asked Maura.

"A brook, wasn't it?" Rath glanced around, his ears pricked for the sound of flowing water. "Why don't you check the map, just to make certain."

"I thought you had it."

Rath shook his head. The last time he recalled seeing it was yesterday night, after they'd climbed the rock stair beside the waterfall. The appearance of the massive goldenwolf who'd led them on the final leg of their journey had driven all thought of the map from his mind.

Maura patted the pouches of her sash, then checked the hidden pocket in the hem of her skirt. "We must have left it back in the Secret Glade."

Rath shrugged. "That could be for the best. I reckon either of us could remember how to find the place again in need. But I would not want that map falling into the wrong hands."

Not that the Han would find anything of value there. But the thought of them invading Umbria's last sanctum set his blood afire and made his sword hand itch.

"True enough," said Maura. "And you were right about the brook. I hear it over that way."

The brook led them back to a small glade, just inside the bounds of Everwood, where they had left their horses the previous evening. So much had changed since then, it seemed much longer to Rath since he and Maura had entered the ancient forest.

"Our mounts are still here." He gave his an affectionate pat on the rump. "And their manes are no more gray than when we left them. I take that as a good sign Everwood has not bewitched our time here."

"Unless the horses were caught in the spell, too." Maura chuckled to show she was only joking, then quickly turned sober again. "I *hope* our time is not out of joint. I would not want the friends who helped us get here to have waited in vain for our return."

Rath nodded, remembering the men he had led in the miners' revolt, the struggling farmer's family from the south and the beggar boy who had reminded him of his younger self. What would they think if they knew he was the Waiting King?

With his mind less than half on his task, he retrieved some food from their saddle pouches. "I reckon we have enough to get us as far as Duskport, if we are careful. I only hope this Captain Gull will not want big pay for taking us to the Islands."

He had heard of smugglers who kept open tenuous ties between the tiny part of Umbria that was still free, and the rest— whispered tales of the lavish ransom they charged to ferry human cargo. Many of whom were rumored never to reach the destination for which they'd paid so dearly. Rath did not fancy putting his and Maura's fate into the hands of such men.

They wasted no time consuming their bread and cheese in thoughtful silence. Now that Maura had persuaded Rath to accept his destiny, she did not want to linger in Everwood for fear he might change his mind...or she might. After washing their breakfast down with swigs of delicious water from the falls, Rath helped Maura onto her mount and they set off for the coast.

Nothing about the countryside beyond the borders of Everwood gave a clue as to how much time had passed in the rest of the world while they had sojourned in the enchanted forest. It was clearly still midsummer, though of the same year Maura could not tell. Yet some vague stirring in her heart told her this was still their own time.

Whenever she glanced at Rath, he appeared to be lost in thought. Though she knew two horses would bear them more swiftly and easily than one, she found herself yearning to ride pillion behind him, as she had through the Long Vale—telling him legends from Umbria's past, sometimes falling asleep with her hands clasped tight to his belt and her head resting against his back.

The sun was high in the sky by the time they came upon a narrow river.

"If we follow this, it will lead us to Duskport." Rath slowed his mount. "Let us stop for a bit to rest the horses."

When he helped her dismount, Maura pressed herself close against him as she slid off the horse's back. And even when she had firm ground beneath her feet, she did not loosen her arms from around his neck. Rath accepted the invitation of her lips as she raised her face to his, but he broke from their kiss far too quickly to suit her.

"This is not Everwood." His answer to her unspoken question trailed off in a tone of regret. "We cannot afford to be caught off guard by the Han or whoever else might be lurking."

Maura did her best to hide her disappointment. This protective vigilance of Rath's was a practical token of his love for her.

"May I hold your hand, at least?" She tried to tease a smile out of him. "And stand close to you? Or will that interfere with your efforts to keep watch?"

The tense furrow of his brow eased. He raised his hand, then let the back of it slide down over her hair. "Both will distract me worse than I can afford, but I will do my best to bear it."

Maura laughed. "You favor me with your tolerance."

"So I do." Rath feigned a stern look, but the flesh of one cheek twitched from the effort to maintain it. "Do not impose upon it more than you can help."

"How far is Duskport from here?" Maura wedged herself into the cleft under Rath's arm so he had no choice but to drape it around her shoulder.

He stared off downriver. "It has been a long while since I last made this journey. After Ganny died, I was fool enough to reckon I might make an honest living crewing on a fishing boat."

"And?" Maura scarcely needed to ask. If he had succeeded in finding honest work after the death of his foster mother all those years ago, she would never have encountered him that day in Betchwood, fleeing a Hanish ambush with his outlaw band.

Rath's lips curled in a sneer at his own childish stupidity. "I was lucky to escape the place with my throat and a few other parts of me unslashed. I know the Han spread many false rumors to frighten ordinary folk of wizards, outlaws and smugglers, but I believe the one about Duskport fishermen using human flesh for bait. I swore I would never go back again."

Maura shuddered. It was no use saying she wished Rath had told her all this before she'd urged him to take her to Duskport. She would not have let it stand in her way...at least she *should* not.

"Then again," murmured Rath, tilting his head to rest against hers, "I've done a good many things I never thought

I'd do before I met you, enchantress. Are you sure you haven't bewitched me?"

"If I had, it would only be a fair exchange for you stealing my heart, outlaw! Now, are you going to tell me how far it is to Duskport? A day's ride? A week's?"

"If we can keep up the speed we have this morning I reckon we should reach the coast in two or three days."

As it turned out, their ride to Duskport took every hour of three days, because Rath refused to risk the least chance of them meeting up with Hanish patrols in open country.

"How can your hundredflower spell make us blend in with the crowd when there's not another Umbrian around for miles?" he demanded, leading her in a wide loop to avoid a ford he guessed might be guarded.

They passed a few scattered farms and two small villages, both of which Rath insisted upon giving a wide berth. "It is warm enough to sleep out of doors and we have supplies to last us until we reach the coast. I'd rather not draw any more attention to ourselves than we have to. Besides, if anybody nasty comes following our trail, I'd just as soon the folk around here have nothing to tell them."

Was that all? Maura wondered. Or did Rath not want anyone else guessing who they might be and raising hopes he feared he could not fulfill?

"Well, there it is," he said at last as they crested a bit of rising ground.

"There is what?" Maura peered down the far slope toward a thick bank of dark fog. If she squinted hard enough, she fancied she could make out a cluster of rooftops rising from the mist.

"Duskport." Rath pointed in the direction of her rooftops. "The rest of the year, it is a good deal warmer than most towns this far north. But in summer, that gray fish soup of a fog rolls in. Haven't you heard the saying, 'Better a winter in Bagno than a summer in Duskport'?"

"Cold, is it?"

"Aye." Rath gave his horse a little nudge forward, and they headed down into the fog. "The kind that settles right into your bones after a while. The smugglers and cutpurses like it well enough, though, for it hides their crimes…or hides *them* if they get caught. Whatever you do, stick close to me, and maybe pull a wee bit of something from that sash of yours to have handy in case of trouble."

Swallowing a lump that rose in her throat, Maura edged her horse as close to Rath's as she dared without risk of their hooves getting tangled and pitching both riders to the ground. After weighing the merits of a few defensive magical items she carried in her sash, she extracted a generous pinch of madfern and cradled it in her clenched fist.

Bless the *twarith* of Westborne who had refilled the empty pockets of her sash! A pity they'd had no cuddybird feathers. Where she and Rath were headed, it might be very useful to be able to disappear at the first sign of trouble. As it was, they'd have to make do with confusing any enemies they encountered. Fortunately, it was a good strong spell if the madfern was fresh—capable of befuddling quite a large crowd.

Once they reached the edge of town, Rath signaled Maura to slide down from their saddles and lead the horses. "We'll draw less notice that way. Besides, most of the streets are narrow and crooked—easier to get about on foot."

They met only one Hanish patrol—three soldiers and a hound, whose gazes roved warily, as if expecting an ambush at any moment from any direction. For all their heightened caution, the soldiers took no notice of Rath and Maura thanks to the hundredflower spell she had cast on them both before they'd entered town. The hound seemed aware of them, though, straining in their direction on the end of its short chain, a menacing growl rumbling in its throat.

Once the patrol passed without challenging them, Maura breathed easier—though not for long. She and Rath spent the next little while approaching some of Duskport's less threatening citizens. To each, Maura murmured a phrase in Old Umbrian that followers of the Giver might understand and respond to.

But the people she spoke to only gave her puzzled, frightened looks before hurrying on their way.

"There's no help for it," Rath muttered at last. "We'll have to leave the horses at the stable we passed on the way in to town. It looked halfway respectable—like they might not sell the beasts off to somebody else before we're all the way out the door."

So they tracked back to the stable, almost getting lost in the cold fog. When they asked to leave the horses with him, the proprietor gave them a suspicious look.

Suspicion changed to something else when Rath asked him, "Is there an eating and drinking place handy where the fisherfolk gather?" He lowered his voice and glanced behind him. "One where the patrols don't visit too often?"

The stable owner looked around, too, before answering. "You mean the Monkey, down on Wharf Row? You'll find plenty of sea-goers there. Though you might soon wish you hadn't, if you take my meaning."

Maura knew better than the man might suppose. She pictured a sea-going band of outlaws rather like the ones who had held her captive in Aldwood. Why would the Vestan wizards instruct her to seek out a man of that sort?

"The Monkey it is." Rath grabbed Maura by the wrist and pulled her out into the thick, chilly fog that smelled of rotten fish.

He led her through a maze of narrow, fog-shrouded lanes and alleys. The only way she could tell they were getting closer to the water was that the fog became even thicker and the smell of fish more rank, until it nearly gagged her. When she struggled to fix her attention on something besides her writhing belly, Maura realized she could hear the rhythmic slap of waves against wood.

"This looks like the place." Rath pointed up at a hanging sign, barely visible in the fog. It bore the crude likeness of a Tolinese monkey.

From within the building came sounds of raucous laughter, angry shouts and the high-pitched tinkle of breaking glass.

As Rath pushed the door open and tugged Maura into the place after him, she heard him mutter, "May the Giver watch over us…if it can see through this fog."

The common room of the Monkey reminded Maura a little of the tavern in Westborne were she'd gone seeking help from the secret followers of the Giver, who called themselves *twarith*. But only a little.

The smell of strong spirits overpowered the ever-present stench of rotten fish, but that came as no comfort to her suffering stomach. Somewhere on the other side of the crowded, noisy room, someone was torturing wheezy music out of an instrument Maura had never heard before. Most of the patrons huddled on low wooden benches that ran along either side of three long, narrow tables. There, they guzzled some drink from earthenware mugs and either argued or laughed loudly with their neighbors.

It eased Maura's fears just a little to realize they were not speaking in Comtung, the language her people used to communicate with their Hanish conquerors. Instead, they spoke native Umbrian, though with a strange accent unlike any she'd heard before.

The noise did not quiet as Rath threaded his way through the crowd, towing Maura behind him. No one turned to look at them. Even the people they brushed against as they made their way toward the counter seemed to stare through them. Yet the flesh between Maura's shoulder blades prickled, as if sensing many curious, hostile gazes aimed at her back.

When he reached the counter, Rath spent a while trying in vain to catch the eye of a short man dispensing drinks behind it. Reaching the end of his limited patience, he lunged forward, grabbing the man by the front of his shirt and lifting him off the floor until they were nose to nose.

Having succeeded in gaining the fellow's attention, Rath spoke in a quiet, mannerly voice quite at odds with both his actions and surroundings. "I'd like to see a Captain Gull, if you please."

Maura braced for the surrounding hubbub to fall into an expectant hush, as everyone's attention fixed on her and Rath. The prickling sensation between her shoulder blades intensified, but the noise continued as loud as ever.

The barkeep did not answer, though his face grew redder and redder. His gaze skittered to a large man standing beside Rath, whose shaved scalp bore a tattoo that looked like a map.

The big man leaned toward Rath and spoke in a friendly tone that surprised Maura. "You fancy seeing Gull, do you, inlander? I can take you to him."

"When?" Rath eased his grip on the barkeep's shirt, lowering him back onto his feet.

The man with the tattooed head shrugged. "As soon as you like, inlander. Now?"

"Now." Rath let go of the barkeep.

"Follow me, then," said the man, his tone still affable.

A month or two ago, his obliging manner would have eased Maura's apprehension. Since then, a little of Rath's wariness had rubbed off on her.

The big fellow turned and began to make his way through the crowd, which parted to let him pass. With Rath and Maura following close on his heels, he strode toward the opposite end of the room. As they approached, Maura could see that a shadowed corner was in fact a shallow alcove. Their guide pulled back a bit of curtain to reveal a door, which he opened and entered.

Maura clutched Rath's hand tighter when he drew her toward the doorway and the dark passage beyond. He glanced at her, brows raised, as if to ask what other choice they had.

"At least we knew there *is* a Captain Gull." He gave her hand a reassuring squeeze. "You haven't lost faith in that destiny of yours already, have you?"

"*Our* destiny," Maura corrected him, trying to sound more confident than she felt. How could she expect Rath to place his fledgling trust in that baffling power when her own doubts were all too evident? "Lead on."

She reached back to shut the door behind her—no easy task with the madfern still clutched tight in her fist. A glance back showed that it was not necessary. Several more people crowded into the narrow passage after them, their sinister-looking forms lit from behind by the flickering candle flames in the tavern.

Rath's grip on her hand betrayed the tension that clenched the rest of his body as he led her into the darkness. They seemed to shuffle along the dim, narrow passage for a long time. It twisted several times, confusing Maura as to the direction they were headed. Would they emerge somewhere behind the tavern…or down the street from it?

Suddenly a light appeared ahead of them and the passage opened into a room. Rath lurched forward, stumbling on something. An instant later, a raised doorsill caught Maura's foot and made her stumble, too. As she squinted against the light, she felt Rath's hand wrenched out of hers.

Before she could open her other hand to release a cloud of powered madfern into the air, Rath cried, "No!"

"In case you haven't noticed, inlander," their tattooed guide chuckled. "You aren't in any position to be giving orders."

Maura knew Rath had been speaking to her—not that it mattered. For at the same instant, someone grabbed her hands and pulled them tight behind her back. She concentrated on keeping her fist clenched around the powdered madfern until she got a better opportunity to use it.

"Well, well, what have we here?" asked a voice.

Maura glanced up at the speaker as he rose from a chair and turned to look them over. He was a small, slender man, a bit less than her own height, which was tall for a woman. The man wore black breeches and leather boots that reached halfway up his thighs. His shirt, the color of dark blood, billowed in loose folds over his arms and upper body, while a long strip of the same cloth had been wound around his head. It covered all his hair except for a long, black plume that stuck out of an opening in the top—a mockery of the way Hanish soldiers pulled their pale hair through the tops of their helmets.

For a moment Maura thought he had a fur collar draped around his shoulders. Then the "collar" raised its head, stared at her and hissed. She flinched from the creature, a long-legged hillcat with sleek brown fur.

"Mind your manners, Abri." The man raised his hand to caress the beast.

He wore snug-fitted leather gloves with holes through which his bare thumb and fingers poked. Only three fingers, though. The smallest on each hand was missing.

"This inlander strolled into the Monkey," said the tattooed man, "with a wench twice too pretty for the likes of him. Said he wanted to see Captain Gull."

"Indeed?" The little man sauntered toward Maura.

When he lifted his hand, she flinched, but he only tilted her chin with the gentle pressure of his fingers to turn her head to one side.

"Tell me, inlander, was that all you wanted—to *see* me?" He let go of Maura, stepped back and struck a pose. "Now you have seen me."

He glanced toward the tattooed man, and in as mannerly a voice as he might have used to bid them be escorted away, he ordered, "Kill them."

"We wanted more than to see you!" Rath cast Maura a sidelong glance that she sensed meant, *"Get ready!"*

She flashed him one back that she hoped he would understand meant, *"This is not going to work."*

Oh, she could mutter the spell under her breath and drop

the madfern. Perhaps even kick it up into the air. But in this small, crowded room, there was a good chance she and Rath would become as befuddled as everyone else. Or the others might do them some harm while in the grip of their confusion.

"We were told you could take us to the Vestan Islands," said Rath. "Can you? Will you? It is vital we reach there!"

Captain Gull looked from Rath to Maura and back again. All the while he petted the cat draped around his neck. "You must know it is death for any Umbrian to sail more than five miles from the mainland. My friends and I are but humble fisherfolk."

Maura could not bite back a retort. "You do not look like any fisherman I ever heard of!"

"Ha!" Captain Gull let out a laugh that seemed far too deep and loud for his slender frame.

"A bold wench!" He remarked to the cat. "I like that."

The cat looked over at Maura and hissed again.

"Mmm, I reckon you're right, Abri." Gull shook his head, a look of deep regret shadowing his fine features. "These two must be Hanish spies."

He glanced toward the large tattooed man and amended his previous order. "Kill them slow."

As Rath listened to Captain Gull order their deaths in such an offhand tone, he sensed the strange little man was more truly dangerous than the outlaw Vang Spear of Heaven, with all his bluster.

He should never have brought Maura here, Rath chided himself. He should have left her somewhere safe while he'd come in search of the smuggler. In truth, the notion had crossed his mind, but he'd worried what harm she might come to if he was not there to protect her. Instead, he'd hauled her into danger from which he would be hard-pressed to protect her.

If she could give him the slightest edge by casting her spell, he would try to fight their way out of here…though he didn't fancy his chances.

"Kill us if you must and if you can!" He hurled the challenge at Captain Gull. "But do not let it be because you believe us Hanish spies!"

Though it made him feel unbearably vulnerable, he bent forward, baring the back of his neck for them to see. The flesh still felt tender where the Han had branded him, almost a fortnight ago.

Rath heard Maura suck in her breath through clenched teeth. He had not told her about the brand, though he knew she could have compounded a salve to soothe and heal it. Once or twice, when she'd thrown her arms around his neck too eagerly, he'd had to bite back a grunt of pain.

"Well!" Captain Gull sounded shaken out of his amused indifference. "I have never seen one of those marks on a living man, inlander. How did you come by it?"

"The usual way." Rath straightened up and shot a look around at Gull and his men. "It is the first thing they do to you when you're sent into the mines...after a whiff of slag to dull the pain and sap the fight out of you."

"How do you come to be here, then?" Gull's dark eyes narrowed. "No man has ever escaped the mines...unless he made a bargain to spy for the Han in exchange for his freedom."

"You disappoint me, Gull." Rath hoped the insult would not cost him his head.

"Do I?" Gull sounded intrigued rather than enraged. "How so?"

"I took you for a man who makes it his business to know what's what in the world. There have been escapes from the mines, though not many and not much talked of. The Han try to keep word from spreading, in case it should inspire more miners to try. And the men who escape are not eager to call attention to themselves by bragging."

The hillcat rubbed its head against Gull's cheek. He reached up to pet it, but his gaze never left Rath's. "Do not flatter yourself that I let you see all I may or may not know."

Perhaps the time had come for Rath to try a little flattery. "It does not take a clever man to guess that the first must far outweigh the last, Captain."

Gull chuckled. "Believe it, inlander. A man like me does not survive in this town unless he is well armed with the right knowledge."

"Then you must have heard rumors of a revolt at the Beast-mount Mine. A successful revolt."

"Amazing if it is true."

"It is true." Rath could not keep a ring of triumph from his voice. "And it was amazing."

Feeling the hold on his arms loosen, he tugged them free, but made no rash move to draw his weapons. "I led those men and now the lass and I have been summoned to the Vestan Islands. If you cannot take us, let us go so we may seek passage elsewhere."

Gull took some time to reach his decision...or to announce it, at least. While everyone stood waiting, he sauntered around the room, petting the cat and feeding it small scraps of what looked like raw fish from a heaping platter on the table.

At last, when Rath had prepared himself for another casual death order, Gull looked up at him and Maura as if wondering what they were still doing there. "Lucky for you the summer Ore Fleet has already sailed with its cargo of metal back to Dun Derhan. Otherwise nothing could persuade me to venture those waters."

He directed his next words at the tattooed fellow standing behind Rath. "Don't just stand there, Nax, find our guests food and a place to sleep."

"You will accept my hospitality, I hope?" he asked Rath and Maura. "We will need to be on our way very early tomorrow."

Before Rath could reply, Maura spoke up, "You honor us with your kindness, Captain. May the Giver's favor fall upon you."

Gull accepted her blessing with a wry smirk and an exaggerated bow.

Rath guessed the man did not risk his life keeping open tenuous links between the Umbrian mainland and the Islands out of duty to the Giver. Likewise, his offer of food and shelter was an act of caution, not kindness. If they were spies, Gull would not give them a chance to steal away and tell the local garrison about the forbidden voyage he had agreed to make.

Rath suspected Maura knew it, too. But since they had no money and knew no one in Duskport, even a smuggler's hospitality beat sleeping out in the fog. Perhaps destiny was taking care of them, after all.

The man called Nax led them through a maze of narrow hallways and up two flights of stairs to a snug, windowless room. The latter did not sit well with Rath, who preferred open spaces and always liked to have an avenue of escape. But he hid his misgivings from Maura, who seemed pleased enough with Captain Gull's "hospitality."

"Luxury!" She threw herself down onto the thick straw mattress in one corner of the room. She sniffed. "The straw's clean, too, strewn with honeygrass and pestweed."

Rath forced a smile and nodded. The most comfortable cage in the world was still a cage.

"There's plenty of room for us both." She patted the mattress.

"A good thing," he teased. "I would feel bad making you sleep on bare floor."

The door opened and Nax entered bearing a well-laden tray. "I hope you're hungry. There's plenty here."

Maura scrambled up from the mattress. "This looks like a feast for twice our number! Give Captain Gull our thanks for his generosity."

"Very good, mistress." The large, menacing smuggler sounded so meek, Rath could scarcely keep from chuckling. "If there's anything more you need—anything at all—just give a call."

That cordial invitation did not reassure Rath. It only confirmed his certainty that one of Gull's men would be standing guard outside the door. He hoped the cozy straw mattress would not put any amorous notions in Maura's head. Much as he wanted her, he could not abide the thought of someone listening in on them, perhaps thinking about her that way.

Nax set the tray down on a low table in the opposite corner of the room from the mattress. Once he had gone, Maura pounced on the food.

"Hold a moment!" Rath grabbed her hand on its way to her mouth bearing a biscuit of some kind. "How do you know that's not poisoned?"

"Don't be daft." Maura jerked her hand free and took a bite before he could stop her. "If Captain Gull decided to have us killed, he had no need to go to all this bother. He could just have let his first order stand."

"Or his second," Rath muttered. How could she talk about threats of cold murder as if they were trifles?

"Just so." Maura swallowed her first bite and took another. "It would make no sense for him to pretend he was going to take us to the Vestan Islands, then waste perfectly good food by using it to poison us."

She stared at her left hand, which was still clenched in a tight fist. "I had better wash off this madfern, though, or I could do myself worse harm than our host means us."

Her tone reminded Rath of the gentle scoldings he used to get from Ganny when he was a young fellow. Maura was probably right. Somehow, when it came to her safety, caution got the better of his good sense.

He picked up a fried patty of some kind and gave it a suspicious sniff. "Smells all right, I reckon."

Maura shook her head and chuckled as she washed her hands in a small basin beside the bed. "I'm certain this food is no more poisoned than the barleymush I fed you the night I brought you to Langbard's cottage."

How foolish it seemed, looking back, for him to have suspected her and her kindly wizard guardian of treachery.

"That was different," Rath growled, taking a nibble of the patty, which turned out to be a toothsome mixture of fish and vegetables. "I had no good reason to mistrust you, except that the Han had made me suspicious of all magic users. Placing your trust in a fellow like Gull is a quick way to get yourself killed. You mark me."

He'd only meant to take the one tiny bite, then wait to see if it made him ill. Now Rath looked down at his hand to find he'd wolfed the whole patty.

"I mark you very well." Maura stole up behind him and wrapped her arms around his waist, pressing her cheek to his back. "I did not trust you, in the beginning, any more than you trusted me, remember? I was certain you would murder Langbard and me in our sleep on the road to Prum. As it turned out, I could not have been more wrong. So if I have become less wary of dangerous-looking men, you have only yourself to blame."

Bad enough she was right. Did she have to remind him he was the rogue who'd taught her this dangerous lack of caution?

He echoed what he had said to her after she'd tricked him into eating that barleymush. "Oh well, if the food is poisoned and the room a trap, we are done for anyway. Might as well die with a full belly and a decent sleep."

"Anything else?" asked Maura, sliding one hand up under his vest.

Rath glanced toward the mattress in the corner. Perhaps if they were very, very quiet...?

A loud banging jolted Maura from the warm haven of sleep in Rath's arms to the baffling fright of impenetrable darkness and hard limbs thrashing around her.

Then a blessed sliver of light appeared and a deep, hoarse voice called, "Time to rise! Sea-going folk cannot afford to loll in bed till all hours, like inlanders."

Rath's thrashing stilled. He must have remembered where they were, as Maura had.

Someone—Nax by the sound of his voice—thrust a lit candle into the room and set it down on the table.

"Take these—" he tossed a soft, bulky bundle onto the mattress "—and make ready to go as quick as you can."

Despite the need for haste, Rath gathered Maura into a swift embrace. "I didn't do you any harm just now, did I?"

When she assured him she had only been frightened by their abrupt waking in the darkness, Rath cursed. "I hate not knowing where I am when I waken. It does not happen to me often, but when it does, it gives me a wicked fright and makes me lash out at whoever is nearest at hand."

He pressed a kiss on her brow, "I entreat your pardon."

"It is yours, now and ever." She clung to him an instant longer then turned to peel open the bundle.

"A change of clothes for us, I reckon." Rath grabbed a shirt that appeared to be his size and pulled it on. "So we do not look quite so much like inlanders."

Maura picked up the smaller of two pair of breeches. "And I do not look so much like a woman. How do you put these on?"

With Rath's help, she dressed in boy's garments then hid her braided hair beneath a cloth cap. Not knowing if they would be given any breakfast, they ate some of the food left over from the previous night.

"At least now we can be certain it is not poisoned," Maura teased Rath as he gobbled up several cold fish patties.

He replied with a menacing growl that only made Maura laugh. Then he lifted the candle and looked her over with a critical stare. "If we meet up with anyone who might cause trouble, keep behind me. You won't fool anybody who looks too close."

He began to gather their clothes into a bundle, when another knock sounded on the door and Nax pushed it open without waiting for an invitation. "You ready?"

"Aye." Rath tucked their bundle of clothes under his arm and bid Maura bring the candle.

"Hold on, now." Nax pointed toward Rath's scabbard. "You'll have to leave that behind, and the clothes, too."

As the first sounds of protest left Rath's mouth, the man nodded toward Maura's sash. "And that. Off with 'em."

"Damned if I will go unarmed!" cried Rath.

Maura dug a pinch of spider silk from its pouch. She had been stripped of her sash once by an enemy, and she had no wish to be rendered so vulnerable again.

"Captain Gull don't care whether you're armed," said Nax, "so long as the weapon's not metal or you will damn us all!"

The way the two men glared at each other, Maura feared they would soon trade blows unless someone stopped them. Fighting her ingrained instinct to flee or hide from conflict, she pushed herself into the middle of their quarrel.

"Metal will damn you all? What does that mean? My companion's blades have been tempered of mortcraft, I promise you."

"Your pardon, mistress." Nax shook his head. "But tempered is not good enough." He glared at Rath over Maura's shoulder.

"Not good enough for what?" she persisted. "Forgive our ignorance—we are inlanders, as you know."

He should know, for he had reminded them of it often enough in a tone that proclaimed his contempt. Did all coast folk in Umbria look down on inlanders? Maura wondered. The way people from the Hitherland accounted all Dusk Coasters smugglers and pirates? And folk in Norest poked fun at Tarshites for their rustic speech and manners? Before Umbrians could hope to throw off the yoke of the Han, they would need to forget such prejudices and come together.

"You do not know?" A look of doubt softened Nax's fierce countenance. Had he thought Rath opposed his order out of arrogance or stubbornness?

Maura shook her head.

"It's the Islands, see?" Nax explained. "Do you not know why the Han haven't overrun them along with the rest of the kingdom?"

"I have heard the waters are treacherous," said Maura, "and the Han are not the best of sailors."

"The Islands have nothing the Han want," snapped Rath. "If they were riddled with metal and gems like the Blood Moon Mountains, they would have fallen to the Han long ago."

Maura stabbed backward with her elbow and made forceful contact with some part of Rath. She loved the man to the depths of her heart, but that did not mean he had lost his power to try her patience.

She directed an apologetic smile at the fierce-looking smuggler in front of her. "Is there more keeping the Han from the Islands than those things?"

"Aye. The waters around the Islands have a powerful warding spell upon them. They sense the presence of metal, and when any come too near, they swallow it up. After losing a few ships, the Han had sense enough to give the Islands a wide berth."

"Of course," Maura whispered, wondering why the idea had never occurred to her before.

"Then how are we to reach the Islands without being swallowed up by the sea?" asked Rath. "Does Captain Gull have a ship that is held together with string?"

Maura turned to skewer him with a look. This sort of bravado had worked last night to win the smuggler's cooperation. Now a little courtesy would take them farther.

Suddenly, from behind her, she heard Captain Gull's voice. "You may soon see how my ship is held together, inlander. If you have wit enough to leave behind your blades and other metal. If you will, then come. You have wasted too much time in talk."

Spinning around to face him, Maura saw no sign of the colorful character who had ordered their deaths last night. Instead, only a gray-bearded old man stood beside Nax, clad in tattered garments that looked to have been woven with a waterproofing spell. Her heart went out to him, for his back was pitifully bent with a cruel hump deforming one shoulder.

As she watched, the hump seemed to swell and ripple. Maura's gorge rose.

Then Rath let out a burst of scornful laughter. "That disguise won't fool anyone, Gull, unless you keep that cat of yours from moving about."

Maura chided herself for a gullible fool.

The smuggler performed a mocking bow. "Do not fret, in-lander. The wharf guards are so used to seeing me shuffle past, they would not notice if Abri turned tumbles under my coat. I'm more uneasy about sneaking your wench by them. It'll take more than a pair of breeches to make her look like a proper boy."

He flashed her a smile that might have been meant to look admiring. His false beard and several blackened teeth quite spoiled the effect.

Rath brought his hands to rest on Maura's shoulders. "I've already told her to stay behind me."

"Do not fret about me!" Though Maura knew he only meant to watch out for her, sometimes Rath's intense protectiveness vexed her. "If I dose myself with enough hundredflower, the wharf guards will pay me no more heed than the garrison at Windleford used to."

"Hundredflower?" murmured Gull. "You're an enchantress?"

Maura nodded and patted her sash. "Which is why I cannot surrender this. You have my word it contains no metal. But now that we understand about the warding spells around the Islands, my companion will gladly surrender his weapons."

"Not *gladly*," Rath muttered under his breath.

But Maura heard him ungird his scabbard and hurl it onto the mattress. Then he stabbed his knife deep into the wood of the doorjamb. It occurred to her how defenseless he must feel surrendering his weapons.

"You *will* be glad," she assured him, "when we do not drown in the Sea of Twilight."

"Come on, inlanders—" Captain Gull started down the hall "—or we will never get to sea this morning!"

Maura grabbed Rath's hand and followed. A quiver of excitement gripped her belly. To think she would soon be sailing upon the great ocean!

Once the small fishing boat pushed away from the wharf, Rath felt as though he could breathe properly again, without iron bands of dread tightening around his chest. Passing under the scrutiny of the Hanish wharf guards without even the tiniest knife to protect himself and Maura was one of the hardest tests of nerves he'd ever undergone.

For a moment, he'd glimpsed a flicker of heightened interest in the eyes of one of the guards, perhaps seeing through Maura's hundredflower spell to pick out a pair of unfamiliar faces among the regulars. When the guard approached, Rath had tensed, preparing for the worst.

But before the Han could challenge him, a scuffle had broken out in another part of the crowd, distracting the guard long enough for Rath and Maura to slip past and board a boat with Gull, Nax and another man.

"Stay to the back," Gull muttered. "Make like you're tending to the nets. Keep your heads down until we're out of sight of the shore."

He climbed up into the prow of the boat and detached the loop of rope that held it to the wharf pilings. Nax and the other fellow had taken their places on a wide bench in the middle of the craft and commenced to wield a pair of broad oars in strong, rhythmic strokes.

"Where are we bound for?" asked Rath as they drifted out into the foggy darkness, the lights of the wharf growing dim behind them. Off in the mist, he could hear the dip and splash of other oars, and above them, the screech of seafowl. "We aren't rowing all the way to the Vestan Islands in this, are we?"

Though he had heard plenty of tales about the Islands, he

did not have a clear idea how far off the western coast of Umbria they lay.

"Inlanders!" Gull let out a hoot of mocking laughter as he peeled off his false beard of brushed fleece. "This poor little dory would not last more than a mile or two off the coast. Which is why the Han will not let us fish in anything bigger."

He did not offer any further explanation, but continued to remove his disguise.

Rath glanced sidelong at Maura. Did she guess whatever Gull was not telling them?

She only shrugged and murmured, "We will find out soon enough, I suppose."

True, but Rath did not like surprises. What would *he* do in Gull's place, to get around the Hanish edicts that bound seagoers so tight to the coast?

By the time he had come up with a couple of possibilities, the fog did not seem quite as thick as when they'd pulled away from the wharf. Behind them, dawn had begun to light the sky for another day.

"Ease off, lads," Gull ordered his oarsmen, peering into the mist. "We're getting close."

True to his word, a large, dark shape reared up out of the fog before them. Someone called out a challenge, to which Gull bellowed back an answer, neither of which Rath understood. They sounded a bit like the Old Umbrian language, *twara,* of which Maura had taught him a few words.

Now he understood what was happening and reckoned himself a fool for not guessing earlier. "They must keep a sea ship anchored in some hidden cove," he whispered to Maura, "then they sail the little fishing boats out to meet it."

Gull made a sound between a chuckle and grunt. "You're clever enough…for an inlander. The Han still haven't figured it out after all these years. Mind you, we keep the local garrison busy enough that the officers aren't eager to stay on the Dusk Coast a day longer than they have to. Before they guess our little scheme, they're back to Venard or over the mountains where the locals don't give so much trouble."

Perhaps Maura resented the smuggler's tone of contempt for the region that had been her home. Rath heard a sharp edge to her tone when she asked Gull, "Do the wharf guards not get suspicious when the small boats don't come back at night?"

Someone on the deck of the ship tossed down a rope, which Gull caught and tethered to their boat. "Never fear, wench, we make certain the same number return at night as sail in the morn. And with a good catch, too. That's all the Han care about. They never notice if each boat is missing a man or two."

Grudging admiration for the smugglers of Duskport began to grow in Rath. He knew the penalties for their trade were as gruesome as those for attempting to escape the mines.

A rope ladder rolled down the hull of the ship. Gull scrambled up it with the hillcat still clinging around his neck. Motioning for Rath and Maura to follow, he called. "Welcome aboard the *Phantom,* inlanders. The most elusive vessel in the whole Sea of Twilight!"

Rath scrambled up the ladder behind Maura and climbed onto the deck. There he found Captain Gull with his arm wrapped around her waist and his hip pressed tight against hers. With the speed of events since they had wakened, Rath hadn't had enough time or light to fully appreciate the tantalizing way those breeches and that shirt clung to the sweet, womanly curves of Maura's body.

Gull glanced up at Rath with an impudent grin. "The wench is a mite unsteady on her feet. Common for inlanders."

"I'll take her, then." Rath struggled to hide his jealous temper. It would only amuse Gull and vex Maura. "You must have plenty of tasks to oversee before we sail."

"True, alas." The smuggler lifted Maura's hand and pressed a slow, provocative kiss upon it. "Else I would be tempted to linger here all day in such comely company."

The hillcat on Gull's shoulder gave a hiss that Rath was

tempted to echo. When the creature swiped its paw toward Maura, she drew back and he was able to pull her into his own arms without too obvious a tug-of-war.

"Mind your ship, Gull," he growled, "and I'll mind my wife."

Gull's dark brows shot up as he mouthed the word *wife*. Then he strode away calling orders about hauling anchor, hoisting sails and other sea-going cant that meant nothing to Rath.

He eased Maura out of the way as Gull's crew swarmed over the deck of the *Phantom* and up the rigging of the large, three-cornered sails. Meanwhile, the small fleet of fishing boats that had borne them from shore dispersed. A stray breeze caught the sails and the ship began to move.

"Did you mean what you said to Gull?" asked Maura. "Or were you just trying to make him leave me alone?"

That sounded like a worthwhile reason for saying...whatever it was he'd said.

"You don't even remember, do you?" She shook her head. "I suppose that answers my question."

"You mean about being my wife?" A flash of heat kindled in Rath's cheeks. "Your pardon if I got ahead of myself, but you are...at least you're meant to be. You will, won't you?"

She had to, didn't she, if he was the Waiting King and she the Destined Queen? That was the one part of all this that made the rest almost bearable.

"Of course I will." Maura leaned into his embrace. "Once we reach the Islands, I think we should have a proper wedding with one of the wizards to bless our union. Perhaps even the Oracle of Margyle."

At that moment, the *Phantom* broke through the last tatters of fog. It surged out into a vivid, sparkling world of blue, white and gold. The majesty of it took Rath's breath for a moment.

No wonder Captain Gull and the others risked their lives to ply this trade. Rath sensed it was not only for riches, but for the tang of adventure they smelled on the sea air. He could almost feel it stirring *his* blood.

He closed his eyes and inhaled deep, invigorating breaths.

A while later a young crewmen approached them. "Captain says he'd show you around the ship if you care to see."

Rath was more than eager. The only watercraft in his experience were small rafts of the kind he and Maura had used to cross the Windle. He wanted to know where and how the *Phantom* had been built, how Gull and his crew navigated the vast, open stretches of water and made the vessel take them where they wanted to go.

"Shall we?" he asked Maura. She didn't look quite as anxious as he for a tour of the vessel. In fact, she looked pale and a little...green.

But she nodded, just the same. "Perhaps it will help me keep my mind off my belly. It feels like everything inside me is sloshing around and trying to get back out."

"Don't fret," said the young crewman who'd been sent to fetch them. "I had that when I first sailed. Comes back now and then when the sea is rough. Here." He rummaged in his trouser pocket and pulled out a tight-packed little brick a disgusting greenish-brown in color.

Rath made a face when he caught a whiff of it, for it stank of salt and fish. "What is that?"

"Dried sea grass," said the lad. "Once you get used to the flavor, it's a treat to chew. Calms a sick belly better than anything else I've ever tried."

"Thank you." Maura took it from him and broke off a small pinch. Then with a dubious look, she shoved it between her back teeth and began to chew.

She grimaced at the taste but did not spit it out or hang over the deck railing retching up her breakfast. After a few moments, she even managed a wan smile. "Perhaps this stuff is like cheeseweed—the smell is a sign of its potency. I believe I feel a little better already."

She kept up a valiant appearance of interest while Captain Gull showed them over his ship.

Rath did not need to pretend. "Amazing that you were able to build a craft this size without any metal at all!"

Gull shrugged. "The sea is not kind to iron. Wooden pegs swell in the wet and hold better than nails that will rust away. The *Phantom* was built in a shipyard on Galene. Some of their trees produce wood that is almost as hard as metal. And some bits have been treated with strengthening spells."

He ran his hand down the middle mast in a proud caress such as a father might bestow on a beloved child he was praising.

"Why do your sails run the length of the ship and not its width?" asked Rath. "Would they not catch the wind better that way?"

Gull grinned. "When the wind is blowing in your favor, that is true, inlander. The Han rig their sails as you describe. That is why their fleet must sail only at certain times of the year. Like now, to take advantage of the Midsummer Blast."

"Midsummer…?"

"…Blast." Gull shook his head. "You are sadly ignorant of the sea. The Blast is a fast, cool wind that whips down the coast this time of year. The Han ride it with their big waddling tubs full of ore. Slow as oxen, they are, and just as stubborn to steer. But the wind is more fickle than a beautiful woman with many suitors. When we set our sails, we become masters of the wind, not slaves to it. If the wind blew against them, we could dance rings around anything in the Hanish fleet!"

Picturing it made Rath grin. "That sounds like fine sport! Do you often harry them?"

"Do I look like a fool, inlander?" Gull held up his hands and wriggled his eight fingers. "I am fond of the ones of these I have left and mean to keep them. My handsome head, too, for that matter and a few other bits I will not mention in the presence of your queasy lady."

"But if you could dance rings around them?"

"Around the galleys, aye. But the Han are no fools—they do not send their precious ore back to their homeland unprotected. The fleet is escorted by fighting ships that would soon crush a greater threat than my pretty *Phantom*. They're sleek and narrow, fast as demons when the wind is behind them. And if they catch a wooden craft like this one, they have a sharp iron prow that could slice through our hull like a hot blade through pudding."

The smuggler's warning put Rath in mind of the hounds the Han used to terrorize the people of Umbria—fast, sharp and vicious.

By the time Gull finished showing Rath and Maura around the vessel, the wind had risen and the clouds had massed on the eastern horizon, dark and threatening.

Gull sniffed the air. "Smells like a storm. Most often they come out of the west, but now and then the Blast will send one down the coast. It will get us to the Vestan Islands all the faster. I only hope it does not push us up the tail of the Ore Fleet."

Before Rath could reply, Maura spoke. "Did you not say the Han sail faster when the wind is behind them? The storm should push them farther ahead of us."

"Aye, wench!" Gull gave her a hearty slap on the back. "So you did mind what I was saying. We'll make a sea-goer of you yet!"

Maura shook her head, chewing the sea grass harder as she clutched the little block of it in her hand. "I think not."

The storm broke just as night began to fall. Rath took Maura below, where they huddled in dark, mute misery on a narrow shelf that folded down from the inside of the hull.

Time slowed to a crawl, until it seemed that day would never come again, and they would be trapped forever in the bowels of the pitching ship, deafened by the howl of the wind and the crash of the waves. The *Phantom's* hull shuddered with every flex of the sea's formidable strength. Soon Rath lost count of how many times they slipped between the jaws of death, only to slide out again before its sharp teeth gnashed. Each time left his heart pounding fit to burst, his belly churning, and a fine dew of sweat prickling on his brow.

The weight of his own helplessness and uselessness ground down his courage. If only there had been something he could *do*! He heard the muted thunder of footfall on the deck above his head with longing. Even if it had meant treading closer to the slippery edge of disaster, at least being up there with duties to perform would have given him some tiny illusion of control.

The knowledge that he would be worse than useless up on deck kept him below. And the conviction that Maura needed him.

"There, there, *aira*." He held her head as her belly gave another violent heave and she spewed what little she'd eaten into the hold of the *Phantom*. "You'll feel better once you get it all out."

He didn't have enough experience of the sea to be certain of that. But right now, he'd say any daft thing if it might ease her. He wished their places could have been reversed. He would rather endure this himself, than watch her suffer. No doubt she'd have tended him better, all deft and gentle and reassuring—unlike his rough, awkward efforts on her behalf.

She subsided against him, gasping for breath. "I'm sorry, Rath…should have listened to you and gone home to Windleford. What good will we do anybody…dying out here on the ocean?"

"Hush, now. We're not going to die!" Had he ever spoke words he believed *less*? "Mind what you told me about believing in our destiny? Why, you *were* dead, or near as. Yet you came back to me."

Somehow, his faltering effort to convince Maura began to have a true effect upon him—as if someone had thrown him a rope to cling to in this storm-tossed night. He did not know where the other end might be anchored. But as the night wore on, a feeling of certainty grew in him that it must be somewhere firm and true.

At last Maura fell into an exhausted doze, a blessing for which Rath muttered a garbled but grateful word of thanks, that somehow lulled him to sleep when the storm was at its worst.

He woke some time later, astonished to find Maura and him-self alive. For a while he sat holding her, savoring the simple luxuries of quiet and calm, and the soft light of dawn stream-ing through the open hatch. A powerful sense of belief took hold of him, as it had in the mines and on midsummer night in the Secret Glade. Though he knew it would not last, he wel-comed it just the same.

A while later, Maura stirred, stretched and opened her eyes.

"It's so quiet," she whispered. "Are we in the afterworld?"

Rath chuckled and dropped a kiss on the crown of her head. "Your ears might make you think so, *aira,* but your eyes and nose will tell you the truth."

He grimaced at the reek of bile that had been spewed in the hold last night—not all hers by any means. "Shall we go up on deck and get a breath of fresh air?"

She gave a weary nod then leaned heavily against him as he helped her aloft. There they found the crew making repairs to the ship and going about their other duties in a mute daze. Most looked as if they had not yet recovered their wits from a hard blow to the head.

Only Gull had a relaxed, well-rested appearance, though Rath doubted he had left the deck all night. His clothes and his hair still looked a bit damp, though the cat lolling around his neck seemed dry enough. Rath wondered how it had weath-ered the storm.

Gull perched on a raised platform near the front of the ship that was girded by a waist-high railing. He scanned the horizon through a long tube that might have been carved from very pale wood, or perhaps ivory. Rath guessed what he was looking for.

"Any sign of the Ore Fleet?" he called to the captain.

"Not a glimpse, inlander." Gull lowered the tube from his eye and leaned back against the platform railing. "I reckon it is too much to hope that the storm might have blown them east into the warding waters around the Vestan Islands. They were likely long past the Islands before it hit."

Maura sighed. "I wish *we'd* reached the Islands before it hit."

"We have a saying where I come from, wench." Gull climbed down the short ladder from his perch with a jaunty step. "'*The worst wind is better than none at all*'. This one blew us toward our destination all the faster. By my reckoning, we might make Margyle before nightfall."

"The sooner the better," Maura muttered under her breath.

After the tempest of the night, the day passed quietly. Late in the morning, Rath and Maura watched in fascination as a herd of sea beasts called *nieda* swam past the ship, lunging up into the air with surprising grace for their size. Now and then two of the larger ones would butt each other with their great, curled horns that put Rath in mind of Hitherland wild goats.

Through the warm hours after midday, Rath and Maura curled up in a quiet, shaded corner of the deck and let the motion of the ship and the soothing music of the waves lull them to sleep.

Later, the sound of a voice calling down from high on one of the masts startled Rath awake. Though he didn't understand the words, the tone warned him it was not good news. The sudden, urgent rush of the crew confirmed it.

Maura stirred, too, as several men ran by in different directions. "I wonder what's wrong."

Rath had a good guess, but he did not want to alarm her.

Then the young crewman who had given Maura the sea grass dashed up to them. "Captain says you're to go below and stay out of the way. We've spotted ships coming up fast behind us—the Ore Fleet, Captain says."

The boy spat on the deck. "Slag the scum! If they catch up, grab something heavy and jump overboard with it. I'd rather be food for the fish than let the Han get hold of me!"

Rath could not concur with the lad's dire advice, he realized as he hoisted Maura up from the deck. More than once when faced with the choice between death and capture, he had not hesitated to choose death. Now, when he looked within himself, and found a fragile bud of belief taking root, he knew that death was no longer an honorable choice for him.

Would it never end? Maura wondered as Rath helped her up from the deck. Would the two of them never know more than a stolen moment's peace before they were plunged once again into turmoil and peril?

Her belly no longer pitched and heaved as it had last night. Instead, a deep hollow seemed to gape inside her as she stared at the ominous dark shapes growing larger behind them. It was not as though she'd never faced the Han before. She had been running from them, hiding from them, and fighting them in one way or another ever since that fateful day the messenger bird had arrived for Langbard. Yet none of those encounters had shaken her in quite the way this one did.

Out on this vast water with nothing between the sea and the sky, there was no place to hide—nowhere to run. And the number of enemies was far greater than the few she and Rath had so far overcome on their travels. Only at the Beastmount Mine had they encountered anything like this. Then, they'd had time to plan surprise attacks.

This time, the surprise was on them.

Around her and Rath, the crew scrambled, adjusting sails and performing other tasks, the purposes of which she did not understand. The air was charged with a sense of alarm, ready to erupt into outright panic at any moment. It felt contagious and Maura feared she might be the first to catch it.

"Come." Rath tugged on her arm. "Let's get you somewhere safe. Then I will see if I can do anything to help."

Maura braced her feet on the wooden decking. "You heard the boy. If the Han capture this ship, nowhere will be safe. I would rather stay with you and do what I can to make sure that does not happen."

For a moment, Rath looked ready to argue.

She did not give him the chance. "We must trust in the Giver and in our destiny. They have never let us down yet, no matter how bleak things looked. I cannot believe they led us all the way to the Secret Glade only to abandon us so soon."

Her words worked—on herself at least. A strange, potent energy swelled to fill the void of doubt within her. All the challenges she and Rath had overcome to get here flooded through her memory, magnifying that power. Looking back, it almost seemed those obstacles had been contrived to increase in difficulty and risk. Each time testing them harder, calling forth greater wit, strength, courage and faith. Preparing them to meet the next trial—to seize the next opportunity.

As she spoke, Maura could see every blow of Rath's inner battle between doubt and trust reflected on his rugged features. Hard as all this had been for him to accept, he had never let her down, either. Nor did he now.

He nodded toward the stern of the ship. "Let's go talk to Gull. Find out what he means to do and how we can help. The Giver knows, we've had plenty of practice fighting the Han."

Hand in hand, they moved toward the rear of the vessel, trying to stay out of the way of crewmen rushing here and there. They found Captain Gull standing on a raised section of the deck peering through the strange instrument Maura had seen him use earlier.

Langbard had told her about such devices. The far end of the tube was enchanted with flesh from the eye of a great north-awk preserved in a thin coating of clear sap from the giant hith-erpine. It allowed the person who looked through it to see as far, and as well, as one of those keen-eyed birds perched atop that tallest of trees.

First Gull peered behind to the east, then behind to the west. "Slagging scum!" he muttered, just loud enough for Maura to hear. "They should have sailed a week ago, rot 'em!"

Maura and Rath exchanged a look. Had the sailing of the Ore Fleet been delayed by the miners' rebellion?

"East southeast!" cried Gull. "Can you get me no more speed?"

From high in the rigging a crewman called down, "Not with these sails and this wind, Captain! Do you reckon it'll be enough to let us slip through their noose?"

Gull laughed. "The Han have been trying to get a noose around my neck for a while now and never succeeded. They will have no better luck today!"

Again Maura met Rath's gaze. Did Gull's crew recognize a desperate boast when they heard it?

"How close are the Han?" asked Rath. "And what is this 'noose' you are trying to dodge?"

"What are you doing here?" Gull lowered the seeing tube and stared at them, a look of puzzlement and annoyance wrin-kling his brow. "Did I not order the pair of you belowdecks?"

He sounded much more vexed than when he'd ordered their deaths, yet Maura did not find herself intimidated. "Answer Rath's question! Our lives are as much at risk as any on board. Perhaps more. We have a right to know what is going on!"

"Very well, wench. I will tell you what is going on." Gull pointed off to the east with one hand and to the west with the spy tube. "A line of Hanish fighter ships from either side of the ore convoy is moving up like a pair of pincers. Damned if I know how they signaled one another to spring this trap, nor do I care. Unless we can break through one way or the other, they will catch us between and crack us like a roasted bristlenut."

His gaze flickered in a strange manner as he spoke. Maura wondered if it was a sign of the fear he dared not show his crew.

Rath glanced toward the setting sun. "Did you not say we might make the Islands before nightfall? Can we outrun the Han long enough to reach the enchanted coastal waters you told us about? The ones that can sense metal and sink Hanish ships."

Gull shook his head. "To repeat my crewman—not with these sails and this wind. I don't suppose your pretty enchantress could make the wind change course for us?"

"I wish I could." As Maura reached toward her sash, rough hands seized her from behind and she heard Rath cry out.

Too late, she realised Gull's skittery eye movements had been wordless orders to his crew.

"What treachery is this?" She put up a token struggle and shot Captain Gull an indignant glare. "Our enemy is out there! We have done nothing but offer you our help against them!"

Glancing at the cat draped around his shoulders, the smuggler addressed his next words to it. "Ah, but is our enemy *only* out there? I wonder. Or was I right about this pair in the first place—figuring them for Hanish spies? Perhaps we had better toss them overboard."

"Gull," Rath growled, "you do not have time for this. If we were spies, we would have jumped into the sea already. I am not a strong swimmer, but I could stay afloat long enough for one of those ore tubs to retrieve me, rather than stay here to be cut to pieces by their warships!"

An instant of silence greeted his words, as if Gull and his men were trying to work out whether they might be true. In that instant, an idea blossomed in Maura's mind. Seizing the chance to be heard, she blurted it out before she could question her own ignorance of seafaring or reject the notion as madly dangerous.

"Turn on the Han!" she cried. "You said they are too fast for you with the wind behind them, but the *Phantom* is nimble and can sail against the wind. Prove it!"

Time seemed to slow as Gull took a step toward her, his mouth opening. Maura thanked the Giver there were no metal weapons aboard the *Phantom*. If Gull had held a sword, she feared he would have run her through for daring to tell him what to do with his ship.

The words that came out of Gull's mouth were the last she expected. "You heard the wench! Turn and dart in among the galleys. That should take the Han by surprise."

The crew leaped into action and slowly the *Phantom* swung about to meet the Ore Fleet head-on.

"Captain," called the man holding Maura, "does that mean we can let go of these two?"

Gull looked from Maura to Rath and back again. Then he nodded. "But keep a close watch and seize them again if they make any move to jump overboard. I swear, if this goes awry, I will kill them with my own hands."

Rath shook off the hold of the two large crewmen it had taken to restrain him, then gathered Maura into the shelter of his embrace.

"A bold plan, love!" He chuckled. "Ordered like a true—"

"I know," muttered Maura. That jest had no power to amuse or soothe her now. "Like a true outlaw."

"Nay." Rath shook his head, then lifted her hand to his lips. "I was going to say, ordered like a true *queen*."

It *was* a bold plan. Rath pressed his lips to Maura's hand, in admiration and homage. But would it work?

The *Phantom* was only one ship and small compared to the monstrous vessels bearing down on them. Her crew was not even armed to repel boarders. It was one thing for Gull to boast of sailing circles around the Hanish ore galleys. If the *Phantom* were caught in a squeeze between two of those big iron hulls, the wooden ship would be smashed to splinters.

"Oh, Rath—" Maura gripped his fingers so tight that he almost cried out "—what have I done?"

"Only what you needed to do and what you bid me do." For her sake, Rath cast all his doubts adrift. "Trusted in the Giver and in our destiny."

"But what if…"

Rath knew what she was feeling—the weight of leadership pressing down upon her. The fear that a bad decision of hers might harm more than just herself. He had no advice to give her for he had never learned how to overcome that feeling. The best he'd ever been able to do was ignore it until the crisis passed.

He pressed his forefinger to her lips. "We have no time for what-ifs now. Besides, the plan may have been yours but the decision was Gull's. I do not reckon him a man to heed bad advice when it comes to his ship and crew. He must believe this is our best chance."

Or perhaps he had decided, since there was no hope of escape, he would rather die in some grand, hopeless attack on the Ore Fleet. Rath remembered the day he had turned to face a whole host of Hanish warriors, and how astonished he'd been when they had all run past him. He also remembered a small battle with the Han at Raynor's Rift and an idea he'd feared he would not live to try.

But he had lived and here was his chance to give it a go.

"Have you any madfern left in your sash?" he asked Maura.

She looked puzzled by his question. "Two or three pockets full. Why?"

"Come!" He tugged her toward Captain Gull. "Perhaps there is something we can do to help, after all."

Action was the best antidote he had ever found to the paralysing venom of doubt and fear.

"Are you daft?" demanded Gull when Rath asked if there

were any bows aboard the ship. He pointed toward the front-most of the ore galleys, now close enough for their bulk to strike cold terror into the stoutest heart. "Do you reckon those hulks will feel a few pinpricks?"

Either their crews had not seen the small wooden ship turn to charge them, or they could not believe their eyes. Rath was eager to foster that disbelief. In as few words as possible, he explained his plan to sow confusion with Maura's madfern.

"Very well," snapped Gull between issuing other orders, "we have bows, but I am not fool enough to place one in your hands."

He called four of his men, bidding them to arm themselves and take their orders from Rath…provided those orders did not endanger his ship.

As the men rushed off to find their bows, Rath turned to Maura. "Have you any more of that linen for binding wounds?"

She had listened to what he'd told Gull, so she did not ask why he needed it. Instead, she lifted the flap of a large pocket at the base of her sash and pulled out a roll of the bleached cloth. She handed it to Rath, who began tearing the linen into small scraps. When he gave these back to her, she placed a large pinch of madfern into each one, then tied it closed with a bit of thread pulled from the torn edge of the binding cloth.

"This may not work, you know," she muttered as she knotted the last fragment of thread.

"We will never know unless we try." In truth, Rath did not care a great deal whether the plan worked. As long as it gave him and Maura something to think about besides the danger into which they were sailing and over which they had not the least control.

The *Phantom* slipped between two of the ore galleys as Rath fitted the first of the madfern bundles onto a wooden arrowhead.

The archer grimaced. "It won't fly well with that thing on the tip. An arrow head must be sharp to cut the air."

"Do your best." Rath pointed toward the mast of the nearest Hanish ship. "It does not have far to travel. Loft it as high at you can and try to hit something so the arrowhead will burst the pouch."

"Aye." The young archer did not sound very confident. He fired off the arrow, while Maura chanted the madfern spell.

Rath wished he could borrow that seeing tube of Gull's to watch the arrow's flight and be certain it hit. Since he doubted Gull would lend it and since everything was moving so swiftly around them, he murmured a plea for the Giver's help, instead. Then he bid the other archers to fire as the *Phantom* threaded its way among the ore galleys. Maura's madfern supply was soon exhausted, with no effect that Rath could tell.

Then one of the archers nudged him. "Look back there!"

Rath surged up on his toes and craned his neck. At first he could see nothing remarkable. Then he noticed that one of the ore galleys they had passed was drifting toward the one nearest it. The other ship did not make any effort to avoid being hit. Closer and closer the two vessels drew with lumbering grace until they slammed together in a thunderous shriek of metal.

The deck of the *Phantom* erupted in cheers. A dozen hands appeared out of nowhere to thump Rath on the back. The crewmen suddenly looked at Maura with the respect she deserved.

"Well done, inlanders!" Captain Gull cried.

Rath caught Maura by the hand and the two of them exchanged a questioning look. Had those little packets of madfern caused the ore galleys to collide?

Perhaps they would never know, but for now Rath was more than willing to take the credit. A new energy seemed to sweep over the deck of the *Phantom,* as if the wind had suddenly begun to blow in a more favorable direction.

"Look sharp, men!" shouted Gull as the galleys on either side of them edged closer together. "Don't get cocky!"

From high in the rigging, a scream pierced the air and a crewmen plunged to the deck below, knocking down one of his mates who had been standing near the mast.

"Hanish archers!" someone called. "Firing from the galley!"

Rath pulled Maura down as an arrow whistled over their heads, ripping through one of the *Phantom's* sails.

She shook off his protective grasp and began crawling across the deck toward the tangle of twitching limbs. "I must see if I can help those poor men!"

The four bowmen on the *Phantom* returned fire and Rath had the grim satisfaction of seeing a Hanish archer plunge from his ship into the sea.

Maura quickly checked the injured men lying on the deck. "They're both still alive." She unwadded more linen from her sash to staunch the bleeding of the man who'd been hit by the arrow. "It is in his shoulder and may have hit bone. I won't be able to push the barb through, the way Langbard did for you…even if I knew how."

Both men had been knocked senseless. Now the fellow who had been struck by the falling body began to waken, moaning.

"We must get them belowdecks," said Rath, "where you can tend them properly."

And where she would be in a little less danger…for now.

The rest of the crew were occupied, returning bow fire and navigating the *Phantom* through the perilously narrow strip of water between ore galleys.

Rath reached for the arrow shaft sticking out of the wounded man's shoulder. Grasping it near the base where it stuck out of the flesh, he snapped off the rest of the shaft, thankful the injured man could not feel what he was doing.

"So it will not catch on anything when we move him," Rath explained to Maura as he hoisted the injured man under his arms. "Can you get his feet?"

The words had barely left his lips before Maura lifted the fellow's ankles. Fortunately, he was not too heavy and the hatch that led down to the ship's hold was not far off.

"Set him…right here," Maura gasped when they had wrestled the unconscious man down the ladder, "so I will have…some light coming through the hatch…to see what I'm doing."

Rath did as she bid him, laying the injured man out to one side of the ladder. "You stay here and see to his wound. I'll go back for the other fellow."

"Are you sure you can manage on your own?" Maura rummaged in the pockets of her sash for healing herbs.

"If I can't, I will fetch you to help me," Rath lied. He would find some way to get the man down here without bestirring Maura from the relative safety of the hold.

As he squeezed past her to reach the ladder, his hands closed over her shoulders in a swift caress.

She reached up to cover his hands with hers, making him linger for a moment, which he was glad to do. "The other man may have broken bones. Check if any of his limbs are twisted at odd angles. If one is, tie it to a piece of wood or anything you can find to keep the break from shifting worse."

"Aye, *aira*." He dropped a fleeting kiss on her neck before heading off. "I may not have your gentle touch, but I will do my best for him."

"Water," he heard her mutter as he climbed back up to the deck. "A whole sea out there, but not a drop where I need it."

"There's a barrel over in that corner." Rath pointed. "If it is empty, I will find you water as soon as I get back."

He had just crawled out of the hold when he met two crewmen carrying their injured comrade toward the hatch. The fellow was conscious now, his features twisted in pain.

Rath caught the injured man's eye. "The lady will soon set you to rights, friend. She has healed me of a good many wounds and always left me better than I was before."

He made a hasty circuit of the deck, looking for more wounded he could send down to Maura, but he found none.

When he asked Gull, the captain shook his head and answered in a tone of grim pride, "The Han are better swordsmen than archers. They got one lucky shot. We hit four times that many. You know, inlander, I am beginning to think we might get out of this alive, after all."

Gull pulled hard on the rudder and the *Phantom* veered to squeeze between another pair of ore galleys.

How many did that make? Rath had lost count. He wondered that there was any ore left in the Blood Moon Mountains, with this much hacked out and shipped away every year since the Han had conquered Umbria. How many men had sweat, bled and retched away their lives to fill this fleet with its vile cargo year after year?

Impotent fury seethed within him. His fist ached for a weapon powerful enough to channel and purge it, but even the Han did not possess one that destructive.

A harsh chuckle from Gull roused Rath from his fruitless rage. "Do my eyes lie, or is that open sea beyond those cursed tubs?"

Rath peered ahead, his rage ebbing for a moment. "I am only an inlander, so you might not want to take my word for it. But that looks a good deal like open sea to me."

Something about the tone of Gull's laughter told Rath it was partly directed at himself. "I *will* take your word for it. And I reckon I had better find something else to call you…friend."

"I like the sound of that."

Gull thought for a moment, then he grinned. "So do I. And to think this was all the idea of a pretty wench. If you ever tire of her…?"

"The lady will tire of me long before I tire of her." Though Rath meant the words only in jest, somehow they turned back to sting him hard and deep.

He did not have time to fret about it, though, for just then the *Phantom* broke through the final row of ore galleys.

"Slag!" muttered Gull. "Nothing's ever that easy, is it?"

Rath glanced up to see one last Hanish cutter sailing toward them.

"We didn't come through all that to let them get us now!" Gull snagged Rath's arm and hauled him toward the tiller.

"Hold on to this and keep it pulled as far that way as you can until I tell you different. Aye?"

"Aye!" Rath struggled to hold the tiller that had seemed to take no effort at all from Gull.

Meanwhile, the captain strode the length of his ship, calling out orders for setting the sails. From what little Rath had learned about wind and sails, he reckoned Gull was putting the *Phantom* on a course that would force the Hanish ship to veer out of the wind. But would it lose speed quickly enough to keep it from ramming the smaller vessel?

Rath guessed it would be a near thing one way or the other. With each passing moment, as he strained to hold the rudder firm, his fear grew that they would not make it. He glanced toward the hatch, willing Maura to climb up looking for something she might need to tend the injured men.

With danger so near at hand, he wanted her close so he could be certain she was all right. And so he could do whatever he must to protect her, if it came to that.

He did not dare leave the post Gull had assigned him, or he would have gone to her at once. Instead, he made frantic plans how he would reach her and what he would do if the Han boarded Gull's ship, or if their sharp prow caught it broadside.

As the latter seemed more and more likely, Rath braced for the crash. Then suddenly, the Hanish cutter veered back to its original course and the *Phantom* slid past.

Rath sagged under the warm weight of his relief—so much that he almost lost his grip on the tiller. What had made the Han flinch at that last instant? Surely they did not fear a collision with Gull's little *Phantom*.

Could this be the working of his and Maura's destiny?

Gull soon appeared to give Rath a few answers. He fairly danced over the deck in his excitement. "Look, man, look! Slag the tiller—let it go and look!"

He pointed past the Hanish cutter to the bulk of the Ore Fleet in the distance. Though the sun had dipped near the western horizon, it was still possible to make out what was happening to the Hanish ships. Galleys and cutters alike, they floundered as if each were caught in its own private squall. The wind blew no harder than it had all day, yet some invisible tempest churned up giant breakers that tossed the huge, heavy-laden vessels about like wood chips.

Only the ship that had been chasing the *Phantom* seemed not to be ensnared...yet. Seeing the rest of the fleet in trouble must have made its crew veer away so suddenly. Now they furled sails and slowed.

"I have heard of the warding waters." Gull shook his head in wonder. "But never thought to see them at work with my own eyes." He pointed toward the cutter. "The Han cannot decide whether to go to the aid of the others, or hang back so they will not be caught in whatever this is."

Whatever this is. Those words set a chill gnawing deep in Rath's bones—his old wariness of magic. During his travels with Maura that fear had eased as he'd come to understand how she channeled the special power of living things for modest feats of healing and defense. But he'd never seen Maura unleash anything like this. Rath hoped he never would.

Gull appeared to have no such reservations. "The whole Ore Fleet! And to think my little *Phantom* lured them into it. Why this will be talked and sung of on the Dusk Coast for a hundred years!"

Rath did not point out that last night's storm had likely played a part, as well. No harm in letting Gull savor his triumph. If the Han had not been so distracted by the Umbrian vessel sailing in their midst, they might have noticed the first of their own ships running into trouble while they still had time to avoid it themselves. The little madfern missiles might have played a part, too.

One by one the sea began to swallow the floundering Hanish vessels. What would the loss of the Ore Fleet mean for the Han and for Umbria? Rath wondered. A growing shortage of weapons for the garrisons, perhaps? A whisper of crippling uncertainty among the Han that rust was beginning to erode the iron grip in which they had long held his country?

"What will we do now?" he asked Gull.

The captain chuckled and took the tiller from Rath. "Quit gloating, I reckon, and head for harbor before whatever's left of the Ore Fleet tries to come after us."

He called out to his crew, "Trim those sails one last time, lads, then we'll sleep and feast tonight in Margyle!"

The crew seemed to fancy that idea, for they scrambled to obey Gull's orders. Soon the *Phantom* sailed west in a wide arc that kept plenty of distance between it and the ravenous stretch of water that had engulfed the Ore Fleet.

Rath headed off to find Maura. She might need his help tending those wounded men. He was also anxious to tell her what he had just witnessed and what he thought it might mean.

He found her holding a mug to the lips of the man who'd been struck down by his fallen comrade. She had strapped his right arm close to his body with long strips of linen and bound his left leg to what looked like the handle of a mop.

She glanced up when she heard Rath on the ladder, smiling when she saw it was him. "I hope all that cheering means we are out of danger at last."

Rath nodded as he sank down beside her. "Gull says we'll sleep and feast on Margyle tonight."

He did not tell her about their close brush with the Hanish cutter. He would save that for later, when they had firm, dry ground beneath their feet and deadly warding waters between them and any Han who might wish them harm.

"You should have seen what happened to the Ore Fleet." He began to describe it. "For once, they met a force even more merciless than themselves, rot them!"

The man with the arrow in his shoulder stirred and moaned, though his eyes did not open.

Maura cast an anxious glance his way. "I hope the poor fellow will not waken until we've reached Margyle. They must have more skilled healers than I who can remove that barbed arrowhead from his flesh."

"Arrowhead?" The thought paralysed Rath for an instant.

The unconscious crewman had a chunk of metal in his flesh. Metal, like the kind that had made the warding waters devour the Hanish Ore Fleet.

"Gull!" He leaped to his feet and surged up the ladder toward the deck. "Turn back! Arrows! Metal! The warding waters!"

Rath hurled himself up through the open hatch and staggered toward the tiller. The moment he saw Gull's face, he could tell the captain had understood his garbled warning.

But when a huge wave rose out of nowhere to slam across the *Phantom's* bow, he also knew his warning had come too late.

Rath's cry of alarm and his hurried footfall on the ladder made fear tighten around Maura's throat. For a moment, though, she did not understand what had driven him toward the deck shouting at the top of his voice.

Then she heard the crash of a great wave and the *Phantom* reeled like a fighter struck hard on the head. The sudden pitch of the ship flung her sideways on top of the unconscious man. She just managed to keep from hitting the poor fellow's shoulder and driving the arrowhead deeper into his flesh.

The arrowhead! Rath's words echoed in her mind and finally made sense. Could one tiny shard of metal truly be to blame for the tempest now tearing at the *Phantom*?

The injured man moved and groaned when Maura landed on top of him. "What happened? Where am I?"

She pulled herself off him, but kept low, with her arms splayed out to brace her against the next roll of the ship. "You're in the hold. A Hanish archer from one of the ore galleys shot you down from the rigging."

The other injured man spoke up, his voice a bit slurred from the pain-easing brew Maura had given him. "You might be dead, now, if I hadn't broken your fall. Say, lady, why is the ship rocking? Are the Han ramming us?"

The *Phantom* gave another great heave…and so did Maura's belly. She rummaged in her sash for the rest of the sea grass, popped a piece in her mouth and began chewing furiously. She'd be no good to anyone huddled in a corner retching her guts out.

"It isn't the Han." Maura mumbled the words around a mouthful of sea grass.

"No." Rath's voice rang out from above. "It's that arrow."

He climbed back down the ladder, stopping halfway and clinging to it when another huge wave lashed the ship, sending a shower of spray through the hatch. "There are more stuck into the masts and the deck. Gull has his crew scouring the ship for them now."

He jumped down the last few rungs, landing on his hands and knees near Maura. "Can you get this one out?"

"I told you, I don't—"

Before she could finish, Rath leaned close and whispered, "If we cannot get it off the ship any other way, Gull will have this poor fellow thrown overboard!"

She had to try, then. She could not let a man drown because he'd had the bad fortune to be shot by a Hanish arrow. Whatever she might do to prevent it, she would have to work quickly. The ship could not take much more of this violent buffeting and still remain afloat.

If only she had not woken the poor fellow by falling on him! Anything she did to dislodge that arrowhead was sure to cause him great pain. Maura shrank from that.

"What can I do?" she asked Rath in an urgent whisper. "I have nothing sharp I can…cut it out with. Remember what Langbard said about Hanish arrows, how the barbs catch in the flesh if you try to pull them out."

"Push it through, then, like Langbard did for me!"

"I don't know how!"

She heard voices overhead. Gull must be sending someone to fetch the wounded man.

"You may know more than you think." Rath clutched her hand. "Did Langbard share any of that skill with you in the passing ritual?"

As she chided herself for not thinking of it, Maura marveled that Rath had. The passing ritual was the first stage of a journey between this life and the afterworld. When the spirit of a living person accompanied a dying one, a sharing of memories took place, so that part of the dying person would live on.

Maura's passing ritual with her wizard guardian had been too brief, rushed by the threat of lurking danger. But since then, she'd discovered unexpected memories of Langbard's among her own, stirred by a chance word or experience. She had never yet tried calling upon a memory she could not be certain was even there.

She heard someone scrambling down the ladder.

"Hold them back," she begged Rath. "Do not let them take him until—"

"Do it!" cried Rath. "I know you can."

If only she could have half the confidence in herself that Rath had in her. Maura crawled over to the wounded man who was moaning in pain. She wished she had time to brew him a draft to ease it, but that would have to wait. Another shower of cold, briny spray crashed into the hold. The boards of the hull groaned under the beating they were taking.

"Lie still," she bid the wounded man. "Take a deep breath and hold it."

She groped for the stub of the arrow shaft sticking out of his shoulder, hoping that action would unearth the memory of what she must do next. She pictured the upstairs chamber of Langbard's cottage with Rath lying on the bed, a Hanish arrow imbedded in his arm. She pictured Langbard perched on the side of the bed, preparing to expel the arrow.

Then, suddenly, she *was* Langbard, seeing the whole scene through his eyes. Knowing what he…what she must do.

Spikeroot—that was what she needed! But did she have any left in her sash? Not knowing its use, she had once thought of emptying that pocket to store something more needful.

The dark, wet, pitching hold of the ship seemed to recede around her. Maura heard Rath's voice as if from a long distance, first pleading, then challenging. "I will not let you disturb the lady at her work. Gull can have my head for it, if he wants."

"The fish will have all our heads and the rest of our flesh, too," the crewman shouted, "if we do not throw that cursed arrow into the sea one way or the other!"

"They want to throw me overboard!" The wounded man thrashed about, then howled in pain as he jerked the stub of the arrow shaft in Maura's grip. "Don't let them take me!"

"Be still!" she ordered him, startled to hear the words came out in *that tone*—the one Langbard had only used on rare occasions to compel instant obedience.

When the man froze, she turned to the one who was trying to push past Rath. "Stay back!"

The sounds of a struggle between the two men ceased.

A heady sense of power pulsed through her. Might the warding waters heed her if she ordered them to calm? Maura decided to save that as a last resort.

Her fingers fumbled in her sash pocket. The spikeroot—she had not thrown it way after all! Perhaps Langbard's slumbering memory had roused just enough to prevent her.

Pulling out as much of the powdered root as she could hold, she held her palm to catch a few drops of water spilling through the hatch. The seawater bound with the spikeroot powder to make a thick paste that Maura packed around the wound.

Then the words of the incantation whispered through her mind. Maura spat out the sea grass and began to chant them, hoping she could hold her gorge long enough to recite the whole spell.

The nub of the arrow shaft began to vibrate beneath her fingers and the wounded man screamed in torment until all Maura wanted to do was jam her fingers in her ears and flee from the awful sound. She stumbled over some of the words.

Then she felt Rath hovering behind her. "Don't stop now!"

He wrapped one arm around her, then reached with his other hand to grip the arrow shaft. What was he doing?

Maura chanted the spell louder, trying to drown out the man's screams. The arrow shaft vibrated harder and harder until she feared it would shatter.

Then something taut snapped.

The screams choked off and the butt of the arrow shaft thrust through flesh and bone to gouge into the floorboards of the hold beneath. Maura slumped forward, gasping for breath as if she had just run many miles or hefted a weight far beyond her strength.

Rolling the injured man out of the way, Rath pried the arrowhead from the wet wood. Then he lunged up, twisting around to shove it into the hands of the waiting crewman. "There—go! Get rid of it!"

The man clambered up the ladder as huge waves pounded the *Phantom* from every direction at once. The ship's hull quivered like the arrow shaft had. Then the unbearable tension broke with a shudder that sounded like the ocean had heaved a great sigh. A breathless, exhausted calm settled over everything.

"Well done, *aira*!" Rath spun Maura around into a swift, hard embrace, with a kiss to match.

She yielded for a sweet, delirious moment, then pushed him away with pretended annoyance. "Enough of that! Let me tend this poor man's wound while he still has a drop of blood left in him. What a mercy he swooned when the pain became too great. I'm not sure I could have kept up much longer if he hadn't."

Pulling another strip of linen from her sash, she wet it with the seawater now dripping more slowly through the hold. Then she sprinkled the damp cloth with candleflax to staunch the bleeding. While she was busy with that, Rath moved the man with broken bones to a drier part of the hold and fetched him a blanket.

"What were you doing," asked Maura "when you put your arm around me and grabbed hold of the arrow shaft?"

Rath chuckled. "I remembered some wise words an old wizard once told me."

"Langbard said many wise things. Which one do you mean?"

Why was she blinking back tears after all this time and everything that had happened? Was it the strange drooping of spirits that often came after danger had passed? Or was it the fleeting but intense connection she had felt with her beloved guardian while she'd worked his spell?

Whatever provoked such intense feelings, Rath seemed to sense and understand them. He made his way back to her and dropped to his haunches, raising his hand to rub up and down against her arm.

"I did not get to hear many of Langbard's wise sayings in the little time I knew him. But I do recall him saying, 'Spells are all very well, but sometimes there is no substitute for a swift application of physical force.'" He imitated Langbard's husky, resonant voice so well, it made Maura laugh and sob at the same time.

Rath brought his hand higher, to rest against her cheek. "I reckoned your spell could use some physical force to help it along. It seemed to work."

Maura nodded. Then a stray breeze found its way down the hatch to whisper over her damp clothes, making her shiver. "Not a moment too soon."

"I wonder." Rath fetched a coarse-woven blanket and wrapped it around her shoulders. "If we had needed another moment, something tells me the Giver would have found it for us."

Beneath his wry tone, Maura heard a note of belief, tentative but sincere. Not a high-flown, zealous faith fired by witnessing marvels and doing great deeds, but a sturdy, workaday belief that grew slowly over time. One that would warm a body against the cold of despair and wear well through the years.

"Just think—" she caught his hand and gripped it tight "—if one tiny ship can bring about the destruction of the Ore Fleet, there may be hope for us to liberate Umbria, after all."

Rath drew in a deep, slow breath. "Don't get ahead of yourself, love. The *Phantom* did not sink those Hanish ships—it was the warding waters."

"Perhaps we will find some other great power to turn to our advantage." At the moment, nothing seemed beyond their reach.

Though the hold had grown too dark to see more than shadows, she could make out Rath shaking his head. "I don't know, *aira*. Great powers can be dangerous things."

Then, more to himself than to her, he murmured, "And not only to the folks they are used *against,* either."

Just then, one of the crew called down through the hatch. "Come on up on deck, inlanders! The captain wants you."

"Tell your captain he can wait," Maura called back, "until I have these men properly tended."

Rath smiled to himself, wondering how many of the fierce men on this ship would have the courage to delay carrying out one of Captain Gull's orders.

He tugged on her sleeve. "Listen." From both wounded men came the soft, regular breathing of sleep. "You cannot do much for them now that a good rest will not do better."

"True." Maura's hand fumbled out of the darkness to find his. "I will need light to set those bones and clean that arrow wound properly. No doubt there are healers on the Islands with greater skill than I who can set them both to rights."

Rath hoisted her to her feet. "There may be healers better equipped than you, *aira,* with gardens of rare herbs and such. But I would defy any of them to do half what you have done with only that sash and whatever you could gather along the way to fill its pockets."

Maura gave a weary chuckle. "Langbard often used to say, 'Necessity is a harsh teacher, but a thorough one.' I confess, I never understood what he meant until I began my journey."

She held tight to Rath's arm as they groped toward the ladder, in a way that told him she depended upon him to support and guide her. His heart ached the way his belly had after those few times in his life when he'd eaten more than his fill. Now his love for Maura felt like more than his heart could comfortably contain.

"There is more to it than that," he said as she started up the ladder. "All the skill and supplies in the world are nothing without the will to help folks. I have never seen anyone with as great a store of that as you have."

Maura scrambled up onto the deck, then turned to offer Rath a hand. "Perhaps you should have looked longer in the waters of the Secret Glade. Then you would have seen someone with vast reserves of that will."

Perhaps, Rath admitted to himself, but did he have the courage to tap it? Like every other power, it had its perils.

Several small lanterns hung from the lower masts, shedding a shadowy light over the deck.

Captain Gull stepped out of a patch of shadow and performed a deep bow before Rath and Maura. "I have never met a pair of inlanders so handy to have about when there's trouble. My thanks to you for saving my ship. I am in your debt."

Rath returned the bow with self-conscious awkwardness, though he could not decide how to reply. His past had taught him more about trading threats and insults than accepting courtesy.

Instead, he glanced out into the night where clusters of distant lights flickered. "Will we put in to harbor tonight?"

Gull shook his head. "We'll drop anchor here and wait for the dawn tide. Though if you are anxious to reach shore, I can let you have one of the small boats and a couple of my men to row you in."

"Should we?" Rath whispered to Maura.

He had no wish to hasten their arrival on the Islands. For all its dangers and hardships, this short voyage had been like a welcome return to his old life. To these men he was no Waiting King with a heavy mantel of impossible expectations, just another inlander who had managed to earn their grudging respect. All that would change once he and Maura set foot on shore.

But he knew she must long for the safety and assurance of firm earth beneath her.

Perhaps Maura sensed how he felt, or perhaps she felt something like it herself. "The sea is calm here. Another night aboard ship will do us no harm. Besides, I want to be near at hand in case those wounded men wake and need tending."

"As you will, then." Gull sounded pleased with their decision. "I reckon a little festivity is in order, to celebrate our daring victory over the Hanish Ore Fleet. Will you join us?"

This time Rath did not hesitate. "With pleasure!"

"You heard the man." Gull snapped his fingers. "What are we waiting for?"

All at once the night air bubbled with the rollicking, infectious music of wooden pipes and hand drums. Rath found himself seated on a sack full of something soft, with Maura's even softer backside nestled in his lap. This was definitely better than whatever reception might await them on the Islands!

When someone thrust a tall jug into Rath's hand, he took a long swig that made his eyes water.

"What is that?" he gasped when the liquid had burned its way down his throat, numbing as it went. He was no stranger to strong drink…at least he hadn't thought so. But this…!

"Your first taste of *sythria*?" Gull took the jug from Rath's hand and guzzled the fiery brew without betraying the least distress. "You must have sea-going blood in you. Most inlanders spew their first drink back up and scream for water."

So that was *sythria*. Rath had heard of the stuff and assumed its reputation exaggerated. Now he knew better. His belly felt as if it was full of flaming oil.

Maura grabbed the jug out of Gull's hand and sniffed its fumes. "The stuff doesn't smell that bad. What is it made of?"

Before Rath could stop her, she tipped the jug back and drained it. After what he and Gull had drunk, there could not have been much left. Still, Rath expected her to choke and gag or belch a cloud of steam.

But she only fanned her mouth. "That *is* strong! Remind me not to it drink so fast next time."

"I will try," said Rath, though he wondered if he would remember.

From that single drink, he already felt dizzy and a good deal more carefree than he had in a long time. Perhaps he could stomach another sip of *sythria,* now that the first one had numbed his throat. For some reason that notion made him laugh like a fool. But foolishness felt strangely pleasant. The look on Gull's face as he stared at Maura made Rath laugh, too.

"Your pardon, mistress." Gull blinked his eyes as if trying to decide whether they still worked properly. "I have never before known a woman ask for a second drink of *sythria* after she has had her first."

Maura sniffed the mouth of the jug again and shrugged. "I've tasted worse. My guardian was the most terrible cook in Norest…perhaps in the whole of Umbria. What did you say this was made of?"

"Pardon, mistress, in my amazement, I did not answer your question. *Sythria* is distilled from the rind of sythfruit that grows on the Islands. Folk here brew a very fine wine from the fruit itself, but Duskporters like a drink that has a bit more…brawn to it. Cheap, too, for sythfruit rind is bitter and would only be thrown away. We put it to much more worthwhile use."

The hillcat around Gull's neck rose and stretched. For the

first time Rath had seen, it bounded off its master's back into a shadowed part of the deck.

"Abri must be hungry." Gull seized another jug from a passing crewman and took a long drink from it. "Rats beware!"

He rose from his perch on a small keg and made a sweeping, rather unsteady, bow before Maura. "Will you do me the honor of a dance, mistress? I dared not ask you while Abri had her claws in me. Jealous creature—she would never have permitted it."

Maura made no move to accept his invitation. "I fear it would be less an honor than a torture for your toes, Captain. I have never danced with a partner."

"Never danced?" Gull staggered back. Either he was pretending to be shocked by Maura's words, or those two long, fast drinks from the *sythria* jug were having an effect on him.

It must have been the first, for he recovered quite nimbly to swoop forward and grab Maura by the hand. Before she or Rath could protest, Gull pulled her to her feet and thrust another jug at Rath to keep him company in her absence.

"That is a grave misfortune we must put right at once." Gull tucked one hand around Maura's waist, while the other, outstretched, gripped hers. In that hold, he galloped her several times around a small circle of deck where none of the crew were sitting.

At first Maura squealed with a mixture of excitement and dismay as Gull whirled her around. Those squeals soon gave way to breathless laughter and her stiff, reluctant posture relaxed. By their last circuit, she appeared to be leading Gull a merry dance.

Rath took several slow drinks from the jug in his hand. In between them, he sat scowling while the *sythria* kindled a blaze in his belly.

Gull? Hmmph! The man's name should be *Gall*, for he had plenty of it. More than enough to suit Rath.

What did the scoundrel think he was playing at, plying Maura with strong drink, then dragging her out of her husband's arms for a wild jaunt around the deck? Did he not have the sense to know that she would draw the lecherous gaze of every man on board, the way her ripe curves filled out that boy's shirt and breeches? Or did he not care?

Rath tipped the *sythria* jug again. He was beginning to enjoy its burnt, musky taste. Curses—the jug was empty!

He lurched to his feet only to find them as contrary as a mismatched team of balky horses. Each wanted to go its own way and neither would move in the direction he wanted them to go. Rath was not about to be thwarted by parts of his own body. So he started forward, letting each leg do what it wanted while he concentrated on keeping his balance.

He had managed to stagger a few steps when a clever idea occurred to him. If he waited at the edge of the ring of crewmen, Gull and Maura's spinning dance would bring them right to him. He congratulated himself on getting stopped without pitching face-first onto the deck.

When Gull and Maura pranced past, Rath stopped them with a heavy hand on Gull's shoulder. "I reckon you've done enough dancing for one night, friend…with my wife at least."

Gull winked at Maura and laughed. "Fie, he's almost as bad as Abri! We should have sent him off with her to hunt rats."

"Sit down, Rath." Maura lifted his hand off Gull's shoulder. "Before you fall down. Don't spoil the celebration."

Her gently chiding tone did nothing to soothe Rath's temper. Besides, his mind was so fixed on Gull's last words that he scarcely heeded what she said.

"Hunt rats, you say?" He grabbed Gull by his long plume of dark hair and wrenched him high on his toes. "I won't need to go far to find a rat, will I?"

"Leave off, you daft inlander!" cried Gull. "No man lays hands upon me aboard *my* ship!"

Suddenly, Gull heaved his feet from the deck, making Rath bear his full weight with one arm. Before Rath could let go of him or lose his balance and topple forward, Gull swung by his hair, driving his feet hard into Rath's belly.

The air whooshed out of him as pain exploded within. He collapsed onto the deck, writhing and gasping for air that would not come fast enough. But pain and even air meant little to Rath Talward when his fighting blood was roused. Gull had roused it to a blazing pitch—first with his insults and now with this attack.

"Let that be a lesson to you, inlander." Gull pulled himself up from the deck where Rath had dropped him. "Most men I'd have killed for what you just did, but…"

Did Gull reckon he meant to lie there and swallow such humiliation? Ha!

Rath swung his arm in a wide swath and caught Gull by the ankle, jerking him off his feet. Before he went down, Gull kicked Rath in the face with his free foot. Rath flinched, blood spewing from his throbbing nose.

The little demon could fight better with his feet than most men twice his size could with their fists! A distant, detached part of Rath's mind acknowledged it even as he kept hold of Gull's foot and landed a good hard blow to some part of the smuggler's compact body.

For a few moments, the two men rolled around the deck, thrashing away at each other with feet, fists, knees and elbows.

"Stop this at once!" Maura cried out in a tone of ringing rage. "Both of you!"

To his credit, Rath did hesitate for an instant. But Gull took advantage of that hesitation to drive his sharp little knee hard into Rath's groin. Rath let out a savage bellow of pain but managed to get his hands around Gull's slender throat and squeeze with all his strength.

Just as he was savoring the bulge of Gull's eyes, a familiar but detested sensation stole through his flesh, making his hands fall slack and freeze motionless along with the rest of his body. The same must have happened to Gull, for he did

not take advantage of Rath's paralysis to land another un-
sporting blow.

Instead, he channeled his hostility into a black glare.
"What have you done to me, inlander? I will not stand for
this, curse you!"

"You have no choice but to stand for it," Rath growled. "Or
lie for it. And it is none of my doing." He tried to turn his head
to glare at Maura, but his neck refused to move any more than
the rest of him. "It is *hers*. Curse those fool cobwebs!"

"Hers?" Gull's gaze shifted sidelong, but he had no better
luck making his head turn than Rath had. "You mean…"

At some point during their brawl, the music had stopped,
but Rath only noticed the silence now. He expected Maura's
voice to fill it, with a firm rebuke to him and Gull.

Instead, a male voice sliced through the silence, speaking
Umbrian, but with a distinctive *twaran* lilt. "What is the meaning of this, Gull? You fouled our warding waters beyond further use by leading the whole Hanish Ore Fleet into them.
Now you anchor offshore, engaging in all manner of violence
and debauchery."

Something about the fellow's tone made Rath forget his good-
natured tiff with Gull. Perhaps it was his outlaw nature to re-
sent any figure of authority. Or perhaps the *sythria* made him
spoil for a fresh fight.

Into the cowed hush that followed the man's words, Rath
muttered, loud enough for all to hear, "You ought to try a little debauchery now and then. It might be just the thing to
loosen those tight bowels of yours."

The silence that greeted *his* words put Rath in mind of a very
thin-shelled egg tethering on the edge of a high wall. Even the
waves seemed to stop their quiet lapping against the hull of the
ship to listen. In that brittle stillness, the soft, deliberate approach of a pair of leather-soled boots sounded louder than the
earlier thunder of the hand drums.

It occurred to Rath, not for the first time, that taunting a mobile opponent while he lay helpless was a stupid thing to do. He could not help himself, though.

The slender leather toe of a boot hooked under his chin, turning Rath's head as he was unable to do for himself. A good-size foot poised above his throat. Long ago he had learned to hide fear, and he flattered himself that he'd become good at it. But it never got easier.

He stared up at a man who appeared very tall and lean…at least from his angle. Clad in tight leggings and a long pale brown tunic, the man had piercing dark eyes and features so straight and perfectly proportioned Rath's fist ached to knock something askew. Or at the very least, to muss the fellow's close-cropped dark hair from its unnatural tidiness.

"And who are you," asked the owner of the boot, "to fling insults about without having either the courage or manners to rise and say them to my face?"

"I'm the Waiting King," Rath growled as if it was only a contemptuous jest meant to shock the other man. He would have had a harder time uttering the words as if he meant them. "Who are you?"

"Don't mind him, Lord Idrygon!" cried Gull. "You can't hold an inlander responsible for the blather he spews on his first bellyful of *sythria*."

Lord Idrygon? Well, well. Lord of what? Rath wondered. He tried to stifle a traitorous notion that Lord Idrygon looked the way he'd once pictured the Waiting King.

Rath shifted his gaze to Maura. When she finally stopped gaping at Idrygon long enough to spare him a glance, he mouthed the word *please?*

She made a face, as if she had bitten into something sour. Then her lips began to move in a silent incantation and soon Rath was able to make his fingers wiggle.

In the meantime, Lord Idrygon had withdrawn the toe of his boot, letting Rath's head fall slack again. "A man who cannot curb his tongue when he drinks too much should not drink at all."

His hand now free to move, Rath seized Idrygon's foot before it reached the deck. He held it an inch or two in the air, enough to keep the other man off balance. Except that Idrygon seemed more poised and steady standing on one foot than most men looked on two.

Since the move was clearly not achieving its purpose, Rath let go of Idrygon's foot and staggered upright, hauling Gull along with him. He swiped his shirtsleeve across his lower face to wipe away some of the blood dripping from his nose.

"I'll make you a bargain, *my lord*. If you curb your tongue, I will try to curb mine." Rath jerked his head in the direction of the warding waters. "If you had asked before casting blame, we could have told you Gull did not *lead* the Ore Fleet here. A storm blew them nearer your coast than they usually come. We are guilty of nothing more than some damn fine sailing to wriggle out of their clutches."

"I saw what happened." Idrygon's well-shaped mouth compressed into a thin, rigid line. "If this ship had not distracted the Han, they might have seen how close they'd strayed to our coast and made some effort to avoid the warding waters. Gull should know better than to come here so near the time when the Ore Fleet sails."

With all the anticipation he would have felt pulling a bowstring to return enemy fire, Rath drew breath to reply.

Before he could summon the right words, Maura appeared at his side, looking pale and agitated. "Are you saying you did not summon us with that messenger bird? But Langbard told me the first one came from here. And the second message said Captain Gull would bring us."

"Messenger birds?" murmured Idrygon in a flat, dazed-sounding voice. His haughty features twisted in a grimace of disbelief as he looked from Maura with her boy's clothes and wild hair to Rath, all beaten and bloody. "But that cannot be."

Much as he relished making this arrogant lordling squirm,

Rath also wished it *could not be*—that somehow this was all a huge mistake.

"We send those fool birds out all the time." Idrygon's contemptuous tone left no doubt what he thought of the practice. "No one has ever answered their summons."

Maura's shoulders slumped and Rath sensed what she must be thinking—that Langbard's death and all their struggles had been for nothing.

He wrapped his arm around her and gave a heartening squeeze. He might not be very promising king material, but he wasn't a man to give up without trying, either.

Leaning toward Lord Idrygon, he flashed his most impudent grin and announced, "Someone has now."

6

What did Lord Idrygon mean about sending messenger birds *all the time?* The fiery *sythria* seethed in Maura's belly until she feared she might make a complete fool of herself by retching on the Vestan lord's elegantly shod feet.

She'd assumed that she and Rath would be expected and welcomed here—find answers to all their doubts and questions. Now it appeared their arrival might pose far more questions than it answered.

When Rath wrapped his arm around her, Maura could not decide whether to savor his clumsy gesture of support or to turn and throttle him for making such an ass of himself! No wonder Lord Idrygon looked so dazed. Any high-flown visions the poor man might have had about the Waiting King and Destined Queen must be dying a painful death.

To give him credit, he rallied his shaken composure quickly.

"Your pardons for beginning our acquaintance on a sour note." He made a stiff bow to them. "These are…surprising tidings indeed. I think you had better come ashore with me now.

No doubt you will desire an audience with the Council of Sages as soon as one can be arranged."

Maura gave a tentative nod. She supposed they would. Was it the Council of Sages who had sent the messenger birds? Would they be able to answer *some* of her questions, at least?

"And you will surely wish to prepare yourselves for the audience," continued Lord Idrygon. "Rest, groom, tend your hurts. I offer you the hospitality of my house for your stay on Margyle."

On the still night air, Maura fancied she heard a hushed buzz spread among Gull's crew. The tone of that murmur told her Lord Idrygon's offer of hospitality must be a great honor.

But his mention of tending injuries reminded her she had other obligations. "Our thanks to you, sir. But two crewmen were wounded during our fight with the Han. They may need me in the night." She patted her sash. "I am a healer, though perhaps modest in skill compared to many on the Islands."

"The wounded men should be brought ashore now, as well," said Lord Idrygon almost before Maura finished speaking. The haste of his offer suggested eagerness, but the set of his well-bred features looked more as though he was compelled to swallow some foul tonic. "They will be taken to a place where they can receive the best possible care."

Put that way, Maura couldn't very well refuse the man's invitation, could she? She glanced at Rath, her brows raised.

He replied with a repentant shrug. His earlier belligerence seemed to have deserted him. "Go, stay, it's all the same to me. Whatever you think best, *aira*."

"I believe we should accept Lord Idrygon's generous invitation. He is right that we ought to make ourselves presentable before we meet with anyone else."

She did not want to risk making as unfavorable an impression on the Council of Sages as they had on Lord Idrygon. At least he appeared willing to give them a second chance. Others might be less forbearing.

"Very good." Lord Idrygon bowed again. This or less apt to crack his spine. "The wounded crewmen, we would find them belowdecks?"

When Maura nodded, he turned and gave some hushed but forceful orders to three men he had brought on board with him. All wore the same boots with slightly curled toes, tight-fitted leggings and high-collared tunics, though theirs were shorter than Idrygon's.

The instant he finished speaking, two of his men headed toward the hatch while Idrygon and the third man escorted Rath and Maura to a long slender boat moored beside the *Phantom*.

As they climbed down into the craft, Maura heard Idrygon call over his shoulder to Captain Gull, "Make sure you do not sail until we have had a chance to talk!"

Rath tried to protest that none of this was Gull's fault, but Idrygon gave no sign he heard…or cared.

They rowed ashore in silence. By the light of the waning midsummer moon, Maura could make out a large number of pale-colored buildings clustered on gently sloping hills that surrounded a small bay. A sense of safety and tranquillity hung about the place. It seemed to open its arms and welcome her, perhaps recognizing how deeply she craved what it offered.

Langbard's cottage and Hoghill Farm had once seemed like peaceful havens to her. But even there, peril had always lurked. Kept at bay by Langbard's power, it had skulked in the shadows waiting for a moment of weakness or inattention to strike. Here, she sensed true peace, unlike any she had ever known.

At last the boat tied up to a small wharf. Idrygon disembarked with quick, lithe movements then turned and extended his hand to Maura. Once he had helped her ashore, he offered his hand to Rath, who ignored it, almost tipping the boat as he staggered onto the wharf.

A mild sea breeze wafted up from the bay, but it did not smell of brine and fish like the air in Duskport. Instead, the subtle mingling of flowers and herbs reminded Maura of her garden behind Langbard's cottage and the warm spring in the Blood Moon foothills where she and Rath had rested on their journey.

Idrygon froze for a moment, as if watching or listening for something. Then he strode off into the night calling softly, "This way."

Though Maura had no idea where they were going, it seemed Idrygon might be taking them by a roundabout, little-used route. Now and then he would stop for a moment and listen before going on. He acted as if he was smuggling something forbidden, and possibly dangerous, onto the island.

After walking uphill for a time, then doubling back, at last they reached a large pale-colored house. Again Idrygon stopped, listened and peered into the darkness before pulling open a door of elegantly carved latticework and ushering them inside.

A single tiny lamp burned in a sconce beside the door. By its light, Maura could see they had entered an enclosed courtyard at the center of which a small fountain gurgled softly. A number of potted shrubs stood in clusters, giving the place the air of a forest glade transplanted indoors.

"It's beautiful!" she whispered. "I could sleep quite comfortably here."

She could sleep comfortably anywhere the ground was not rocking beneath her. Ever since they'd stepped off the boat, she had relished the firm foundation of solid earth under her feet.

"No need for that." Idrygon sounded mildly shocked at the idea of their spending the night in his courtyard.

His reaction made Maura grin to herself in the darkness. This would be a far more comfortable sleeping place than most of the ones she and Rath had shared on their journey.

"There is a guest chamber you may use." Idrygon took the lamp from the wall sconce and started toward a wide archway in the right-hand wall of the courtyard.

After a few steps, he stopped so suddenly that Maura and Rath almost bumped into him. When she peered around their host, Maura could see a faint light coming toward them. It flickered and grew brighter as someone approached, also bearing a lamp.

An instant later a man emerged through the archway. At first glance, he looked so much like Idrygon that Maura fancied he might be some enchanted reflection.

The other man startled at the sight of them. "You are late coming home!"

"And you are late going to bed, Delyon," replied Idrygon in a chiding tone. "What keeps you up?"

Delyon held out his right hand, which gripped a scroll. "Reading." He sounded almost guilty. "What else? Have you brought guests with you?"

He held up his lamp to get a better look, which gave Maura a better look at *him*. His clothing was almost identical to Idrygon's, but he had a rumpled air about him. He wore his hair a bit longer, and the way it curled around his face had a softening effect on his fine, regular features.

"I have brought guests." Idrygon took a step toward him, perhaps to block his view. "But the hour is late and introductions can wait until morning."

"I suppose they can." Delyon yawned, then headed across the courtyard, raising his scroll in a kind of salute. "Sleep well, guests. I look forward to meeting you tomorrow."

"My brother," said Idrygon. Then, as if to explain or apologize, he added, "Delyon is a scholar."

They passed through the archway and by several doors on either side of the wide, tiled gallery furnished with clusters of chairs and small tables.

Finally Idrygon stopped in front of one door and threw it open. "I hope this will serve you for tonight."

Behind her, Maura heard Rath give a snort of laughter. She knew what he was thinking. This spacious chamber would be easily the most luxurious place in which they'd ever spent the night...apart from the Secret Glade, perhaps.

A wide, low bed thrust out from the opposite wall with a canopy of fine netting draped over it, suspended from a hook in the ceiling. A pair of chairs and a small table occupied one corner, in front of a shuttered window, while another corner held the most elaborate washstand Maura had ever seen. Finely woven rush matting covered the floor, from which rose a faint aroma of dried flowers.

"This will do very well, my lord." Maura tried not to laugh. "We thank you for your hospitality."

"It is an honor." He set the lamp down on the elaborate washstand. "I believe you should find everything here that you might need for the night. I would ask that you remain here in the morning until I come for you."

A simple enough request, but it made Maura uneasy somehow. Before Rath could take it into his head to protest, she answered, "If that is what you wish, you are our host."

"Very good." Idrygon stepped back out into the hallway and drew the door closed behind him. "Sleep well."

Maura turned to find Rath had pushed the netting aside and settled onto the bed.

"Ah! Hope this will serve, indeed! We could have brought back half of Gull's crew to sleep with us!" He winced as he raised his arms to tuck behind his head, but his features soon lapsed into a roguish grin. "I'm glad we didn't, though."

"You can stop looking at me that way, Rath Talward!" Maura investigated the washstand where she found a ewer of the most delicate glazed pottery filled with water, as well as a matching basin and some washing and drying cloths. "If you reckon I mean to let some battered brawler have his way with me, you had better think again."

"But Maura…"

"But what?" She filled the basin and carried it to the bed, some cloths spread over her arm. "Gull did not sully my honor this evening. He only showed me how to dance…which is a good deal more than I can say for you."

In a gentler tone she added, "Now peel that shirt off so I can see how badly you're bruised."

She set the basin on the floor beside the bed and wet one of the cloths. As Rath struggled out of his shirt, she swiped at the dried blood all over his lower face. "You must remember you are not an outlaw anymore. You are a king. You cannot answer every imagined insult with your fists."

"We have had this talk before." Rath threw his shirt onto the floor, then clamped his hand around her wrist. "Besides, I thought you liked the outlaw." He drew her toward him, as much with the shimmering heat of his gaze as with the tug of his hand. "Thought you *burned* for him."

Maura tried to hold on to her anger, but it slipped through her grasp like a greased rope—greased by Rath's rough-edged charm and by the long-forbidden feelings she was now at liberty to indulge. It did seem a shame to have such a fine bed at their disposal and not make use of it.

"Behave yourself, now!" She swooped to kiss a spot on his neck she knew was ticklish. "At least let me clean you up and apply a poultice where Gull kicked you—that'll teach you to pick on a man half your size!"

Removing her sash, she mixed a potent compound of laceweed, marshwort, moonmallow and winterwort, bound with a bit of water warmed over the lamp flame. Then she smeared it on Rath's belly and bound it with the last of her linen strips.

"This reminds me of the time you tended me after I fought Turgen." Rath chuckled. "When I squirmed under your touch, you worried that you were *hurting* me." This time he made no effort to hide his true response.

"Make fun of my innocence, will you?" Maura rinsed her hands, then let them stray down his body to torment him further.

When she had him writhing beneath her touch and a low growl of desire rumbling in his throat, she rose from her perch on the edge of the bed. She trimmed the lamp as low as it would burn yet still cast a faint light. Slowly, she removed her clothes and wiped a damp cloth over her naked body. It did nothing to cool her desire, but the sight clearly stoked a hotter blaze in Rath's flesh.

"Come to bed, *aira*," he pleaded. "I am sorry I picked that fight with Gull. It was a daft thing to do. I should have known such a little fellow could never command the way he does without being able to fight like a demon. I swear I'll beg his pardon the next time I see him."

"I suppose..." Maura circled the bed, draping the fine netting back over it. "Will you promise to make better use of your wits after this before you let your fists fly?"

"Aye!" He held out his arms to her. "You have my word."

"The word of a king?" Maura lifted the edge of the canopy and slipped under it. "Or the word of an outlaw?"

"Why, the outlaw, of course." Rath reached to caress her bare breast as she crawled toward him. "He's the one who needs your help to mend all his wild ways."

Maura gave a deep, purring chuckle. "I am not sure I want *all* his wild ways mended." She straddled his hips, bearing her weight on her outstretched arms to hover over him, inviting his touch. Then she leaned toward him, grazing his chest with her breasts, but sparing the sore muscles of his belly.

Nuzzling his ear, she whispered, "I will make you a bargain."

Rath arched his hard, lean body toward her. "Anything!"

"If you will promise to play the king in the council chamber," she vowed, "I will let you play the outlaw in the bedchamber."

Play the king in the council chamber. Play the *king* in the council chamber. Rath repeated the words over and over in his mind like an incantation for one of Maura's spells. He feared it would take stronger magic than hers to turn him into a king.

Would the sages of the Vestan Council think so, too? He could feel the weight of their curious, uneasy stares resting upon him while Lord Idrygon explained how the Hanish Ore Fleet had come to flounder in their warding waters.

After a miserable night's sleep, Rath had woken with a headache so fierce none of Maura's remedies could do more than blunt it. All their preparations for this appearance before the Council of Sages had not helped his head…or his temper.

He craned his neck and twisted it, trying to relieve the pressure around his throat. Though Vestan tunics flared out below the waist, the chest and arms were close fitting, as was the high collar. The one Idrygon had lent Rath fit very snug on his muscular torso, and like a noose around his neck.

Maura caught his eye and flashed a reassuring smile. She looked every inch a queen in her loose, sleeveless gown of pale blue-green linen with slender filets of matching ribbon twined through her hair.

She'd admired *his* hair, too, after Idrygon's mother-in-law had washed it and cut it in the Vestan style. Rath had no illusions this short trim suited his shaggy mane the way it did Idrygon's straight hair or Delyon's crisp curls. But he'd stopped fretting about his hair when the forceful old lady had proceeded to shave him so close he feared she would scrape all the skin off his lower face.

No question—this being a king was an uncomfortable business. Rath wondered why a war-leader needed to look well groomed any more than an outlaw did. But Idrygon had insisted with some confusing talk about Council factions and support for an invasion. Though Rath had not warmed to him since their first meeting, he knew enough to respect Idrygon as a man of ability, drive and vision. The kind of man who might be able to make the dream of a free Umbria come true if he put his mind to it.

"To conclude—" Idrygon's words drew Rath's attention back to the council chamber "—we cannot hold Captain Gull and his men responsible for what happened when they acted on instructions from this Council. How do we know the storm that blew the Ore Fleet toward our coast was not the Giver's will at work?"

Though Idrygon spoke in a tone of hushed reverence, Rath questioned whether the man felt any more true belief in the Giver than he once had.

"Your pardon." A voice of quiet authority drew all eyes to a tiny old woman sitting three places to the right of Idrygon. "I am not aware of any instructions from this Council that might have summoned Captain Gull to our shores at such a hazardous time. I hope you have not taken it upon yourself to act in the Council's name without our knowledge or consent, Idrygon."

Her cheeks were sunken, her dark hair heavily frosted with white and she looked as though a hard gust of wind might blow her off the island. But her penetrating gaze and regal bearing told Rath she was *not* someone a smart man would cross if he had a choice. He wondered if anyone else on the Vestan Islands dared address the forceful Lord Idrygon in that chiding tone.

"I protest, Madame Verise!" Idrygon looked so offended, Rath knew he must be guilty of whatever the old lady had hinted at. "My aim has always been to serve this Council, the Vestan Islands and the kingdom of Umbria."

This, Rath sensed, was altogether true.

Madame Verise must have known it, too. For she waved a withered hand. "Oh very well, then be plain, lad. What summons of ours brought that ship from the Dusk Coast? And while you are at it, who are these guests you have brought before the council?"

She did not sound as though Rath's sacrifices in the cause of good grooming had impressed her much.

"How astute of you to pose those two questions together, madame." As Idrygon looked around at the council, he did not rub his hands with glee at the opening he'd been given. But Rath sensed he wanted to. "For they are inextricably bound."

Rath wondered if *inextricably* meant what he thought it did.

"The summons," said Idrygon, "is one we have sent out so often, in vain, that some here may have forgotten we do it. While others, including me, to my shame, may have come to believe it was all a fool's deed and that those messages would never be answered."

A fevered whispering broke out around the Great Circle. By watching who whispered to whom, Rath could guess which side they supported. Idrygon's talk of factions, which had only aggravated Rath's headache first thing this morning, suddenly began to make sense.

There seemed to be two generations of sages—elders like Madame Verise, roughly the age Langbard had been. They made up the majority of the council. Perhaps a third were closer to Rath's age, including Idrygon and his brother, Delyon.

According to Idrygon, many of the older generation had become content with their peaceful, prosperous life on the Islands and were in no hurry to go to the aid of their suffering countrymen on the mainland. When pressed for action by younger members of the council, they urged delay until the coming of the Waiting King and the Destined Queen.

Well, the Council of Sages was in for a surprise today!

As Maura listened to Lord Idrygon speak, she felt as if she were teetering on the edge of Raynor's Rift, with that terrifying chasm gaping before her.

"Every year, spring and midsummer, we send out those messenger birds." Lord Idrygon looked around the Great Circle, fixing each of the sages with his forceful gaze. "'Her time has come. Come at once. Gull of Duskport will bring you.' Only the name of the captain has ever changed with the passing years. We have never known where these birds were bound, nor had any assurance they did not simply fly away to become food for hawks."

Maura's heart sank. She had thought herself special…chosen. Her fears had eased as her faith in their destiny had taken root. Now she wondered if that destiny had all been an illusion. As she remembered the disasters she and Rath had so narrowly escaped, all the times they had poised on the brink of death and worse, she grew dizzy and bilious with fear.

She could not sit still or remain silent a moment longer.

"I don't understand!" She leaped to her feet, not caring that she had interrupted Lord Idrygon and drawn the stern gazes of more wizards, healers and scholars of the Elderways than she'd ever imagined could exist. "The first messenger bird found its way to our little cottage in Norest a few months ago on my twenty-first birthday. Langbard told me it had come from you. He told me you had studied the ancient writings and determined the time had come for me to begin my quest. Now are you saying it was all a mistake?"

If Lord Idrygon's words had shaken her world, Maura's outburst appeared to shake the Council of Sages even more. The great chamber buzzed like a wasp's nest under attack.

Maura braced for a stern rebuke from Lord Idrygon. After his first hostile exchange with Rath, the man had extended them every courtesy. But she suspected, if she turned quickly enough, she might catch him wrinkling up his well-bred nose at the smell of them. Now he stood silent and calm, at the center of the tempest she had created, looking strangely pleased with it.

Maura turned toward Rath. He replied with a look that told her destiny might let her down but he never would.

Before Maura could say anything to him, the tiny woman who had spoken so sharply to Idrygon appeared before her. "My dear, you mentioned Langbard a moment ago. My sister, Nalene, is his wife. Are you…their daughter?"

The anxious glow in the woman's eyes made Maura wish she could say yes, for both their sakes. Growing up with only Langbard, she'd secretly yearned for parents, but never thought of a wider family…aunts, uncles, cousins.

"Though I loved Langbard as dearly as any daughter, he was my guardian. My mother died when I was very young and she entrusted me to his care."

The woman's eager gaze faltered when Maura spoke of Langbard in the past.

"I call for silence!" Idrygon's tone of authority quelled the tumult of voices. "We all have questions that want answers, but we will never hear those answers if we do not listen."

The Council appeared to see the wisdom in that. Many who had risen sat down. Several who had moved from their accustomed places returned to their seats, including Madame Verise.

Once quiet and order had been restored to the chamber, a stout wizard with a wild shock of red hair cleared his throat loudly.

Idrygon motioned for him to rise. "You wish to speak, Trochard?"

"So I do. I believe there is one question most pressing on all our minds." He swung to fix a stern gaze upon Maura. "Young woman, do you mean to tell us *you* are the Destined Queen?"

His tone of disbelief shook Maura. She'd expected it from Rath and people like Captain Gull. But the wizards of the Vestan Islands were the ones she believed had sent her on her quest. The ones who had summoned Rath and her once she'd completed it. If they did not believe...?

"*Am* I the Destined Queen?" She looked around at them. "I thought I was. I did what she...what *I*...was meant to do. Yet everything I have heard today makes me question if it can be true."

"By *what you were meant to do*," said Trochard, "I take it you mean finding the Waiting King?"

Before Maura could reply, Rath rose and stood beside her. "Why?" he challenged her inquisitor. "Is there some *other* quest the Destined Queen was supposed to undertake?"

"Please, Rath..." Maura begged him through clenched teeth. Had he so quickly forgotten his promise to play the king in council chambers?

Well groomed and wearing the regal Vestan garb, which forced him to stand tall, he looked more like a king than she had ever imagined possible.

In a few blunt words, he told the Council of Sages how

Maura had found and rescued him within hours of the messenger bird reaching Langbard's cottage. He went on to speak of Langbard's murder and their flight to Prum, where they had discovered Exilda, the guardian of the map, murdered, also.

He cast a challenging glare around the Great Circle. "The Echtroi seem to place more faith in this legend than the lot of you."

Trochard's face flushed redder than his hair and others among the older sages betrayed similar signs of chagrin.

While they chewed on that tough crust, Rath went on to recount the rest of their adventures. As he spoke, Maura noticed how the older members of the Council winced and paled at the dangers they had faced. Meanwhile, younger members like Idrygon hung on every word, an eager glow in their eyes. All looked equally perplexed when Rath told what he and Maura had discovered in the Secret Glade.

"So *you* are the Waiting King?" murmured Madame Verise. "How can that be? You did not lie sleeping in the Secret Glade for hundreds of years."

Rath shook his head then cast a sidelong glance at Maura. How could he explain what they had not fully fathomed?

Then Delyon rose from his seat. "I believe I can answer that, if I may speak."

"Go ahead." Rath tried not to let his relief show, but Maura could sense it as he sank into his chair beside her.

"As most of you know," Delyon looked around the Great Circle, "I have worked for several years to decipher our oldest scrolls which are written in a language that predates *twara*. I believe that language may have been spoken by the Great Kin before the Sundering, which divided the children of Umbria from the children of Han."

"Speculation!" muttered Trochard, loud enough for all to hear.

Delyon pretended not to. "My study of these works leads me to believe that Queen Abrielle used the Staff of Velorken to work her enchantment upon King Elzaban."

Trochard leaped to his feet. "We asked for answers, not star-tales, upstart cub! Everyone knows the Staff of Velorken was destroyed during the Sundering."

Delyon ignored him. "Abrielle was a powerful enchantress, wise beyond her years, having served as apprentice to the Oracle of Margyle. I believe she knew or discovered the whereabouts of the Staff of Velorken and used it to keep Elzaban's spirit alive in this world. When a young child or a pregnant woman entered Everwood, Elzaban's spirit might be reborn within that body, waiting to be fully woken by a future daughter of Abrielle."

A fresh buzz greeted Delyon's explanation. The tone of some comments sounded doubtful and hostile, but more sounded guardedly accepting.

Maura was not certain what to think. Did this mean there had been other men who'd lived and died, never knowing the spirit of the Waiting King slumbered within them? Other women, destined to call forth that fallow potential for greatness, only to fail? The possibility chilled her.

"I smell a conspiracy!" Trochard pointed a finger at Delyon. "This *research* of yours everyone thought so harmlessly foolish has been nothing but a ploy to justify your brother's machinations!"

"Enough, Trochard."

Madame Verise fixed him with a reproachful stare as she rose from her seat. "We may question young Delyon's scholarship, but I am satisfied as to his integrity. And I can vouch that the man who raised this young woman..."

She glanced toward Maura. "Your pardon, my dear. I do not believe you were properly introduced to us."

"I am Maura." She rose and made a self-conscious bow to the Council. "Maura Woodbury, ward of the wiz—"

But she did not get to finish, for the Vestan Council of Sages suddenly erupted in a more fevered clamor than before.

Maura cast a questioning look at Rath. He only raised his

brows and shrugged, clearly as puzzled as she. When she shifted her gaze to Idrygon, hoping for some explanation, he replied with an approving nod and a cold smile that did not allay her confusion…or her misgivings.

7

"I finally have Trochard where I want him!" Idrygon beamed at Rath and Maura as they ate their evening meal in the fountain courtyard of his villa. "Exposed to the Council for the carping old hypocrite he is."

"Explain this faction business to me again." Rath took another big bite of a tasty dish of eggs, cheese and vegetables. Now that he had seen the Council in session and knew the names of some members, it all might make more sense to him.

"With pleasure, Highness." Idrygon raised his wine goblet in a salute that made Rath almost as ill at ease as Idrygon's use of the title. "It is quite simple. As you saw today, many among the Council are elders. Some made their home here before the Hanish Conquest, others fled here to escape it. The years since have been full of trouble and danger, but the elder sages provided prudent, cautious leadership that has served us well."

"But times have changed," said Maura.

Idrygon looked surprised by her comment. His wife and mother-in-law were eating in silence, which Rath guessed was their custom when Idrygon started on this subject. Delyon had a scroll draped over his knees. Reading while he ate, he scarcely seemed to notice the conversation or the food that he popped into his mouth at regular intervals.

After an instant's hesitation, Idrygon recovered his composure and nodded to Maura. "True, Highness. Times *have* changed. In recent years, younger members have joined the Council. Members who grieved the oppression of our kin on the mainland and who believed we should take measures to aid them."

Rath raised his goblet in a salute to Idrygon. So there *had* been folk on the Islands who thought beyond their own peace and comfort to care what happened in the rest of the kingdom. That came as welcome news.

Idrygon shook his head. "I regret, our efforts have been thwarted by Trochard and his followers, always protesting that we must take no action until the coming of the Waiting King."

Beneath the table, Rath clenched his fist. He'd once despised the whole notion of the Waiting King for just that reason—because his countrymen might linger idle and passive in their misery waiting to be delivered from the Han, rather than seizing the chance to rise up on their own behalf.

"To be fair," said Idrygon, "some of the elders, like Madame Verise, were sincere in their beliefs and would endorse necessary action if and when the Waiting King answered their summons. I suspected all along that the others had no true faith in…you. All they wanted was to protect their own interests."

"It all makes sense now." Rath unfastened the top button of his tunic and leaned back in his chair. "Why that Trochard fellow and some of the others were so unwilling to believe Maura and I could be who we say we are."

"Casting unfounded aspersions upon my brother's integrity as a scholar!" Idrygon glanced at Delyon for the first time since the meal had begun. "Brother! The king and queen of Umbria are our guests. Can you show them the small courtesy of *not* reading at the table?"

"Your pardon!" Delyon hastily rolled up the scroll and dropped it beneath his seat. "When I read something that takes my interest, I become blind and deaf to everything around me."

Maura chuckled. "I take no offense, Delyon. In fact, it makes me feel quite at home. My guardian was the same. He did not even need a scroll to read—he could just as easily get lost in his own thoughts and never hear a word I said. You remind me of him."

For some reason that notion did not sit well with Rath. Perhaps because he could not read the simplest scroll in modern Umbrian, let alone some ancient language. Even if he was able to help liberate the kingdom, how could a man with so little schooling and experience hope to rule it?

After a despairing look at his brother, Idrygon was quick to turn the discussion back to his favorite subject. "Speaking of your guardian, Highness, it is fortunate he was the brother-in-law of Madame Verise. She is well respected by all factions of the Council. If she endorses you, Trochard will have to go along, or risk being exposed for the cowardly fraud he is."

From what he'd seen of her during the Council meeting, Rath had formed a good opinion of Madame Verise. It was clear she held strong opinions from which she would not be easily swayed, but neither was her mind completely closed to new ideas. Rath could imagine Maura maturing into just such a wise old lady.

"It was canny of Madame Verise to suggest consulting the Oracle," said Idrygon. "Even Trochard will have to abide by *her* decision."

But so would Idrygon and his faction. Rath sensed a shadow of apprehension in their host.

Maura set down her goblet after a deep drink of *sythwine*. "Why did they all start talking so loudly after I told them my name?"

"Do you not know, Highness?" Whatever it was, the notion seemed to restore Idrygon's confidence. "The Woodburys of Galene are a family of noble lineage, descendants of Queen Abrielle. They've lived quietly since their patriarch Brandel died. He was a strong force on the Council and much respected."

Maura lowered her gaze to her lap for a moment and Rath sensed her struggle for composure as she whispered, "Then I do have a family?"

That would mean a great deal to her, he knew. Enough, perhaps, to keep her here on the Islands if the Oracle determined there had been some mistake and the Council ruled against aiding them? Or was that wickedly selfish for him to hope?

"Would you like to go to Galene and meet them?" asked Idrygon. "I am not certain what relation they might be to you, but their endorsement could only strengthen our position with the Council."

"I should like that very much, thank you," replied Maura. "Once I have met with the Oracle."

"Of course." Again Idrygon looked unsure. "The Oracle."

Rath had sensed a similar hesitation from several of the sages when the Oracle of Margyle had been mentioned. What lay behind *that*? he wondered.

Back on the mainland where life was a raw struggle for survival, he'd enjoyed a measure of confidence. Here on the Islands, Rath felt far out of his depth.

"Follow this lane. It will bring you to the dwelling of the Oracle." Delyon pointed to a gated trellis between two high banks of hedging. It was so overgrown with twilight vines that it almost blended into the shrubbery walls on either side.

"Are you not coming with me?" asked Maura. The prospect of meeting this mysterious woman whose memory reached deep into the past and who could also catch glimpses of the future intimidated her.

"I wish I could." Delyon sighed. "I have been trying to arrange a meeting with her for the longest time—to talk over my research and find out if I am on the right track. But the Oracle is getting more and more reclusive as time goes on, Madame

Verise says. I wonder how the Council persuaded her to see you and His Highness?"

For a moment Maura wondered who Delyon was talking about. Then it dawned on her that he must mean Rath. She found it difficult to get used to everyone in Idrygon's household addressing them by title.

"I can wait for you here," Delyon offered, "if you think you will not be able to find your way back afterward. I wish I'd thought to bring a scroll with me to read."

"I will not keep you hanging about here when you have work to do." Maura pointed toward a lower hill. "Besides, I can see your house from here. I'll have no trouble finding my way back."

This was not the mainland, after all, where a young woman had to be careful about walking alone. Perhaps one day that would change. And her dreaded meeting with the Oracle of Margyle might help pave the way.

That thought gave Maura courage to smile and nod when Delyon said, "You're sure?"

She did not wait to watch him go, but squared her shoulders and pushed open the vine-covered gate. Once through, she followed a path that wound through a bit of woodland until it opened near a cottage with white plaster walls, like those of Idrygon's elegant villa. Its thatched roof made the place look much more homey and inviting to Maura. Perhaps she did not need to be so anxious about meeting a woman who lived in a modest dwelling like this one.

"Hello." The sound of a child's voice startled Maura.

She spun around to see a young girl with a mane of wild dark curls picking mushrooms by the edge of the wood. She looked no older than Noll Howen back in Windleford, perhaps ten or eleven.

"H-hello." Maura pressed her hand to her chest to quiet her pounding heart. "Do you live here?"

A ward of the Oracle, perhaps, as she had been of Langbard.

"I do." The girl rose from the ground, dusting off her skirts. "You've come from the mainland, haven't you...Mistress Woodbury?"

"That's right." Maura wondered how the child knew her name. "To see the Oracle. I have heard people talk about her since I was your age and younger, but never thought I would meet her face-to-face. Is it true she is hundreds of years old?"

The child laughed so hard she practically doubled over. When she had finally mastered her mirth, she picked up her mushroom basket. "What queer ideas people get! Though I reckon it isn't so far wrong, in a way."

The door of the cottage opened just then and a middle-aged woman bustled out carrying a bundle of washing.

"Is *she* the Oracle?" Maura whispered to the child. It was difficult to imagine such a famed personage stooping to a mundane chore like laundry. Then again, people might think the same of her and Rath—the Destined Queen compounding liniment and the Waiting King cutting hay on Blen Maynold's farm.

"No, silly!" The child began to laugh again as she shook her head. "*I* am."

Maura almost laughed at that jest until the woman with the laundry called, "Is that the guest you were expecting, mistress? If you want to bring her inside, I can fetch you some cakes and lipma cordial."

"Cakes!" squealed the Oracle like any other child her age at the prospect of a treat. "I should have guests more often!"

While Maura tried to recover from her shock, the servant woman shook her head. "Now, mistress, you know the Council doesn't approve of you being bothered too often. Madame Verise said this lady is a special case."

"Your pardon, great Oracle!" Maura made a deep bow to the child. Her face felt as if she had a bad sunburn.

"It's all right." The child shrugged. "You gave me an excuse to laugh. I don't get those often enough lately."

In her large misty-gray eyes, Maura caught a glimpse of wisdom and sadness far beyond her years.

"Will you come in for cakes and a drink?" The Oracle nodded toward the cottage. "The cordial is from a batch the last oracle put down two summers ago. We had a fine harvest of *lipma* fruit that year."

"The…last oracle?" Maura followed the girl into a snug cottage, where she immediately felt at home. "Is a new one chosen when the old one dies?"

"Oh, no." The Oracle laid her mushroom basket on the table. "That wouldn't do at all. Then the memories would be lost."

The memories? Maura wanted to ask, but refrained lest the Oracle get tired of hearing herself repeated over and over.

Perhaps the Oracle divined her question anyway, for she beckoned Maura through the cottage to a large open porch with a spectacular view down to the sea. "Come, sit down and I'll tell you how it is."

Maura sank onto a cushioned chair that looked to be made of many slender branches woven together into a light but sturdy seat. She wondered what other astonishing revelations the young Oracle had in store for her.

The child seated herself on the chair opposite Maura's. "Like every other oracle for hundreds of years, I was brought to this house when I was a baby to be raised by the last oracle."

"Do you ever see your other family?" Maura thought of the Woodburys of Galene, whom she could hardly wait to meet.

"I have no other family. That's how the Council knew I was the one. An orphaned girl child born at the right time."

Maura nodded. That made a kind of sense.

"Have you ever performed the passing ritual?" asked the Oracle.

"For my guardian, Langbard, this past spring."

"Langbard?" The Oracle's eyes took on a far-off look and her innocent young lips curved in a not-so-innocent smile. "He was a fine-looking fellow. If we'd been twenty years younger…"

Realizing what she'd said, the Oracle hid her face in her hands. "Your pardon! Please do not think ill of me. That name brought back such vivid memories that, for a moment, I could feel the old oracle within me."

Maura wondered what *that* meant.

The child hastened to explain. "When an old oracle raises her successor, every day is like a prolonged passing ritual. There would never be time to share all the memories going back so many generations, otherwise. By the time the old oracle is ready to depart this world, the new one has received the accumulated wisdom and experience of all those who have gone before her."

"Amazing!" Maura whispered, not aware she'd spoken aloud.

"It can be." The Oracle sighed. "When all goes as it should."

The child's wistful words jolted Maura upright in her chair. "But your oracle died too soon, didn't she, before your training was completed?"

With a wary nod, the child drew her legs up onto the chair and hugged her bent knees. "Just a few months ago, she got very ill suddenly and the healers could do nothing to help. At the end I was with her all the time while she poured memories into my mind until I was afraid my head would burst."

Maura rose from her chair and knelt beside the child. "That must have been a sad and frightening time for you."

"It isn't fair!" The young Oracle struck the side of her chair with her fist. "This never happened to any of the others—why me? These are restless times. So many things will change. So many important decisions will need to be made. People will want my advice. But what can I tell them and how can they trust me? I am not ready, and so much wisdom gathered over the generations has been lost."

How long had the poor little creature been brooding about this? Maura wondered. Though she might be the custodian of memories stretching back hundreds of years, she was still only a child. A child who had lost her beloved foster mother too soon. A child with no one to confide in but her servant and perhaps some Council members who might not want to hear their Oracle voice such doubts about her abilities.

The child rested her forehead against her knees and her delicate frame shuddered with sobs.

"You're right." Maura wrapped her arms around the child. "It *isn't* fair. If it helps, I know a little of how you feel."

While the child wept, Maura told of Langbard's surprising announcement on her birthday and of events that had overwhelmed her since then.

"So you see," she said at last when the child's sobs had quieted, "when I started out, I felt unready for such a big task and afraid I would fail and let everyone down."

She lowered her voice to bestow a confidence. "I still feel that way sometimes. If I dwell on it too much, it can freeze me worse than a spidersilk spell."

The Oracle wiped her eyes with the hem of her gown and sniffled. "How do *you* keep yourself from thinking about it all the time?"

Maura pondered the question for a moment. "I remind myself to trust in the Giver's providence. I try to keep moving ahead and doing what I need to do. Each little bit of success I gain makes me feel more confident, even if it is only a few miles closer to where I'm going."

She ran her hand over the child's hair, wondering if anyone else dared to show the Oracle of Margyle a little affection. At that moment, the most comforting thought settled over her. "Do you suppose the Giver's will might work *better* through people like us, who aren't fully prepared for what we must do?"

The child gave a final sniff as she regarded Maura thoughtfully. In her soft gray eyes glowed the accumulated wisdom of many generations—fragmented but still sound.

After a moment she nodded. "There would be more room for the Giver's power to work."

Just then the Oracle's servant bustled in. "The wash will dry in a trice with that sun and the breeze. Here are the cakes I promised you."

She stopped in her tracks, staring at Maura and the child. "Is everything all right, pet? Is this too much for you? Should I send this lady away?"

"No, Orna!" The Oracle clasped Maura's hand. "We were having a fine talk. I hope she will come and visit me often while she is on the Islands."

"Orna?" Maura smiled at the woman as she returned to her chair. "That is a very dear name to me. The mother of my dearest friend was named Orna, too. You remind me of her."

Clearly the woman was much more than a servant in the Oracle's household—a warm, protective caregiver who did not forget that this special, troubled little girl was a child first.

"Orna's a real common name over Norest way." The woman beamed at Maura, clearly reassured by her young charge's words. "My folks came to the Islands from there when the war started. Now I'll fetch that cordial."

"What does this *lipma* cordial taste like?" asked Maura. "Anything like *sythwine*?"

The child wrinkled her nose. "It will make your mouth pucker but it's very refreshing. Now tell me about this friend of yours from Norest. What kinds of things did the two of you do when you were my age?"

For the next little while they talked like any two new friends getting better acquainted. Orna's cakes proved delicious with their glaze of fruit and honey. At first Maura wasn't sure she liked the sour *lipma* cordial, but each time she took a sip, she found the flavor improved from the time before.

As the Oracle plied her with questions about her friend Sorsha and the town of Windleford where they'd grown up, Maura wondered if she felt embarrassed over betraying her uncertainty to a stranger she should have been trying to awe.

Gently she steered their talk back to the task they had been set. "Do you know why Madame Verise sent me here?"

The child drained her glass of cordial with an air of resignation that their pleasant social time had come to an end. "I'm supposed to talk to you and to that man. Then I must tell the Council if you are truly the Destined Queen and the Waiting King."

Why had Idrygon's rivals on the Council agreed to these interviews? Maura wondered. Did they hope the young Oracle would be too uncertain of her own judgment to give a decisive answer? If she endorsed Rath and Maura, would Trochard's faction try to discredit her because of her age and unfinished training?

Maura did not envy her young friend the task. "Are there any questions you need to ask me?"

The Oracle tapped her forefinger against her chin and her clear brow wrinkled with concentration. "You said Langbard was your guardian. Did he have any other children?"

"None." Maura plundered her memory for everything Langbard had told her on the fateful afternoon of her birthday. "He said the Oracle had told him he would be father to the Destined Queen."

"She did." The child squeezed her eyes shut. "I can picture it as clear as anything. I wish you could have seen the look on his face!"

"I can imagine it." Maura chuckled. Delyon would probably look the same—eyes wide with horror at the prospect of a destructive little creature getting muddy hands on one of his precious scrolls! "I wish the Oracle had told Langbard I might not be his daughter by blood. He went through a terrible time after his wife died without bearing a child."

"Poor man!" The girl winced as if she knew something of such pain. "The way oracles are fostered, we know it is love and care that make a family bond, not blood alone. She would never have thought to remark upon the difference."

Rising from her chair, the young Oracle approached Maura with a solemn gait and laid a hand on her head in the manner of a benediction. "You are Langbard's daughter and you come from the line of Abrielle. I may not be certain of many things, but I *know* you are the latest Destined Queen."

"Latest?" The word trickled down Maura's spine like a drop of water from a cold, black well. "That is something *I* do not understand. The sages spoke of sending out messenger birds every year and of King Elzaban's spirit having dwelt in other men before Rath. Does that mean what I fear it might? Have there been other Destined Kings and Waiting Queens before us who failed?"

The young Oracle nodded with an air of regret. "Those were some of the most important memories Namma passed on to me. We spoke of it, too, though I am not sure I understood it all. You see, before the Han came, there were troubled times, but not the very darkest hour. Some Destined Queens laughed off the whole notion of what they were meant to do. Others were too frightened to stir from their own doorsteps."

Maura could not condemn them. "I laughed at first. I was afraid. If Langbard had not offered to go with me, then Rath, I might still be hiding in Windleford hoping destiny would get tired of waiting for me and choose someone else."

She gazed up into the child's face, for the first time wishing she *had* found a wise old woman here to advise her. "That's what I cannot understand, though. If those others were truly destined, how could they fail? It took me such a long time to learn to trust in my destiny—now you're telling me it doesn't matter?"

Maura tried to blunt the sharp edge of frustration in her voice. It wasn't the child's fault, after all, or anyone else's. And she did not truly expect an answer that made sense. As Langbard had once said, *"Look around you, my dear, at all the marvels of the Giver's creation. How can simple creatures like us hope to fathom its plan or purpose?"*

Maura wished she could understand a little at least.

The Oracle held out her hand. "Will you come for a walk with me before you have to go?"

The burden of too much knowledge had left her eyes, and she looked like any child her age, eager to run and play. No doubt she was tired of all this grave talk and hearing words come out of her mouth that she did not fully understand.

"I would like that." Maura took the oracle's hand and rose from her chair with what she hoped was a convincing pose of enthusiasm.

Together, they left the porch and wandered out into the meadow that sloped down toward the sea. But the Oracle did not go that way. Instead, she led Maura toward a wooded hill.

She pointed toward the summit. "Up there is the most beautiful place of meditation in all the Islands. I go there often when I'm troubled. Everything seems clearer there, somehow. If there is anyplace in this world where you might find the answers to your questions, it will be there."

Answers—Maura could do with a few of those. The hill looked steep and quite thickly wooded, though a gap between the trees at the base of the hill might be the beginning of a footpath. "Very well. Let's go."

The child released her hand and ran ahead, calling, "I'll see you at the top!"

"Wait for me!" Maura did not relish the prospect of a race up the steep, wooded hill. Hiking up the hem of her gown, she ran after the child, who had already disappeared into the trees.

"Oh, these shoes!" Maura bit back a mild curse when the curved toes almost made her trip. The stout walking boots Sorsha had given her when she left Windleford would have been much better for climbing this hill.

Darting through a gap in the trees, Maura saw that the path divided almost immediately. Which way was she to take?

She peered down each branch as far as she could see but both curved after a few yards and the Oracle was already out of sight.

"Hello!" Maura called. "Which way am I supposed to go?"

No answer came, but she heard laughter off in the distance.

The right-hand path seemed to lead in that direction so Maura followed it, grumbling to herself about inconsiderate hostesses.

Before long, she was doing more than grumbling. The wooded path wound its way up the hill in a complicated maze, twisting, branching, turning back on itself, sometimes coming to a dead end. Would she ever find her way to the top?

Maura considered turning back, or sitting down and staying put until the naughty little tease of a child came looking for her. She did stop for a short rest, but soon grew bored with waiting and started off again. If she'd been sure she could find her way back to the cottage, she might have given up. But by this time she had made too many turns and was hopelessly confused.

So she kept going, encouraged that she seemed to be climbing higher. The nearer she got to the top, the less space there would be for the path to branch. As long as she kept going she must reach the top at last.

And, at last, she did. Footsore, out of breath and very much out of temper.

She found the Oracle sitting in something that looked like a little house without walls—stout beams holding aloft a roof. Only when she drew very close did Maura realize the beams were living trees, their branches concentrated at the top and turned inward to twine together, creating a roof shingled with broad leaves.

The structure stood in the middle of a meadow carpeted with wildflowers of the most vivid and varied colors Maura had ever seen. Springwater bubbled up from a tiny stone fountain beside the little house of trees. A soft breeze wafted and swirled about the summit of the hill, stirring the fresh, sweet perfume of the flowers.

By the time Maura reached the Oracle, most of her irritation had been soothed away by the peace and beauty around her. Understanding blossomed within her, as unexpected and breathtaking as this place.

"You meant to leave me behind, didn't you?" she asked the Oracle.

The child nodded gravely. "I'm sorry. I know it is bewildering and tiresome. This was one of the first lessons Namma taught me when I was old enough to understand."

She pointed to the fountain. "You must be thirsty. Have a drink. It will make the long climb seem worthwhile."

Maura stared around the summit glade. "It already does. But you're right, I am thirsty." With cupped hands, she lifted the water to her lips and drank until she could hold no more.

The Oracle had spoken true, for the water was so cool, fresh and sweet, it would have been worth the long, wearying climb all by itself.

"Namma told me this path through the woods is like our destiny," explained the Oracle while Maura drank. "We cannot tell which way it may take us, and we may make many wrong turns."

Maura nodded. The frustration she'd felt while trying to grope her way to the top of the hill echoed some of the feelings she'd experienced during her quest.

"The path could not pick you up and bring you here against your will or with no effort on your part," the Oracle continued, "and you had many choices to make. Some of those would have led you away from the top of the hill, others were dead ends. If you had become too discouraged to continue, you never would have reached the top."

Once Maura finished drinking, the Oracle beckoned her to take a seat beneath the living canopy. "Did you notice that some of the path doubled back upon itself?"

Maura nodded.

"This path may confuse the person who climbs it for the first time." The Oracle patted Maura's hand. "But for those who keep trying, there are not as many wrong choices as may first appear."

But there *were* wrong choices and Maura could not abdicate

her responsibility for them. The specter of failure returned to haunt her. Others before her had failed and she sensed that the closer she and Rath came to their goal, the greater their opportunities for disaster would be.

A dark whisper of temptation slithered through her thoughts as well. If she and Rath abandoned their destiny, another Waiting King and Destined Queen would come after them some day.

But in the meantime, how much darker could Umbria's *darkest hour* get?

"So, what did the Oracle tell *you*?" asked Maura the following evening while she and Rath prepared for dinner at Idrygon's villa.

Rath wondered if the evening meal was always such a formal occasion in Idrygon's household, or whether it was in honor of visiting royalty—uncrowned though they might be.

"Well?" Maura prompted him. "Did she make you walk up that hill maze to teach you about destiny? Did she promise to tell the Council of Sages you are the *latest* Waiting King?"

When he did not answer right away, her gaze became more searching. "Did the Oracle look into your future?"

Oh, she had looked, all right. And what she'd seen had shaken Rath to the core. He tried to convince himself that, though she might hold the memories of countless generations, the present oracle was still only a child. One whose training had been cut short, at that. Perhaps she had taken the wrong meaning from whatever she'd glimpsed in his future.

For all his doubts and denials, he could not escape a chilling fear that the child *knew* what the future held for him. He wished she had kept that troublesome knowledge to herself, though, for he feared it could mean only one thing—that he would lose Maura.

Could the Giver be so cruel, to rob him of the happiness he'd so lately found? Rath tried to believe otherwise, but his faith was still new and untested. He had far more experience with the impersonal cruelty of whatever forces shaped the lives of folk like him.

Maura's voice broke in upon his brooding, like a ray of sunlight penetrating some dark dungeon cell. "She did foretell your future, didn't she? Come, what did she predict? Something dire, I reckon, by that grim look on your face."

"I do not look grim!" he snapped, then repented his quick temper. "All right, perhaps I do. But it is not on account of that young seer."

Not for all the world would he burden Maura with the foreboding that weighed upon him. He could worry enough for both of them. "It's all the talk of an invasion and this business of playing off one Council faction against another. Here I reckoned the Vestan Islands would be so peaceful, with folks all getting along and having not a care in the world!"

"I cannot say I like that much, myself." Maura laid down the ivory comb with which she had battled her unruly hair into temporary submission. "But is it so hard to understand? Trochard and his followers just want to look after their own interests…like a certain outlaw I once knew."

Rath grumbled something about how he'd been forthright in his selfishness, at least. Then he craned his neck. "Can you help me fasten this miserable collar button without throttling me. Thank the Giver that Idrygon plans to have his soldiers kitted out in gear that will let them move…and breathe."

"Whose soldiers?" Maura asked with a teasing lilt in her voice as she fastened the troublesome button. "You will be leading them—will that not make them *your* soldiers?"

Rath shook his head and dropped a kiss on the tip of her

nose. "Idrygon has been planning all this for a great while. Gathering supplies, amassing weapons, training men. This army will be his to command, which is just the way I would have it. What do I know about leading any force bigger than the band of outlaws you first saw me with in Betchwood. Look what happened to them, poor devils."

"That was not your fault!" Maura reminded him.

Rath tried to pretend he believed her.

She quickly changed the subject. "I thought it strange at first that Idrygon should care so much what happens on the mainland."

So had Rath. He did not reckon Idrygon had planned and schemed so long to liberate the mainland out of the goodness of his heart. After watching their host the past few days, he'd concluded that the man was a born commander, a role with limited scope on these islands. Much as they delighted Rath and Maura with their beauty, peace and plenty, to a man of Idrygon's forceful personality, they must seem like a luxurious prison.

"You said *at first*." Rath wetted a comb and tried to tidy his hair. "What changed your mind?"

"Something Delyon told me." Maura dipped her fingers into a tiny crock of delicate pottery and drew out a drop or two of scented oil to anoint her neck and wrists. "He said their parents put him and his brother on the last Umbrian ship to escape the mainland. The boys were raised here by their grandparents, who were both members of the Council. Only many years later did they find out their parents had been killed by the Han."

Rath winced at Maura's account, though he'd heard plenty worse stories of things that had happened to Umbrian children after the Hanish conquest. He'd lived worse, himself, come to that. Though Idrygon and Delyon had been orphaned, at least they'd gotten beyond the reach of the Han and into the care of folks with the means to look after them properly.

Would he have switched places with them, though, if he could have changed the past? He'd tasted his share of guilt after Ganny died and found a bitter brew. How much worse might it have gnawed his belly if he'd ended up somewhere safe and prosperous? Might it have driven him to do whatever it took to oust the Han from Umbria?

"I'll admit," he said, "I was wrong in thinking the island folk came to no harm on account of the Han. I reckon it's harder sometimes to know somebody else is being ill used and not being able to aid them than it is to take the lumps yourself."

"You're a wise man, Rath Talward." Maura took his arm. "Now we had better get to dinner before Idrygon sends a search party after us. Delyon told me important guests will be dining with us tonight."

"Delyon tells you all sorts of interesting things, doesn't he?"

Maura seemed not to hear anything beneath Rath's bantering tone. "I have to get my news from someone and Idrygon's wife always looks so busy I'm afraid to stop her long enough to ask."

She lowered her voice as they stepped out in the wide, elegant gallery that ran between two sets of bedchambers. Rath could see people gathered talking in the courtyard. He recognized several Council members.

As they walked toward the company, Maura leaned closer to him and whispered, "There is one drawback to relying on Delyon for information."

He cast her a sidelong smile, struck afresh by her delicate beauty. "And what might that be?"

Maura's lips twitched. "He doesn't seem to know what is going on half the time, himself."

A hoot of laughter stuck in Rath's throat when he saw the formidable Madame Verise bowing to them. Did that bode well?

Apparently so, for Idrygon appeared beside the old lady,

looking more cheerful than Rath had ever seen him. He held a goblet in each hand, which he offered to Rath and Maura. "We have cause to celebrate, Highnesses! Madame Verise informs me that the Oracle has declared you are indeed the Waiting King and Destined Queen of Umbria!"

So this dinner was a celebration. Rath glanced around at the other guests. Unless he was hopelessly confused, they belonged to the group Idrygon hoped would support them against those who opposed going to war. If Idrygon's painstaking preparations were not to be in vain and if Rath was to get the help he needed to fulfill his destiny, these folks would need to be convinced that he was the king they had been waiting for.

The weight of responsibility pressed down on Rath's shoulders, like the heavy pack he'd carried into the Waste.

"The Giver does work in strange ways." Madame Verise looked him up and down, shaking her head. "To think, King Elzaban's spirit in the body of an outlaw."

Again the high, stiff collar of his Vestan tunic tightened around Rath's throat. He struggled to frame a reply that would not curdle on his tongue.

Then Maura spoke in a tone of quiet dignity befitting a queen. "Considering the present *law* of that land, madame, do you not think better of His Highness for having been outside it than in?"

Rath bit back a grin, remembering how he'd flung those words at her soon after they'd met. That she'd recalled them after all this time and summoned them at a crucial moment to come to his defense sent a fresh surge of love for her through his heart.

"Now, Highness…" Idrygon's dark eyes flashed. Clearly he did not want anything to threaten this vital alliance.

"No, Lord Idrygon." Madame Verise made a dismissive gesture with her delicate, withered hand. "Her Highness is right. Outlaws, smugglers and that ilk are the only ones who have kept a spirit of resistance alive in our poor captive land. Perhaps it *is* fitting that the spirit of King Elzaban should return to us in such a one."

She bowed to Rath with an air of sincere deference. "I beseech your pardon if I gave offense with my thoughtless remark, my lord. I fear we on the Islands have grown self-righteous in our good fortune. We forget how hard it may be to serve the Giver in harsher circumstances."

"I cannot claim I have always served—"

Before Rath could finish, Idrygon shot him a warning look and interrupted. "I am certain His Highness understands, madame. Now, I see our meal is ready. Shall we be seated?"

He steered Rath toward the head of the long table, while his wife drew Maura to her place of honor at the other end. On their way, he muttered, "Take care what you say to Verise. Without her support, we are lost. Let me do the talking. I have learned how to handle her."

Rath nodded. He had never felt so out of place in his life—like a bird thrust underwater and expected to swim, or a fish tossed into the sky, to fly or perish trying. He wished they'd let Maura sit near him. He felt a little more confident with her by his side, knowing she had seen him at his worst, yet still recognized a spark of nobility within him.

A feast was served, fit for a king. But the king barely managed to eat a bite for fear he would commit some glaring lapse in table manners. He tried to follow what Madame Verise and Idrygon were talking about but they might have been speaking that ancient language from Delyon's scrolls for all he understood.

Finally he gave up and stared down the table to where Maura sat laughing and talking with the person seated to her right...Delyon. So the fellow could make conversation when he didn't have his gaze fixed on some ancient scroll. Now he had his gaze fixed on Maura, which made Rath's pulse pound in his ears.

It was pounding so loud he did not notice Madame Verise rise from her seat until Idrygon gave his foot a nudge under the table.

She looked up and down the table, her gaze settling at last on their host. "I believe I speak for all your guests this evening, Lord Idrygon, when I say how overjoyed we are to welcome the king and queen for whom we have waited so long. I promise you our full support in the Council for a campaign to liberate the mainland."

Idrygon rose and picked up his wine goblet. But before he could propose a toast to their alliance, Madame Verise continued, "We have only two conditions to make."

"May I ask what those might be?" Idrygon's fingers tightened around the stem of his goblet until Rath feared it would snap.

"Can you not guess?" A dry half smile arched one corner of the old lady's tiny mouth. "A proper royal wedding for our king and queen, of course, and a grand coronation."

"Agreed!" cried Idrygon without bothering to consult Rath or Maura. "Now, a toast to our newfound monarchs. May their reign be long and victorious!"

As the company drank to them, Rath tried to look properly pleased and dignified. He liked the idea of having his union with Maura blessed, but he wasn't so sure about a *proper royal wedding*. The thought of a *grand coronation* made him itch all over.

A few days later Maura's palms grew suddenly clammy and her belly churned as the island of Galene filled more and more of the horizon, beckoning her to glimpse a missing part of her life.

She turned to Captain Gull. "How much longer until we get there? It was kind of you to bring me."

"Not long now." Gull stroked his cat's head. "And no thanks needed. This beats being moored off Margyle and told to sit tight, though not told what's going on. I don't suppose you could let me know what *is* going on—just between us?"

"I wish I could." Maura gave a rueful shake of her head. "But Lord Idrygon said I mustn't and…"

"And," Gull finished her thought, "Lord Idrygon is not a man you want to get on the wrong side of. Ah well, I reckon I can content myself with being left in the dark a while longer. Just answer me this, if you can—the Council aren't going to hold it against me for luring the Ore Fleet into their waters, are they?"

"Of course not!" Maura wondered why a man who seemed to fear nothing else cared what the Council decided or what Idrygon decreed. "Rath explained to them about the storm and how you only brought us here because of a summons from them. They still aren't happy about it, mind you. Delyon told me having so many ships sunk there will make that part of the warding waters useless for a long time, and if the Han ever find out…"

Was that another factor in deciding the Council to support an invasion? she wondered. Even Trochard and his supporters? With the security of the warding waters breached, they could no longer afford to tolerate a menacing Hanish presence so nearby.

"I see where that could be trouble sure enough." Gull made a face that soon twisted into a grin. "It was a fine sight, though, all those big ore-tubs being tossed about like the leaf-boats I used to sail in puddles when I was a lad."

"At least until the *Phantom* started getting tossed along with them!" Maura shuddered, remembering. It had only been a fortnight ago, yet it felt much longer.

She had quickly grown accustomed to island life. To eating hot meals at a proper table instead of snatching a quick bite from a pack. Sleeping in Rath's arms on a real bed rather than taking turns keeping watch through the night. Clean clothes. Water to bathe. And the most precious luxury of all—freedom from lurking fear.

If only this were the end of their journey instead of a pleasant way station on a long, twisting, uphill road.

A short while later, the *Phantom* made harbor at a small port. Gull offered to accompany Maura in search of her relatives, but she declined with thanks. She wasn't quite sure what her mother's kin might make of the flamboyant smuggler. She wished Rath had been able to come with her, but he was busy with Idrygon, studying old maps and discussing strategy for the coming invasion.

A few children gathered near the wharf to see what manner of visitor the ship had brought. They reminded Maura of the boys and girls back in Windleford. But these carefree younglings never had to worry about picking up a pain spike or running into a Hanish hound that had slipped its chain.

"Good day, mistress," said the oldest boy, nudged forward by his friends. "Are you looking for someone? We can show you the way."

"Why, thank you, young sir," said Maura. "I have come looking for the Woodbury family."

The children laughed until the boy shushed them. "Any special one, mistress? There's Woodburys aplenty on Galene." He motioned forward a small girl, her ruddy hair plaited in four long braids that looked to be the fashion here. "Jophie is a Woodbury. Quilla's ma was born a Woodbury and so was Gath's. Both my granddames were."

"Really?" Maura looked around at them, a smile stretching her lips wide, while a tear tingled in the corner of her eye. This was the first time she had met anyone with her kin-name. "No wonder you are all so handsome, then! My mother was Dareth Woodbury and I was told she came from Galene. Perhaps if you could take me to one of the elders of the family who might remember her."

The boy thought for a moment. "My house is near and my granddames are smart as anything. They tell me lots of stories about the old days. I reckon they'd know about your mother if anybody would."

"Very well, then." Maura took two small girls by the hand. "Lead me to them, if you would be so kind."

The children conducted Maura down a narrow path that wound through the village to a house that looked like Idrygon's, only less grand. Thick vines climbed over the stippled white walls, and a fragrance of wholesome sweetness from the tiny blue vine flowers perfumed the air.

"Granna Lib! Granna Jule!" The boy's voice rang through the center courtyard of the house. "Visitor to see you!"

"Visitor?" A tall, slender woman strode into the courtyard carrying a basket of flax tow in one hand and a distaff spindle in the other. "Who would be visiting at this hour?"

Another woman, grayer and a bit more stooped, followed the first. "What did the boy say, Lib?"

The woman with the spinning gear turned and shouted, "Visitor, Jule!"

"Oh. Who'd be calling at this hour?"

The two women peered at Maura.

She bowed. "Your pardon if I have called at a bad time. I have come from Margyle in hope of finding some of my kin. My name is Maura and my mother was Dareth Woodbury."

Lib's basket dropped to the tile floor of the courtyard with a soft thud, followed by the clatter of the falling spindle. She seemed not to notice as she stared at Maura. Her hand trembled as she raised it to her lips.

"What did the lass say?" demanded Jule.

"The girl claims—" Lib's voice cracked with emotion "—she's Dareth's daughter."

"Dareth?" Jule picked up the fallen spindle and basket. "Oh, that can't be. There must be some mistake."

"Look at her, though. The very image."

Jule stepped closer, her head cocked like a bird's, staring. "So she is. But how can it be?"

Lib recovered her shattered composure. "Well, don't stand there like a stranger, my dear." She took Maura's arm. "Come in! I am your mother's aunt and Jule here is a cousin of ours."

"Run off and play," she called to the children. "All but you,

Bran." She beckoned her grandson. "You were a good smart lad to bring the lady here. Now I want you to go around and fetch Auntie Zelle and Uncle Mayer..." She rattled off a list of names so long it made Maura's head spin.

"Are those *all* my kin?" she asked when the boy had run off on his errand. After years of having no one but Langbard, and him no blood relation, the thought of such a large family overwhelmed her...but in the most pleasant way.

"Oh my, no, dear." Lib chuckled. "That's not half of them! Only the ones nearest related that live handiest."

"Dareth's child?" Jule shook her head as Lib drew Maura toward some chairs clustered in a shaded corner of the courtyard. "Whoever would have thought it? What became of poor Dareth? The last we heard, she and Vaylen had been captured by the Han. Then never a word until now."

Maura took a seat between her kinswomen and told them everything she knew of her mother, which was pitifully little. She concluded with a question that left her breathless and a little dizzy. "Who was this Vaylen you spoke of? And how did my mother come to be on the mainland for the Han to capture?"

The two women looked at each other, as if silently arguing who should be the one to break the news.

Finally Lib spoke. "Vaylen was the son of the last Margrave of Tarsh. He led a rebellion against the Han. Oh, it must be all of twenty years ago. For a time Tarsh was free."

Tarsh, free? That came as surprising news to Maura.

"My brother, Brandel—" Lib's voice caught for a moment "—your grandfather, was fierce in his support of Vaylen. He said if Tarsh could hold on to the freedom it had won, then Norest might rise up next, then Southmark or the Hitherland. He was forever urging the Council to send more aid to Tarsh, but many of the sages felt it would put the Islands in danger if the Han found out we were abetting the rebels."

No wonder Idrygon had spoken well of her grandfather,

Maura thought. Brandel Woodbury sounded like a man very much after his heart. But where did her mother fit into all this?

Lib wasted no time coming to that. "After a great deal of secret communication with Tarsh, Brandel agreed to send one of his daughters to marry Vaylen. He thought if there was a Vestan-born descendant of Abrielle on the throne of Tarsh, the Council might find a little more courage and generosity in its dealings with the rebels."

"So this Vaylen was my father? And you say both he and my mother were captured by the Han?"

The two old woman gave weary nods, as though this grief were a weight they had carried on their hearts for many years.

"Libeth should have been the one to go." Maura's great-aunt sighed. "But she was a delicate creature, so Dareth offered to take her place. She had met Vaylen years before, when he'd come to the Islands as a guest of her father, and she thought well of him."

"I warned Brandel," Jule grumbled. "Told him he had no business sending his daughter off to marry a man she hardly knew. And into such danger."

"Hmmph!" Lib clearly did not hold with criticism of her brother. "What a waste you weren't apprenticed to the Oracle of Margyle! You know very well Dareth had her heart set on going."

"She'd have done *anything* to please her father," Jule muttered, just loud enough for Maura to hear.

For the first time Maura sensed a true connection with the mother she had never known. She'd felt the same way about Langbard. In fact, all that had kept her moving forward during those first difficult days of her quest had been the determination not to let him down.

"None of the Council knew," Lib continued, "but the ship that carried Dareth to Tarsh was loaded with weapons and supplies to aid the rebels…"

Her voice trailed off and her eyes took on a distant look, as if she were watching that ship from long ago sail away.

After a few moments, Maura's curiosity got the better of her. "Then what happened?"

"Oh!" Lib roused with a start from her pensive daze. "By and by the ship came back. So we knew Dareth had reached the mainland safely. After that we heard no more for the longest while. Then word came that Tarsh had been overrun by the Han. The Margrave had been killed and the Han had captured Vaylen and Dareth."

Even in the shade, the courtyard was warm. Yet a chill rippled through Maura.

"Brandel wouldn't believe they were dead." Jule shook her head. "He used to get provoked when anybody spoke of them as if they were. And whenever a ship sailed into the harbor, he'd be the first one down to the wharf in case Dareth might be aboard."

"The old fool." Lib wiped her eyes with the back of her hand. "I wish he'd lived to see Dareth's daughter set foot on Galene."

Maura wished so, too. There were many questions she would have liked to ask him.

A muted clamor of voices and footsteps approached.

Lib heaved a sigh and rose from her chair. "That'll be some of the rest of the family come to see you for themselves, my dear. I hope you don't mind my sending for them?"

Maura shook her head. "I have waited such a long time to meet all of you."

More and more Woodbury relatives poured into the little house, until the courtyard could scarcely hold them. Maura's head began to spin from all the names and faces and convoluted connections.

"...this is Wildon Broadroot. His mother was a first cousin of your grandmother's. And here's Cousin Kedrith. She's one of the Westbay branch of the family..."

Yet in each eager, smiling face, Maura caught a glimpse of something strangely familiar. A bit of her mother, or of herself, perhaps. As the hours passed, she listened to endless introductions, received bashful bows and vigorous embraces, heard stories of Dareth Woodbury's younger years that brought her mother alive to her for the first time.

She remembered the night she and Rath had stopped in the foothills of the mountains and soaked their aching flesh in a warm spring pool. This gathering of her family was like a warm spring for her spirit—reviving and renewing her in places she had never realized were empty or weary.

Yet part of her remained detached from it all, mulling over the brave, tragic account of her parents. No wonder her mother had died of a broken heart that even Langbard could not heal, even with all his skill and devotion. And what had become of her father? Had he been tortured to death by the Echtroi? Or sent to the mines where his spirit had perished before his body?

Though part of Maura wished she could stay on peaceful Galene forever, basking in the quiet joy of kinship, another part itched to get back to the mainland. Liberating Umbria had become something more than her destiny. It was now a hallowed duty she owed her parents—to finish the task they had begun. A task that had cost them everything.

9

"When you found your family, you didn't do it by half measures, did you, *aira?*" Rath wrapped his arms around Maura from behind, resting his chin on the crown of her head. "If we must have a big, fancy wedding and crowning ceremony, I reckon this is a good place for it."

They stood in the large courtyard of the house that had belonged to Maura's grandfather. The house in which her mother had been born. A festive celebration swirled around them as twilight dappled the vast western horizon. Merry music from string and wind instruments floated on the evening air along with the mouthwatering fragrances of fresh bread, roasted meat and fruit stewed in honey.

Maura's past two weeks on the island of Galene had been like a dream come true—going wherever she liked, whenever she wished without the smallest fear. A perfect blend of safety and freedom. She'd been rapturously welcomed by her kin, a precious boon indeed after growing up with no family and few friends. Only one thing had been missing to complete her happiness.

Then Rath had arrived from Margyle aboard the *Phantom,* along with the Oracle and the whole Council of Sages to take part in their wedding and crowning ceremonies.

Now Idrygon stood in one corner of the courtyard involved in a grave discussion with some of Maura's uncles and cousins. Madame Verise danced by in the arms of Captain Gull, looking as if she was enjoying herself immensely. Beyond the courtyard, the Oracle of Margyle was playing a hiding game with young Bran and some other Galeni children. Delyon perched on the edge of the fountain, poring over an old scroll from Brandel Woodbury's private library. Gull's hillcat sat on Delyon's lap, content to suffer the occasional absentminded scratch behind the ears.

Maura's happiness should have been complete. But the brooding distraction she had sensed in Rath before she'd left Margyle had not lifted, hard as he tried to hide it. Maura wished he would confide in her whatever was troubling him. Was she a fool if she could not figure it out for herself? Or did she guess the truth but not want to face it?

"Shall we steal away for a walk on the beach?" She reached down to twine her fingers through one of the hands Rath had clasped around her waist "We've hardly had a moment alone since you got here, and the shore is so beautiful."

For an instant, Rath seemed not to hear her. Then her words must have sunk in, for he squeezed her hand and he spoke with forced brightness. "That sounds like a fine idea. Let's go."

It took them a little while to wend their way through the crowd. Some of Maura's cousins who had not met Rath stopped them for introductions. They waved to the children who were running to hide from their new playmate.

"You had better find good cover," Rath teased, "if you hope to stay hidden from an oracle who can see the future."

"Why did you have to remind them she's the Oracle?" Maura chided him. "She is still only a child, after all—one who doesn't often get to enjoy games with others her age."

"You're right." Rath scowled and kicked the turf as they walked. "It just doesn't seem right—a child that age with a head full of memories she can't understand and a gift of foresight she can't make sense of."

"People might say the same of you and me. A king who has never commanded an army. A queen who has never set foot in a palace. We cannot help those limitations and we're trying our best in spite of them."

"So we are," muttered Rath as they picked their way down a steep slope to the shore. "I only hope our best will be good enough."

"It has been so far." Maura told him what she and the young Oracle had concluded, about how the Giver might work all the better through flawed instruments like them.

Rath mulled over her words as they pried off their shoes. "It would be comforting to believe that."

"Can you not believe it?" Maura tugged him toward the edge of the shore, where fine, wet sand welcomed their feet with its cool caress and white-foamed waves rolled in one upon the other in a ceaseless, soothing rhythm. "Here, of all places?"

Rath stared into the distant, broad horizon blushed with twilight into the vivid hues of the island flowers. Even its serenity and splendor could not ease the subtle tightness around his eyes.

"My mother stood here once," said Maura, "and looked out at a sunset like this one. It is the most vivid memory Langbard passed to me from her. When I first saw this place with my own eyes, it took my breath away. Not just because of its beauty, but because of the closeness I felt to her."

They ambled along the beach, the cool surf breaking over their feet, and the tangy ocean breeze whispering through their hair. Overhead, seafowl wheeled and glided, their haunting cries echoing through the gathering dusk. Her hand holding tight to his, Maura told Rath as much of her mother's story as she had learned from her kinfolk.

"Your mother was a brave lass," said Rath when she had finished. "Like her daughter. Your father sounds a noble fellow, too. It is a shame you never knew them, and that they gave their lives for nothing."

"But don't you see?" Maura turned toward him. "It wasn't for nothing. If my mother had never gone to Tarsh and begotten me, then somehow escaped from the Han and found her way to Windleford, all those prophesies of the Destined Queen would never have come true. The ones about my being descended from Abrielle and raised by Langbard. If we succeed in liberating Umbria, my parents will not have died in vain."

Her words did not dispel the cloud that hung over Rath.

"What is troubling you, *aira*?" She reached up to brush the backs of her fingers against his cheek. "And do not insult my wit by pretending nothing is."

"Taken lessons from your little friend, the Oracle, have you?" Though his voice sounded gruff, he leaned into her caress, nuzzling her hand with his cheek, which was shaved closer than she had ever felt it before. It seemed almost to belong to another man.

"You are not so hard to read," she teased him, "like one of Delyon's ancient scrolls. You are more like a tavern sign, with the words writ large and plain, and a picture carved above them for good measure. Out with it, now. Perhaps it is not as bad as you think."

"All right, then." He inhaled a deep breath of the briny ocean air. "There is something I must know from you, and it *must* be the truth, mind."

"Rath Talward!" She jerked her hand back as if he had stung it. "Do you think I would lie to you?"

"To spare my feelings? Aye, you would. Or if you felt you had other good reason. Remember how you strung me along on our journey to Prum, with tales of an old aunt and an arranged match you had to make?"

"That was different!" Maura protested. "I hardly knew you back then. And it would have been dangerous to go about telling everyone I met that I was the Destined Queen. Now that we are to wed, you will have the truth from me, I promise."

A chill wave of worry broke over her, quenching her flash of anger. What question could he mean to ask that he feared she might not answer truthfully?

"We are soon to be wed," Rath repeated. "And I need to know, are you wedding me because I am your heart's choice? Or is it like your mother, who went to her marriage for the sake of duty and destiny? You promised me the truth, remember."

Relief swamped Maura with such force she might have crumpled onto the sand if Rath had not caught her by the arms.

Instead, she collapsed against him, giving his broad chest a token swat. "You fretted yourself and me over *that*? Of course you are the choice of my heart! It almost tore me in two when I thought the Waiting King would come between us."

"But you chose him before you knew we were one and the same. I remember our journey to the Secret Glade and how you were prepared to sacrifice your happiness for the sake of your people. I cannot accept such a sacrifice from you, *aira*."

Maura raised her face to meet the challenge of his gaze. "*We* made that decision together, remember? I cannot swear how I might have chosen if you had set yourself to change my mind."

"Truly?"

Did he *want* to doubt her? Or was it just that doubt and distrust were still stronger in him than belief and hope?

"How can I convince you? Being your destined partner is the one part of my fate I can embrace with a joyful heart and no reservations. Have you forgotten our joining of spirits, when you saw yourself through my eyes and tasted the flavor of my love for you?"

"Perhaps I had forgotten, a little." He canted his head and

leaned toward her. "Looking back now, it all seems like a dream—too good to be true."

"Perhaps this will remind you." Maura slid her hand up his chest and around his neck, pulling him toward her.

Her lips met his, parting in welcome. He kissed her with all the hoarded yearning of their journey, when it had seemed impossible that they would ever be together like this.

Even as she responded to his anxious ardor, Maura could not help wondering if there was something more troubling him. Something he could not bring himself to share with her. Perhaps something he had not fully acknowledged to himself.

She pulled back from him just far enough to murmur, "What about you?"

"Me?" He lifted her off her feet and spun around until she squealed with laughter. "Can you suppose for a moment that I am not eager to wed you?"

"Not that," she said when he had finally set her back on her feet. "I practically dragged you out of Everwood. But I do not want you to accept the crown and all that goes with it only for my sake."

"Not such a bad reason, is it?"

Perhaps he had made himself dizzy spinning around. Now he clung to her for support, as she sensed he would in the years to come. He was a strong, forceful man, but there were other kinds of strength and Maura knew there might be times ahead when he would need to call upon hers.

"Not a bad reason, just not good enough. I want you to do this because it is the right thing to do. And because it is *your* destiny."

"Do not fret yourself." He leaned down and pressed a kiss to her brow, like a benediction. "I wasn't thinking right that morn in Everwood. The whole notion of being the Waiting King had thrown me off balance, like that spinning did just now. And I had a good many wrong ideas I've since learned the truth of."

Maura listened for a false or forced note in his voice, but heard none.

Rath took her face in his hands and gazed deep into her eyes by the dying light of day. "Now that I have seen what life is like here on the Islands—what it *could* be like on the mainland—I cannot rest until I have done everything in my power to make it so."

"Spoken like a true king," Maura whispered.

"I still doubt we can oust the Han from Umbria all by ourselves. Though, who knows…if the Giver wills it? But we will not be alone. Idrygon has been preparing for this day for years. Waiting and hoping that I would come to lead the force he has assembled."

His words stirred and reassured Maura. "You're convinced we can prevail now, aren't you?"

"I am." Rath looked so regal in his confidence, she wished she had the crown in her hands to nestle on his windblown hair.

Then the banished shadow returned to darken his gaze. He gathered Maura close again, as if she were a frightened child in need of his comfort. Or perhaps the other way around.

"I am convinced we can prevail," he repeated in a harsh whisper. "But at what cost?"

At what cost? Those words haunted Rath's dreams on the night before his wedding and crowning ceremonies.

What Maura had told him about her parents did nothing to ease his dread. Quite the opposite. He might have reconciled himself to a heroic death like the kind her father had suffered. But to endure the loss of his beloved, as her mother had—the thought of it sapped his courage.

He rolled over in the narrow bed he'd been provided by one of Maura's relatives, cursing the custom that they must sleep apart during the days leading up to their wedding. He had not minded it so much while she'd been off to Galene visiting her kin. Now that they were on the same island again, he could scarcely bear to be parted from her.

If she'd been sharing his bed now, he could have held her close, soothed by the warmth of her body, the whisper of her breathing and the murmur of her heartbeat. He could have convinced himself to savor whatever time they had and trust to the Giver's providence that it would not be cut short.

No matter what the young Oracle prophesied.

Thinking back over his talk with Maura on the beach, he burned with shame for questioning *her* honesty when he had been hiding something from her. But he could not blight her happiness by telling her the truth. From now on, he must keep his worries better hidden from her—not writ large with pictures like a tavern sign!

"Highness!" Someone shook Rath's shoulder.

He came awake with a violent start, to find his hand around Delyon's neck.

"Your pardon!" He let go at once. "Don't ever wake me sudden like that."

"No harm done." Delyon's voice sounded hoarse as he rubbed his throat. "My brother sent me to fetch you. It will soon be dawn—time for the ceremony."

As Deylon set down the candle he was carrying on a small table beside the bed, Rath thanked the Giver that the young scholar hadn't dropped it on the bedclothes during their brief struggle.

"Your robes are all laid out over there." Delyon pointed to a low chest in the far corner. "You'd better hurry."

Rath scrambled out of bed. "I'll be right along."

As he headed for the door, Delyon paused and turned. "Highness?"

"Yes?" After two weeks in Idrygon's household, Rath was slowly getting used to answering to that title.

"I wish you every joy in your union, sire." Delyon bowed. "It will be an honor to witness the joining and crowning of the Waiting King and the Destined Queen."

"Um…thank you." Rath knew he sounded gruff and awkward, but he couldn't help himself.

The young scholar was a decent enough fellow, but the two of them were as unalike as men could be. And given a choice between them, Rath had no illusions about who was the better man.

After Delyon left, Rath quickly slipped into his wedding robes, relieved to find they were a good deal looser than the tunics he worn on Margyle. Delyon had told him their brown color symbolized the fertile earth. When he emerged from his chamber into the courtyard, it was packed with men, talking quietly by candlelight.

Idrygon stepped forward with a woven circlet of leaves and placed it on Rath's head. "We had better get going to reach the wedding grove by dawn. I hope you slept well, Highness. This is going to be a grand day."

Rath nodded, stifling a yawn. This would be a grand day and he must do nothing to spoil it for Maura or these good folks. He tried to approach it as he might a coming battle—concentrating on the tasks at hand, while firmly locking away any distracting worries.

With his usual efficiency, Idrygon mustered all the men into a procession that headed off toward the wedding grove. As they walked, they sang a ritual chant in *twara,* of which Rath could make out a few words. It did not matter, though, for he'd been told the bridegroom took no part in the singing. He brought up the rear of the procession, following the bobbing lights of many candles through the predawn darkness.

Soon they reached the wedding grove, a cultivated ring of trees, shrubbery and flowers with four openings—one each for north, south, east and west. The bridegroom's procession entered through the eastern one into a large grassy circle that sloped to a low mound at the center. The men walked around the rim of the circle, moving westward, while Idrygon led Rath to the middle of the grass, where they waited.

The moment he stopped, Rath could hear a high, clear chorus of women's voices coming from the west. Soon the first women began to file into the grove through the western entrance, their chant weaving a haunting harmony with the men's voices. They walked around the circle in the opposite direction the men had, while Madame Verise and one of Maura's aunts led her toward Rath.

Maura wore a gown the color of spring leaves. Her ruddy curls hung loose over her shoulders and down her back, crowned with a wreath of flowers. By the flickering light of a hundred candles, and the first rays of dawn, she was a vision of near-unbearable beauty.

Suddenly the chanting stopped, and all the candles were blown out.

"Let us meditate with one pure will," said Madame Verise in a quiet but resonant voice. "And ask that the gracious spirit of the Giver may hover over this holy place and bless the union of this man and woman."

In the expectant silence that followed, Rath heard the distant pounding of the surf, the whisper of the breeze through the leaves and the first clear, sweet notes of birdsong to herald the rising sun. As he had on the swift, treacherous ride down that river from the mines, Rath felt a presence enfolding and uplifting him.

When at last Madame Verise began to pronounce the ritual of union, he was able to meet Maura's gaze with a warm, untroubled smile.

"Elzaban and Maura. As you embark upon a lifetime voyage across the uncharted ocean of the future, we gather today to witness your compact of union and to invoke the Giver's blessing upon you."

She nodded to Rath, who held his right hand out to Maura, palm up, and spoke the words he had worked hard to memorize. "Maura, I offer myself to you—all that I have and all that I am. I promise to protect you, defend you, support and cherish you as long as I live."

"Elzaban…" Maura stumbled a bit over the unfamiliar name and her voice sounded thick with unshed tears. "I accept you as my lifemate, with a joyous and thankful heart."

Her right hand was cold as she laid it palm down upon his.

Madame Verise led the guests in a chant, asking the Giver to bless Rath with the strength, wisdom, tenderness and patience to fulfill his vows.

Then Maura extended her left hand to Rath. "Elzaban, I offer myself to you—all that I have and all that I am. I promise to sustain you, heal you, support and cherish you as long as I live."

She had scarcely finished speaking when Rath laid his left hand upon hers. "Maura, I accept you as my lifemate, with a joyous and thankful heart."

This time the company chanted a blessing upon Maura, while Rath stared deep into her eyes and silently begged the Giver to endow his bride with an extra measure of patience. She would need it.

When the chant ended, Madame Verise nodded to Rath and Maura, who raised both pairs of clasped hands toward the sky—a symbol of growth.

"All here witness," proclaimed Madame Verise, "that Elzaban and Maura have freely pledged themselves to one another for life. May their union grow and flourish. And may it bear an abundance of sound, sweet fruit in the years to come."

Rath flinched at the mention of the fruits of their union, but quickly shoved that renegade worry into a deep, dark corner of his mind. By the time he and Maura had lowered their clasped hands and she could see his face clearly, Rath flattered himself that she glimpsed nothing but what he wanted her to see—his joy, his pride and his love.

With hands still clasped between them, he leaned forward and sealed their vows with a kiss.

The rings of men and women ranged around the edge of the grove broke as the guests surged toward Rath and Maura to offer their blessings. Those already wed hung back to let the younger folk reach the center of the circle first.

Untangling their hands, Maura lifted the circlet of flowers from her hair while Rath removed the garland of leaves from his. Then they threw the wedding wreaths into the air, where they broke apart, showering down on the approaching guests. Young men lunged after the falling leaves, while the maidens each tried to catch a flower that meant they would one day find true love.

Rath laughed with a full heart as he watched the merry scramble. Just then, he wished everyone in the kingdom could know the surpassing happiness he had found with his destined bride.

Maura had only ever witnessed one other wedding—her friend Sorsha's. And it had been very different from this splendid ceremony. She and Langbard had gone with Sorsha and Newlyn to a tiny glade in Betchwood where the two had made their vows. All the while, they'd listened for any sound of a Hanish patrol or an outlaw band. Rather than tossing her bridal wreath in the air, Sorsha had carefully lifted it off her head and placed it on her friend's, saying she hoped the Giver would bless Maura with a fine husband someday. At the time, Maura had judged the chances of that very slight.

Her eyes misted with tears.

"What is it, love?" Rath stopped laughing at the antics of the young folks scrambling for groom's leaves and bridal blossoms. "Nothing wrong, is there?"

She shook her head. "I've never been happier. I only wish Sorsha could have been here today."

For all she was delighted to have been welcomed into the bosom of a large, loving family and to have her Woodbury kin witness her ritual of union, Sorsha was her oldest and dearest friend. A friend who was still in danger of having her family torn apart, if the Han should discover the secret of Newlyn's past. A friend who had to observe the rituals of the Elderways in secret.

"Maybe it's just as well she couldn't be here." Rath's voice lilted with teasing humor. "I'm not sure Sorsha would have approved you wedding a dangerous character like me. She wasn't too happy about you going off with me in the first place."

His jest lifted Maura's spirits as they received congratulations from all the company. "Sorsha would change her colors soon enough, I reckon, once she got to know you. You and her Newlyn are a good deal alike."

Hand in hand, they led a merry procession that wound in and out through all the entrances to the grove. Finally they departed through the northern one, to signify that their union would endure through adversity. Remembering the hardships it had already withstood to reach this moment, Maura felt confident she and Rath could weather whatever storms the future might bring.

From the wedding grove, they walked back to her grandfather's villa. A bountiful feast awaited them there, with food spread on long tables from which everyone could help themselves. Before anyone else could eat, Maura and Rath peeled two hard-boiled eggs decorated with *twaran* letters and fed them to each other.

"Well, this is fitting!" Maura chuckled. "Do you remember the morning after we left Windleford, how you peeled those eggs Sorsha gave us?"

"I do." Rath's dark eyes twinkled with glee. "Though if I'd known then what it meant, I might have thought twice."

Afterward, they helped each other to more of the food—strands of bread twisted into fanciful shapes, wedges of flavorful cheese and pieces of island fruit threaded on wooden skewers in colorful patterns. *Sythwine* and *lipma* cordial flowed freely along with other delicious drinks Maura had never tasted before.

After Rath and Maura had eaten their fill, Idrygon and Ma-

dame Verise summoned them away to change into their coronation robes for the ceremony that would take place at noon.

Madame Verise smiled through tears as she helped Maura
into a gown the color of midsummer sunshine. "Bless the
Giver that I should live to see the Destined Queen crowned.
I only wish Nalene and Langbard could be here. They devoted
their lives to making this happen. Though you are not their
daughter by birth, your coronation still honors them and ful-
fills their hope."

Maura clasped the old woman in a gentle embrace, and in
their shared tears, the spirits of Langbard and his wife seemed
very near, bestowing their special blessing upon her.

"Enough now." Madame Verise at last thrust a handkerchief
at Maura. "Dry your eyes, child. We cannot have the Destined
Queen blubbering through her coronation."

The crowning ceremony took place in the same hallowed
glade as their ritual of union, which was fitting, Maura thought.
In a way, she and Rath were being united with their people into
one very large family. Rath looked so regal in robes that seemed
to have been woven from threads of the deep blue Vestan sky.
Maura even found herself thinking of him as *Elzaban*.

Delyon read from a scroll that prophesied the coming of the
Waiting King. The uncanny parallels between what had been
foretold so long ago and the adventures she and Rath had
shared to reach this moment gave Maura chills of wonder.

There were several chants by the assembled witnesses, calling down the Giver's blessing on the new king and queen. Rath
spoke his vows, similar to the ones he had made Maura, to protect and defend his kingdom. Then it was her turn to promise
she would sustain and nurture her people.

She and Rath knelt before the young Oracle of Margyle, who
looked a little uncertain. Maura flashed the child a reassuring
smile, to remind her that they were no better prepared for this
than she. Yet the Giver was with them, and all would be well.

The child stood a little taller as she looked out at the assembled crowd. "I am perhaps the only one here with memories of other Umbrian kings and queens crowned." Her high young voice rang with the accumulated wisdom of all her predecessors. "But never has an oracle placed the crowns of our realm on the heads of two worthier sovereigns."

She turned to Madame Verise and took from her a crown of ivory, carved to resemble the flower wreath Maura had worn in her hair that morning. Placing it on Maura's head, she said, "Wear this crown, Destined Queen, in token of the Giver's wisdom, courage and compassion. May your reign be long, peaceful and prosperous."

Then she took a larger crown from Idrygon, also of ivory and carved as a ring of leaves. So skillful had been the artistry of the carver that Maura almost fancied it had been fashioned from real leaves, bleached to the color of fresh cream.

"Wear this crown, Elzaban, Waiting King, in token of the Giver's wisdom, courage and compassion. May your reign be long, peaceful and prosperous."

Signaling the newly crowned monarchs to rise, the Oracle turned to those gathered and cried, "Umbria waits no more!"

10

"What shall we do next, *aira*?" Rath leaned back in the gently swaying hammock suspended between two tall tree trunks, shaded by a high canopy of broad leaves. Maura nestled against him. "Go for another swim in the lagoon? Catch some fish? Or wander through the woods to see if we can spot any monkeys?"

Following their coronation, they had spent a blissful week on the tiny island paradise of Tolin, where Madame Verise told them Langbard and his wife had spent their *nectarnights* many years ago. They had been given the use of a cozy little villa, with a breathtaking view of the lagoon from its bedroom balcony. The pantry had been stocked with all the food they would need for their stay. As well, there was plenty of fresh fish for the catching and an amazing variety of ripe fruit just waiting to be plucked.

But the thing Rath liked best about the place was its seclusion. Ever since Gull and his crew had brought them from Galene, they had not seen or heard another living soul. Unless you counted the monkeys, which they had not seen, either, though they'd heard haunting calls from the forest at night.

"Why must we go anywhere or do anything?" Maura ran her hand over his bare chest in a provocative caress. "For weeks and weeks, we've been on the move, always with something urgent to accomplish. I think we owe ourselves these nice lazy *nectarnights*."

Rath chuckled. "I love it when you're right, lady wife."

He had a faint suspicion there was something they ought to be doing, or planning to do, but he could not remember what. And he was not sure he wanted to remember.

Madame Verise had given him and Maura a potion to bring with them to the island. She'd told them it was her wedding gift and said they were to drink a special toast with it as soon as they arrived. He and Maura had dutifully followed her instructions, though Rath hadn't cared for the taste of it. The potion was supposed to do something, but Rath could not recall what.

Never mind! He had the most desirable woman in Umbria in his arms and a beautiful private paradise in which to enjoy her.

Maura looked up at the summer sky, or such bits of it as they could see through the thick leaves overhead. The wind had blown a vast billow of clouds over the island. "Perhaps we ought to go inside. It looks like another downpour is coming."

"So it does," said Rath. But he made no move to rise from the hammock.

The island weather was strange, with its brief but intense showers that left the ground steaming when the sun chased them away. Now that he was getting used to it, Rath preferred it to the long days of gray drizzle that sometimes blanketed the Hitherland, or the parching heat of the Southmark steppes.

"You know—" he wound a strand of Maura's hair around his finger "—it's hardly worth the bother of going in, the rain will be over so soon. And it isn't cold."

"But our clothes will get wet."

Rath shrugged. "They dry out quick. Or…"

"Or…?" Maura hoisted herself up enough to rest her chin upon his chest.

"If you're that worried about them getting wet, we could always take them off and put them underneath something. That, maybe?" He pointed to a large empty fruit bowl, woven from thin slats of wood. "If I turn it over on top of our clothes, they'll be dry after the storm passes."

"But *we'll* be wet." Maura shot Rath a mischievous grin to match the one on his face.

"Mmm." He ran his hands over her body, guessing the sensation would feel even more delicious on her moist, naked skin. "Sounds tempting, doesn't it?"

Maura's eyes shimmered with the sultry heat of rain-drenched leaves after the sweet tempest of a storm. "You make anything sound tempting, outlaw."

A distant roll of thunder echoed the rumble of Rath's chuckle. "We'd better strip off quick, then, or we won't have a choice."

Luckily their clothes were easy to shed. Maura wore only a length of light linen that wrapped around her body and tied over one shoulder, while an even shorter scrap of cloth sheathed Rath from hip to thigh. After a bit of twitching and twisting, the small mound of linen soon lay sheltered under the bowl, while the newlyweds lay tangled in one another's arms, flushed with desire that the approaching rain could not hope to quench.

As they exchanged hot, hungry kisses, they scarcely noticed the first drops of rain that spattered on their bare bodies. Rath hoisted Maura on top of him, so her legs straddled his belly and her firm, generous breasts nestled against his chest, while the tempting roundness of her backside was perfectly positioned for his hands to fondle.

The storm quickly gathered force. In spite of the thick awning of branches above them, warm summer rain soon teemed down over the lovers. Maura's hair fell like a wet veil around Rath's face as her lips ranged hungrily over his.

He strained to reach her breast with his mouth, and she obliged, arching up until he was able to catch the drops of rain that trickled from her nipple on his tongue. Each one set him pleasure-drunk with its musky sweetness. He ran his hands over her body, caressing the enticing curves and probing the beguiling clefts. The hammock swayed gently in time to their movements, two creatures in a primal garden giving and receiving the most potent pleasure.

Rath's pulse galloped like the swift rolling drum of the rain on the roof of their villa. Desire swirled inside him, with the thrilling savagery of an ocean gale. His body roused to the touch, scent and taste of Maura until it was taut and fevered with need. When she lowered herself into him, he thrust up to meet her. Storm-tossed on a sea of sensation, powerful waves bore them up and swept them along ever higher and faster. Until one wild surge crested and broke over them, drowning them both in a vast ocean of ecstasy.

Rath subsided, just as the rain eased, his chest heaving as if he *had* barely escaped drowning. The raindrops trickling down his face heightened that feeling, but no matter—he knew as long as he held fast to Maura, they would wash up together somewhere he wanted to be.

As quickly as it had begun, the rain stopped and the sun seemed to shine all the brighter for the brief squall. The slow sway of the hammock lulled Rath and Maura into a lazy doze of peaceful contentment.

Whether an hour passed or only a moment, Rath could not be certain. But the sound of a voice calling a friendly greeting jarred him awake.

"Hello?" The voice belonged to Delyon—curse him. "Highnesses? Are you there?"

As both Rath and Maura tried to grab their clothes, the hammock twisted, dumping them onto the ground. Rath growled a curse under his breath. Maura shoved the loincloth into his hand. He fumbled to wrap it around him.

They'd just got themselves decently covered when Delyon appeared. "Oh, there you are! You had me worried when you didn't answer. Were you caught out in that rain?"

Rath and Maura stammered out different replies at the same time, but Delyon showed no sign of guessing what he had almost interrupted. "Bad luck. Oh well, you have time to dry off before we have to leave."

"Leave?" Rath wanted to throttle the handsome young scholar for even suggesting it. "We have to leave now? So soon?"

Delyon gave an apologetic nod and his bronzed complexion seemed to redden a little. Perhaps he was beginning to guess what they'd been up to. "It has been a week, after all. Preparations for the invasion are almost complete. I hope you got a good rest to ready yourselves."

"Invasion?" Rath and Maura stared at one another and then at Delyon, as though he'd gone daft.

"The invasion to liberate the mainland…remember? It's the reason you came to the Vestan Islands in the first place."

Suddenly Rath did remember. That potion from Madame Verise had made him and Maura forget. Rath could now recall being doubtful it would work. But he'd been willing to try, for the sake of a few elusive, unshadowed days with Maura.

As it turned out, the potion had worked well. Perhaps too well. Suppressed memories flooded his mind now that they had been roused. A host of worries landed upon him like packs dropped from a high window. He staggered under their weight.

And the burden of his destiny felt all the heavier for having escaped its crush a little while.

To think only yesterday she and Rath had been taking their pleasure out in the rain, with not a care in the world!

As she sat by her husband's side in the council chamber, Maura fought to suppress a sigh. How tempting it was to wish they could return to that secluded island paradise with a lifetime supply of Madame Verise's potion. But that would be cowardly and selfish.

Maura summoned thoughts of her friends Sorsha and Newlyn Swinley, Blen and Tesha Maynold, Boyd Tanner, Snake and Angareth. All those people were counting on her and Rath, whether they realized it or not. Then she remembered Langbard and Nalene, Exilda and her parents. She must do everything in her power to make certain their sacrifices had not been in vain.

Those thoughts acted like a magical tonic on Maura's courage and will. With renewed concentration, she listened while Idrygon explained the details of his invasion plan.

He had brought a large wooden slab to lay on the floor in the center of the chamber, upon which a map of Umbria was molded in clay. Maura's gaze swept over it, tracing the path of her quest to find the Waiting King.

"Your pardon, Idrygon." The wizard Trochard rose from his seat and pointed to the tiny model ships being pushed across the board toward the Dusk Coast. "Your preparations have been most thorough, but the number of ships you have available and the number of fighters you have been able to raise will be but a pittance to the Hanish legions now occupying the kingdom. I fail to see how this invasion of yours can possibly succeed."

He turned and made a curt bow toward Rath. "Not even with the Waiting King to lead them, for he has no magical army or special powers to…"

Rath's hands clenched around the arms of his chair. Maura knew he must be struggling to "play the king in the council chamber" as she had bidden him.

"*If* you will permit me to continue, Trochard," Idrygon snapped, "I believe your objections will be answered."

"He is right, Trochard." Madame Verise nodded for the redheaded wizard to sit down. "It has always been the custom of this Council to listen and consider before raising objections."

Glaring at Idrygon, Trochard resumed his seat with a loud huff.

"As I was saying…" Idrygon pushed the tiny ships nearer the coast. They did look pitifully few. "Our strategy is not to meet the Han on an open field of battle. They are many, but they are spread thin over a wide area. By concentrating our small force in surprise attacks on key positions, I believe we can prevail."

He gestured toward Rath. "And you are wrong to say His Highness has no special weapons or powers. The power of his legend is one of the most potent weapons any army could wish for. It will rally the mainlanders to our cause. They may not be well trained or equipped, but they could be a mighty force, properly wielded. And make no mistake—they *will* flock to the banner of the Waiting King!"

Maura had never warmed to the forceful, ambitious Idrygon as she had to his scholarly brother, but at that moment she could cheerfully have kissed him. Trochard squirmed in his seat as whispers of agreement passed among the Council members, even some of his own supporters.

With an air of grim triumph, Idrygon described how his force would attack Duskport and secure it as their base. From there, they would march across the Hitherland, liberating every town and village and gathering strength. "By the time we have cleansed Tarsh, Norest and Southmark of the Han, we will be ready to sweep down upon Westborne."

Rath rose, drawing the gazes of all the Council.

"You wish to speak, Highness?" Idrygon asked.

"What about the mines?"

"Your pardon, Highness?"

"The Blood Moon mines." Rath pointed toward Idrygon's map. "You have heard of them?"

"Of course, Highness. What about them?"

"They must be one of our first targets. They are…" he searched for a word and winced when the best he could think of was "wrong. They are…" He tried again, his rugged features contorted with the effort.

"An affront." Maura rose to stand beside him. "The mines are an affront to the Giver, and the Precepts and all it once meant to be Umbrian. The king is right. The mines cannot be allowed to continue their evil work if we have the means to stop them."

Rath's hand closed over hers with a grateful squeeze.

Idrygon's features tightened into a scowl, which he was quick to subdue. "Your Highness's concern for the most oppressed of your subjects is laudable. However, I fear a premature bid to liberate the mines would not only be doomed to failure itself, but might imperil our whole campaign."

When Rath looked ready to object, Idrygon changed tactics. "You and I can discuss this further in private, Highness. Perhaps some way can be worked out to speed our liberation of the mines without jeopardizing our greater objective."

Did Idrygon mean what he said? Maura wondered. Or was he just trying to keep Rath quiet so Trochard could not take advantage of a rift in their alliance? Glimpsing Rath's thoughtful frown, she guessed he must be asking himself the same thing. He glanced at her and they resumed their seats without further protest while Idrygon outlined the rest of his plan.

"May I be permitted to speak *now*?" asked Trochard when Idrygon fell silent at last.

Madame Verise nodded, then cast an apologetic glance at Rath. "If it please Your Highness?"

"Have your say, Trochard." Under his breath Rath muttered, "Before you burst from bottling it up."

Maura bit the inside of her cheek to curb a most unqueenly chuckle.

"Your plan is quite clever, Idrygon," said Trochard in a patronizing tone, "as far as it goes. But you cannot hope to avoid open battle with the Han forever. Once you make your first attack, they will mass and come after you. I fear you are too young to remember the tactics they used to conquer Umbria in the first place."

"How would you know any better, Trochard?" asked one very old wizard whose name Maura could not recall. "You were on the first ship to Margyle after the Han attacked."

The mocking laughter that greeted the old wizard's comment made Trochard's face flush almost purple. Unable to answer the charge, he hit back at Idrygon's plan instead. "Besides, you have given the Council no hint of how you mean to handle the Echtroi. Their power is terrible, and we have no means to combat it!"

Idrygon smiled—a strangely chilling expression. "No means *yet*. This is the other vital part of our plan. With the Giver's blessing, each will work to abet the other." He butted his fists together. "To crush our foe."

This was the first Maura had heard of another part to Idrygon's invasion strategy. She caught Rath's eye and arched her brow in a silent question. He replied with a subtle shrug that told her it was new to him.

"If I may beg the Council's indulgence a little longer," said Idrygon, "my brother can better explain what must be done."

"Very well," grumbled Trochard. "Let him speak."

Idrygon yielded the center of the Great Circle to his brother, returning to his own seat beside Rath.

Delyon looked far less confident than his brother, speaking before the full Council. Maura caught his eye and flashed him an encouraging smile.

It seemed to help. Delyon bowed toward her and Rath. "Highnesses, members of the Council. Trochard raises an important question—how *are* we to combat the Echtroi? It is true they channel powerful forces of destruction, but there is a power even greater that we might use against them, if we can find it. And I believe we can."

"And what is this power, pray?" asked Trochard, his tone thick with scorn.

Delyon hesitated for a moment, as if wary of even speaking its name. "The Staff of Velorken."

"Rubbish!" Trochard cried after a moment's stunned silence. "If the Staff of Velorken ever truly existed, it was lost ages ago during the time of the Sundering."

"What was lost can be found." Suddenly Delyon sounded far more confident. He gestured toward Rath. "The Waiting King, for instance. Many questioned his existence…or only pretended to believe. Yet here he sits among us after being lost for ages. I believe the person who restored him to us can also restore the weapon only he or she can wield."

Maura could feel all eyes in the room fixed upon her.

"As I have told the Council," said Delyon, "my study of the ancient scrolls leads me to believe Queen Abrielle used the staff to free King Elzaban's spirit, allowing him to be reborn until his destiny could be accomplished."

Trochard muttered something Maura could not make out, but a cool stare from Madame Verise silenced him.

"The writings say Abrielle later hid the staff in the castle," continued Delyon, "which is now occupied by the Hanish High Governor. I believe that our Destined Queen, a direct descendant of Abrielle, has the power to recover what her foremother hid."

A shiver ran through Maura as some baffling intuition told her it was true.

She braced for Trochard's retort, but instead heard a hostile rumble from Rath. "You mean to send my wife into the High Governor's palace to poke around in search of some magic weapon *you reckon* might be there and *you reckon* she might be able to find?"

He leaped to his feet, assuming the stance of a warrior under attack. "It is too dangerous. I will not allow it!"

"B-but, Highness—" Delyon flinched from Rath's fierce anger "—without the staff…"

"Slag the staff!"

The sages of the Council all gasped at once.

"*Aira.*" Maura laid a hand on Rath's arm and felt the straining tension of his flesh. "The *king* in the council chamber, remember?"

Idrygon rose and joined his brother. "Highness, if you and the Council will only hear us out." His tone begged Rath to show a little solidarity, at least until they could discuss the matter further in private.

"Very well." Rath dropped back into his chair, slightly chastened. "But there is nothing you say that will convince me to put Maura in danger."

What had riled him so? Maura wondered. It wasn't as though he'd never seen her in danger before—sometimes on his account. She didn't *like* the idea of probing the black heart of Hanish oppression, but she doubted Delyon would have suggested the idea if he'd seen any other way.

"No!" Rath paced the courtyard of Idrygon's villa. "There must be some other way."

Idrygon remained seated at the table with Maura and Delyon. The supper dishes had been cleared away, and the ladies of the house had excused themselves.

Rath had made a valiant effort to restrain himself until now. But it had been a long wearying day stuck inside the council chamber. He was a man of action—all the talking and arguing back and forth made him feel as if the walls were closing in on him. He had to vent his pent-up feelings before he exploded!

"Now, Highness," said Idrygon in a tone Rath hated—as if he were trying to soothe a fractious beast. "You heard what Delyon and I told the Council. We must have the Staff of Velorken if we are to defeat the Echtroi. Our attacks in the north should draw troops and death-mages away from Venard. Her Highness will not undertake this mission alone. Delyon will go with her."

"Much help he'll be," Rath muttered.

He had finally been able to stop brooding about the Oracle's prophesy by vowing he would do everything in his power to keep Maura from harm. Then this whole business had ambushed him, as if to prove he could not fight destiny. So much for hill mazes and the notion of folks having some control over their lives!

"It isn't as if we'll be marching up to the gates of the castle and demanding entry." The smirk on Delyon's face made Rath want to pitch him headfirst into the fountain.

Maura's safety was no laughing matter, damn it!

"Tell me more, Delyon," said Maura, "about this new magical agent that will make us invisible."

What was this *will* and *us* business? Rath's scowl deepened. Why was Maura talking as if she meant to do this?

"It isn't new," said Delyon. "In fact, it was known and used many years ago, but the *genow* became scarce and folk had little need for invisibility, so gradually the spell was forgotten. It was one of the things I discovered while deciphering the ancient scrolls. It proved to a number of people that I was truly able to read them."

Rath had caught a fleeting glimpse of a *genow* while he and Maura were on Tolin. At least he thought he had. The tiny creatures had an uncanny ability to make the color of their skin match the cover in which they hid.

"So the spell uses scales from the *genow*—like the cuddybird spell Langbard taught me?"

"Better than cuddybird feathers." Delyon leaned back in his chair and sipped the last of his wine. "*Genow* are much more plentiful than they used to be, especially on some of the smaller islands. And their spell lasts longer."

Rath strode back to the table and pounded his fist on it. A show of temper like this had often won him his way back in his outlaw days. "Being invisible isn't the same as being safe! The Han have ears, too, remember. And their hounds have noses. You might bump into somebody or something."

Maura didn't look as if his outburst swayed or alarmed her. The gaze she fixed on him reminded Rath of Ganny's when he'd misbehaved as a child.

"We won't march around the place in the middle of the day looking for the staff, will we?" she asked Delyon as if she hadn't heard Rath at all. "We'll use the invisibility spell to steal into the palace at a quiet time. Then we'll find someplace to hide during the day while we search by night."

"Just so, Highness!" Delyon lavished Maura with a smile of unmistakable admiration that Rath would have liked to smack off his handsome face…except that would probably make her angrier.

Why should it vex her so that he wanted to keep her safe? Hadn't he promised her something like that during their joining ceremony? What was the good of a man making such a vow if he didn't mean to keep it?

"I doubt we will have to search long," continued Delyon. "Once we find the staff, we will bring it to His Highness with all speed and prevent any more bloodshed."

"What is the great power of this staff, anyway?" Once the question was out of his mouth, Rath wished he could recall it. It sounded too much as though he meant to go along with this risky plan of theirs.

"The power of the staff is very simple, but potent, sire," said Idrygon, who had been unusually quiet until now.

"Aye?" Rath crossed his arms in front of him. This had better be good.

"A wish, Highness." Idrygon seemed to relish the flavor of that word upon his tongue. "A single, unlimited wish."

11

One wish. If Maura had been given one wish in the days following the Council meeting, it would have been for Rath to stop being so pigheaded!

They had been over and over it—in the Council, in private with Idrygon and his brother and just between the two of them. Finding the Staff of Velorken was vital to liberating Umbria with the least destruction and loss of life.

"What *I* do not understand," said Maura as she Rath and Idrygon rode toward the west coast of Margyle to launch a pair of ships, "is why the invasion and battles are necessary."

Both men looked at her as if she'd gone daft, but she refused to be daunted. "If the Staff of Velorken has the power to rid Umbria of the Han, why does Rath not come with Delyon and me to Venard? We could search the palace, find the staff, make the wish and all would be well."

She glimpsed a hint of agreement in Rath's gaze, but Idrygon replied with a chuckle that sounded faintly contemptuous. "If only it were that simple, Highness. Trust me, this has all been many years in the planning. Our invasion of the north coast is essential to draw Hanish reserves away from West-borne so you may reach Venard safely."

When Maura still looked doubtful, he added, "It is also a necessary demonstration for the mainlanders that the Waiting King has come to deliver them. If they simply woke one morning to find the Han gone, I fear there would be chaos. This way, by the time His Highness wields the staff, his subjects will have rallied to his cause and be prepared to settle down peacefully under his rule once the kingdom is liberated."

Maura had to admit his reasons made sense. In addition to his leadership abilities, Lord Idrygon was a very persuasive man.

It had rained that morning, but the clouds had blown away and the summer sun now shimmered on the water of a snug inlet. Two ships rested on wooden platforms by the shore, ready to slide down into the embrace of the waves. They were similar in shape and rigging to Captain Gull's, but larger. Today they would be given their sailing names.

The sight of them made Maura shrink from the prospect of crossing the sea again, especially without Rath. She wished he could accompany her on this quest to find the Staff of Velorken. With him by her side, she felt she could do anything...if only he would let her.

As they rode down the gently sloping road to the shipyard, a child called out, "Here they come!"

Folks rushed out of their houses. Reedpipe music lilted on the gentle breeze along with laughter and calls of welcome. Some young girls tossed a soft, colorful rain of flower petals over the royal visitors from the upstairs windows of a house.

Maura smiled and waved to the people, while Idrygon acknowledged their jubilant welcome with dignified nods. Rath looked as though the whole spectacle made him ill at ease.

"Smile!" Maura coaxed him. "Try to look as if you're happy to see them."

He did *try,* raising his hand in a rather stiff salute. No one seemed to mind, though. They continued to cheer. And when the royal party had passed, the crowd fell in behind them, parading down to the dock.

There, Idrygon gave a short speech, thanking the villagers for their vital contributions to freeing the mainland. A small troop of soldiers raised from the surrounding countryside assembled for review by Rath and Idrygon.

All her life, Maura had never seen soldiers except Hanish ones. Fortunately these warriors reminded her little of the Han. Their padded leather armor was designed more for stealth and swiftness of movement than for strength, though an old wizard proudly informed her that he had placed a spell of hardness on it, using sap from local trees.

The weapons, too, were very different from the cruel metal blades of the Han—mainly bows and staffs of various types. Rath looked a good deal more relaxed and lively as he moved among the men, stopping to ask questions about their armor and weapons.

Once the troop review had finished, Idrygon ushered Rath and Maura to the dock where he explained what they must do. Vestan folk, he told them, always had some sort of ceremony to mark the launching of a new vessel, though not often as grand as this one.

Maura was given a tiny basket in the shape of a boat. It was filled with dried flowers, leaves and bits of sea plants. As Rath spoke the ritual words of blessing, prompted by Idrygon, Maura sprinkled the plant matter over the bow of each ship.

Finally Rath announced in a ringing voice, "I declare the sailing name of this ship the *Destined Queen*. May it find fair winds and good seas. And may the Giver protect all who sail it."

Props were cut away, and the ship glided down into the water with ponderous grace, throwing up great waves on either side. As the village folk cheered, Maura caught Rath's hand in hers.

For a moment, his awkwardness and brooding anger lifted as he seemed to catch the spirit of the crowd. Was he imagining the same thing she was? Maura wondered. Picturing this scene played out in Windleford or Prum—with everyone looking well fed, safe and happy?

They launched the second ship, named the *Waiting King* with the same ritual, then Rath and Maura were rowed out for a tour of the two vessels. Afterward they were guests of honor at a feast. Night had fallen by the time they rode back to Idrygon's villa, but Maura did not feel tired.

When Idrygon suggested he and Rath talk over more details of their attack on the Dusk Coast, Maura drew her husband away. "Tomorrow, my lord. It has been a long day."

The bedchamber door had scarcely closed behind them when she turned and slipped her arms around Rath's neck. "Wasn't that splendid? Here we thought we might have to fight the Han all by ourselves. It turns out there are plenty of people wanting to help. They just needed a little spark from us to get started."

"*You* were splendid today, *aira*!" Rath wrapped her in a warm embrace. "Everything a queen ought to be and better. I felt like a fool…looked like one, too, I reckon. I couldn't help wondering if all those folk would cheer if they knew who I really am and some of the things I've done."

"You did look a little…severe, perhaps." Maura kissed one corner of his lips, then the other, until she coaxed them to curve in a smile. "But kings are allowed to look that way. They have a lot on their minds. No one took it amiss."

She yielded to his kiss—a tender, lingering one.

"Besides," she said when they drew apart a little, "who you were and what you've done is all in the past. What matters is the man you are now and the king you'll become. This was your first real test since our crowning. You'll become more at ease with a bit of practice. You did fine with the soldiers."

Rath shrugged. "I wasn't thinking about this king business, then. Just wanted to find out about their armor and weapons."

"Perhaps that's the secret of it." Maura tugged him toward the bed. "Showing a little interest in folks."

The past few nights Rath had seemed so sullen and distant

after his talks with Idrygon. And she'd been so vexed with his stubbornness that they'd scarcely exchanged cool pecks on the cheek before rolling to opposite sides of the bed.

Perhaps Rath guessed her thoughts, for he murmured, "I haven't been showing enough interest in *you*, my queen. At least not the proper kind for a bridegroom."

He let go of her hand just long enough to shed his tunic and kick off his shoes, then he hoisted her in his arms and carried her the last few steps to the bed. "Will you give me leave to win your pardon?"

"You already have it." Maura ran her fingers through his hair as he eased her onto the bed. "I know how hard it has been for you to go from outlaw to king. I of all people should have shown you more patience."

Rath gave a deep melodious chuckle. "Funny you should mention patience, for you will need it tonight."

He draped the netting around the bed. Then he made love to her with slow, gentle whispers of his hands, lips and tongue, as if she were a delicate treasure that might shatter if handled too roughly. The deliberate restraint of his touch teased her to greater heights of pleasure until her body quivered and pleaded for release. When at last he eased himself into her, she did shatter in a fierce, frenzied spasm of delight that sparked an answering one in him.

Rath cradled Maura in his arms after their lovemaking. The intensity of his long-delayed release had drained him of all the pressure that had been building within him of late. He hoped the tenderness of his seduction had given Maura a glimpse of how deeply he loved her. That might make her understand how cruelly he feared losing her.

She nestled against him, caressing his cheek with her hand. "You know I must do this, don't you, *aira*? The legend says the Destined Queen and the Waiting King will work together to save the kingdom in its darkest hour."

"But you have already done your part and more." Had she only let him make love to her to appease him? "You found me. You made me come to the Islands when I would rather have run from this destiny of mine. It will drive me mad with worry to think of you wandering around the High Governor's palace."

In the darkness, he felt Maura prop herself up on her elbow. "This will be far easier than my quest to find the Secret Glade. This time, I know where I am supposed to go, and the distance from the coast to Venard is not great."

Rath shook his head. "But I will not be there to rescue you from the Han…or from your own misplaced kindness."

"I will have Delyon with me."

"I don't trust Delyon to protect you as I would!" Rath clenched his fist in helpless fury and pounded it on the mattress. "I don't trust him…"

His own words turned and caught Rath by the throat. Could there be another meaning to the Oracle's prophesy? Might Maura not be lost to him by death…but by betrayal?

She'd often said the handsome scholar reminded her of her late beloved guardian. Rath knew from experience that the shared adventure and danger of a quest could kindle passionate feelings between a man and a woman. If it could work between such opposites as Maura and him, what stronger bond might it forge between his beloved and a man far worthier of her?

"Don't trust Delyon?" Maura pulled away from Rath, her voice cold as a Hitherland wind. "Or don't trust me?"

Before he could overcome his shock at hearing her voice his most private fears, she continued, "Do you doubt I am capable of helping you overthrow the Han? Do you expect me to stay placidly on the Islands doing needlework while you go off to risk your life? I would go mad with worry!"

He reached for her. "As I will if you go ahead with this!"

She shook off his touch as if it were some kind of shackle. "You will have battles and such to keep you occupied. Why can you not see how perfectly all this fits? You will be doing your part to liberate Umbria in the way you are best suited, by a swift application of force."

Her tone warmed a little as she quoted Langbard's words. "And I will serve in the way I am best suited—with guile and magic and faith in the Elderways."

And another man. The thought burned in Rath's mind but he did not say it.

"I must do this, and I will." There could be no mistaking the finality in Maura's tone. "I wish you could support my decision, but I cannot let you stop me. You are my husband, not my master who I am bound to obey in everything."

Though he told himself it was useless, Rath could not keep from trying one last time. This would be the last, though.

"Not *everything*." His hand fumbled toward her in the darkness and brushed against her bare arm. "Just this one."

He steeled himself for her answer.

"Sleep well, Highness." Maura rolled away from him to the farthest edge of the bed.

When he could think of nothing to say that would not make things even worse between them, Rath silently turned his back on her and tried to sleep.

Their quest to find the Waiting King had brought Maura and him together. Rath heaved a sigh in the darkness. Would their battle to liberate the kingdom tear them apart?

He woke the next morning to find her already gone. It did not surprise him to discover her taking breakfast with Delyon. Planning their little adventure together, no doubt.

Fortunately Idrygon strode into the courtyard before Rath could say anything he might regret. "Highness, there is one final matter we must discuss, if you would come with me."

"Might as well." Rath shrugged. "Nothing better to do."

He followed Idrygon out of the villa and along a narrow path that climbed uphill.

"For this invasion to succeed," said Idrygon, "it is vital we present mainlanders with the kind of Waiting King the legends have primed them to expect."

Rath made a vague sound of agreement. He wasn't sure what Idrygon was talking about, but he hated to expose his ignorance. From the direction they were walking, he wondered if Idrygon was taking him to see the Oracle of Margyle again.

"I fear they will not rally to the cause of a reformed Hitherland outlaw." Idrygon took a different turn, leading to a part of town where Rath had never been before. "Not even one who claims to be the reborn spirit of King Elzaban."

"*I* made no claims," Rath muttered. "It was your daft brother who came up with that Staff of Velorken business and the Oracle who said—"

"Precisely. You saw for yourself how difficult it was to persuade Trochard and his followers that you are the Waiting King. And they are sages who have awaited your coming all their lives. Think how much harder it will be to convince a nation of backward mainlanders whom the Han have made suspicious of all magic and doubtful of the old legends."

"The way I used to be." Rath glanced out at the harbor where more ships were gathering each day, bringing troops from other parts of the Islands. "What do you plan to do about it?"

Idrygon would never bring up a problem if he had not already worked out a solution. "Sire, I propose we help your subjects believe, by giving them exactly what they've been led to expect."

Rath arched a brow. "And what is that?"

Ahead of them stood a villa like Idrygon's, only smaller. A scent wafted from it that reminded Rath of Langbard's cottage.

Idrygon nodded toward it. "We must give them a hero."

Rath gazed at the house. "You expect to find one here?"

"In a manner of speaking. I do."

A woman strode out to meet them. She was almost as tall as Rath, dressed in a plain brown robe with a floss of fine white hair floating around her head.

"Fair morning, Lord Idrygon," she called.

"Fair morning, Dame Diotta." Idrygon bowed. "How goes your work for me?"

"Done as you commanded, my lord. All that's left is a final test of my spells."

"Then we have come at a good time." Idrygon gestured toward Rath. "This is His Highness, King Elzaban. Or will be when you are through with him."

"What's that supposed to mean?" Rath scowled at the faint edge of mockery in Idrygon's voice.

"It means Dame Diotta has prepared several spells and magical items that will make you appear to be everything your people will expect from their Waiting King."

The old enchantress rubbed her wrinkled hands together. "I have a lovely potion that'll make you grow a foot taller. When folks call you *Highness,* they'll mean it!"

She clucked with laughter at her own wit. "I have a draft you can gargle that will make your voice carry ten times as far as normal. I can outfit you with armor that will stop any blade, save one forged of ice gems. A sword of rare hernwood honed with powerful spells that will make it harder and sharper than most metals. It's a thing of beauty, too—the hilt all inlaid with ivory and coral."

"We have a special mount for you as well, sire," said Idrygon. "The beast will also be fed Dame Diotta's growth potion to make it large enough to bear you."

"You want me to lie?" Rath looked from Lord Idrygon to Dame Diotta. "Pretend to be some great hero to dazzle folks into following me?"

"Not a *lie,* Highness." Idrygon bridled. "You are the Waiting King. We simply want to give the people what they will expect—give them hope. Is that so wrong?"

"I reckon not." Rath scratched his chin, thinking hard. "I just don't like the idea of pretending to be something I'm not."

From the moment he and Maura had arrived on the Islands, he'd felt as if he was only pretending to be a king. Would these magical aids make him feel more like King Elzaban and less like Rath the Wolf? And was that truly what he wanted?

"Besides, Highness," said Idrygon in his most reasonable, persuasive tone, "this is only necessary for a short time—until we drive the Han from our shores. Once they are gone and you are secure on your throne, you may tell the people whatever you like, with my blessing. No doubt they will forgive this small ruse once it has served its purpose."

Likely Idrygon was right, as he seemed to be about so much else. Yet to Rath it felt wrong somehow.

"I reckon I could do it for a little while." Here was a tool he could use to bargain with Idrygon. "On one condition."

"And what is that?"

It was on the tip of Rath's tongue to demand that Maura not be sent to recover the Staff of Velorken, but he feared she would never forgive him if he prevented her. "The mines. Once we free the Hitherland, I want our army to attack those cursed mines."

Idrygon shook his head. "It is too great a risk."

"Then the Han won't expect it, will they? And think what a blow it would be to them losing all the ore and gems they get out of the mines."

For once Idrygon seemed to rethink a decision he had made. "True enough, but…"

"Will you make up your minds?" Dame Diotta glared at them. "I don't fancy having gone to all this work for nothing!"

Rath bit back a grin to hear Idrygon scolded so. "What do you say? Do we have a bargain?"

"Oh, very well." Idrygon wrinkled his nose. "Perhaps the Giver will smile upon us and we will have the Staff of Velorken in our possession by that time. Now have a drink of that growth potion and see how it works."

Maura glanced up from the scroll she and Delyon had been looking over. If they could manage to decipher the writing, it might contain a spell to help her unlock the buried memory of where Abrielle had hidden the staff.

Idrygon entered the courtyard looking more than usually pleased with himself. Behind him strode a man so tall he had to duck his head to keep from hitting it on the archway.

Who was their guest? she wondered, glancing at his fine armor. And why had Rath not come home with Idrygon?

Then the huge man pried the elaborate leather helm off his head. A cup of wine slipped from Maura's hand, crashing to the tile floor.

"Rath Talward!" she cried. "What in the name of the Giver have you done to yourself?"

Before Rath could answer, Idrygon spoke. "Does he not look magnificent?"

Several words came to mind as Maura stared up at her husband. Magnificent was not among them.

Unfamiliar. Intimidating. However it had come about, this troubling transformation matched too closely Rath's recent shift in temperament. A shadow of wariness crept back into her heart—the kind she'd felt toward him when they first met.

"It was Idrygon's idea," Rath growled. His voice was deeper than ever, with a husky rasp that made the flesh between Maura's shoulders crinkle.

He no longer looked or sounded like the man she had grown to love so dearly. The thought of sharing a bed with this gruff, hulking stranger filled her with unease.

Idrygon appeared to approve the changes in Rath as much as Maura questioned them. "*This* is what the mainlanders will expect from their Waiting King. This is what they will rally behind—a hero of legend come to life."

He went on to explain at some length the reasons for the changes in Rath, and how they had been accomplished.

"So it will wear off?" Maura was relieved to hear that, though not too surprised. Most life-magic worked only for a limited time, then had to be renewed.

"Both the growth and voice spells will last from dawn till dusk," said Idrygon. "And we have plenty of the magical agents to affect the change. Once we reach the mainland, it should not take long for word to spread that the Waiting King has woken—a hero of fabled proportions that no Han can stand against."

"No *ordinary* Han, you mean," Maura corrected him. "I do not think the Echtroi take much account of size. It is just that much more flesh for them to torment."

Idrygon picked up a piece of fruit from a bowl on the table, tossed it in the air and caught it. "Which is why you and my brother need to find the Staff of Velorken and get it to us as quickly as possible."

Those words deepened the scowl on Rath's face. Though he did not launch into another tirade against her quest, Maura could tell his opposition had not softened.

Why could he not see this was something she *must* do? For all her oppressed country folk. For her parents and for Langbard, so their sacrifices would have some meaning. For him and his small army, so not one more drop of their blood would be shed than need be.

As long as she could recall, she had been a healer. The thought of so many wounds and so much death appalled her, even if it would be in the worthiest of causes. If the Staff of Velorken could bring it about with less bloodshed, then she would search in the High Governor's bed, if she had to!

Rath brushed aside the canopy of netting over his bed and rolled out to face another day. If only he could sweep aside the invisible net of destiny that had trapped him in its web!

He did not even need to glance at the other side of the bed to know Maura had crept out before he woke. Muttering a curse, he ran a hand through the close-cropped hair that no longer felt as if it belonged to him. Too many things in his life felt that way these days.

Foremost, the big, ungainly body he grew whenever he took

that vile draft. Slag! Dame Diotta should consider selling that stuff to the Echtroi. When it went to work, the pain equaled anything he'd suffered from the wand of a death-mage. It felt as if every bone in his body were breaking at once, every joint being wrenched apart and a crippling ache in his muscles bringing him to his knees. The sour potion that deepened his voice was no better, for it left his throat raw and stinging.

He wasn't going to take either of those cursed brews today, Rath decided as he began to dress. If Idrygon objected, too bad about him!

After spending almost his whole life going where he wanted and doing what he wanted, Rath now found himself forced to do too many things he didn't want. That made him feel trapped, a sensation he hated above all others…except one, perhaps.

He glanced toward the bed, wishing Maura had lingered there this morning. His deepest, most secret fear was of being forsaken. His parents, whoever they'd been, had left him before he was old enough to remember. Then Ganny had died, leaving him to fend for himself long before he should have had to. For years he'd never let anyone get close enough for him to miss them if they went away.

He'd fought against his growing feelings for Maura, believing she would have to leave him for the Waiting King. Those feelings had taken deep, stubborn root in his heart after she'd come to rescue him from the mines when she should have abandoned him to complete her quest. When she'd defied even death to return to him, his feelings for her had become something more powerful and frightening than even love.

Not that she would have known it by the way he'd been acting lately! As he always did when cornered or trapped, he'd lashed out at whoever was nearest. Haunted by the specter of losing her, he'd gone from clinging too tightly to pushing her away in a vain effort to lessen the dread of her going.

Little wonder Maura avoided being alone with him. She could fight when she had to, but given a choice, she'd been brought up to hide or flee from trouble. Did she think of him as *trouble*?

Rath had to find out and he had to make it right between them. Their time together was running out too fast for him to let this poison it.

Barging out of their bedchamber, he nearly barreled into Idrygon's wife. The small, birdlike woman was so quiet and submissive, Rath had paid her no more notice than the tasteful furniture in her elegant villa.

"Highness!" she gasped, fumbling the basket of neatly folded laundry in her hands. "Is something wrong?"

"Wrong?" Everything was wrong. "No. I'm just looking for my wife. Have you seen her? I need to talk to her."

"I'm afraid she's gone, Highness." Idrygon's wife backed away from Rath as she delivered the news.

He bit back a curse better suited to an outlaw than a royal guest in the lady's home. "Do you know where she went?"

"With my husband and his brother, Highness. Idrygon said something about getting your wife equipped for her mission."

That must mean they'd gone to Dame Diotta's. Rath muttered a quick word of thanks to his hostess as he strode off.

She called after him, "Will you have something to eat before you go, Highness?"

"Later perhaps." Food could wait. Though the growth potion made him ravenous, Rath was more anxious to break this strain on his marriage than to break his fast.

He climbed the hill to Dame Diotta's villa at a dead run, arriving out of breath and in a sweat.

"Highness." The old enchantress bowed when she recognized him. "How are those potions I gave you working?"

Rath resisted the urge to tell her what he thought of her potions. "Well…enough," he gasped. "My wife…is she here?"

"Was," said Dame Diotta. "She came with Lord Idrygon and his brother. I refilled that sash of hers with everything I had on hand, as well as a few herbs she'd never heard of. She was quick to learn the incantations, I must say. If I had her to apprentice with me for a few months, I could make a first-rate enchantress of that lass. I don't suppose that would do for a queen, though. Pity."

Before Rath could catch his breath to ask where Maura had gone, she rattled on, "I made sure they had plenty of those *genow* scales. But I didn't put them all in one big sack. Oh my, no. A dozen small pouches I gave them and warned them to hide the things in as many different places about them as they could find—sashes, pockets, the toe of a shoe if one would fit."

"Please!" cried Rath when her torrent of talk slowed. "How long ago did they leave? Do you know where they went?"

He should just go back to Idrygon's house and wait for Maura to return, Rath told himself, rather than chasing all over the island after her. The tension between them had been mounting for days. Would an hour or two more make any difference?

"It hasn't been long since they were called away," said Dame Diotta.

"Who called them away?" Rath's mission gathered fresh urgency. It *did* matter. He could not stand for any more time to pass with ill will between them.

The old enchantress pointed over his shoulder. "The Oracle of Margyle. It sounded important. Then again, young ones do get anxious over trifles, don't they? A shame about the old Oracle passing before her time. It's an awful burden for a child that age to carry, don't you think?"

"Aye, it is." Rath backed away. "My thanks. Good day to you." He turned and strode off to the Oracle's cottage.

The child's serving woman nodded readily when he asked about Maura. "The little one sent me to fetch them, and by good fortune I spied them yonder with Dame Diotta. Had some sort of vision, the child did, that she wanted to warn them about."

Vision? Warning? Cold fear stabbed Rath in the belly. Had the child seen more of the troubling future she'd told him about? If he'd thought a warning from the Oracle would keep

Maura from going on her perilous quest, Rath would have told her, himself. But he feared she was too determined to be daunted now.

"Are they with the Oracle?" he asked.

The woman looked around. "I fetched them here. Then I went into the cottage to check if the bread had burnt while I was away. I wonder if the Oracle took them up to the hill. She likes talking to folks up there."

"I'll go see." Rath headed toward the tree-girt hill calling Maura's name. Was he going to have to puzzle his way through that miserable maze again to reach her? Its twisting, branching paths were no more baffling than his own feelings.

Rath had not gotten far when he spied the child coming toward him.

"If you are looking for Maura," she said, "you must just have missed her. She and the others hurried away as soon as I spoke with them."

They must have gone while he'd been talking to Dame Diotta. A pity they hadn't been as sharp-eyed as the Oracle's waiting woman, to glimpse him off in the distance.

"Did they say where they were headed?" he asked. "What did you tell them?"

The child flinched from his fierce tone.

Rath regretted his gruffness. He dropped to one knee, so as not to tower over her, and softened his voice. "Did you tell Maura what you told me…about my heir?"

The Oracle shook her head. "Perhaps I should have. But she's been so kind to me, I did not want to grieve her. I warned her about something else. I had a vision of Maura's ship floundering in a bad storm coming. I warned them to wait until it passes before they sail."

Idrygon would not be pleased to hear that. His plan called for Maura and Delyon to sail in two days' time, so they could slip ashore before the Han started keeping a sharper eye on the coast—as they were bound to once his forces landed in the north.

This delay would give Rath a few extra days in which to make things up with Maura. Or would it?

He scrambled to his feet. "Thank you for telling me." Before he hurried off, something made him add, "You're doing a good job, you know. I was left on my own when I was your age, and I got myself into all sorts of trouble."

"I know." The child looked as if she was trying to keep from grinning. "Namma had a vision of you. Something about setting fire to a Hanish sentry post. She feared you would get yourself killed ten times over before you got any sense knocked into you."

Rath's scalp prickled. He hadn't thought about the Hanish sentry post in years. Yet an old woman hundreds of miles away had seen it and fretted over him. It gave him an even greater respect for the Oracle's power...and made it harder to dismiss what she'd seen in his future. It also gave him a clearer insight into her daunting duty. How frustrating it must be to catch only tiny glimpses of things to come, disturbing and hard to interpret, then have to deliver warnings folks might not heed.

Pushing aside the weight of his regrets and worries for a moment, he answered the child's grin with a wink. "I am still getting sense knocked into me."

A few moments later, he strode back down the hill to Idrygon's villa, wishing he'd had the sense to stay there and wait for Maura's return, rather than trying in vain to chase her down.

The more he thought about it, the more certain he became that Idrygon would never stand to have his plans delayed. By waiting until the storm passed to send Maura and Delyon, he would have to wait longer still before he dared send troops against the Dusk Coast.

Rath's spirits sagged when he saw no sign of the others at Idrygon's villa.

"They came not long after you left." Idrygon's wife sounded apologetic. "I'm surprised you didn't meet them on your way.

I told my husband you were looking for Her Highness. Perhaps they went off trying to find you."

Rath doubted it. If Idrygon wanted Maura to sail ahead of the storm, he would not waste time scouring the town for her husband so she could bid him farewell. And that was assuming she wanted to. Rath wished he could be certain she had.

"If they come back here, tell them I've gone to the harbor." He set off running as if chased by a party of Hanish soldiers.

The streets of the town wound back and forth up the hills to avoid steep slopes. So the fastest way down to the harbor meant cutting between houses. Rath drew more than a few curious stares as he vaulted fences and raced through yards. No doubt Idrygon would be vexed when he heard of it, but Rath did not care.

His frantic inquiries at the wharf revealed that Maura, Idrygon and Delyon had departed by barge a short while ago.

"A boat," Rath muttered, searching for a small craft he could commandeer.

By this time it was near noon, and most of the boats were busy ferrying gear out to the fleet. At last he found a tiny one that did not look very seaworthy. Rath untied it, jumped in and grabbed the oars.

Only when he'd rowed toward the ships did he realize he had no idea which of them would take Maura and Delyon to the mainland. It would have to be a small craft—one that would not draw too much attention if it were spotted off the coast.

"Hey, there!" he bellowed to a young crewman on the deck of the nearest small vessel. "Is this ship...?"

He hesitated. What should he say? Is this the ship that's taking the Destined Queen on a secret mission to the mainland? No, for it was a secret, known only to the Council of Sages.

"Is this ship what?" the lad called back.

"Is this ship sailing with the rest of the fleet?"

The lad gave an eager nod. "I reckon we all are. Except the one that just set sail. Don't know where it's bound."

Rath did.

"There it goes." The lad pointed westward.

Though he knew there was no chance of even getting close enough in time to signal, Rath kept on rowing, threading his way among the fleet until he reached open water. There he met Idrygon, being poled back to shore in his barge. Off in the distance, the sails of Maura's ship billowed in the breeze.

Taking her away from him. Perhaps forever.

Maura stared back toward the shore of Margyle through a mist of tears. After several long days of growing estrangement between her and Rath, she had left with so much unresolved between them. They had parted without even a proper farewell.

She did not hear footsteps on the deck, but she sensed a warm, watchful presence beside her. "I am sorry we had to leave all of a sudden like this," said Delyon, "without a chance for you to see His Highness."

Maura acknowledged his words with a nod, keeping her face averted slightly from him.

"Don't fret." Delyon's sensitive sympathy turned hearty. "The two of you will be back together before you know it."

Maura barely resisted the urge to pitch him overboard.

Don't fret? Only someone who'd never known the sweet anguish of love could say something so heartless! And how could he be certain she would soon be reunited with Rath? They each faced many dangers in the days to come, with no assurance that both—or indeed, *either* of them—would survive this battle to liberate their kingdom. None of the old legends told what became of the Waiting King and his Destined Queen afterward.

Paying no heed to her stony silence, Delyon rattled on, "I'll go do some more reading. I'm making progress in deciphering that scroll I showed you the other morning."

His words made Maura forget her regrets and worry for a moment. "You brought along ancient, sacred scrolls—where we are going? Are you daft?"

"Only one." He shrank from her outburst. "And it is not the original. Give me credit for a little sense."

"Your pardon, Delyon. I did not mean to snap at you." She'd been seething with frustration and fear, and he had been the nearest person upon whom she could safely vent those feelings. It did not mean she thought ill of him.

Suddenly she could see Rath's recent behavior in a new light. More than ever she wished she could order Captain Gull to turn the *Phantom* around and head back to Margyle. But if she did that, she might never be able to make herself leave again.

"No harm," said Delyon. "I know most people think my fascination with deciphering old scrolls is daft. My work has come in handy, though, and I hope it may again."

"Indeed?" Maura wished he would go away and let her brood in peace. But after speaking so rudely to him, she felt obliged to abide another of his wandering discourses on ancient writing.

"Oh, yes." Delyon leaned closer to her. "The part I've managed to translate so far suggests it may contain a special spell for deep meditation."

"Oh?"

With no more encouragement than that, he launched into a rambling explanation of how he had come to work out the meaning of some symbols, while others continued to baffle him. His words washed over Maura like the endless roll of the waves as she watched Margyle grow smaller and smaller in the distance.

A fragment of Delyon's words caught her attention for a moment. Something about using a sort of ritual trance to unearth any buried memories that might have been passed down to her by Queen Abrielle.

"If it is that important," she said at last, "I should not keep you from your work. If you'll excuse me, I must speak to Captain Gull."

"As you wish." Delyon did not appear to regret losing her company. "I hope I can find a quiet spot out of the wind to work."

A stab of shame hit Maura. Delyon was a nice, harmless fellow, and he had taken her mind off her regrets just when they'd threatened to overwhelm her. "May the Giver bless you with enlightenment."

Maura wished the Giver might bless her with a little peace of mind, though she feared she did not deserve it. After all those fine promises she had made to Rath on the enchanted daybreak of their wedding, the first gathering of storm clouds and rumble of thunder in their marriage had made her turn away from him. She would not take all the blame—he had been unreasonable and short-tempered and pigheaded. But she had been impatient, quick to take offense…and perhaps a trifle pigheaded, too.

Rath had only been worried about her safety, after all. Instead of dismissing his fears and pointing out all the reasons they were groundless, would it have hurt to reassure him that she felt the same way about him, and pledge to exercise every possible caution if he would promise her in turn? Of the two of them, he would face far greater danger.

Maura startled as something smooth and warm rubbed against her ankles. She lifted the hem of her gown to find Captain Gull's hillcat slithering around her legs, purring.

"There you are, Abri!" Gull suddenly appeared behind Maura. "Naughty girl, you mustn't pester the queen."

He scooped the cat back up onto its accustomed perch around his neck.

"I don't mind." Maura managed a shaky smile. "It just surprised me to see Abri acting friendly. It's the first time she's come near without hissing at me."

Gull reached up to scratch the cat behind its ears. "I told you, she's a jealous creature. I reckon she knows you belong to somebody else now and aren't any threat to her."

His words made Maura's eyes sting again. She belonged to Rath—even a smuggler's pet cat knew it. When a tear slid down her cheek, she did not feel so compelled to hide it from Gull as she had from Delyon, though she was not sure why that might be. Perhaps because the tough little smuggler reminded her of her big rugged outlaw in many ways. The harsh climate of Hanish rule had made them hard, clever and sometimes ruthless, but it had not destroyed their capacity for love.

Gull reached out and brushed away her tear with a gentle touch usually reserved for his cat. "Abri might have been thinking there are times when females need to stick together. I don't know what it is you and Lord Idrygon's brother have to do on the mainland, but I reckon it must be important."

Maura nodded.

Looking back toward the island, Gull murmured, "That doesn't make it any easier, does it?"

Tears sluiced down the back of her throat. "What if I never see him again?"

"That could happen, I reckon." Gull did not try to make light of her fears, which Maura found comforting in some perverse way. "If it'll do you any good to wallow in worry, while you're aboard my ship you may fret to your heart's content."

His words coaxed a moist hiccup of laughter from Maura.

"Once we reach the mainland," said Gull, "you'll need to forget about that and keep your mind on doing whatever you have to do and staying out of harm while you're doing it."

That reminded her of something she and Rath had once talked about. She'd asked if feelings were something to pack away when they were inconvenient, then bring out to air when a body had time for them. She recalled his answer so clearly, she fancied she could hear his voice. *You make it sound like a bad thing.*

"Folks might say that's no way for a smuggler to talk to a

queen." Gull pulled a face that made Maura laugh again. "But you're aboard my ship, where I'm king, so you'd better heed me."

Heartless as it might sound, Maura decided he was right. Worrying about a future she could not control and fretting about a past she could not change would only hinder her ability to carry out the tasks she must accomplish now.

So much depended on the success of her mission—perhaps even Rath's life. She could not afford to put that in jeopardy by letting her thoughts wander. Somehow she must channel the power of her emotions into her present quest, the way she had harnessed her grief for Langbard to strengthen her resolve during her last one. She must have faith that Rath would cheat death as he had so many times before, and she must get back to him as quickly as possible with the staff.

Only then could they heal the breach between them.

"There's a storm brewing out there, all right," said Gull, late on the third day after they'd set sail from Margyle. "A good job we put out to sea when we did. Remind me to get a little present to thank the Oracle. Do you reckon she'd like a kitten?"

"I think she'd love one." Maura chuckled. "Why, is Abri…?"

"Aye, the naughty creature." Gull gave the cat's tail a gentle tug. "Don't ask me how she got ashore and back again…or what sort of creature she found on the island to dally with. Just what we need on the *Phantom*—a litter of kittens!"

The notion made Maura smile, but that smile froze on her lips when she glanced behind her. Dark clouds poised on the western horizon like hungry beasts ready to pounce.

"Can we race the storm?" Her belly gave a lurch at the thought of enduring another tempest at sea.

"Don't fret," said Gull, "we haven't far to go. I'm making for a wee island off the coast where we can anchor and ride out the storm away from Hanish eyes. With luck, the rain will hit just as night falls—perfect cover to smuggle you and Lord Delyon ashore."

The captain proved something of an oracle himself in that guess. The first drops of rain were beginning to spatter against the deck when the *Phantom* dropped anchor in a small cove. The island scarcely deserved that name for it was little more than a bit of rock sporting a sparse crop of trees.

On a clear day, nightfall might still have been an hour or more away. But with the western horizon shrouded in storm clouds, the sky had already grown dark enough to suit Gull.

"Let's go!" In his disguise as a hunchbacked old fisherman, he motioned Maura and Delyon toward the edge of the deck. "Before it gets any worse."

A gust of wind whipped Maura's hood back as she scrambled down the rope ladder into a boat that bobbed alongside the *Phantom*. By the time she settled herself in the bow of the small craft, her hair was so wet, it was hardly worth pulling her hood back up again.

The splash of rain and spray on her face and the struggle to keep the wind from sucking away her breath took her mind off the anxious churning in her belly. The choppy sea was only partly to blame for that. During her stay on the Vestan Islands, she had quickly grown accustomed to the peace and safety of the place. Now the Hanish-occupied mainland loomed more dangerous than ever.

Two of Gull's brawny-armed crewmen took up the oars and began to pull for shore. They did not have to work very hard on the inbound journey, for each wave lifted the small boat and bore it landward with relentless, primal power. Maura did not envy the men their return trip, rowing against the incoming breakers.

A cry rose in her throat when the sea slammed the boat onto the shore. In the deepening darkness, she could just make out the two oarsmen scrambling from the craft and hauling it farther up the beach, before the waves could claw it back.

Gull swatted Maura on the arm to get her attention. "Step lively!" he hollered to be heard over the howl of the wind and the pounding of the surf. "And stick close to me!"

Delyon hopped out of the boat, then reached back to help Maura out.

"Don't forget these!" Gull shoved bulky bundles into their arms.

With the haste of their departure from Margyle, Maura was not even certain what the bundles contained. Nevertheless, she clung to hers as she and Delyon staggered up the dark, storm-swept beach after Captain Gull.

She hoped the smuggler knew his way. With almost no light, she could not tell where they were going, or how soon they might reach their destination. The darkness did not alter from one stride to the next, neither did the rhythmic thunder of the sea or the gusting sheets of rain.

All that changed to give her any assurance they were making progress was the feel of the ground beneath her feet. It soon shifted from wet sand to a springy turf riddled with clumps of shore grass. Then it changed again to slippery rocks on which Maura had to concentrate mightily to keep from losing her footing. After an endless time groping up the shallow slope, she felt firm ground beneath her boots, and shoots of wet meadow grass slipped under her gown to whisper against her legs.

Even with a waterproof cloak wrapped around her, she wondered if she would ever be truly dry again. All the same, she thanked the Giver for the Oracle's warning. The only thing worse than being lashed by this storm on land would have been to endure it on a pitching ship out in the middle of the sea.

She reached toward the vague shadow of Captain Gull and tugged on a bit of his cloak. "Is it much farther?"

"Not much!" he shouted back. "Can you make it?"

Maura gave a grim nod. "I will."

Forcing one foot in front of the other, she kept moving until at last they stumbled into some manner of shelter.

Maura dropped her bundle and sank to her knees. "What is this place?"

Gull groped for her hand, thrusting a twig into it. "Can you make greenfire?"

"Since I was no higher than Langbard's knee." She concentrated on the twig, chanting the simple spell.

As a soft green glow kindled in the tip of the wood, Maura could see they were standing in a small empty cottage with no windows and only a gaping hole that had once held a door. Now the rain blew in through it, leaving a large wet patch on the floor. The corners looked dry enough, though.

Maura lurched to her feet long enough to drag her bundle into one. She cast a wistful gaze at the low hearth opposite the door, wishing she had a few sticks of dry wood to light a fire. Gull and Delyon joined her in the corner. Abri crawled out from under Gull's cloak and began to groom herself.

"Welcome," said Gull, his voice laced with wry mockery, "to your new home for the next week or so."

"What is this place?" asked Maura.

"It used to be called Ven Gyllia…"

"Gathering of the Wise," murmured Delyon. "I have heard of it. It was a community of scholars and sages, and a training academy for young wizards and enchantresses."

"I suppose they all went to Margyle after the Han invaded," said Maura. The twig in her hand was almost exhausted of greenfire. She looked around for another but could see none.

In the rapidly fading light, she saw Delyon shake his head. "When the Han invaded, Ven Gyllia was one of the first places they attacked. It was a slaughter. Only a few escaped."

Maura could picture it all too vividly. Like the slaughter of outlaws in Betchwood from which she'd rescued Rath. Perhaps it was fitting their campaign to drive the Han *out* of Umbria had begun here. Perhaps it was…destiny.

Destiny. The word drummed in Rath's thoughts as he stared eastward over the prow of the ship Maura had launched in his name. Every muted crash of the waves droned it, while every circling seabird screeched it.

Even after all that had happened, did he believe in it? Rath could not decide. It was a seductive notion to trust that his victory over the Han in the battles to come was assured. But if he believed that, then he must also believe the Oracle's prophesy about his personal future.

Rath's oversize fist clamped down on the deck railing. He would rather suffer a little uncertainty.

Sensing someone standing beside him, he glanced over to find Idrygon staring toward the horizon, as lost in thought as he'd just been.

"I've waited and worked thirty years for this day," Idrygon murmured. "There were times I wondered if it would ever come."

Rath's gaze swept over the small but formidable fleet that now sailed to reclaim their homeland. All those years he had been thinking of nothing beyond his next theft, Idrygon had been laboring to make what was about to happen come true. Rath had seen enough in these past few weeks to know it had not been a quick or an easy task.

"I remember looking back at the coast as our ship sailed away," Idrygon mused. "Watching smoke rise from some buildings our enemies had put to the torch. I swore then I would return someday with an army and scourge them from our shores."

Why had the Giver not chosen Idrygon as the Waiting King? Rath wondered. The man was far more eager and better suited for the daunting burden of command than he would ever be.

His gaze strayed southward, pulled in the same direction as his thoughts and his heart. "Do you reckon they reached the coast ahead of that storm?"

While it had raged, he'd walked a lonely strip of Margyle beach, gazing out at the rampant waters and willing them not to harm Maura.

Idrygon stirred from his thoughts. "I regret you were not able to bid her farewell. Thank the Giver for the Oracle's warning, otherwise they might have been caught out at sea. I have never had much use for Captain Gull, but I respect his sailing ability. Rest your mind—knowing the danger, he will have raced the storm."

A tiny ember of hope rekindled in Rath's heart. Perhaps the Oracle's vision of his future was like her warning about the storm—something he could escape with proper caution.

"Do not fret," said Idrygon. "You will see Her Highness soon enough. In the meantime we must draw the Hanish forces northward to make the way to Venard safer for her and my brother."

His fingers clenched and unclenched, as if around the hilt of an invisible sword. "I can hardly wait until the fighting begins! I have never drawn the blood of an enemy. Never drank the sweet wine of vengeance."

"I have done both." Rath shook his head. "Far too often. Vengeance *is* like strong drink. It makes you all dizzy and daft for a while, but it soon sours in your belly."

"Maura," said Delyon, "look at this symbol and see if you can make anything of it."

The sudden sound of his voice made Maura start.

"Hush!" She waved him toward the corner of the cottage beside the door. "I thought I heard something out there."

Perhaps she only fancied it after so many long days with little to do but worry and imagine approaching danger. It did not help that Delyon seemed oblivious to any peril. More than once, while lost in thought, he had almost wandered out of their hiding place in broad daylight.

Before he'd returned to his ship Gull had told Maura that the Han hereabouts thought Ven Gyllia was haunted—a belief he and his fellow smugglers did everything possible to foster. Though patrols seldom came near, they surely would not hesitate to search if they spied or heard anything suspicious. Maura was determined to give them no reason to venture closer.

With a huff, Delyon gathered up his scroll and moved to the

corner as she had bidden him. Maura ignored his sulky look, listening with every particle of concentration.

Finally she admitted, "It may not have been anything after all. A small animal, perhaps."

Before Delyon could reply, she wagged her finger at him. "Just because it was nothing *this time,* does not mean we can let our guard down."

The man hadn't exactly let his guard down, she reminded herself. The problem was he'd never bothered to put it up in the first place.

With a rueful shake of his head, Delyon moved back near the door, where he had more light for reading. "Is everyone on the mainland as wary as you?"

"The ones who survive any length of time," she snapped. "If you hope to remain among our number, you'd do well to exercise a little wariness yourself!"

How much longer would it be until the sun set? she wondered. Once it got dark enough, she could venture outside to stretch her legs and get a bit of air. Between that and sleeping, the nights passed quickly. But these past days of waiting and hiding were some of the most tedious Maura had ever endured.

Was there such a thing as *too much* peace and quiet? She fancied the walls of the little cottage were closing in on her a bit more each day—as were the worries that haunted her.

Delyon had enough sense not to argue with her, but had gone back to studying his scroll with furrowed brow.

Though Maura knew he would not want to be disturbed until the light faded, she could not keep her fears locked inside her a moment longer. "Gull promised someone would bring us a message when it is time to begin our journey. Do you suppose something has happened to the messenger…or…?"

No. She would not allow herself to think something had gone wrong with Rath's invasion of the Dusk Coast.

"It may be the fleet was delayed longer than they expected by the storm." Delyon spared only a crumb of his attention for her. "Some of the ships may have been damaged and needed repairs before they could set sail. Perhaps news of the invasion has not traveled as fast as my brother hoped."

That all made sense, Maura conceded grudgingly. Still, she could not help resenting Delyon's lack of concern.

He dug out a charstick from his pack and scrawled a note on the scroll. After staring at it for a moment, he shook his head and rubbed the marks off with a lump of sandstone.

"I could use a few more days of peace and quiet," he muttered, "to decipher this spell of deep meditation. It could save us a great deal of time once we reach the palace."

"I will give you three more days." She stared out the door opening at another deserted cottage, its thatched roof caved in. "After that, we must head for Venard and keep our ears open for news as we go."

The words had scarcely left her lips when some movement behind the deserted cottage caught her eye.

"Get back again, Delyon!" she ordered in an urgent whisper. "There *is* someone out there!"

Grumbling under his breath, Delyon picked up his scroll and moved back to the corner where he would not be seen unless someone entered the cottage.

Maura dug a pinch of *genow* scales from her sash and chanted the invisibility spell under her breath. Many times in the past few days, she'd been tempted to make herself invisible so she could wander abroad in daylight. But Idrygon had given strict orders not to use the spell except in emergencies.

Well, this qualified. If someone was lurking about Ven Gyllia, she must find out if it was Gull's messenger. If she'd only fancied seeing something, then she needed to get out of the cottage before the waiting drove her daft.

Maura knew when the invisibility spell took effect, for Delyon let out a soft gasp.

"Keep quiet," she whispered as she slipped through the door, fumbling in her sash for some madfern.

If someone other than Gull's messenger was out there, a little madfern together with a tap on the shoulder and a disembodied voice should be enough to bolster Ven Gyllia's reputation for being haunted.

The moment she stepped out of the cottage Maura heard someone chopping wood nearby. She followed the sound to a wooded area where she found a man attacking the slender trunk of a whitebark tree with a hatchet. While he chopped at the tree, he grumbled to himself in a voice loud enough for Maura to hear.

"'Take the news to Ven Gyllia,' Gull tells me. 'What news might that be?' says I. 'Ye'll know what news when ye hear it,' says he. A pretty riddle that."

In her excitement, Maura forgot the caution about which she'd lectured Delyon. "What news have you heard?"

"Who's there?" The man spun about, holding his ax in front of him. "Show yerself!"

"I cannot." Maura backed away, taking shelter behind a tree. "But I am a friend of Gull's. Please tell me the news he bid you bring."

The man's grip on his ax eased a little. "The Han are all in an uproar and folks say the Waiting King has come with an army to set us free."

Weak with relief, Maura slumped against the tree, savoring the rough caress of its bark against her cheek.

"It is true," she breathed.

The messenger must have heard her, for his ax fell slack. "Well, I never...the Waiting King? I reckoned he was no more than a tale for the younglings."

"Spread the word among your neighbors," Maura bid him. "And tell me how I can reach Venard from here without drawing unwanted attention."

"Stay in the woods as far as you can." The man pointed east. "Then you'll see the main road. It goes to Venard...like all the main roads do. Stay as far back from it as you can while still keeping it in sight. Many Hanish soldiers may be heading north to fight the Waiting King, but the ones who are left will be making sure no Umbrians go to fight at his side."

"You have my thanks," said Maura, "for bringing this welcome news. When the Waiting King is restored to his throne, come to court and you will be well rewarded."

The word *reward* seemed to remind the messenger of something. Laying down his ax, he pulled a small pouch from his pocket and tossed it in Maura's direction. It jingled when it hit the ground near her.

"Gull said I was to give you that. In case you need to buy supplies or bribe your way out of a tight spot."

After thanking him again, Maura grabbed the little purse and ran back to the cottage. Delyon had moved closer to the doorway in her absence, the better to study his scroll. But Maura was too happy to scold him for his lack of caution.

Instead, she stooped and threw her arms around his neck. "It's all right! The invasion has begun well!"

Only when Delyon let out a strangled scream and tried to fight her off did Maura remember he could not see her.

"Delyon, stop!" She could scarcely get the words out for laughing—a release of her tightly wound nerves. "It's only Maura. I'm sorry I frightened you."

"Maura?" He sank back to the floor of the cabin, his chest heaving and his voice shaky. "Of course. I should have known. But you gave me such a start."

She tried to stifle her heartless mirth, reminding herself how she would have felt in his place. Another part of her wondered if Delyon might have needed a good scare to make him a little more cautious. She told him what she'd learned from Gull's messenger.

"Study your scroll to your heart's content while the light lasts." Maura rolled up in her blanket. "Or try to get some sleep. Once the sun sets, we must be off. Until we reach Venard, we'll travel by night, then hide and sleep by day."

The next thing she knew, Delyon was nudging her. "Wake up, Maura. You said we must go once the sun set."

Maura yawned and rubbed her eyes. "Did you sleep?" she asked Delyon. "I almost wish I hadn't. I feel more tired now than I did when I lay down."

"I meant to." Delyon knelt beside her in the rapidly deepening darkness. "But I got caught up studying the scroll. I am almost certain I have figured out another of the words. It looks like the *twara* symbol for the ritual of passing, which makes me wonder if—"

"Tell me later." Maura jumped up and began to roll her blanket. "We must be on our way now. Are you ready to go?"

She regretted her rudeness for interrupting him, but if she didn't he could go on for hours.

"All my supplies are packed." Delyon did not sound offended. Perhaps he was accustomed to people not sharing his passion for ancient languages.

"Let's go." Maura fished a leaf of quickfoil from her sash and began to chew it. As the sharp tang suffused her mouth, the fog of sleep lifted from her mind and her senses sharpened.

She and Delyon made good progress that night. They found the main road just where Gull's messenger had said they would, then followed it until the first tentative glow of dawn kindled on the eastern horizon.

"This looks as good a place as any to hide and rest for the day." Maura pointed to a barn at the far edge of a field of ripening grain.

Delyon replied with a soft grunt that did not sound fully awake.

"Get a good sleep today," Maura scolded him gently. "I won't have you studying that scroll so many hours that you cannot keep your wits about you at night. Understand?"

"Mmm-hmm."

They had scarcely crept into the barn and settled themselves in a far corner of its loft when Delyon's breathing settled into the quiet buzz of sleep. Maura meant to keep watch until he woke, but the early-morning twitter of the birds outside and the dry warmth of the barn lulled her.

When she roused some hours later, Delyon was studying his scroll again.

"Don't fret." He glanced up at her with a smile. "It has been quiet. I hope the rest of our journey continues this well."

Maura hoped so, too. But she knew better than to expect it.

Sure enough, they emerged from their hideout that night into a steady drizzle of rain. Lights bobbed on the road—perhaps movement of Hanish troops, forcing her and Delyon to keep even farther away. They had to wait a long time before it was safe to cross a road that wound up from the south to meet the main one. Dawn caught them far sooner than Maura would have liked, and the only hiding place they could find was a damp, smelly root cellar.

The next three days were no better. The fourth got worse. Would they ever reach the capital? Maura wondered. Or would they rot first?

On the fifth night a warm wind blew up from the south, finally drying their damp clothes. But they made slower progress than ever when they reached a river and had to walk far out of their way to find a safe fording spot. Then they had to double back on the other side of the river to find the road again.

The next morning, Maura chose a hiding place on the edge of a crossroads town. When Delyon woke, she told him they were going to the market.

"Our food has almost run out," she explained. "And I want to find out how much farther it is to Venard. I wish there was some way we could get there faster without drawing Hanish notice."

"Must we both go to market?" asked Delyon. "Could I not stay here and work? I had the most interesting idea last night and I'd like to give it some more thought."

"Delyon!" Maura could scarcely believe her ears. Perhaps Rath had been right not to trust him. "We must stay together always—to guard one another's back. To help the other one out of trouble if need be."

The Giver help her if she ever needed Delyon to come to her rescue!

"Very well." He shouldered his pack.

"Leave that here," said Maura. "We do not want everyone who sees us to know we are travelers."

She showed him where she'd hidden her pack behind a pile of firewood. With a shrug, he lowered his to the floor and dug inside.

"What are you doing now?" Maura asked.

"Getting this." Delyon pulled out his precious scroll and tucked it into his belt. "Han or no Han, I do not mean to take the chance of losing it."

"Have your own way," Maura muttered as he stashed his pack beside hers. "Just do not stroll down the street reading it like you would on Margyle and walk into a Hanish patrol."

Delyon glared at her. "Have a little respect for my good sense!"

"I will as soon as you show some!" The moment the words left her lips Maura regretted them. "Your pardon, Delyon! I did not mean it. This journey is wearing on me and I am so worried we will reach Venard too late to do Rath any good."

Delyon nodded his acceptance of her apology. "Let's go. It may do us both good to get some sun and mix with other people."

They headed toward the center of town where they found a busy market. Maura was relieved to see few Hanish soldiers in evidence. She made her food purchases at a number of different shops and stalls so as not to rouse suspicion of her well-laden coin purse.

Just as she was paying for a parcel of flatcakes, Delyon tugged on her sleeve. "Maura, look! That sign!"

"In a moment, Delyon." She tried to keep the impatience from her voice, but it was not easy.

The vendor woman was jabbering on in Comtung about the distance to Venard. It was difficult enough for Maura to follow without Delyon pouring a rapid stream of Umbrian in her other ear. She glanced over her shoulder to see what had him so excited.

A large sheet of coarse parchment had been nailed to the side of a building across the street. The message on it was written in Umbrian and another language...Hanish most likely. It urged people to ignore rumors and to report any suspicious activity.

Maura gave a derisive chuckle. "I wonder who they reckon will be able to read that."

The Han had discouraged all use of the Umbrian language. On this side of the mountains, they had been all too successful. As far as Maura knew, there was no written form of Comtung, the bastard language that bridged the gap between Umbrian and Hanish.

For now, she was having enough trouble understanding spoken Comtung. She turned back to the vendor to collect her change.

Meanwhile, Delyon kept talking with rising excitement. Something about ancient *twara* being the parent of both Umbrian and Hanish and how the sign might be the key to...something.

Maura could not concentrate properly, for the vendor woman was repeating something about the distance to Venard, holding up fingers to reinforce her words. Ten...twenty... thirty...Maura's heart sank further every time the woman clenched her hands then opened them again to add another ten miles.

She had signaled sixty and did not look ready to stop soon, when Maura heard the sound of a scuffle behind her.

She spun about to see Delyon being restrained by a Hanish soldier. It looked as if he'd been caught trying to take down the sign. With a groan, Maura dropped her parcels and reached for her sash.

"Maura!" Delyon cried, staring straight at her. The fool!

She had a pinch of *genow* scales in her hand, ready to cast the invisibility spell, when rough hands seized her.

13

"Maura, do something!" Delyon cried.

Do something? If the *zikary* who held her had loosened his grip for an instant, Maura would have done something, all right—grabbed the cursed sign out of Delyon's hand and flogged his fool head with it!

What had possessed him to tear an official Hanish sign down off a building? Had he not thought how that would look to them and what it would provoke them to do? If only he had not looked straight at her and called her name, she might have had time to aid him somehow. Now she could only wait and hope for an opportunity that might never come.

She tried to break free from the man who held her, just long enough to grab a pinch of *genow* scales, but the vendor woman seized her right arm in a powerful grip. "I knew there was something not right with this one. Asking how far to Venard. Talking strange, like."

What would Rath do if he were here? Maura wondered. "Delyon!" she called in Umbrian. "Make yourself invisible!"

But it was too late. He had gotten into a tug of war with the

Hanish soldier over that cursed sign when he could have let go and used his hands to dig out some magical ingredient.

Instead, the soldier let go first, then used *his* free hands to grab Delyon by the neck and slam his head hard against the side of the building. After the second such blow, Delyon fell limp to the ground.

What now? Panic caught Maura by the throat. Even if she could break free, then turn herself and Delyon invisible, she would never be able to drag him away without leaving a trail a blind man could follow.

Suddenly a bold, impossibly risky plan took shape in her mind. If it succeeded, several of her problems would be solved in a single stroke. But if it failed... She did not dare let herself think what might happen if it failed.

"We are not spies for the Waiting King!" she cried, praying the soldier would understand her mangled Comtung.

"Spies, is it?" The young Han scowled as he glanced from the unconscious Delyon to Maura and back again.

So he was open to have ideas planted in his mind. Good!

"You must not send us to Venard to be questioned by the Echtroi!" Maura did not have to feign the pleading note in her voice. "I beg you!"

"Silence!" The soldier marched toward her with a menacing stride. "No spy tells me where I can and cannot send her!"

Under her breath, the vendor woman muttered, "Should have kept yer mouth shut, fool. Ye'll be worse off than ever now."

Was she a fool? Maura wondered. Had she only made things worse for herself and Delyon by not keeping silent?

Several more Hanish soldiers appeared, summoned by Umbrian collaborators, like the two who held Maura. The officer in charge questioned the young soldier on the scene, who rattled off his report in Hanish. By the way he pointed to Delyon, the parchment sign and finally to her, Maura could guess what he was saying.

The Hanish officer turned and stared at Maura. His cold,

ruthless gaze made her blood feel as if it were freezing in her veins. He snapped a curt order in Hanish, upon which two of the soldiers hoisted Delyon to his feet, while the other two seized Maura from her Umbrian captors and marched her down the street.

Please, she sent a silent petition winging to the Giver, *do not let them deal with us here!*

Almost as an afterthought, she added, *And please do not let Delyon be hurt too badly.*

Vexed as she was with him for landing them in this predicament, she did not wish him any worse harm. She was a poor one to sit in judgment of Delyon's actions, after all the trouble she had landed Rath in by offering her aid to every person in need they'd met on their journey.

A short distance from the market, they came to the garrison compound, identical to the one in Windleford, though perhaps a little bigger. This was one familiar sight that did not make Maura long for her home village.

At a shouted word from the officer, the garrison gate opened. The soldiers dragged Maura and Delyon inside, across a wide bare courtyard, through a door and up a steep flight of stairs to a large room with windows facing out onto the courtyard. Several tall, flaxen-haired soldiers were standing around a table upon which was spread a crudely drawn map. Even from across the room, Maura could make out the familiar crescent shape that gave the Blood Moon Mountains part of their name.

The men looked up when Maura's party entered, and the one who looked to be in charge barked a question at the officer who had brought her. The officer made some kind of salute with his fist then spoke rapidly in Hanish. Maura wished she knew what he was saying.

The commander dismissed the other men with a glance and a nod. Once they had departed, he strode toward Maura. She flinched in fear as he reached beneath her cloak, but he only grabbed a corner of her sash and pulled it toward him for closer inspection.

"What is this?" he demanded. "What does it contain?"

"Only harmless herbs, my lord, for healing."

He let go of the sash as if it had turned into a hissing serpent. "The strong who are sick or wounded heal without stinking poison herbs. Weaklings who need such things are better left to die!"

Maura clamped her lips shut. She dared not argue the point with this man, who held her life in his hands. But neither would she give the smallest sign of agreement.

Fortunately, the commander did not appear to want an answer from her. He turned his attention to Delyon instead, hauling the scroll from his belt and unrolling it. For a moment he stared at the markings, his full brows knit together.

"What is this?" He thrust the scroll under Maura's nose. "What does it say?"

She was able to answer truthfully, "I know not, my lord. If you wish to find out, you must let me tend my friend and hope I can revive him to answer your questions."

"Pha!" The Hanish commander dropped the scroll and kicked it aside with his foot. "It will take more than this to make me care whether some Umbrian lowling lives or dies. There are too many of your kind as it is. We do your race a service by winnowing out the weak."

"You mistake tyranny for strength." The words came out before Maura could stop them.

Fortunately, they came out in Umbrian, and the Hanish commander ignored them. "Lurgo tells me you are spies."

"No, my lord." Maura hoped her denial sounded false enough to rouse suspicion. "Only harmless travelers, detained by mistake."

"When it comes to detaining your kind, my men never make a mistake! *Travel* except in the service of the empire is forbidden. If you do not know that, you are far from harmless. Where have you come from and where are you bound?"

"We come from the south, my lord." Maura offered a lie she hoped the commander would recognize as such. "A village called...Woodbury, and we are bound for...Talward."

"Never heard of either." The Han sneered, as most of his race did when speaking to *lowlings*. "What is your business in this Talward place?" He nudged Delyon's unconscious form with his foot. "And why did this one tear down an official notice?"

"An unfortunate mistake, my lord. My friend...merely wanted a closer look." Fie, but lying was a tiresome business— even when she did not want to be believed! "As you see from the scroll, he has a great interest in written words."

"Lying sow!" The commander lunged toward Maura, thrusting his face within an inch of hers. "If Oseck were here, he would soon bleed the truth out of you, and enjoy doing it, I daresay."

He laughed, a sound like falling splinters of flint. "But since Oseck has been summoned to Venard just when I need him most, I believe I will send you *there* for him to question."

"Please, my lord! Not Venard!" Maura willed her muscles to tense even tighter, rather than relax with relief at his words. "Not the Echtroi!"

His lips curled with cruel pleasure at her pretended distress. How could such a handsome surface encase such ugliness of spirit? Maura wondered.

The commander's large, hard hand thrust out to take her by the throat. "Tell *me* the truth, and I will spare you the *pleasure* of Oseck's attentions."

"I swear, my lord." Maura's eyes bulged and she gasped for breath. "What I have told you *is* the truth!"

"Weak, deceitful and stupid, like all your kind." The commander shot her a look of bottomless contempt as he released his grip. "You have decided your own fate."

Maura slumped forward, her chest heaving. If not for the soldiers who held her arms, she would have pitched to the floor.

The commander barked some orders to the other soldiers, who dragged her and Delyon from the room. She kept her head bowed in case her face should betray her true feelings. It looked as if her desperate gamble might pay off after all.

When she glanced at Delyon and saw a trickle of blood oozing down his forehead, a dark shadow fell across her fragile hopes. If he did not waken soon with his wits intact, what chance did she have of finding the Staff of Velorken?

"If this keeps up, we may not need the Staff of Velorken to win Umbria's freedom." Idrygon strode into Rath's tent looking better pleased than Rath had ever seen him.

"Could you call out next time to let me know you're coming in?" Rath growled to cover his alarm at being burst in upon.

The hour was late and his daily dose of growth potion was wearing off. He'd feared that one of his men might catch him in his true, unimposing form.

Idrygon laughed. "Who else would dare walk into your quarters, unannounced, at this hour? Never fear. The lads I have guarding your tent know their orders well. You won't be disturbed by anyone but me after you retire for the night. In an emergency, I will come and fetch you."

"Is this an emergency, then?" Rath sank back down onto his bedroll. "What's wrong?"

He'd been so startled by Idrygon's sudden appearance that he hadn't paid proper attention to what the man was saying.

"Wrong?" Idrygon dropped onto a large canvas cushion that served as a seat. "Why, nothing in the world. My plans are unfolding better than I dared hope. Today's battle was a stunning victory for us."

"That wasn't a battle. It was a rout." Rath reached for his drink skin—the one containing *sythria* so potent he was amazed it did not eat through the container. "And it wasn't a victory, either. It was a butchery."

He'd reckoned the life he'd led had hardened him to any depth of brutality. Since landing at the head of his small army in Duskport, he'd discovered otherwise. "We never should have let it happen like that. Did I not make it plain after the blood-letting in Duskport, I wanted no more of it?"

Idrygon threw up his hands. "*My* men had their orders, and obeyed them as far as I could see. The slaughter was all the mainlanders' doing—today and back in Duskport. They have decades of hatred boiling inside them. You of all men have reason to know that."

Rath tipped his drink skin and let a long draft of *sythria* scald its way down to his belly. He hoped it might purge his mind of some of the sights he'd seen today.

"I do know. I suffered plenty from the Han. Still…" He shook his head.

Idrygon shook *his* head, clearly bewildered by Rath's attitude. "Do you suppose our enemies would have shown us any mercy if the tables had been turned?"

"I know they would not." Rath took another drink. "How does that make it right?"

"What would you have us do?" Idrygon's voice took on a tone of calm, rational persuasion. "Offer them terms of surrender? You know we do not have enough men to guard prisoners or the means to feed them. Even if the Han would accept, which you must know they would not. They are a warrior race. Horribly as many of them died today, I believe they would have chosen such deaths over the dishonor of surrender."

Rath replied with a grunt. Idrygon was a hard man to dispute. He seemed to have an endless cache of solid, sensible reasons for everything he did or wanted to do. And he had barely begun to tap his supply when it came to this matter.

"To fight warriors—" Idrygon's fist clenched "—we must think like warriors. We must *become* warriors. True, we have had strength of numbers in our battles so far—that was always our aim. But we do not have sufficient force to stand against the whole Hanish army of occupation. We must weaken them in small bites. You knew our battle plan before we set out from Margyle. I thought you approved."

"I…I did." But those had been tiny wooden markers moved around on that map board. Not men who screamed and bled and had their bodies torn apart for sport.

He leaped to his feet and began to pace the tent, still clutching the drink skin.

"I know all this, Idrygon." He jabbed his forehead with his thumb. "Up here, I know it. But here and here—" he thumped his chest and then his belly "—it sickens me. I have spilled plenty of Hanish blood in my day—but never like this. When I had no other choice but to kill, I always tried to make it as quick and as clean as I could."

"Very noble of you." Idrygon's voice betrayed no obvious mockery, but Rath sensed it just the same.

"If we are to become no better than the Han—" Rath shook his drink skin at Idrygon "—what are we doing all this for? Will Umbria be any better off?"

He heard his voice beginning to slur and he still had enough sense to know he should quit talking and go to sleep before his runaway tongue got him into trouble.

"Calm yourself," said Idrygon. "And sit down before you fall. I am certain this…savagery on the part of the mainlanders is a passing fever that will soon burn itself out."

"A fever, is it?" Rath planted his feet wide to keep his balance. "Then they need a good physic, and if you will not dole it out, I will. Tomorrow, I will issue orders about honorable conduct in battle and set penalties for any who disobey."

"Don't be a fool!" Idrygon sprang to his feet and grabbed the drink skin out of Rath's hand. "The mainlanders have flocked to you just as I said they would. Without their numbers, we might have had a more *honorable* fight on our hands today, but we would have lost a good many more of our own men. Is that what you want?"

"No, but—"

"In case you have not noticed, the mainlanders outnumber our Vestan soldiers these days. If you try to prevent them from taking their legitimate revenge, they will turn on you, *Waiting King*. And if they do, the Han will be the least of our worries."

He pointed to Rath's bedroll. The fierceness of his tone and stance eased. "Now lie down and get some sleep. You are too…overwrought to be making any plans just now. Tomorrow everything I've said will make better sense to you."

It wasn't that, Rath wanted to protest. Idrygon's arguments all made sense, but they did not change the way he felt about any of this. It was not the kind of glorious, honorable conquest he'd imagined they would make. Perhaps there was no glory or honor to be found in conquest.

He settled himself onto his bedroll as Idrygon had bidden, hoping the *sythria* would numb him to sleep and keep his nightmares at bay.

"Enough talk for tonight." Idrygon pulled the blanket over Rath. "We must be on the move tomorrow. Up into the mountains as I promised you. Perhaps when you see the mines again you will not feel so sorry for the poor ill-used Han."

"This is not about the Han," Rath murmured as drink and sleep joined forces to overpower him. "It is about us."

That was it—not that the Han should be slaughtered the way he had seen today, but that his countrymen should take such brutal delight in killing.

Idrygon rose and headed off, tossing the drink skin aside.

As Rath surrendered to sleep, he heard Idrygon mutter, "I thought an outlaw would have a stronger stomach."

Rather than waking *from* a nightmare, Maura woke *to* one.

She found herself astride a horse—her feet tied to the stirrups of its saddle and her hands lashed to the pommel. The horse's reins were attached to the mount of her Hanish escort.

Twisting around in her saddle, she could see Delyon trussed

to the back of another horse like a piece of cargo. She almost envied his continued stupor. At the same time it worried her.

Would she be able to revive him before they reached Venard? If not, what would she do then?

No need to go searching for trouble, she reminded herself of an old Norest saying. *It always finds its way home.*

Plenty of trouble had already found its way home to her. Behind them the sun was setting, but their Hanish escort detail did not show any sign of stopping to sleep or eat. Overhead a fat bundle of clouds threatened rain.

On the bright side—at least they were moving toward Venard many times faster than they had been. Since leaving the town where they'd been captured, Maura judged they had traveled a distance that would have taken her and Delyon many nights of hard walking.

Shaking herself fully awake, she looked around. There were many other soldiers on the road besides their small party— some marching in groups, others riding. Maura had never seen so many Han. Were they *all* on their way to battle Rath's forces? How many other roads in the kingdom were flooded with troops?

To have any hope of prevailing against such a host, Rath would need the magical Staff of Velorken. Somehow, she must find a way to revive Delyon and make their escape before they fell into the hands of the Echtroi.

The soldier guarding Maura glanced up at the sky and said something to the one guarding Delyon, who replied with a curt word and a nod.

What was he agreeing to? Maura wished she understood a little Hanish. If only she had asked Rath to tutor her—that would have been a far more productive use of their last days together on Margyle than arguing with him and avoiding him. Now she concentrated on remembering that every mile the horse carried her was a mile closer to Rath.

Before the sun had fully set and before the clouds had done

more than spit a few drops of rain, Maura's party reached a village about the size of Windleford. As they approached the local garrison compound, the soldiers slowed their mounts and halted. Both climbed down from their saddles. Delyon's guard held the reins of both horses, while Maura's guard went inside. He returned shortly and motioned for them to enter the courtyard.

"We bide the night here," he informed Maura as he unbound her hands and feet from the saddle.

Her feet prickled fiercely when the ropes came off. She clung to the horse as she slid down from the saddle, fearing her legs would not support her. Pride would not allow her to lean upon a Han—she would sooner fall.

"Come." Her guard took her by the arm and marched her toward one of several cells that faced onto the courtyard.

Hearing a soft grunt of exertion and a heavy tread behind her, she glanced back to see the other guard with Delyon slung over his shoulder.

"My lord," she begged her guard in Comtung. "I pray you put me with my friend so I can tend him tonight."

She could tell by his deepening scowl that the Han meant to refuse her.

Before he could rap the words out, she rushed on. "I am only his guide. I know nothing of value to the Echtroi, but he might, *if* he can be revived."

"Anxious to spare yourself the attention of the death-mages, are you?" The guard gave a dry, mocking chuckle.

Maura nodded. "And you, my lord. Will they thank you for bringing them a dead man who is beyond their power to question?"

The Han was quick to disguise the flicker of fear her warning kindled…but not quick enough.

"It matters not to me." He pushed her through the cell door one of the local soldiers held open. "The lowling will be less bother to Urgid if he can sit a horse and walk."

He muttered something to the other guard, who hoisted Delyon off his shoulder and shoved him into the cell with Maura. As Delyon's dead weight fell against her, Maura crumpled to the hard-packed earth floor. Though it knocked the wind out of her, she congratulated herself on having spared him another blow on the head.

After making him as comfortable as she could with her rolled-up cloak for a pillow, she inspected their tiny cell. It had stout stone walls on three sides, while thick metal bars made up the fourth. There was no furnishing of any kind, not even a wooden slat attached to the wall for a bed. There were two metal cans about the height of her knee. One held water that dripped from a small hole in the roof. It was filling now with a steady, high-pitched trickle as the rain gathered force.

The other container looked and smelled like a privy bucket. Holding her nose, she made hasty use of it, then returned to Delyon. His heartbeat was steady, though a little slow, and he was breathing well—good signs both.

When Maura looked more closely at the water can, she found a small metal cup resting at the bottom of it. Emptying it of all but a small amount of water, she pulled out some of Dame Diotta's quickfoil. She had been afraid the Han might take their sashes, as Vang Spear of Heaven had done when he'd captured her. But after a quick inspection revealed their contents of plant and animal matter, the officer had dismissed them with a contemptuous shrug. If only he knew!

Now Maura rolled the leaves between her palms to release their most potent essence and dropped them into the water. Next she added a liberal pinch of laceweed and moonmallow. She wished she'd been able to give them to Delyon earlier. She also wished she had some means to heat the water for this tonic. Ah well, there was no help for it. She could only do what she could do and appeal to the Giver to supply the rest.

Sliding her arm under Delyon's shoulder, she lifted his head and began to dribble the tonic into his mouth. It brought back painful memories of the night she had worked over Langbard in a similar fashion, trying to revive him. Then, she had been too late. Would she be too late for Delyon?

She was beginning to fear so, when suddenly his gorge rose and fell to swallow the tonic. By the time she had emptied the cup, his eyelids were beginning to flicker and he gave a soft groan of pain.

Under other circumstances, Maura would have given him a draft of summerslip, but she did not want to risk knocking him out again when she had just succeeded in rousing him. Instead, she mixed up a poultice of marshwort, candleflax and winterwort and gently applied it to the painful-looking bump on his head.

By the time she had finished binding his injured head with strips of linen, Delyon had come fully awake.

"What happened?" he groaned. "Where are we?"

Maura told him.

"I remember now—the sign! The Hanish letters reminded me of some of the symbols on my scroll. I believe they could be the key to deciphering the rest of it." Delyon reached for his belt. "My scroll—where is it?"

"The guards have it." Maura restrained him when he tried to sit up. "The Han seem to think it may be some coded plan or spy message. They are taking it, and us, to Venard where the Echtroi are gathered."

"We must get it back!" Delyon struggled to rise from the floor of their cell. "And we must escape from here! We cannot fall into the hands of the Echtroi!"

"Hush! Lie still." She spoke *twaran,* in case they might be overheard. "We are in no danger at the moment. I do not fancy being interrogated by the Echtroi, either. But I am not opposed to accepting a ride to Venard, even if it is in the company of Hanish soldiers."

Delyon mulled over the notion for a moment or two, then he gave a grudging nod. "With our supplies and coins gone, what choice have we? I beg your pardon for landing us in this trouble."

"What's done is past." With an effort, Maura let her resentment go, recalling something Langbard had often said. "We cannot go back and fix it, we can only move forward and make the best of it."

Delyon lifted his hand to clasp hers. "How much longer do you think it will take us to reach Venard?"

Maura shook her head. "Another day, perhaps two. By then we must have you well and fit and ready to make our escape." She thought for a moment. "We may not get another chance to talk before then. So let us lay our plans now and hope the Giver will send us an opportunity."

The rain fell all that night until the water can in Maura and Delyon's cell overflowed. Maura gave thanks that the wind was blowing from the west and not in through the bars on the open wall of the cell. Perhaps minding her warning about the Echtroi not wanting dead prisoners, the Han fed them.

It was not a very appetizing dish, especially after being half drowned on its way to their cell, but Maura ate every bite and coaxed Delyon to do the same. They could not afford to faint from hunger when their chance to escape presented itself.

Their guards seemed surprised the next morning to find Delyon alert and able to walk. They set off early in spite of the continued rain. As they rode, Maura beseeched the Giver to make the sun come out before they reached Venard. Her escape plan depended upon the invisibility spell. Though Dame Diotta had assured her *genow* scales were less vulnerable than cuddybird feathers to water, she did not want to take any chances.

The answer to her plea came so swiftly Maura could hardly believe it, though she chided herself for not having better faith. Without warning, the wind shifted. It soon blew all the rain clouds away and, combined with the sun's warmth, rapidly dried her clothes.

After several hours their party halted for a quick meal of bread and some meat. While they were stopped, Maura pretended to tend Delyon's head wound as an excuse for exchanging a few words in *twaran*. "How are you feeling today? Any better?"

Delyon nodded. "Thanks to your tonic. My head aches with the jolting of the horse's stride, but I can bear it."

"Good, for I dare not dose you with summerslip. We will both need our wits about us when our chance to escape comes."

"This may be the best chance we get." Delyon pointed to his head, as if he were still talking about his injuries.

Maura unwrapped the poultice binding for a quick look, pleased to see the swelling had gone down. "I wish I knew how far we are from Venard. I'd rather not part company from our *escorts* too soon."

Gathering up her nerve, she asked one of the guards, "Will we reach Venard today, my lord?"

"Why do you ask?" The Han gave a mocking chuckle. "Anxious to meet a death-mage and see his pretty gem before the day is over?"

"Too bad." The other guard laughed at his jest. "You will have to wait until tomorrow, lowling sow."

Maura turned back to Delyon. "We will have one more night on the road, by the sound of it. I think we should delay our escape as long as we dare."

"Very well." Delyon sounded uncertain, but willing to follow where she led. "And we must find some way to get my scroll back. That spell may be our key to recovering the Staff of Velorken."

Several hours later they stopped at the Hanish garrison in another village. Maura's guard went inside, then came out a short time later muttering what sounded like curses. He snapped a few words at Delyon's guard, then climbed into his saddle and the party kept riding. The same thing happened at the next village.

Though the scowls of the two soldiers warned her not to ask them what was wrong, Maura could guess. With so many troops on the road, all the officers must be commandeering quarters with local garrisons along the way, leaving no room for their party.

When they finally stopped for a quick bite to eat, Maura slipped Delyon a leaf of quickfoil. "Tuck that in your cheek until you need it. I reckon we will be pressing on to Venard tonight after all."

She could see a number of possible advantages to that…as well as several drawbacks.

The sun set and the wind grew cool as they rode on. A sickle moon and great swaths of twinkling stars bathed the great plain of Westborne with their pale, bluish light. Straight ahead of her on the eastern horizon, Maura could see the gleaming star group called the Sword of Velorken, its blade pointing north.

Could it truly be that Velorken's staff still existed and lay waiting in Venard for her to recover it? Doubt gouged a cold hollow in her belly until she remembered how many other impossible legends she had seen come true of late.

On and on they rode until Maura began to nod and reel with fatigue. Then a faint cluster of lights appeared in the distance. Hearing one of the guards call something to the other, Maura thought she heard the familiar name "Venard" among all the other unintelligible words.

Shifting the quickfoil leaf with her tongue, she worked it between her back teeth and began to chew. Gradually the fog of weariness lifted from her mind and her pulse quickened. She hoped Delyon had been paying attention and recognized the time had come to revive himself.

When they reached the gates of the city at last, the watchman called down a wary challenge. Maura's guard responded in a tone of angry impatience. A few moments later, one of the huge metal gates swung open to admit their party.

The winding streets of the city were nearly deserted as they rode through them. Maura had never seen a place this size before. Would she and Delyon be able to find their way out again once they had completed their mission? Save that worry for its proper season, she reminded herself.

A while later the party came to a halt before another, smaller gate that Maura guessed must lead to the High Governor's palace. Once again they answered a challenge and were admitted.

By now, Maura's heart was pounding hard and fast against her ribs. Her throat felt as if she were wearing one of those high-collared Vestan tunics Rath complained about. She wriggled her hands and feet to work out the stiffness before she had to call upon them. Would the risk she had taken prove inspired or dangerously foolhardy?

14

They rode into a huge courtyard with a fountain in the center that reminded Maura of the villas on the Vestan Islands. She had managed to get them delivered right to the doorstep of the High Governor's palace. If she and Delyon managed to escape custody, she would congratulate herself.

The two Hanish guards reined their mounts to a halt, then climbed down. One shook his head hard, as if to banish his fatigue. The other one yawned. They approached Maura and Delyon and began to go through the familiar motions of untying them from their saddles. First release one foot, then move to the other side of the horse, untie the other foot, then the hands.

"Let's go," muttered Maura's guard, stepping back to let her climb down. "You don't want to keep the Echtroi waiting."

Maura pretended to sag in her saddle from weariness. The moment her hands were free, she reached into her sash for the *genow* scales and chanted the invisibility spell under her breath. "Gracious Giver, hide me from the eyes of my foes."

Sprinkling the scales over herself, she scrambled down on the other side of the horse and staggered as far away as she could so no one would blunder into her. She looked around for Delyon, vastly relieved when she could not see him.

Shouts from the guards told her they'd realized something was wrong. They raced around the horses looking for their vanished prisoners, making the beasts whinny and rear. If the situation had not been so dangerous, Maura might have been tempted to chuckle at their bewildered frenzy.

"Delyon," she called softly in *twaran,* "meet me by the fountain."

As soon as the words had left her lips, she scooted away in case the soldiers homed in on the sound of her voice. But they only looked around, more confused than ever. Their noise drew more and more of the palace guards until the whole courtyard fairly boiled with confusion.

"Delyon?" Maura called again in an urgent whisper as she circled the fountain hoping to bump into him. "Where are you?"

She *must* find him so they could stay together. Otherwise they would waste precious time blundering around the palace looking for one another. Just when she was about to risk calling louder, the commotion among the Han intensified, drawing her gaze to that part of the courtyard.

The soldier who had been guarding Delyon was flailing about, one hand clasped around the end of a stick or…a scroll. It took only an instant for Maura to realize Delyon must be pulling on the other end—the fool! How hard would it have been to have waited until all the fuss died down and someone left the scroll lying on a shelf or a table, ripe for the plucking?

Though tempted to let Delyon suffer the consequences of his folly, Maura got a firm grip on her anger and launched herself into the fray. As she slipped between the horses, she gave each a good hard swat on the rump. One beast reared, hooves churning. Two others took off running around the courtyard.

While this drew the attention of the palace guards, Maura sprang at the Han who was using Delyon's scroll for a tug-of-war. She grabbed the long plume of flaxen hair trailing from the top of his helmet and yanked on it hard.

With a loud bellow of shock and pain, the Han lost his balance and fell backward, arms thrashing. Maura skipped out of his way, her gaze fixed on the scroll, which he had let go. She must act fast before the other soldiers noticed it had not fallen to the ground with him.

She pounced on it, relieved to feel the solid shape of Delyon and smell the faint aroma of Vestan wildflowers that clung to his cloak.

"Hide the scroll under your cloak!" she hissed, groping for his hand. "Let's get out of here before someone trips over us!"

Keeping a tight grip on him, she fled to a deserted corner of the courtyard. With all the noise and fuss, she doubted it would stay deserted for long.

"What now?" Delyon whispered.

"We must make our way inside and find a hiding place before we become visible again. That door looks as good as any. Come."

They had almost reached the entrance, when a dark-robed figure stalked out. The green wand in his hand gave off an aura of menacing power. Maura could not stifle a gasp as she checked her stride and yanked Delyon out of the death-mage's path.

Perhaps he heard her or sensed her presence, for he came to an abrupt halt and looked around. Maura held her breath, clamping her lips together to stifle a whimper of terror. Though she had fought others of his kind, she knew with certain dread that they had not possessed half his power.

A desperate litany rolled over and over in her mind—the words of the invisibility spell. *Gracious Giver, hide me from the eyes of my foes.* The death-mage stared straight at her, and for an instant Maura felt his icy gaze stripping away the flimsy protection of her vitcraft spell.

Then one of the soldiers ran up to the death-mage and began jabbering in Hanish. When he turned his attention from her, Maura hauled Delyon toward the door. Long after they had found a safe hiding spot in a distant, quiet corner of the palace cellars, her heart continued to race and her hands to tremble.

"Where are the death-mages?" Rath muttered to himself as he sheathed his blade and stared around the mining compound his army had just liberated.

Off in the distance he could still hear scattered sounds of fighting as his army overran the last fierce pockets of resistance. Miners were emerging from the depths of the mountain, dazed and shielding their eyes against the daylight. Rath had a detail of men out scouring the mountains for freshwort to help wean them off the slag.

"Another glorious victory!" Idrygon sucked in a great draft of the cool mountain air. "I'll admit, I had my doubts about venturing into the mountains, but you were right to insist. Attacking the greatest symbol of Hanish domination—I hear it has inflamed the whole kingdom with a spirit of rebellion!"

"You make it sound like a stunt staged for effect." Rath stared out over the plain of Westborne. "It was meant to be more than that."

"Of course it was, Highness." Idrygon's agreement sounded exaggerated. "It *is*. We have rescued the most oppressed people in all of Umbria. It is a heroic deed. One that will be told and sung of for generations."

"Worthy it may be." Rath shook his head. "But heroic?"

When his small band of miners had risen up to gain their freedom against impossible odds, that had been the true stuff of legend. This well-planned campaign had seen some hard fighting, but the outcome had never been in question. At least not once it became clear the Echtroi had deserted their posts.

"This has been too smooth a ride for us," Rath warned. "I smell a trap."

"Perhaps the Han are hoping to lure us down to open combat in Westborne," said Idrygon. "If so, the surprise will be on them."

A young Vestan soldier approached Idrygon. "My lord, some mainlanders wish to speak with His Highness."

Rath glanced up to see three men standing a ways off, staring at him with a look of amazement and awe he had come to know too well since his return to the mainland. It never failed to make him uneasy, for he did not deserve their homage. The success of this invasion was Idrygon's doing, not his. His imposing appearance was nothing but a trick. There were times when he felt a stirring of King Elzaban within him, but he was not the Waiting King legends had led these men to expect.

"Tell them the king has important matters to oversee." Idrygon tugged on Rath's arm to pull him away. "He cannot be disturbed. If it is urgent I will speak with the mainlanders."

As Rath turned away, something about the men stirred his memory. Could it be? Anulf, Odger and little Theto?

Rath felt the first sincere smile in weeks warm his face. Shaking off Idrygon's hand, he strode toward them.

He only got two steps when Idrygon leaped into his path. "Highness, what are you doing?"

"It's all right, Idrygon. Those are my mates from the Beastmount mine. To think they came here." His throat tightened.

"They know you as Rath Talward?" Idrygon's eyes widened and his nostrils flared. "Get them out of here!" he ordered the young soldier. "I will come and speak with them shortly."

He hauled Rath away to a distant outcropping of rock, muttering curses. "You were going to talk to them? Have you gone daft?"

"What's daft about it? Of course I mean to talk to them. Invite them to dine and drink with me tonight. They are good fellows—the best. If I had a whole army of their kind, we could defeat the Han with or without that Staff of Velorken."

"You *have* gone daft!" Idrygon shook his head so hard and so fast, Rath wondered he did not swoon from dizziness. "It must be this thin mountain air. You know we cannot afford to have anyone recognize you as the outlaw Rath Talward."

"Is *that* all you're fretted about?" Rath chuckled, his humor buoyed by the unexpected appearance of his friends. "Anulf and the others will keep quiet if I ask them to. I would trust any of them with my life."

"That is all very well. *I* do not trust them with the success of this war."

"Are you forbidding me to speak to my friends, Idrygon?"

"Yes! I mean no. Not forbidding, Highness—begging. Once the war is won, then you can drink all night with them or anyone else you fancy. For now, you agreed to play the legend and it is working. Do not balk at the most critical moment and put all we have worked so hard for in jeopardy."

Rath looked from Idrygon's compelling stare to Anulf and the others being led away. He felt like a frayed rope in the middle of a fierce tug-of-war.

Beyond Idrygon, he could make out the distant shape of Umbria's capital. Was Maura down there now, risking her life to find the Staff of Velorken? What business had he to fret about delaying a drink or two with his friends?

"Very well." He gave a resigned nod. "Rath Talward will trouble you no more. But see those fellows are used well and treated with respect."

Idrygon bowed. "I knew I could depend upon your loyalty and discretion, Highness. I will make certain your friends are treated with the honor they deserve."

"Good." As Idrygon strode away, looking vastly relieved, Rath called after him, "If they should ask about…Talward, tell them he is on a special mission for the king, and that he will be pleased to see them when his task is done."

"A politic message, Highness. I shall be pleased to convey it."

For some time after Idrygon had left, Rath stood on the outcropping, staring down toward Venard.

"Giver, keep her safe and bring her back to me," he murmured. "Do I trespass on even *your* generosity to ask so much?"

Perhaps, for he had not properly cherished the gift of her presence when he'd had it. Now he swore to himself that he would never make that mistake again if he should be granted the most priceless gift of all—a second chance he did not deserve.

"We cannot afford any more mistakes like last night," Maura warned Delyon the next morning. "We cannot assume we will get a second chance if we do not take care."

Delyon looked up from the scroll, which he was studying by the light of a greenfire twig that had almost spent itself. "What I did last night was not a mistake or carelessness. I had no intention of letting this scroll out of my sight. What if it had fallen into the hands of the Echtroi? I hear they make it their business to know things."

"Not those kinds of things." Maura tried to keep her mind off her empty stomach.

"How can you be sure?" Delyon squinted at the markings on the scroll as if willing them to reveal their meaning to him. "They might have thought this was some coded message being sent to the Waiting King. I doubt they would have left such a thing lying around for us to recover easily."

Maura sniffed the air. The kitchens must be nearby. The aroma of roasting meat made her mouth water and her stomach rumble worse than ever. "Perhaps you are right. You might have warned me, though, so you didn't catch me all fumble-footed."

The twig in Delyon's hand gave a final flare of pale green light then went out, plunging the cellar storeroom into darkness.

He sighed. "I thought you would say it was only a fool piece of parchment, not worth risking our necks for."

"I know this scroll could be very important." Maura groped her way toward the sound of his voice, moving carefully so as not to knock anything over. "But without you to decipher it or me to use the spell, it will not be much good to anyone, will it?"

She sank onto the floor, wishing they had found a nice cozy larder to hide in. The first place she intended to hunt for the Staff of Velorken, tonight, would be the kitchens!

Delyon's voice wafted out of the darkness, edged with bitterness. "I may not be the great planner and leader my brother is, but I have worked every bit as hard to see the kingdom reclaimed and restored to its former glory."

"You can keep your glory." Maura yawned. "As long as we can have peace and good harvests, I will be content. Now let us sleep while we have the chance so we will be fresh and alert for our search tonight."

"You sleep." Softly, Delyon chanted the greenfire spell. A faint pale glow began to shine from a fresh twig he clutched. "I doubt we will find the staff with an ordinary search, though you are welcome to try. What I intend to look for tonight are samples of Hanish writing. I wonder if they might have one of those signs about with both Hanish and Umbrian letters."

"Perhaps." Maura settled herself on the floor beside him. The rush of fear from their escape had finally ebbed. Now a warm drowsiness stole over her. "I will keep a lookout for one when I search tonight. Or perhaps we could find the engraver's shop in the city where they were printed."

"Yes, of course!" cried Delyon in an excited whisper. "That would make sense. You are a very clever woman, Highness!"

"Do not call me that?" she murmured. "We are not on Margyle anymore, needing to convince the Council of Rath's and my claim to the throne."

To think this palace belonged by right to them. Maura had never felt *less* like a queen than she did now—curled up on the floor of a cellar storeroom.

"Your pardon. It is a hard habit to break." Delyon spoke in an absent tone, as if only a small part of his mind was on their conversation.

When Maura half opened one eye, she could see he was studying the scroll so closely that his nose was almost pressed against the parchment.

"Do try. The last thing I need is for someone who understands Umbrian to overhear you addressing me by that title."

She rolled over so she was not facing the light. "Wake me when you want to sleep and I will sit guard."

Delyon was too engrossed in his task to heed or reply. And Maura was too weary to bother repeating her instructions. The next thing she heard was the sound of a door closing softly. A surge of alarm brought her instantly awake, all her senses aquiver.

Curse Delyon! He should have warned her if he heard anyone coming.

As she fumbled in her sash for *genow* scales, Maura reached with her other hand to give Delyon a nudge. No doubt he had fallen asleep poring over that precious scroll of his.

"Oh, slag!" she muttered when her finger poked empty air. Where could Delyon have gone without telling her, and why?

She stifled a groan. Of course…he must have gone off looking for an engraver's shop to see if he could find a copy of that sign. She should have known.

Scrambling to her feet, she cast the invisibility spell over herself. She would have to go after him. The Giver only knew what sort of trouble he might land himself in. Her stomach gave a loud rumble to remind her that she should look for something to eat while she searched for Delyon.

By the time she stole out into the dimly lit corridor, there was no sign of Delyon. Of course she wouldn't be able to *see* him, Maura reminded herself. But she did not see any suspicious shadow flicker or hear the muted sound of invisible footsteps, either. She pictured him blundering through the palace and the city, perhaps frightening someone half to death by stopping them to ask directions.

Plundering her still-drowsy memory to recall the route they'd taken to get here, she set off after Delyon. With every step, she promised herself she would have his hide for this latest folly. Her anger intensified when she mounted a narrow stairway and emerged in broad daylight to find a palace full of people coming and going. Why could he not have waited for nightfall, at least?

When a pair of serving wenches passed her, talking rapidly together in Comtung, Maura pressed herself against the nearest wall, hardly daring to breathe. She brought her hand up and wiggled her fingers in front of her face, reassured when she could not see them.

All her senses alert, she stole through the palace, trying to remember the way to the courtyard that led out into the city. She must have taken a wrong turn, though. For she suddenly found herself wandering down a wide gallery that did not look the least bit familiar.

Do not panic, Maura told herself. *Just turn around and go back the way you came until you find a spot you do recognize.*

But as she turned to go back, she saw a large party of men striding toward her. Most were high-ranking Hanish soldiers in uniform. Several death-mages walked together in silence, including the one with the green wand Maura had almost run into the night before. He was not one whit less alarming by daylight.

The members of the party who most caught Maura's eye were two men who appeared to be Umbrians. What were they doing here? They did not look frightened or particularly ill at ease. They must be *zikary,* Umbrians who curried favor with the Han. How she wished she dared stick out her foot and trip them!

Instead, she backed away, determined to stay ahead of them until they reached wherever they were going. She got several steps down the gallery when a Hanish soldier approached from the other direction with a black hound on a leash.

Maura froze. The hound would not need its eyes to find her.

For an instant she considered trying to thread her way through the party of men coming toward her, but they filled the width of the gallery, walking close together. Caught between the hearth and the griddle, she dived through the nearest open doorway and found herself in a large room. A long marble-topped table occupied most of the room, with a great many wrought-iron chairs huddled around it.

Maura had scarcely entered when the throng of soldiers and

Echtroi came in behind her and spread out to take their places around the table. The only way she could avoid the press of milling bodies was to dive under the table.

A sharp, raspy voice cut through the low rumble of conversation. It surprised Maura that she could understand the words. "We have a great deal to discuss, so let us not squander our time. Take your places, everyone, and we will begin."

Begin what?

She did not want to find out, but it appeared she would have no choice as the men took their seats, blocking her escape.

No, wait! There *was* still one way out from under the table. At the very end, one seat remained empty.

Maura crept toward it as quickly as she dared. Luckily the racket of so many men taking their seats and pulling their chairs into the table drowned out the furtive sounds of her movement along the floor. She stifled a cry when the toe of a boot dealt her a glancing blow, but the owner of the boot only muttered something in Hanish. Probably an apology for kicking whoever was seated next to him.

She was just emerging from under the table, hoping the door had been left open to aid her quick escape, when one last man strode to take his seat. He wore a rich-looking robe of silver-gray and all the others jumped to their feet when he appeared. This must be the Hanish High Governor himself.

Maura crawled back a ways and resigned herself to being trapped beneath the table until this meeting finished. That was the *best* she could hope for. The worst did not bear thinking about.

The High Governor did not take his seat at once, but stood at the head of the table and addressed those gathered. He had the firm, decisive tone of a man accustomed to making plans and having them executed without question. It put Maura in mind of Lord Idrygon.

"All the northland is in chaos." Maura startled to hear a

quiet murmur of Comtung echoing the High Governor's Hanish speech. "Now a rebel horde overruns our mines."

The words were coming from nearby. One of the *zikary* must be translating for the other. Maura edged closer to that voice, straining her ears to catch familiar words.

From what she could gather, the High Governor was informing everyone of recent events, the *rumors* they were trying so hard to discredit among the Umbrian people.

When he finished speaking, the High Governor took his seat and the man at the other end of the table rose. Maura knew he must be a death-mage. Even if she had not been able to see the lower part of his distinctive dark robes, she would have known by the hollow rasp of his voice.

"For some time the Echtroi have known rebellion was brewing," murmured the translator. "Our warnings fell on deaf ears, so we took matters in hand ourselves and had some success crushing dangerous rebel agents."

Dangerous rebel agents? Like Langbard and Exilda. Maura jammed her mouth shut to keep from screaming her outrage.

She almost screamed in fright when something heavy slammed down upon the tabletop. It must have been the High Governor's hand, for he shouted in response to the death-mage's words.

"How can *this* be called success?" The *zikary* translated his challenge. "You claimed to be searching for a young woman. How could we take such a threat seriously?"

The death-mage responded in a cold but dispassionate tone. "Sometimes the greatest threats take on the most harmless appearance, Excellency. It is all part of some ridiculous ancient prophesy. Often the more preposterous such rubbish, the more power it has to rouse the ignorant. I have brought someone who can tell us more about it, so we know what we are fighting."

The *zikary* translator and the man sitting beside him rose. In bald, simple terms, they recounted the legend of Elzaban and

Abrielle, and how the Destined Queen would one day waken the Waiting King to rescue his kingdom in its darkest hour.

Several of the military officers interrupted with questions about the Waiting King and the nature of his powers. Most of which the Umbrian could only answer in the vaguest terms. Still, it was enough to send a ripple of apprehensive muttering up and down the table.

The High Governor rapped out a single word, which Maura could understand without translation. *Enough!* perhaps. Or *Silence!* A heavy hush fell over the room.

At just that instant, Maura felt an insistent tickle at the back of her nose. Oh, no! She couldn't sneeze now! She pinched her nose and held her breath. Her eyes watered furiously as she nearly stifled herself in an effort to hold back the sneeze. But it would not be stifled. It came in a muffled rush that felt as though it would burst her head.

It might have betrayed her presence. But at that moment the two Umbrians took their seats again. Even with the cover of their noise, Maura was certain someone must have heard her. Her heart fluttering frantically, she tensed to flee for her life.

To her amazed relief, the High Governor began speaking again as if he had heard nothing.

Again the *zikary* translated for his comrade and, unwittingly, for Maura. "So the leader of these rebel invaders is this Waiting King?"

One of the officers answered, "It would seem so, Excellency, from our reports."

The death-mage at the end of the table added, "There are rumors circulating among the Umbrians that this hero of old has returned to lead them. The countryside is crawling with men running off to join his rabble. We do not have enough troops to battle the rebels and still keep a tight hold on the lands under our control."

"We must put a stop to this nonsense," said the High Governor as if he had only to declare his wishes in forceful enough terms and they would be successfully discharged at once. "Before this whole stinking country rises up against us. We should never have let the rebels get into the mountains and attack the mines."

"On the contrary, Excellency," said the death-mage. "As long as we continue to protect the mines, keep them operating, and send a steady supply of ore back to Dun Derhan, the Imperium will see no need to give us the kind of aid we need to put down the uprising."

"How can you be so certain what the Imperium will or will not do, Nefarion?" The *zikary* translated it in more respectful language. But hearing the High Governor's tone, Maura guessed that was closer to his true meaning. "Have you spoken with any officials in Dun Derhan lately?"

"I have been in contact with imperial officials. Last week and again last night."

Though the tone of the death-mage's remark sounded perfectly casual, as if referring to something he did often as a matter of course, it had a potent effect on the gathering. The buzz around the table put Maura in mind of the Council of Sages on Margyle, when Idrygon had introduced her and Rath. Perhaps Han and Umbrians were not as different as they liked to believe.

One voice rose above the others, instantly translated by the *zikary*. "How is that possible?"

"I have mastered the spell of farspeech," replied the death-mage, setting off an even louder buzz. "And a good thing, too. Did you know the summer Ore Fleet never reached Dun Derhan? All but a handful of escort vessels were wrecked off the Vestan Islands."

At that point Maura could have shouted at the top of her lungs without being heard above the clamor. She wished they would all quiet down! Voices rose above the uproar, but any translation was drowned out.

At last the High Governor called for silence again and

Maura could hear the *zikary* translating for the death-mage. "The Imperium approves our caution in withdrawing all Echtroi from the mountains," he announced with obvious satisfaction. "They were appalled to hear of the number we have lost already."

"And what business had you telling them that?" demanded the High Governor.

"Are you saying I should have given a false report to my superiors?"

The High Governor replied with a snarl that could not readily be translated. Nor did it need to be.

"What are our orders from the Imperium, then? Withdraw and let some *star tale* king and his lowling rabble take back the land our fathers fought and bled to conquer?"

If only it could be that easy! Maura thought.

"We are instructed to bide our time and not risk worse losses," said the death-mage. "Keep a strong hold on the territory we still control. We are to lure the rebels into the eastlands."

It would not take much luring. The back of Maura's neck prickled. Rath and Idrygon had already planned to move east.

"What happens then?" asked the High Governor.

"Once the rebels take our bait," said the death-mage, "we are instructed to raise as large a force as we can spare and march over the mountains. The Imperium has already dispatched a fleet of fresh troops to put down this uprising. They will land on the east coast within the next fortnight. We will be the hammer, and the new troops will be the anvil upon which we crush this Waiting King."

Maura clamped her hand over her mouth to muffle a gasp. In all his plans, Idrygon had never considered the possibility of the empire sending troops until it was too late. If only she could learn the farspeech spell of which the death-mage had boasted, she would warn Rath and Idrygon that they were walking into a trap.

Since that was not possible, she and Delyon must waste no

time finding the Staff of Velorken and carrying it to Rath along with an urgent warning.

Before the earth of the eastlands was soaked in Umbrian blood!

15

Images of a horrific lost battle for Umbria haunted Maura as she cowered beneath the meeting table. How she wished the men would all stop talking and go away!

Hunger gnawed at her stomach with sharp teeth and her nerves were stretched tight by the peril of her position. What if the invisibility spell wore off before the meeting ended? Did she dare use more of their precious supply of *genow* scales? She had dipped into hers three times already, though she had not yet begun to search the palace.

When chair legs finally scraped against the floor and the men rose to leave, Maura could scarcely contain a sob of relief. Once most of the men had moved toward the door, she checked herself over, heartened to discover she was still invisible.

All the same she emerged from under the table like a meadow-hare poking its nose out of its safe burrow, sniffing the wind for the warning scent of predators. If she could have smelled it, no doubt the air in the meeting room would have been pungent with the heavy musk of aggression.

Clustered in small groups, the men drifted out of the room

until only two remained. Peeping out from her shelter beneath the table, Maura recognized the High Governor by his rich robes. On his head he wore a helm like the ones she had seen all her life on Hanish soldiers. Only his was crafted of silver burnished to a high sheen and studded with gems. The luxurious plume of flaxen hair that flowed from the top was so pale it looked almost white.

The other man was the death-mage Maura had almost run into the night before. In his austere black robe and cowl, he could not have cut a sharper contrast to the High Governor. Yet for all that they looked so different, the two men possessed a similar air of tense, coiled power.

Now they faced each other, trading sharply honed words like blade blows. Neither man appeared ready to retreat from their verbal duel anytime soon, and they were so intent upon one another, Maura risked stealing around them to head for the door.

She had almost reached it, when the High Governor suddenly wheeled away from the death-mage and strode toward her. Maura leaped out of his path just in time, but lost her balance. Though she clamped her lips tight to stifle a cry as she hit the floor, the soft thud of her fall must have betrayed her presence.

The death-mage had been staring after the High Governor, his gaunt features twisted in an expression of icy triumph. Now he strode toward Maura, who froze, certain he must hear the thunderous beat of her heart and the deafening hiss of her breath.

His grim, menacing stare paralysed her. But as she stared into the dark depths of his eyes, unable to look away, Maura glimpsed something she had never expected to find and could not be certain she believed. A shadow of doubt…perhaps even fear.

Then a voice rang out from the door, and the death-mage looked away. The harsh Hanish tongue sounded positively sweet in Maura's ears as she stumbled to her feet and retreated to a corner of the room. After a brief exchange with the military officer who had called to him from the door, the death-mage swept the room with a furtive glance then strode away.

Maura sank back to the floor, trembling so hard she did not trust herself to walk. But this was too dangerously public a place to remain for long. After a few moments, she rallied her shattered nerves and made her way back to the cellar. She needed a little quiet and solitude to compose herself before venturing into the city to look for Delyon.

As she crept through the corridors, trying to remember her way back to their hiding place, the scent of roasting meat and baking bread made her stomach give a pained rumble. Might as well make use of her invisible state, she decided, following the savory aromas to their source in the palace kitchens.

There she had to move with care to keep from bumping into servants bustling to and fro. All the same, she managed to slip a few items under her cloak. Hardly able to think of anything but the food, she wandered down to the cellar and soon located the distant storeroom that she and Delyon had made their hideaway.

Relief and vexation warred in her when she pushed the door open and caught a brief flash of greenfire before it flickered out.

"Delyon?" Maura pulled the door shut behind her and released her first easy breath in hours. "Thank the Giver you're safe! What possessed you to go off like that without telling me? I was beside myself with worry!"

"I'm a grown man," he snapped, "not a child! I can take care of myself."

He was still alive and he had found his way back here. Perhaps Delyon had a point.

"Your pardon." She shuffled toward the sound of his voice. "I did not mean to belittle you. But in such a dangerous situation we must work together. The Giver knows, we have no other allies we can count on."

He made a vague sound of agreement. "I fretted when I returned and found you gone. I did not mean to alarm you with my going, I swear. I thought I would be back before you woke."

After an instant's hesitation, he added, "And I was afraid you would forbid me going if I asked you."

"So I might." Maura sank to the floor beside him. "Can we make a bargain? From now on, we will work as a team and stay together as much as possible?"

"A bargain," Delyon agreed. "By the way, you were right about the engravers—they had stacks of those signs. I could have poked about the place all day if they hadn't been so busy."

"I hope you found something useful." Maura took out the food she'd pilfered and shared it with him.

"Several things." Delyon spoke in an eager tone between bites of food. "I can hardly wait until the kingdom is free again and I am able to go back to my studies. I believe an understanding of Hanish may be the key to deciphering even more ancient texts. Who knows what lost wisdom I may rediscover there?"

His words nudged Maura's memory. "What I meant was, I hope you found something to help you read this scroll. It is more vital than ever that we find the Staff of Velorken and get it to Rath."

She told Delyon of the Hanish plans she'd overheard.

"I had better get back to work then." He chanted the green-fire spell and a flush of pale light began to radiate from the twig in his hand.

Her hunger appeased, Maura curled up behind a musty pile of rolled tapestries and slept for a while. That night she and Delyon searched the palace without success, and again the next night. As each hour passed, her frustration and desperation grew. If her ancestress Abrielle had bequeathed her this memory, it was deeply buried indeed, for she did not feel the slightest flicker of recognition.

Blood pulsed hard and fast through Rath's veins as his army marched along the mountain trail toward the last of the Blood Moon mines. All the misgivings that had plagued him of late fell away when he remembered the men they had delivered from those pits of death. Just one more and they could turn their backs on these stark, treacherous mountains to free the eastlands that were the most familiar and dear to him of all parts of the kingdom.

Suddenly he heard the soft, lethal hiss of arrows.

One slammed against his breastplate, bouncing off the magically hardened leather. The sharp pain of its impact made him cry out, even as he heard someone cry, "Ambush!"

Rath pulled hard on the reins of his horse and bent low over its neck, preparing to dismount. In an ambush, his oversize frame made a tempting and easy target for archers.

Before he could scramble down from his saddle, the horse let out a shrill whinny of pain and reared, its great hooves plowing the air. Rath barely managed to keep his seat. He struggled to curb the powerful beast beneath him. If it continued to rear out of control or if it bolted on this narrow mountain track, he could end up plunging over a cliff.

"Take cover!" he bellowed to his troops, for once glad of his enchanted voice. "Return fire!"

As soon as he could safely dismount, he would send a party higher up the mountain to sweep around and outflank their attackers. But would he get the chance? More arrows glanced off his armor, and he could see a number bristling from his mount. The poor beast continued to rear and plunge.

Hearing the ominous sound of rocks tumbling down the sheer cliff, he resisted the urge to glance back and see how close they had strayed to the edge.

A man ran toward him, carrying a cloak or blanket. Idrygon?

"Stay back!" cried Rath.

One strike from the horse's enormous hooves and the rebel forces could lose the man whose vision and daring had carried them further than Rath had ever believed possible.

Idrygon did not heed the order. Dodging one flailing hoof, he threw the cloak out like a fisherman casting a net. As it settled over the horse's head, Rath fumbled his reins to grab one end and hold it in place.

All the furious power of the great beast seemed to subside at once, and it collapsed beneath him. Rath jumped clear and rolled, cursing as another Hanish arrow glanced off his helm. He managed to find shelter behind a bit of rock. An instant later, Idrygon joined him.

"How did you bring my horse down?" Rath gasped for breath. "You could have been killed."

Idrygon leaned back against the rock, his chest heaving. "Better me than you. I was afraid the horse would bolt off the cliff with you. So I sprinkled my cloak with dreamweed. The beast should sleep for hours. If the Han think it's dead, they may stop firing at it."

"My thanks." Rath repented every ill opinion he'd ever had of Idrygon.

He peered around the outcropping, at the nasty sheltered ledge from which the Han were raking the road with arrows. "I must lead a party around behind them, or find a higher spot where our archers can fire down upon *them*."

Idrygon shook his head. "They would see what you were up to in no time. Let me take the flanking party. It is clear you are their target. Stay here and give them a mark to draw their eyes away from us while we get into position."

Though it went against Rath's nature, he knew the plan made sense. He was about to give in, when he noticed a tear in the sleeve of Idrygon's armor. Blood was leaking from it.

"You're hurt!"

"So I am." Idrygon glanced down at his arm. "Not badly, though. Get some linen from my sash and bind it for me."

As Hanish arrows whizzed over their heads, Rath stuffed a small wad of linen through the breach in Idrygon's armor, then bound a long strip tightly over it. "We'll make a better job of it later. For now, you rest here. I will go find one of your captains to lead the flanking party."

"No." Idrygon pulled a leaf from his sash and stuffed it in his mouth. "I may be no good with a bow or sword, but my wits are sound enough. Besides, I'll be safer going behind the enemy's back than down here under their fire."

"Go then. But be careful. We cannot afford to lose you."

"Do not fret." Idrygon crawled past him, chewing on the leaf. He made a wry face to cover a wince as he put some weight on his wounded arm. "A good challenging battle may be just the thing to loosen my tight bowels."

The insolent words he'd flung at Idrygon that night on the deck of the *Phantom* came back to shame Rath.

"Make some kind of diversion, will you?" Idrygon bid him. "So I can get out of here without being stuck with a hundred arrows?"

"Very well." Rath pried off his helm. Sticking it on the point of his sword, he raised it over the rock. "May the Giver go with you."

While a barrage of arrows rained down, Idrygon raised himself to a crouch and sprinted away. Once he had gotten well clear, Rath lowered his helm and began to pry out a few arrows that had managed to stick. Not long afterward, he heard sounds of combat coming from up the mountain.

Unable to stand another moment of being a sitting target, he shoved his helm back on and drew his sword.

"Charge, Umbrians!" He vaulted out from behind the rocks and scrambled up the mountain to engage the enemy.

A brief but intense fight followed as Idrygon, Rath and some of their men routed the Hanish ambush party.

After pausing to reform and treat the wounded, including Rath's horse, they continued their journey. Wary of another ambush, they sent greater numbers of scouts ahead.

But no second ambush came.

"I don't like this," Rath muttered to Idrygon as they marched within sight of the mine.

The place looked deserted. The only sound besides the footfall of his men was the cool, eerie whisper of the wind. The only movement came from a Hanish flag that flew from a pole outside the guards' barracks and a door of the barracks that the wind blew open and shut.

Idrygon looked around then shrugged. "Perhaps that ambush was meant to cover their retreat."

"When have you ever known the Han to retreat?" Rath raised his hand to bring his troops to a halt. "They live for battle and conquest."

Idrygon considered for a moment. "When they are certain of victory perhaps. It has been a long while since they tasted defeat at Umbrian hands. Who knows what they might do."

Rath could not dispute that. "If the Han have gone, then some of the prisoners should have come up—the newest ones at least, who are not yet too fuddled from slag."

"Perhaps the Han have taken refuge below," suggested Idrygon, "and plan another ambush for us when we try to free the miners."

That sounded like something Rath would expect from their enemies.

"Curse this growth potion!" he growled. "I couldn't begin to squeeze down there. But I have an idea how we might repay the Han their nasty surprise with one of our own."

In very short order he had put it into effect.

One party of his warriors crowded around the top shaft, making noises as if they were about to descend. Meanwhile, a second small group, armed with weapons for close fighting and with a supply of dreamweed, was lowered in the huge scuttle used to hoist freshly dug ore up from the depths of the mountains.

Rath waited with those clustered around the mine entrance, listening for sounds of a struggle from below.

At last a voice called up in Umbrian, "Drop the ladder. There are no Han down here."

The other men looked to Rath, a question plain on their features—might this be a trick?

"Lower the ladder," he ordered. "They can only come up one at a time." Only a death-mage would stand a chance against the throng waiting above.

Something about the voice had troubled him vaguely. It had a hollow, lifeless tone when it should have rang with relief. Perhaps the fellow had been spoiling for battle and was disappointed to find no enemies.

A man crawled up the ladder. Rath recognized him as one of Idrygon's Vestan warriors. The young fellow squinted against the light, his gaze roving until it fixed on Rath. He stumbled through the crowd gathered around the mine entrance, which parted to let him pass.

"Highness." He bowed before Rath.

"Aye, what did you find down there?" He didn't like the slack, dazed look on the young fellow's face.

"Death, Highness. Blood. Can you not smell it from up here?"

"Whose death?" Had the miners somehow caught word that a liberating army was closing in and risen up against their captors? "Whose blood?"

"Our countrymen, Highness." The young soldier raised his hand to his mouth and bolted a short distance.

In the heavy hush that clamped down over the pithead, every hollow, agonizing retch slammed home the truth with sharper force than words could have.

That ambush had not only bought the Han time to retreat, but time to rob Rath's army of their victory.

"Go below and fetch them up," he heard himself order. "I do not want a single body left below. And bring water for the passing ritual."

They could do nothing more for those men now. Having failed to free them in life, he and his men must free them in death.

* * *

"May the Giver grant you understanding, Delyon." Maura tried to make the words sound like a casual parting pleasantry rather than the desperate plea they were.

After a week spent fruitlessly combing the palace, she tried to pretend the hollow feeling in the depths of her belly was hunger.

"I'll go fetch us something to eat," she said. "Then I'll have another look around the women's chambers to see if anything there nudges my memory."

Hard as she tried to sound optimistic, the effort failed.

Delyon did not seem to notice, though. Hunched over his scroll by the soft glow of a greenfire twig, he squinted at the strange symbols with rapt concentration.

"Go with care," he muttered, more from habit than from true concern.

Maura heeded his warning just the same. It would be seductively easy to let down her guard now that they'd been here awhile and she was becoming familiar with the palace. She'd begun to recognize some of the palace night guards and took care to avoid the most vigilant. But she must not let herself be lulled by this deceptive sense of routine. Her task had not become less dangerous just because she'd grown used to it.

The sound of women's voices greeted her when she slipped through the wide arched entry into the kitchen. Had she misguessed the time, or were the scullery maids about their work later than usual? For a moment she hung back, wondering if she had better save her nightly foraging until later.

No, she decided at last. She did not want to interrupt her night's work once she started. Nor was she anxious to risk the kitchen's early-morning bustle when her invisibility spell would be wearing off and her reflexes dulled by fatigue. She crept toward the larder, grateful for the rattle of cutlery and the soft babble of voices to cover the pad of her footsteps.

The women were talking so rapidly in Comtung that at first

Maura was able to let it wash over her without understanding. Then a stray word caught her by the ear and made her freeze.

Nadgifo. Mountains.

Maura strained to pick up more.

"Best they do it now before the snows come."

The other two women made noises of agreement that were much the same in any language.

Then one lowered her voice. "Why do you reckon such a great army has marched eastaway if all that talk of the Waiting King is lies?"

"Hush, Yora!" The woman who spoke sounded older than the other two. "None of our business, is it? All's I know is there'll be less work 'round here with so many of the officers gone."

"Wish they'd taken the death-mages with them," said the one called Yora in a loud whisper. "Gives me the shivers having so many of them stalking about the palace lately."

A loud jangle of loose metal hitting the floor made Maura jump.

"Mind your tongue, young fool!" the older woman snapped. "If you fancy keeping it!"

Perhaps to divert the others, the third woman chuckled. "I reckon it's worth cleaning up after this leave-taking feast to have so many gone. I'm just glad I don't have to trek over Pronel's Pass to keep all those warriors fed on their march."

"How long do you reckon they'll be gone?" Yora did not sound chastened by the scolding she'd received.

"Not near as long as I'd like," muttered the older woman, just loud enough for Maura to catch.

The other two scullery wenches responded with laughter that held a sharp note of bitterness.

"Enough now," ordered the older woman at last, "before one of the guards wanders by and hears us."

She began gossiping about some people whose names meant nothing to Maura—her family, perhaps, or some of the other palace servants. Under cover of the women's chatter, Maura stole into the larder and foraged some of the food left from the feast.

Her mind was only half on the task, if that. She hurried back to the cellar.

"Our time has run out, Delyon!" The words that had been boiling inside her gushed out. She thrust the bag of food toward him, too anxious to think of eating, herself. "The army is on the move. That must mean the troops from Dun Derhan have reached the Dawn Coast, or soon will."

As he glanced in the direction of her voice, Delyon did not look as though her news alarmed him. "That may be, but—"

"But? There is no *but*. We have not found the staff—I have not felt the faintest flicker of a memory, though the Giver knows I have tried. Someone must get to Rath and your brother to warn them of the trap the Han mean to spring on them. We cannot afford to tarry here any longer! We must leave tonight if we are to have any hope of crossing the mountains ahead of the army!"

"So we shall!" Delyon shook his scroll toward Maura and almost hit her on the nose with it. "Bearing the Staff of Velorken, just as we planned." He began to chuckle and could not seem to stop himself. "I cracked it, Maura! This cursed, blessed writing. I know what it means, every word. Just as I thought, it is a spell for delving deep into the memory."

His eagerness buoyed her spirits, but it could not banish all her doubts. "Knowing the spell is one thing. Do we have the ingredients we will need to cast it?"

So potent a spell might require some rare herb—perhaps one that had grown in Abrielle's time but had since disappeared.

"We have plenty of everything we will need." Delyon's grin broadened and his voice fairly crackled with excitement. "Summerslip, madfern, dreamweed and queensbalm. The only thing wanting is a bit of hot water for the infusion."

"That will be easy enough to get." Maura told him about the kitchen wenches she'd spied washing dishes in the scullery. Then the significance of his words jarred her. "But you cannot mean to mix madfern with summerslip and dreamweed. That was one of the first lessons in vitcraft Langbard taught me. Such a brew might put me to sleep, but I would never wake up again!"

"Are you certain?" asked Delyon. "Have you ever tried it?"

"Are you daft? Why would I try anything so dangerous?"

Delyon shrugged. "If you have never seen with your own eyes, how can you be sure it is true?"

"Because Langbard told me. As would any life-mage of skill and wit."

"And how did *they* know?" Delyon did not appear swayed by her protests. "Because a teacher they trusted told them, no doubt. How better to guard a spell of such power than to declare it a danger?"

Could it have happened like that? Maura had to admit she'd never seen such a spell used on anyone. And yet…

"Am I to believe you and that scroll over the man who raised and trained me? What if you erred in your translation? What if it calls for laceweed instead of dreamweed? You are asking me to put my life at risk, Delyon."

Her words took him aback, but only for a moment. "Your life has been at risk from the moment we sailed for the mainland. And even before that, when you went looking for the Waiting King. To find the Staff of Velorken will insure us victory. If I could take your place, I would, gladly."

The greenfire twig he clutched in his fingers had grown dimmer and dimmer while they talked. Now it flickered out as Maura could picture her life doing. True, she had ventured into danger before, risking her life for the liberty of her people. If she could be certain this spell would yield the prize they sought, she would risk it again.

"What if you are mistaken, Delyon? What if my mind holds no buried memory passed down from my ancestress? What if the Staff of Velorken *is* only a legend?"

Delyon's voice drifted out of the darkness. "A legend like the

Waiting King? You must have had your doubts about him, yet you went ahead. And the legend proved true."

In its way. Rath had not turned out to be the powerful, mystical warrior she'd sought and expected. Perhaps the Staff of Velorken would not live up to the myth that had grown around it, either. Which might be for the best, if only they did not need it so desperately.

"That was different. I had no choice."

Delyon's reply might not have swayed her, except that it echoed the one from her own heart. "What choice have you now?"

Night held the foothills of the Blood Moon Mountains in its black fist. But its grip was beginning to ease. In another hour or so, a faint blush would creep into the distant eastern horizon and a bright new day would dawn.

Until then, it was safe for Rath and Idrygon to stand on the crest of a humpbacked hill and stare down at a small cluster of lights that was the town of Prum.

"They should be back by now," muttered Rath.

Shortly after sunset he had sent a handful of men familiar with the place down to find out if the Han still held it. It did not take an expert tracker to tell that the guards from the last mine had marched this way after they fled their posts.

Idrygon stamped his feet and chafed his arms. Autumn would soon come to the Southmark steppes and the nights were getting colder, especially to a man brought up in the mild climate of the Vestan Islands. "I still say it was a waste of time sending those men down last night. Attack before dawn—that strategy served us well in Duskport and all those little villages in the Hitherland."

"Prum is a good deal bigger than those villages." Rath cupped his hands around his mouth and let out a moist breath to warm them. "And it has a large garrison, perhaps bolstered by those guards from the mine. I do not want us blundering in there blind, or a lot of innocent townsfolk might be killed in the battle."

"Perhaps so." Idrygon did not sound as if the worry would keep him awake nights.

From a little way off came the sound of a scuffle. A number of darker shadows loomed out of the night. "We think this is the man you sent us after, Highness. We had a bit of trouble tracking him down."

"Boyd Tanner?" asked Rath.

"Might be," came the sullen answer in a voice he recognized. "What is all this hauling a law-abiding man out of his bed in the middle of the night?"

"Were you not told who summoned you and why?"

"Claimed they were taking me to see the Waiting King. Is that you, then?"

"It is." Rath tried to sound certain. "We need you to tell us how things stand with the Han in Prum."

"Are they still in control of the town?" asked Idrygon. "How many are there? Any death-mages? What are their defenses like? Can we count on any help from the townsfolk? Well? Give us some answers, man!"

"How do I know you are who you claim to be?" demanded the tanner. "What if you are Echtroi trying to test my loyalty?"

"You do not need to tell me where your loyalty lies, Master Tanner." Rath reached into the darkness and brought his hand to rest on the man's shoulder. "And if we were the Echtroi, do you reckon we would waste our time with tricks when we could wave a wand and make you beg to tell us everything you know?"

"Never know what they might do," muttered the tanner. "I fancy I've heard your voice before, but I cannot place where from."

"We do not have time for games," snapped Idrygon. "If this

fellow will not tell us what he knows, forget him. We must make ready."

Rath ignored Idrygon. "You would recollect if you had met me before, good man." He lifted his hand from the tanner's shoulder. "You did give aid to friends of mine some months ago."

"Eh?"

"The night they rescued Gristle Maldwin from the death-mage. Tell me, is she as ill-tempered an old shrew as ever?"

Boyd Tanner chuckled. "Oh, she has her days, but she's not…"

The significance of Rath's question must have struck him, for he gasped. "Highness! Are you truly King Elzaban, at last?"

When Rath hesitated to answer to that name, Idrygon spared him the need. "Of course it is King Elzaban! Have you paid no heed to anything we've said?"

"There was rumors, o'course." The man's voice had a hollow, dazed sound. "But I've heard enough of those in my life not to heed every one that gets whispered about."

"These ones are true," said Rath. "Now will you tell us what we need to know? It is urgent. Do the Han still hold Prum? What are their numbers?"

"They hold the town tighter than ever since that new lot marched in. Some folks said they were mine guards chased down from the mountains by the Waiting King. But I reckoned the garrison commander must have sent for them to help keep order during the cattle fair. After the commotion at last year's."

"The cattle fair?" cried Rath. Of course. It was that time of year.

"Aye," said the tanner. "There's herds coming from all over the steppes, and more buyers arriving every day from the Long Vale."

Pitch a battle in among all that, thought Rath, and you had a recipe for slaughter.

Were the Han counting on that? Did they mean to hold an entire town hostage?

"What are your orders, Highness?" asked Idrygon. "Shall we make the attack as planned?"

The upland breeze whispered in Rath's ear. He fancied it carried Maura's distant voice. *Your wits are sharper than your blade, aira. Use them!*

Could there be a way to turn this situation against the Han?

"Well, sire?" Idrygon prompted him when he did not reply right away.

"Let us delay our attack a while." Rath stroked his stubbled chin as he stared down toward the sleeping town. "I reckon there may be an easier way to take Prum."

"Sire?"

More like an outlaw than a king, Rath rubbed his hands together and chuckled to himself. "Good pickings at cattle fairs."

"There." Delyon held out the mug to Maura. Tiny wisps of steam rose from the water she'd smuggled down from the palace kitchens. "I have put in the right quantities of herbs. Once you drink it, we must chant the spell together."

"If I can stay awake long enough." Maura cast a wary glance at the mug as she forced her hands to close around it. "I hope it will not taint the potion to be compounded in a cup made of metal."

"Does the substance truly matter, do you suppose?" Delyon looked thoughtful. "Or is the use we make of that substance? A blade of iron or an arrow of tempered wood will do just as much harm. A goblet of ivory or one of metal are equally useful. Many herbs can heal, but some can poison."

That last word made Maura's throat tighten. What if this potion did as Langbard had warned her and she slipped into a sleep from which she would never waken?

"Promise me, if this goes wrong you will do the ritual of passing, then make haste to warn Rath and your brother."

"Nothing will go wrong!" Delyon flashed an indignant glare in her direction, though she was still invisible. "Show a little confidence in me for once, if you please. I may not be the leader my brother is, but I am a skilled scholar. Now drink the potion before it goes cold!"

Winging a silent plea for the Giver to preserve her, Maura raised the cup to her lips and drained it. If she sipped slowly, sleep would surely overcome her before she had time to chant the spell.

"There." She set down the cup. "Now, quickly, tell me the words."

His handsome countenance alight with satisfaction, Delyon lifted the scroll in one hand and the glowing greenfire twig in the other. Then he spoke a word or two in a language that sounded both foreign and vaguely familiar.

"Repeat after me," he prompted Maura.

She chanted the strange words after him. Already the storeroom and Delyon looked farther away than they had an instant ago, as if she were retreating from them.

Time seemed to slow and thicken around her, like sap over a moonmoth that lingered too long on the trunk of a hillpine. While she still had control of her voice, she fixed her dwindling concentration on the vital task of echoing Delyon's words.

"Well done!" he cried after what seemed like hours of the most difficult mental effort Maura had ever undertaken. His voice sounded distant, muffled and very slow. "I pray you will find what you seek within yourself."

Was she still sitting up? Maura wondered. Or had she crumpled to the floor? She could not feel her body, at least not in the way she was accustomed to. It was as if the spell had loosened the connection between her spirit and her physical form. Now her body seemed like a large empty shell over which she had no control. Was it taking in air? Was her heart beating?

At least her ears still worked, after a fashion.

Delyon's voice reached her, echoing down a long tunnel that seemed to be growing longer and narrower with every word. "I hope you can hear me, Maura. I am holding you, but your body seems frozen."

The faint quaver of doubt in his voice chilled her.

"Sink down into the depths of your memories," Delyon's distant voice urged her. "See what you can find there."

Poised between battling the potent forces that gripped her or surrendering to them, Maura sensed she must free herself from the reassuring ties of consciousness if she ever hoped to find the answers she sought. Releasing her fierce hold on her last link with the outer world, she plunged into a swirling, rushing darkness that shimmered around her.

Color engulfed her in a thousand hues, each luminous strand flickering to the strange music of a thousand melodies that wove themselves into a soft, warm blanket of fragrant, delicious harmony. For a time, Maura forgot her mission, and almost everything else, as she reveled in this sweet, fluid mingling of pure sensation.

Then she found herself thinking how perfect this endless moment would be if only Rath were here to share it with her. The only other time she had experienced anything remotely like this had been at the pinnacle of their lovemaking.

All at once, she could picture Rath with an aching clarity far sharper than memory. His warm, wry chuckle caressed her as his whisker-stubbled cheek rasped against her face, redolent with the familiar scent of smoke and leather. When he turned his dark gaze upon her, it glowed with long-denied love and hard-won trust. Maura subsided into the haven of his embrace with a mute sigh of bliss.

"Remember what you came here to do," he whispered. "What only you *can* do."

This was not the real Rath, Maura reminded herself, pleasant as it would be to tarry here and pretend it was. Reluctantly she let go of him and slipped deeper into…wherever she was.

Sorsha appeared—merry-eyed and bursting with innocent gossip from the village. Then Langbard strode out of their cottage, his blue robe swirling about his feet as the distant aroma of herbs wafted from the preparing room.

"Don't be frightened," said Sorsha. "Think what an adventure this will be! I wish I could come with you."

Maura wished so, too. No feat would be quite as daunting if she had Sorsha's courage and good sense to rely upon.

Langbard cupped her cheek with a worn, loving hand. "Keep searching, but be careful."

Battling the urge to cling to him, Maura wandered on until she found herself in the bedchamber that had once belonged to her. Her mother gazed up at her from the bed, an exquisite face ravaged by illness, exhaustion and heartbreak.

"What a fine young woman you have grown to be," she whispered. "I knew Langbard would not let me down."

Maura longed to stay and ply her mother with all the questions she had hoarded in her heart since childhood. But Dareth Woodbury waved her on. "Another time, my sweet. Now you have work to do. Go with my blessing. But go quickly and do not dally where you have no business."

Before she could ask what that meant, Maura found herself enveloped in a swirl of snow. Just then a slender figure lurched toward her from out of the shadows. The hood fell back to reveal her mother's red-brown hair and haunted gaze. This time she did not seem to recognize Maura.

"Help me, please," she gasped. "I do not deserve to live...but take pity on my child."

With those words she swooned into Maura's arms.

"Langbard!" Maura heard herself call. "Help! Please!"

She kept calling until Langbard appeared, bearing a lantern and looking younger than he had only a moment ago.

"I will see to her." He set down his lantern on top of a shorn tree trunk and hefted Maura's mother into his arms. "Keep going. You have far to travel and not much time."

She watched him leave, wanting to follow, but two long strides carried him out of her view and she found herself peering into a dimly lit cavern. Against the flickering glow of a small fire, a man and woman clung together in an embrace Maura recognized as hungry passion. The sight of it made her long for Rath with fresh urgency.

She tried to draw back, embarrassed to spy upon them in such an intimate moment. The man had his back to her, his head covered by a hood, so she could tell nothing about him except his towering height. But the rich red-brown cascade of the woman's hair drew Maura's gaze even as she tried to look away. The woman seemed to sense her presence, for she stirred from her lover's embrace and cast a furtive glance toward the mouth of the cavern. Her eyes widened and her features contorted in a look of alarm.

Mother? No question it was her. Which must mean the man with his back to Maura...

Before she could move to get a better view of Vaylen, her mother broke from their embrace and dashed toward Maura. "Go! This is not what you are looking for!"

True, it was not what she'd been sent to discover, but it was something she'd been desperately curious about her whole life. Maura tried to peek past her mother for a glimpse of the man as he turned toward her.

"No!" Her mother pushed her backward, sending her tumbling deeper into the well of her memories.

More and more swiftly the scenes shifted as she visited events in the lives of her foremothers. It felt like what she had experienced during the ritual of passing with Langbard, only faster and more intense.

Knowledge that had slumbered unsuspected within her suddenly woke to life. Maura struggled to make a place for it all. Bits of spells and lore Langbard had never taught her now became hers to call upon.

She would like to have taken the time to absorb it more slowly, but some powerful force beyond her control drew her deeper.

"So, one has come at last." With those muffled, echoing words, a richly robed woman held her hand out to Maura.

She wore the carved ivory circlet Maura recalled from her crowning ceremony over a tumble of thick dark curls. "Abrielle?"

The woman nodded. Her features were not those of a great beauty, but of a strong ruler who had learned courage and wisdom from the harsh lessons of adversity.

"Come, daughter. You have not much time." She beckoned Maura to follow her. "And the need must be great if you have risked this search to find me."

Maura followed the long-dead queen through archways and chambers of a castle she had never seen before, but which looked hauntingly familiar. They descended a steep staircase and made their way down one long, dim hallway, then another. At length, Abrielle opened a hidden door and led Maura through a narrow passage to a cavernous room full of tall straight columns. Or was it a grove of towering trees?

Suddenly, the Staff of Velorken appeared before her. It looked as tall as a man, its shaft of tawny wood carved with ancient symbols like those on Delyon's scroll. The top of the staff had been carved from ivory, now yellowed with age. The head of a sunhawk had been crafted with such skill Maura half expected its glittering golden eyes to blink and its beak to open with a shrill, piercing cry.

Abrielle held the staff out to Maura. "Make certain it is wielded with care, my daughter. Wishes can be powerful and dangerous things."

As she reached toward the staff, Maura felt herself borne away, over miles and years and through lives. She heard a voice calling her name.

"Can you hear me, Maura?" Each word grew louder, closer, more distinct. And more anxious. "Have you found anything yet? Maura? Perhaps you had better come back…if you can."

The packed dirt of the floor felt hard and cool beneath her, and the beat of her heart, faint but steady. She sucked in a deep breath of the cellar's musty air. Her eyelids fluttered and she glimpsed Delyon's face, his features clenched with alarm.

She whispered his name.

"Thank the Giver!" Delyon expelled a deep sigh. "You were

so still for so long, I feared you might be… Was it as I said? Did you uncover those buried memories? Did you find out where the staff is hidden?"

"I…think so." It took a great focus of will to make her mouth form the words. "I saw it. Deep under…the castle. In a grove of…tall trees."

All the newly wakened memories swirled in Maura's mind, hampering the proper movement of her thoughts. Her head felt as if it might burst to contain all the new knowledge that flooded her thoughts—the way the melting snow of spring made the waters of the Windle swell and churn.

"Under?" repeated Delyon. "Are you certain? We have scoured the lower levels of the palace for days now. And what did you mean about tall trees? There are no trees under the ground."

Maura lurched to her feet, not certain what made her rise or where she intended to go. "I recognized the place…parts of it. At least I thought I did."

Perhaps if she went out now, while what she'd seen was still fresh in her thoughts, she could find it. She shuffled toward the door and pulled it open. Wandering out into the dim passageway, she searched for anything she had glimpsed in her memory-vision of Queen Abrielle. In a daze she turned this way and that, paying no mind to her direction. Behind her she heard Delyon calling her name in a frantic whisper, but she did not answer.

Meaning to turn, she stumbled into a shallow alcove off one of the passages. As she paused a moment, trying to recover her bearings, a sliver of light caught her eye. It shone through the corner of one sidewall.

Maura reached toward it. But when her hand made contact with the stubbled stone of the wall, it met only the slightest resistance. She pushed. The chink of light widened. Where had she seen a false sidewall like this before? In her vision? Perhaps…

She pushed harder and the false wall swung inward on quiet hinges to reveal a steep stairway. Though they did not look like the stairs down which Abrielle had led her, Maura followed them just the same. Any hidden passage must lead somewhere important.

Hemmed by solid stone walls on each side, the steps led deep into the bowels of the earth beneath the palace. At intervals, small hollows held clear crystals that glowed just brightly enough to light her way. After making two sharp turns, the stairs ended in a chamber that looked to have been hewn out of solid rock.

A giant crystal, which might have been the parent to the ones that lit the stairs, rose from the middle of the floor. Like them, it gave off a pale glow, but not a steady one. Rather it pulsed in an irregular rhythm. A man stood with his back to her, his hands pressed against two facets of the crystal. He wore the black robe and hood of the Echtroi.

Maura's daze had lifted enough that she knew how dangerous it would be to linger here. Stifling a gasp of dismay, she turned to flee. At least she *tried* to.

Something forced her gaze to linger on the death-mage. A wrenching sense of familiarity haunted her and she could not think why. In the past months she had seen more of his ilk than she would have wanted to in a lifetime. In those dark robes, hoods and masks, one looked much like another. Why did she sense a particular connection with this one?

It did not matter. She must get away. The Staff of Velorken was not here. Not in this chamber. Not anywhere in this palace. The certainty of it jolted Maura.

Then a hand settled on her shoulder.

She screamed and ran from whatever had crept up behind her.

A shudder went through the death-mage and his hands parted from the crystal as if they had been pushed away. He spun about and his gaze locked on her.

He could see her! Maura did not need to glance down at herself to know the invisibility spell must be fading, exposing the first ghostly view of her to enemy eyes.

Even as she fumbled to reach the pocket of her sash that held the last of her *genow* scales, Maura feared it would do no good.

She was trapped in this small space with someone who had seen her. If he set his mind to catch her, she would not be able to evade him for long. Especially if he called for aid.

But the death-mage did not.

Instead, the gaunt features visible below his mask contorted in a look that might have been fear.

"Dareth?" The word retched out of him as he took a stumbling step toward Maura. "Why do you haunt me?"

17

Which staggered her more? Hearing her mother's name from the mouth of a death-mage...or realizing that he had spoken in Hanish, yet she could understand his words?

Marshaling her wits from the shock, Maura pulled a tiny pinch of powered scale from her sash and concentrated on re-calling the incantation. If the death-mage tried to capture her, she would not make it easy for him.

She knew the instant she disappeared again. Not because she felt any different, but by the way the death-mage staggered back, his pale eyes widened with alarm that even his sinister cowl could not disguise. Just to be certain, she took a step to the side. But his gaze did not waver from the spot where she'd been standing before.

His hands began to tremble and he sank to his knees. "I am not going mad. I am *not* going mad!"

He seemed to cling to those words, as if they were a slippery rope suspended high above Raynor's Rift.

But how could she understand them, Maura wondered, when he had spoken in Hanish? Did she truly grasp his meaning or was *her* mind playing tricks on her? One thing she knew without doubt, though it puzzled her as much as any uncertainty—the death-mage had called her by her mother's name. Why?

Her deeply ingrained sense of caution told her to fly while she had the chance. Remembering the hand she'd felt on her shoulder, she glanced toward the stairs with fresh alarm. But no one was there. Had she only imagined it?

With no obvious threat, curiosity got the better of her wariness.

"What is Dareth to you?" she whispered, amazed and mildly disgusted to hear her words come out in Hanish. "What did you do to her that she should haunt you?"

Killed the father of her child? Tortured him to death before her eyes? Broken her spirit and her will?

When the death-mage lifted his head to gaze in the direction of her voice, Maura moved again—nearer the stairs this time, in case she needed to make a fast escape.

"What did *I* do to *her*?" The death-mage staggered to his feet. "Ask what she did to *me*. Bewitched me, then betrayed me!"

Betrayed? Maura shook her head. Perhaps she did not understand Hanish after all.

"Fool that I was to be taken in by her lowling wiles." His gaze swept the room. "I *am* going mad. First seeing Dareth, now hearing voices. Worse yet, answering their cursed questions!"

He turned and fled up the stairs as if chased by something more terrifying than Maura could imagine. Half against her will, she followed. The death-mage's answer had not satisfied her curiosity—only roused it more. With the image of her mother so fresh in her mind from her vision, she could not let it go until she had found out more…somehow.

Halfway up the stairs she slammed into something solid and warm. Before she could cry out, Delyon's voice calmed her, though he sounded anything but calm himself. "We must stop the Echtroi before he tells anyone what he saw! I tried, just now, but he pushed me away. You go back and fetch the staff. I will follow him."

"There is no staff here." Maura shook off Delyon's hand and continued up the stairs. "Not in this chamber. Not in the whole palace. I doubt the death-mage will tell anyone what he saw. He thinks he's going mad."

"How do you know?" Delyon's voice followed her. "What did you say to him? I thought you could not speak Hanish."

"I couldn't until you put me in that trance."

At the top of the steps, the false wall hung agape. At the end of the cellar passage, Maura spotted the death-mage scrambling up from his knees. He must have tripped and fallen in his haste.

"If the staff is not here," whispered Delyon behind her, "then where is it?"

"I think I know," Maura called as she raced down the passage. "Go back to the storeroom. I will join you shortly and explain everything. But there is something I must do first."

Hitching up her skirts, she sprinted after the death-mage. Perhaps he heard her footsteps behind him, for he kept turning to glance back.

On he ran and Maura followed, gradually gaining ground. When a young night guard issued a challenge and barred the death-mage's way, she almost barreled into them both, but managed to curb her headlong rush at the last moment.

"Out of my way, fool!" barked the death-mage. "I…have urgent news for the High Governor."

"Your pardon, great one—" the guard stepped aside "—but the High Governor's quarters are that way." He pointed in the opposite direction.

As Maura caught her breath, trying to be quiet about it, she marveled at being able to comprehend the two men's exchange in Hanish. Their tones and gestures matched so perfectly with what she supposed they were saying, she could no longer doubt her sudden baffling ability.

Casting a glance behind him, the death-mage collected his icy composure. "I would not dream of rousing His Excellency at this hour."

"But you said it was urgent..."

"Urgent for me to prepare the report I will deliver as soon as he rises." Fixing the young soldier with a glare, the death-mage stalked off down the gallery with long, hurried strides.

Where was he headed? Somewhere to prepare a report, he'd told the guard. But Maura had become familiar enough with the palace to know this way led to the women's quarters.

She raced after him, catching up just as he halted before one of the doors and began hammering upon it with his fist. "Mother. Let me in. Hurry!"

Did death-mages have mothers? Though Maura knew they must, the notion taxed her imagination.

After a moment, she heard the sound of a lock turning and the door swung inward. She managed to slip in on the death-mage's heels before it was closed again by an old woman wrapped in a fine robe, her thinning white hair pulled back in a tight braid.

She scowled at the death-mage and spoke in a tone so sharp Maura doubted any other Han but the High Governor would dare use it to a member of the feared Echtroi. "What brings you here at this hour, pounding on my door? Are you being sent over the mountains? A good thing it would be. We do not want one of your rivals to steal all the credit for crushing this rebellion."

The death-mage shook his head. "That is the least of our worries. My mind is beginning to break. Soon I will be a babbling simpleton!"

He sank onto an ornately wrought chair. His shoulders slumped and his pale hands began to tremble.

"That cannot be!" With stiff movements, the old woman dropped to her knees beside him and clutched one of his hands tightly in both of hers. "You are young still, and you have always been strong-minded, even as a child."

The death-mage refused to take heart. "Remember Tharled.

He was younger than I when he became a raving madman and had to be locked away!"

"Tharled was always too high-strung for his own good." The woman's sharp features twisted into a sneer. "He should never have been allowed to join the order, let alone rise so high so fast. But he had the House of Zardisvon behind him—the scavengers! There have been others like Tharled who lacked the strength to control the power they wield. But I have known many who kept their wits to a great age and died at the height of their powers."

Huddled in a shadowed corner, Maura listened with a sense of grim justice. So death-mages did not escape unscathed from the pain and terror they inflicted. Even the ones who did not go mad lived in fear that they might. Now she understood why her sudden appearance and disappearance had struck terror into this one.

For a moment the old woman's hand hovered above her son's shoulder, as if she wanted to offer comfort but did not know how.

Instead, she struggled up from the floor and took a seat opposite him, speaking in a brisk tone. "You seem to have all your wits about you now. Perhaps you only dreamed whatever has unnerved you."

The death-mage's head snapped up. "What *is* madness but dreaming when I am awake? I saw her, I tell you! Dareth—down in the low chamber."

Maura watched the old woman stiffen and stare at the mention of her mother's name. "Perhaps she is here. One of your rivals might have found the little wretch and brought her here to discredit you at a crucial moment."

How could her mother discredit him? Maura wondered. Because she had escaped from him all those years ago?

"You do not understand." The death-mage rose from his chair and began to pace behind his mother's. "Dareth did not enter the chamber…or leave it. She just…appeared. But I could see through her like a reflection in a window. She did not look to have aged a day since I saw her last. And when I called her name, she disappeared again and a voice asked what I had done to her that she should haunt me."

With each word he became more agitated. "What *I* did to *her*? Protected her. Hid her."

His voice broke, but not before Maura heard him keen the impossible words, "Loved her!"

She jammed her hands over her ears, but it was too late. Like one small stone rolling down from a mountaintop to cause an avalanche, the death-mage's admission triggered a hail of memories in Maura's mind.

She recalled something Langbard had said before going on to tell her that she was the Destined Queen. The shock of his revelation had chased it from her mind. Now it came back to her.

When she'd asked about the identity of her father, Langbard said her mother had kept that secret from him, even during her passing ritual. Just as she had kept Maura from seeing the face of her lover during her memory vision. Why keep such a secret unless it was a source of regret and shame?

Maura's skin crawled and her gorge rose. She wanted to weep or vomit or smash something, but she dared not do any of those things.

The Hanish woman—her grandmother?—sprang from her chair with surprising energy for her years and gave the death-mage a hard slap on the cheek. "You were mad *back then*—bewitched! Seeing and hearing things is nothing compared with the folly of what that creature compelled you to do."

That creature? Maura longed to fly at the pair of them and give them a haunting they would never forget!

The old woman gentled her tone. "You came to your senses before and you will not take leave of them now. Go get some sleep and try not to tax your powers for a few days. It will be well. You will see."

This mixture of harshness and concern seemed to work on her son, for he grew calmer. "Perhaps you are right. I have not slept well since that incident at the Beastmount Mine. It may be that all this recent unrest among the Umbrians has stirred up old memories."

As he headed for the door, the pair spoke about matters and people that meant nothing to Maura, even if she had been able to concentrate on what they were saying. But she could not.

The notion that she might have Hanish blood threw her mind and heart into paralysing turmoil. She had feared and loathed the Han for as long as she could remember. Any kinship with them would be like a vile parasite invading her body. How could she be the Destined Queen of Umbria if she were tainted with the blood of their most hated foes?

The death-mage pulled open the door but stood a moment taking leave of his mother. Not able to stand being near either of them for a moment longer, Maura risked slipping past them. Once she reached the corridor, she fled back to the cellar as fast as her legs would carry her.

But that was not swiftly enough to evade a question that dogged her thoughts. Was *this* what Rath had learned about her from the Oracle of Margyle? Had it poisoned his trust in her and his love for her?

He would make the Hanish scum sorry for what they'd done to those miners! Righteous rage seethed within Rath as he stood in the secret room of the tannery and tipped the growth potion to his lips. He would make them sorry they'd ever set foot in his kingdom!

Out on the streets of Prum, everything should be ready. Rath had left it up to Idrygon to execute that part of his plan, and Idrygon had proven himself a master of execution.

For once he swallowed the foul-tasting potion with something like eagerness. Perhaps every wrench of pain it inflicted on him might be one less the townfolk of Prum would have to suffer. He kept reminding himself of that as the spell went to work. The thought helped him bear it better than usual.

The pain was beginning to ebb and his head brushed the

ceiling when someone tapped softly on the hidden door. Rath did not call out in case it might be Hanish soldiers searching the building. With quiet movements he drew his sword and raised it.

The door swung inward on well-oiled hinges.

"Giver's mercy!" The tanner shrank back, clutching his chest when he glimpsed Rath's hulking form.

"Your pardon!" cried Rath. "I feared it might be…"

"Of course, Highness." The tanner mustered his composure and sank into a deep bow. "I came to tell you the time is at hand and all is as you ordered."

"The womenfolk, elders and children are off the streets?"

"Aye, Highness. Word has gone round that some cowherders from the north steppes are spoiling for a fight with those from the south. Folk with any sense will be keeping off the streets. Lots do, anyway, at fair time."

Rath nodded his approval. "Then we had better get a move on. I cannot stand to think of Prum under Hanish rule a moment longer."

"Nor I, sire." Boyd Tanner held the door wide for Rath to lumber through, hunched to keep from hitting his head on the ceiling beams. "Right handsome suit of armor ye got there, if ye don't mind my saying—fine work."

"And yours." Rath had become so used to seeing men in armor, he had not noticed the tanner's sturdy jerkin. "Make it yourself?"

"Aye." The tanner chuckled as they descended the stairs. "I've put on a pound or two around the middle since then, though. It's a mite snug."

Rath chuckled. "Let us hope you will soon be able to hang it up and never worry about wearing it again."

They paused at the bottom of the stairs. "Tell me, Highness, if it ain't too bold for me to ask, what became of the lass who was here with you that night—the one Exilda was looking to come. Did she find what she was looking for?"

"She did," said Rath. "Thanks in part to your help. Now she is off looking for something else in a place even more dangerous. I hope she finds someone as brave as you to aid her this time, if need be."

"I don't know about brave, Highness." The tanner flashed him a weak grin. "It's one thing to do a bit on the sly against the Han, but to come out in the open and take up arms? Right now my guts feel like jelly and my palms are so wet I'll be lucky not to drop my blade."

"You'll do fine, I reckon." Rath laid one massive hand on the man's shoulder. "Beforehand is always the worst. Once the fighting starts, you'll be too busy to fret."

"I hope so." The tanner pushed open the door. "After you, sire."

Rath drew his sword as he charged out to meet his foes.

The sun shone bright and warm as he made his way toward the center of town, but the breeze coming down from the north carried a crisp promise of autumn.

When he caught sight of a cluster of Hanish soldiers, he raised his enchanted voice and bellowed in Comtung, "Filthy, slinking cowards! Vile murderers! Are you afraid to take on a foe who can fight back?"

For an instant the Han stared at him, stunned. Then his insults goaded them to action. With roars of outrage, they raised their weapons and charged toward him through the milling crowd. If they all reached him at once, Rath would be in for the fight of his life.

But they did not all reach him, let alone at once.

The milling throng in the street hardly seemed to take notice of either Rath or the Han. But when the soldiers started toward him, two of them only got a few steps before clumsy feet thrust into their paths, sending them sprawling.

That still left three. Out of the corner of his eye, Rath glimpsed reinforcements coming.

"Folk of Southmark!" he cried, bounding forward to engage the first of his attackers. "Rise up and claim your freedom!"

He had no time to watch and see if his rallying call worked, for he was soon fighting as hard and as desperately as he ever had in his life. Back and forth his blade flew, parrying blows. Once he caught the rhythm, he could keep two enemies busy. The third was a problem that would only grow worse as he tired.

He landed one hit, but it only dented the Han's armor. While his sword arm was raised, he felt a Hanish blade thrust in and strike him below the ribs. His enchanted leather armor stopped the worst of the blow that might have slain him otherwise. But the force of it knocked him off balance and his flesh felt the bite of Blood Moon iron.

Rath might have faltered then, but he heard the Han who had struck him give a bellow of pain as Boyd Tanner cried, "That's one less for you to worry about, sire!"

Someone else leaped in to divert his second attacker. He was down to one now—hardly a fair fight for his foe. Except that he was beginning to feel his wound. The movement of his sword arm slowed and the force of his attack waned. To make matters worse, his opponent was young, strong, swift and fierce. Rath staggered and just barely managed to deflect a powerful blow.

Then, as the two blades caught, Rath felt his gaze drawn to the young Han's helm. There was something odd about it. Only a short stub of flaxen hair rose from it, rather than the usual luxurious plume. Perhaps he had been a fool, letting this whelp live to fight him now. But he didn't feel a fool.

At that moment, the Han recognized something familiar in Rath's relentless glare. His eyes widened and his jaw fell slack. "You!"

"Me." Rath grinned and fresh strength surged through him. He shoved the young Han back and gripped the hilt of his sword harder for a renewed attack. "Don't say I didn't warn you, boy. I showed you mercy once. Do not expect it again."

* * *

"Maura, is that you?" Warm with relief, Delyon's voice wrapped around her as she slipped into their hideout. "Praise the Giver's mercy you're safe!"

Through the darkness, he groped his way toward her and clasped her in an anxious embrace. "I feared so for you after what happened. What *did* happen? I still do not understand."

The revulsion Maura had not dared vent before would no longer be contained. Delyon's show of concern shattered her self-control. She began to tremble as harsh, dry sobs shook her. Her knees gave way, and she would have collapsed to the floor if Delyon had not borne her weight.

"What happened?" He sank down slowly as she clung to him. "Are you hurt?"

"No." It felt like a lie. True, she had come to no bodily harm, but she would rather have suffered the Echtrois' worst torture than endure this torment of heart and mind. Her only crumb of comfort came from the warm arms that held her and the concerned voice that whispered in her ear.

Part of her wished it was Rath who held her, or Langbard. Another part rejoiced that it was not. What would either of them think if they knew? How would it change their feelings toward her? Rath had changed toward her during their last days on Margyle…becoming gruff and suspicious. Small wonder.

Delyon raised one hand to stroke her hair. "If you have come to no harm, then what is wrong?" He tensed. "Have the Han found the Staff of Velorken?"

"No!" Maura gasped, glad to be telling the truth about that at least.

"Thank the Giver!" The tension eased out of Delyon as quickly as it had come. "But what has happened to upset you so? It must be dire, for you have been a tower of strength—even when the Han captured us. I know I have been more burden than aid to you on this quest, but whatever is wrong, I promise I will do anything in my power to help."

"You…already have helped." Maura choked out the words. "More than…you will…ever know."

"About time I made myself useful, isn't it?" Delyon's soft derisive chuckle had a strangely soothing effect. "Come now, tell me what grieves you. Keeping it all inside you will only make it worse—I know."

She had no intention of telling him or anyone else—at least not yet. No doubt there would come a time when she'd have to confess the truth. For now she only wanted to protect her shameful secret as fiercely as her mother had—to death and beyond, if need be. But the shielding cloak of darkness and the protective intimacy of Delyon's touch tempted her to unburden herself.

What if she was wrong? False hope added its seductive whisper to the call. A scholar like Delyon might be able to weigh her evidence with calm reason and reach a less damning conclusion.

"The death-mage—he called me by my mother's name." Caution tried to silence her, but she could not stop once she'd begun. "He knew her."

"You think he might have been one of her captors?" Delyon's arms tightened around her. "Perhaps the one who killed your father?"

Maura began to tremble again. In a hoarse whisper she confessed, "I do not believe Lord Vaylen *was* my father."

"What? But he must have been. I mean…who else?"

Her silence gave Delyon the answer she could not bring herself to speak.

"He…the *death-mage*…?" His tone betrayed the grimace that must be on his face. "You think he…defiled your mother?"

That would be easier to accept by far!

"From what I overheard, I believe she may have…seduced him…to gain her freedom."

"There must be some other explanation."

"If you can think of one, tell me, please," Maura begged him. "For I could abide almost anything better than this."

She told him what she had seen in her vision, as well as what she had learned from her mother's family and from Langbard. The only thing she could not bear to tell about was the secret revelation Rath had received from the Oracle of Margyle.

"I'll admit," said Delyon after a moment's thoughtful silence, "what you say does make sense of an appalling kind."

A weight on her heart that had eased a little now pressed down, heavier than ever, but Maura did not resume her weeping. Repulsive as the whole idea was, some small part of her had already begun to accept it. If it was true, all the denial and tears in the world could not change it now.

Delyon's hand brushed down her cheek to cup her chin, "But even if it is true, that does not change who you are. Your parentage and the manner of your getting does not make you one of them and it never will! It is what you believe and how you put those beliefs into action that make you Umbrian."

It was just the kind of thing Langbard might have said if he'd been there. Maura's eyes misted with fresh tears, but of a different kind. These were healing tears.

"Please, Delyon, do not tell anyone else of this. I know it will have to come out, but I want to break the news in my own way and my own time. When it will do the least damage to our cause."

"As you wish. But none of this will matter if we fail in our quest. You said the staff was not in that secret chamber or anywhere in the palace. How can that be? According to the old writings, Abrielle hid it in the castle, and this is the only castle in…"

"No." The back of Maura's neck rippled with an eerie chill. "There is another. A very old one, scarcely more than a ruin now. In Aldwood. I have been there. That must be why it looked familiar."

Could it have been the nearness of the staff's powerful magic that had sparked her courage when she'd been captured by the bandit lord who now occupied the ancient castle?

"Aldwood?" said Delyon. "Over the mountains, you mean?"

"Yes. Near the eastern shore where a great army from Dun Derhan will be landing soon." If troops from Westborne had been dispatched to the eastlands, it must mean the death-mage had received word that the time was approaching to spring their trap.

She jumped up, grabbing Delyon's arm to pull him to his feet. "Come, we must not tarry here another moment! We have to get over the mountains before the army does, to warn Rath and your brother and to search for the staff."

"Curse me," muttered Delyon. "Why did I not think of another castle? Why did I not ask? If the rebellion fails, the fault will be mine!"

"Nonsense. If we had not come to Venard, we might never have known what the Han are planning." And she might never have discovered the truth about her parentage. Could it have been destiny that had led her and Delyon here?

"Put any doubts out of your mind." That applied to her, she realized, even more than Delyon. "We must not let anything distract us from racing the High Governor's army over the mountains."

It was one of the first lessons she had grudgingly learned from Rath when she'd started out on her quest to find the Waiting King. Now she put it into practice, almost welcoming the urgent, demanding mission that would distract her thoughts from the revelation that had turned her world upside down.

"How can we do that?" Delyon sounded defeated almost before they began. "The Han have a head start on us. They will block the high road through Pronel's Pass and we dare not try to steal through their ranks. I doubt I have enough *genow* scales left to make a meadow mouse disappear."

"There must be other ways through the mountains." Maura shrank from the thought of a bridge like the one over Raynor's Rift. "Paths too narrow for an army, but ample for a pair of wayfarers traveling light and swift. It is past dawn. We must start on our way before the invisibility spell wears off."

Before he could protest, she pulled open the door and tugged him out into the passageway.

They found the palace and the city both astir with a great caravan of supply wagons marshaling on the outskirts to follow the army into the mountains.

"I wonder if they're leaving behind any of the harvest in Westborne?" Maura muttered as she towed Delyon toward a low hill just outside the city. In spite of everything, her spirit lightened to be out in the sunshine and fresh air, with their days of hiding and searching behind them. "This looks a likely spot to take our bearings."

"Take them quick," said Delyon. "You are starting to become visible around the edges. I reckon I will, too, before long."

"That road to the southeast—" Maura pointed toward it "—leads in the direction of the mountains but away from the high road the army is taking. At least we can follow it while we make our way through the fields and woods."

"Lead the way," said Delyon, "and set the pace. I will do my best to keep up with you."

They moved steadily eastward all that day, not even pausing to eat what little food they had left from the High Governor's larder.

As night closed in, Maura fretted the short distance they'd covered. "We need to move faster, or we will never find Rath in time once we reach the Long Vale."

By now they were both fully visible, and there was still light enough for her to see Delyon's rueful shrug. "I cannot walk any faster over this rough ground. Shall we risk taking the road?"

After a moment's thought, Maura gave a grim nod. "We have spied little traffic on it, and I doubt the Han can spare many soldiers to guard the way. I wish I still had some powdered stag hoof to hasten our journey."

They made better speed once they reached the road, though Maura kept glancing behind them when she was not peering ahead into the gathering darkness. She had been traveling in stealth for so long, the prospect of meeting up with anyone on the road fretted her. She would have praised the Giver with a grateful heart to find a patch of hundredflowers by the wayside. But even if they did grow on this side of the mountains, their season was past.

The sun had set and the moon not yet risen in the star-dappled night sky when Delyon suggested they stop and make camp.

Though reeling with fatigue, Maura resisted. "Just a little farther, please? Our only chance to gain ground on the Hanish army is if we start earlier than they each morning and keep going later each night."

"But if we exhaust ourselves now, we may not reach—"

"Shh!" Maura squinted into the darkness. "I think I see lights up ahead. If it is a farm, we might be able to barter some healing for a few supplies. Or at least get directions for the quickest way through the mountains from here."

Her weariness lifted at the prospect of encountering another family like the one she and Rath had met in the south—folks hungry to relearn some of the old customs they had lost under the harsh rule of the Han. The gentle glow spilling from a small window beckoned her with a promise of rest and help.

Then, from out of the darkness ahead, came a sound that banished all such hopeful thoughts from her mind. Loud, vicious barking, the kind made only by...

"Hounds!" Maura grabbed Delyon by the hand and began to run.

I he barking drew closer at a terrifying speed. And the night had grown too dark for Maura to spot any means of escape but one.

"Up this tree, quick!" She scrambled onto the lowest branch, then turned to give Delyon a hand up.

They climbed higher among the boughs as the hounds—at least two by their noise—reached the base of the trunk and set up a blood-chilling racket. Likely they were enraged at being deprived of their sport…for the time, at least.

"That must be…a Hanish guard post," gasped Maura. From the direction of the building, she could see the bobbing light of a torch coming toward them. "I'm going to climb out to the end of this branch to see if there is another tree close enough to reach."

Even as the words left her lips, she knew it was probably futile. The hounds would only follow them from tree to tree until they could go no farther.

"What about a spell?" suggested Delyon. "Dreamweed? Spidersilk?"

"Anything is worth a try." Maura fumbled at the pockets of her sash, though she was not very hopeful. Her spells hadn't worked on those lankwolves in the Waste.

The branch beneath her sagged dangerously. One of the boughs around her might have led to another tree, but in the darkness, she could not tell.

The torchlight came closer and a deep male voice called out in Comtung, "Throw down your weapons, then climb down to be questioned! Be warned—I have an arrow aimed at you and I am a good shot."

"Maura!" Delyon called in Umbrian, just loud enough for her to hear over the baying hounds. "Keep still and stay here. I will give myself up. Now that you know where the staff is, you no longer need me. May the Giver go with you."

Maura opened her mouth to protest, then closed it again. If the Han believed Delyon was alone, she might be left at liberty to rescue him.

"I have no weapon!" Delyon cried out in Comtung. "I am but a weary traveler. I would come down but I fear your dogs will tear me to pieces."

"Songrid!" snapped the man in Hanish. "Chain the hounds!"

A woman's voice called out, "Meat!"

It was clearly a word the beasts understood, for the sound of their barking moved away from the tree as quickly as it had come. The torchlight moved away, too, tempting Maura to try running off in the dark. But sense and caution prevailed. The hounds could be set loose again just as quickly. And next time there might not be a tree handy.

A moment or two later the woman returned with the torch and the Han once again ordered Delyon to climb down, which he did.

"Search him for weapons, Songrid," said the Han.

Through the leaves, Maura saw a tall fair-haired woman approach Delyon. She held the torch in one hand and with the other she patted his chest, waist and legs.

"He is not armed," she announced at last.

Why had she made no mention of his sash? Maura wondered. Then, by the flickering torchlight, she spied it hanging from one of the tree branches. A pang of shame gripped her for every unkind thought she'd ever had about Delyon.

"Anyone else up there?" the Han asked him.

"I am alone."

"Indeed?" said the Han. "Then perhaps I should loose a few arrows into the branches to make certain."

Maura kept still. Surely he was bluffing.

Then she heard the snap of an arrow embedding itself in the tree trunk. Still she would have taken her chances, for it was a big tree and she was perched farther out on a branch than the bowman would expect.

But Delyon cried, "Stop!"

The Han gave a harsh grunt of laughter that his threat had worked.

"Come down, Maura," Delyon called in Umbrian. "We will have to find another way. I cannot risk you being killed."

Cursing under her breath, Maura slid down out of the tree. She did not remove her sash, in the hope that she might be allowed to keep it.

But this Han was more cautious than the one who had taken them prisoner on the way to Venard. He immediately ordered the woman named Songrid to take the sash from Maura before marching her and Delyon back to the guardhouse. Once they entered, he kept his bow trained on them while bidding Songrid tie the prisoners into a pair of heavy chairs near the hearth.

"Now…" He aimed his bow straight at Maura's chest, but his words he aimed at Delyon. "Tell me who you are, where you are bound and why you were trying to sneak past this guard post after dark. And no more lies, or the wench will pay for your deceit."

Delyon gave their names. "We did not mean to sneak by your fine guardhouse," he lied, in spite of the Han's warning. "We would have stopped, but your dogs prevented us."

The Han appeared to waver between suspicion and belief. "Where are you headed and why?"

Maura fancied she could see the sweat pop out on Delyon's brow. He hesitated and his gaze shifted restlessly, as if searching for inspiration to weave a plausible falsehood. If the Han had more than half a wit, he would not believe anything that came out of Delyon's mouth.

So she spoke up. "It is no use lying to the man, Delyon. He looks far too clever to be fooled by any excuse."

The Han pretended to scorn her flattery, but his aim with the bow lowered a bit.

"The truth is," she continued, "we heard the mines had been attacked by the army of the Waiting King and that many of the men who toiled there had been set free. I go in search of my husband. He was taken to the mines not long ago, so I have hope he might still be alive."

She infused the story with all her longing to see Rath again. "We mean no harm to anyone. Let us go, I beg you! I fear he may be wandering in the mountains, hurt and hungry."

"Enough!" The Han appeared to believe her story, even if he had no sympathy with it. "These wild tales about an Umbrian army are nothing but lies to stir up gullible folk like you and cause unrest. If your husband was taken to the mines, that is where he belongs. You had better go back where you came from and turn a deaf ear to treasonous tales from now on."

Might he let them go? Maura did not try to hold back her tears of relief, but let them fall in a pretense of despair.

Delyon caught the spirit of the tale.

"I told you it was foolish to pin your hopes on such mad rumors!" he chided her in a convincing tone. "Now will you come home and forget all this nonsense?"

Bowing her head so the Han would glimpse nothing in her

eyes to contradict what she'd told him, Maura gave a nod that she hoped looked reluctant. As the Han mulled over his decision, she silently begged the Giver's help.

"I will fetch you back to Venard for questioning in the morning," the Han announced at last in a tone that suggested he was doing them a favor. "If all is as you say, you can return home from there. For tonight, you will sleep in the haymow over the stable."

One last tiny ember of hope in Maura's heart flickered out when he added, "Bound, of course."

A while later as they lay in the straw, Maura squirmed closer to Delyon. "Let me see if I can untie your hands before my fingers grow too numb."

Back to back, Maura tugged at the tightly knotted rope around his wrists.

"That was quick thinking in there." Admiration warmed Delyon's words. "My mind just went empty."

Maura sighed. "Much good it did us."

When they were taken back to Venard in the morning, someone would be sure to remember a man and woman of their description who had disappeared in the courtyard of the High Governor's palace.

The best they could hope was that the death-mage—Maura still could not bring herself to think of him as her *father*—had already gone to join the army marching over the mountains. If he saw her again, he might guess the truth, and she knew better than to hope for mercy from him.

"I'm not sure this is any use," she said at last, after fumbling with the knotted rope in vain for some time.

Even if, by some miraculous grace of the Giver, their identities were not discovered tomorrow, they would still be back where they'd started, with less chance than ever of reaching Rath in time.

"Shh!" whispered Delyon. "I hear someone coming!"

They wriggled apart, and Maura rolled onto her other side so it would not be obvious what she'd been trying to do.

The flickering light of a small torch shone up through the trapdoor as the Hanish woman climbed into the haymow.

Kneeling beside Maura, she whispered, "What Kez told you is not true. The mines *were* attacked and the prisoners set free."

Maura feigned surprise. "Why are you telling me this?"

"If I help you get away now—" Songrid glanced over her shoulder and lowered her voice further "—will you take me with you?"

"Why would you want to go with us?"

The woman's strong, handsome features tensed. "Do you think your people are the only ones who suffer oppression?"

Maura shook her head.

She had glimpsed enough in the women's quarters at the palace to know better. A race of warriors that disdained healing needed a vast supply of replacements for those killed or injured. Which meant the lot of Hanish women was continuous breeding from a young age. As soon as they were weaned, most children were taken away from their mothers to be raised in an armylike atmosphere that would winnow out the weak and crush any troublesome traits like curiosity, defiance or compassion.

Fearing a trap, she answered the woman's question with one of her own. "If you wish to flee, why not go on your own?"

"If we are caught, I can claim you took me against my will." The Hanish woman looked almost as wary of them as Maura felt of her. "I want your promise that you will take me across the mountains and help me find a place among your people."

"Do you not despise us as your enemies?"

"That is what I was taught." Perhaps as a show of good faith, Songrid began to untie Maura's hands. "But I have eyes and a mind that work better than my womb. There are many things about your people I do not understand, but I know your women are better off than mine, though you are the conquered and we are the masters."

Delyon must have sensed how the woman's words swayed her. "Maura," he warned, "how do you know we can trust her?"

Songrid glared at him. "How do I know I can trust you, *man*? I would just as soon leave you behind. But if we are caught, no Han would believe another woman had managed to take me prisoner."

Having intimidated him speechless, she turned her glittering blue gaze back upon Maura. "There are two horses we can take. Food. Warm clothes for the journey into the mountains."

If this was a trap and Maura went for the bait, she and Delyon would probably be executed right here. But if Songrid was sincere…

Reaching down, Maura began to untie her feet. "The man—Kez—what about him?"

"Maura!" cried Delyon. "Do you mean to place our fate in the hands of this—"

"Watch your words, *man*!"

In spite of the brittle tension and everything at stake, Maura was tempted to chuckle. Songrid and Delyon sounded so much like her and Rath at the beginning of their acquaintance. "Do not forget the First Precept, Delyon. Trust in the Giver's providence."

"How can you be certain this is the Giver's providence and not Hanish treachery?"

Her feet untied, Maura crawled over to where he lay and began to unbind him, since Songrid showed no inclination for the task. "I cannot be certain. If I were, there would not be much reason to trust, would there?"

Delyon replied with a wordless grumble while Songrid answered Maura's question. "Kez is getting ready for bed. He sent me out to let the hounds loose again. Is there something in that sash of yours I could put in a drink to make him sleep deep and long?"

"Please, Maura. Do not trust her." Delyon spoke in *twaran*. Did he reckon Songrid could not guess every word by his suspicious tone?

"Why not? Because she is Han? You claimed to think no worse of me if I had Hanish blood."

"That is different!"

Did she *need* to trust this one Hanish woman? Maura wondered. To begin accepting the part of herself that suddenly felt foreign and untrustworthy?

Perhaps, but was that need worth risking their lives and mission for?

Two nights after his army crushed the Hanish forces in Prum, Rath woke suddenly from a deep sleep. Had he heard that noise or only dreamed it? He lay still and strained to catch it again if it had been real—the deadly whisper of a sharp blade slicing through canvas.

He listened hard for several moments, but all he could hear were the usual noises of the night—the gurgle of a nearby stream, the distant nicker of horses, some snoring that must be deafening to anyone closer. That other sound must have been a dream. Rath rolled over, nestled into his blankets and tried to get back to sleep.

That was another unwelcome effect of the growth potion. Besides the foul taste, the pain and the hunger that made him eat like a starving beast, the effort of shifting that huge body around all day sapped his energy and made him sleep soundly the whole night. That went against the outlaw instincts which had kept him alive for a good many years.

The *kingly* part of him told the outlaw part not to be so cursed foolish. Why should he not enjoy a deep restful sleep? There were soldiers—the cream of Idrygon's Vestan troops— standing guard outside his tent. He would have plenty of warning if danger was near.

Hold a moment! thought Rath the Wolf, remembering the noise he'd dreamed. The guards would only protect him from danger that was fool enough or arrogant enough to mount an attack from the front. His tent had three other sides, and canvas presented no great obstacle to an enemy with a sharp blade and a bit of enterprise. Not for the first time Rath asked himself whether the guards were meant to keep others out, or to keep him in?

Rath's heartbeat slowed down and his breathing deepened. In the morning he would issue orders for the guards to keep watch around the whole tent, not just the entrance.

There! What was that?

It was a different sound than the high-pitched rip of cloth—a rustling, furtive scuttle. This time Rath *knew* it was not a dream. He willed himself to keep his breath slow and even, giving no sign that he had heard. At the same time he roused to defend himself.

The thought of calling for help flitted through his mind but did not take hold. Whoever had stolen into his tent, and whatever they wanted, they had a knife and were no doubt prepared to use it. Besides, he'd spent most of his life relying on his own powers to stay alive. That kind of habit did not desert a man easily.

It was quiet in his tent again—too quiet. But Rath had not been called *Wolf* on account of his fierce fighting skills alone. Among his outlaw brethren, he had been known for his sharp senses. Now his ears picked up the faint hiss of breathing and his searching gaze spotted an unfamiliar shadow among the familiar ones. His nostrils flared and caught the whiff of whoever was crouched nearby, waiting to strike.

Pretending to roll over in his sleep, instead Rath lofted his blankets in a swift, sudden motion, bringing them down over the intruder. That should muffle the knife and give him the very brief benefit of surprise. Taking his advantage while it lasted, Rath seized the intruder who was struggling to escape the blankets.

Strange? The fellow seemed far smaller and lighter than he'd expected. Rath was able to lift him off the ground with ease, at which point a pair of sharp heels began to pummel his knees. Beneath the blanket, the intruder twisted and thrashed like a wild thing.

What he did not do was make much noise. Rath could not

stifle a flicker of grudging admiration. The intruder knew while their fight was one against one, he stood at least a chance of escape. Any cry he made was sure to summon aid for his victim. So even in the midst of a struggle, he had the wit to keep quiet.

Perhaps it was respect for that wit kept Rath silently grappling with the intruder rather than calling for help. Or perhaps he'd have been ashamed to think he could not subdue this wriggling mouse of a fellow on his own.

Rath gave him a really sudden, hard squeeze to get the intruder's attention, then demanded in a soft growl, "Drop the knife."

"Let go," came a muffled counter-demand from beneath the blankets. "My knife is sheathed. I meant you no harm."

Was he imagining things or did that voice sound familiar? "Then why did you sneak into my tent, armed, in the middle of the night?"

"They wouldn't let me in, would they?" At least the intruder stopped struggling. "And I have an important message for you. Wouldn't trust those uppity islanders to pass it along."

"Sire?" called one of those *uppity islanders* from outside. "Everything all right in there?"

Idrygon had given strict instructions the guards were not to enter Rath's tent unless summoned.

"No trouble!" For some reason, Rath found it hard to keep a chuckle out of his voice. "Just a bad dream."

To the intruder he whispered, "A message? Are you sure it's for me? Do you know who I am?"

"Who doesn't? Now let go of me so I can tell you and get out of here."

"First things first. Hold still a moment." Rath laid the intruder on the floor and pinned him with his knee long enough to strike a light.

Then he lifted the blankets.

"You!" The word burst out of them both at the same instant as Rath stared at the beggar boy known as Snake.

"Sire?" the guard called again. "Are you *certain* all is well with you?"

"Oh, aye. Just singing a little song to myself. I do that sometimes when I can't sleep."

Snake rolled his eyes as if he couldn't imagine anyone daft enough to believe a story like that. He glanced around the tent as if looking for someone else. Then he whispered, "So where's the Waiting King? I thought this was his tent."

Rath shrugged. "It's a long story. What message do you have for him. I promise I'll tell him straightaway."

The boy looked doubtful for a moment. "Aye, well, I reckon she'd want me to tell you, too."

"She? Maura?" The words came out louder than he meant them to. Before the guard got suspicious and reported to Idrygon, Rath sang in a hoarse voice, "Oh Maura, my fair one, my lady…"

Snake made a face and pretended to plug his ears. "That might be her name. The one from the hay cart. Pretty. Helping folks all the time."

"When did you see her?" Rath's hands closed around the boy's upper arms. "Where? What did she say?"

"Let go or I'm not saying nothing."

"Tell me before I beat it out of you!" growled Rath. He could imagine the look on Maura's face if she'd heard him.

"Your pardon." He let go of the boy. "I didn't mean that. Just tell me…please. I'm sick with worry about her."

"Then why'd you let her wander around Westborne with that…that…"

"Delyon." Rath whispered the name as if it were a curse. "That's an even longer story. Tell me what you know, I beg you."

"Right. I didn't talk to her, just seen her. Two, three weeks ago. Long as it took me to get here from…" The boy spoke the name of a place Rath had never heard of. "I was in the market that day, lifting...I mean, looking around. I hears this racket and I knew the lady's voice, so I run for a closer look."

Rath hoped the boy's story wasn't leading where he feared it might.

"It was her, all right. The Han had her and that *Delyon*. If she'd kept her mouth shut, they might have got off. But she hollers out right in the middle of the market, 'We ain't spies for the Waiting King.' Might as well spit on a death-mage."

Once Rath got over the feeling that Snake *had* slashed him hard across the belly with his knife, he puzzled why Maura might have done something like that. Now and then she could be heedless when she got caught up in helping someone, but provoking the Han like that was something else again. "What happened to them?"

"Han marched 'em off to the garrison." Snake's hard young features tensed. "Reckon I should've done something. Tried to help, like. Made a row so they could get away. It wouldn't have done no good, though. There was too many Han and *zikary*."

Rath shook his head. "She wouldn't have wanted you to get yourself in trouble, too."

The boy scratched his chin where the first delicate shadow of a whisker was starting to grow. "While I was watching the garrison and trying to figure what to do, a pair of Han rode off with them, tied to horses. Heading for Venard, I reckon. Since I couldn't do nothing else, I thought I'd come tell the Waiting King. If the lady claimed she wasn't his spy, I reckoned that's what she must be."

Snake's news acted on Rath's heart the way the growth potion did on his body.

"That's alls I know," whispered the boy, as if expecting more questions that hadn't come. "Been on the move ever since."

"You...must be hungry." Rath picked up a basket of Long Vale peaches and thrust them at the boy. "Thank you for bringing word." He almost heaved his supper saying that.

"So..." Snake grabbed one of the peaches and took a great,

juice-squirting bite. "What are you going to do? About the lady, I mean?"

What could he do? Order his army over the mountains to besiege Venard? Run off and try to rescue her himself? If she and Delyon had been in Hanish custody that long, were they even still alive?

Snake spit the peach pit into the basket and grabbed another piece of fruit. "I'd go with you."

Their whole exchange had been in whispers, but the boy's last words were even quieter. Caught in a web of dread, Rath almost didn't hear.

"I'd go with you." Snake spoke a little louder. He stared at the peach as if addressing it instead of Rath. "When you go to fetch her back."

A lump rose in Rath's throat that felt as big as one of the peaches. He shook his head. After several tries he managed a gruff whisper. "She wouldn't want that."

"No?" Snake slurped down another peach.

No. She would want him to believe she could fetch herself back, even from the clutches of the Echtroi. She would want him to believe in destiny and the Giver's providence.

For her sake he would try. Though there were few things in the world he found harder to do…than believe.

For the first day after they made their escape from the Hanish guard post, Maura kept glancing back for signs of pursuit, then ahead for fear of ambush. She only calmed when she realized Songrid was every bit as fearful of being caught.

The two of them shared a horse while Delyon rode the other, which also carried their supplies for the journey. Whenever Maura spoke to him, he replied with no more than a word or two. With his handsome features clenched in such a forbidding expression, he looked more like his brother than Maura had ever thought possible. He did not seem to fear falling into the enemy's clutches again—he fully expected it at any moment.

"Let us stop here for the night," said Maura after many hours' riding up a winding mountain pass.

With a glance at the setting sun, Delyon shook his head. "We have another hour of daylight at least. We should press on."

That was more words than he had spoken the rest of the day combined. Was he beginning to relent?

Perhaps not, for he added in a tone of bitter mockery, "Did you not say we must press on an hour after the Hanish army and begin an hour ahead of them if we are to reach the eastlands in time?"

"That was before we had horses." Maura reined hers to a halt. "They carry us more swiftly, but it can be dangerous to take them over such a steep trail in the dark."

She tried to sound both conciliatory and authoritative. She understood Delyon's anger and suspicion, but she would not cater to them.

"There's water here." She pointed to a trickle sliding down the rocks. "And a bit of grass for the horses. We might come across another spot as good as this before nightfall, but I wouldn't want to count on it."

With a grunt of grudging surrender, Delyon swung down from his saddle.

Maura felt a tug on her cloak. She glanced back at Songrid. "Your pardon. I should have asked what you think on the matter. These are your horses, after all."

As he led his mount to drink from a shallow basin carved in the rocks, Delyon grumbled in Umbrian, "*Ask* her, but *tell* me. We'll be slaughtered in our sleep."

Maura ignored him.

"Do you reckon this would be a good place to stop for the night?" she asked Songrid. "Or should we keep going?"

The Hanish woman answered with a question of her own. "What does the man mean about 'reach the eastlands'? Are we not first going to one of the mines to look for your husband?"

"Oh, that." Maura scrambled down from the horse. "Let's talk about it while we eat."

To her relief, Songrid did not seem angry to have been…misled.

"You are a good liar." She sounded as if she approved, even admired Maura for it. "When you told Kez of your husband, it sounded so true."

"It's true I am eager to see him again." Songrid's acceptance of her deceit shamed Maura more than anger would have. "Only, *over* the mountains, not *in* them."

"That is better." Munching some bread, Songrid gazed back the way they had come, on the broad plane of Westborne, lit by the sun's last rays. "I will feel safer when we reach your eastlands."

Maura shot a look at Delyon, but he paid her no mind, as he sat some way off from the women, his back all but turned on them. He continued to eat, but with a different manner, somehow—as if he were no longer *certain* every bite must be poisoned.

"What about your husband?" she asked. "Were you not sorry at all to leave him?"

"Kez is not my husband." Songrid stared into the gathering darkness. "I was given to him as a…sort of servant when my lord cast me off for being a bad breeder."

"I'm…sorry." It sounded so inadequate, but Maura could not think what else to say.

"Do not pity me. My people scorn women like me, but I reckon we are the lucky ones."

No Han attacked them in the night, which seemed to surprise Delyon. He and Songrid did not exchange a single word the next day, and he pretended not to listen when she told Maura more of her story. But when she fell the next evening and twisted her ankle, he whipped up a poultice and bound the injury almost before Maura knew what was happening.

The next morning he hoisted Songrid in his arms and lifted her onto the horse's back. By the time they reached the Long Vale, he'd become positively attentive to her. Did he repent his earlier suspicions? Maura wondered. Or was he trying to prove that not all men were like the others Songrid had known?

As they neared the end of their journey, part of Maura rejoiced that their quest might still succeed and that she would soon see Rath again. Another part dreaded having to face him, knowing what she now knew about herself.

After another long day in the saddle, Rath stumbled into his tent tired, hungry and troubled. He told himself he should be grateful for the Giver's blessings. His army's progress through the Long Vale had been nothing short of triumphal. After their victory at Prum, other Hanish garrisons had fled before them.

He'd kept up the pressure, advancing each day as far as his men could march. The last thing he wanted was to give some vindictive Hanish commander time to organize a slaughter of Umbrian countryfolk like the one he'd found in that mine.

His men were not able to move quite as fast as he'd have liked, though. For every day their progress was slowed by the crowds that gathered to cheer them. Who'd have thought nodding and waving and acknowledging the adulation of his subjects could be so wearying? Rath could have told them.

Every stooped grandam who blew him a toothless kiss, every child hoisted on its father's shoulders to catch a glimpse of the Waiting King, every young man who flocked to join his makeshift army—was another pebble added to a bulging pack he carried.

They were his responsibility—his burden. He worried his hungry troops were depleting their harvest. He fretted that once his army passed by, they would fall prey to outlaws. Most of all, he feared the Han might rally and strike back, leaving them worse off than before the rebellion.

Some nights it was all he could do to keep from stealing out of his tent and slipping off into the darkness to become another nameless outlaw in whom no one placed their hopes and of whom no one expected anything.

He would have managed better with Maura by his side. Almost from the moment he'd met her, the lass had brought out everything that was noble and heroic in him, no matter how deeply buried. But Maura was not here. After what he'd learned from young Snake, each day that passed with no word of her made it harder for Rath to hope that he might see her again.

His armor was beginning to hang loose on him. Rath pulled it off and wrapped himself in a woolen robe that seemed snug at the moment but would become ample once he returned to his proper size. Then he turned his attention to a heaping tray of food that had been left for him. Though the growth spell made him constantly hungry and Long Vale farmers sent him the choicest fruits of their harvest, he hardly tasted what went in his mouth.

Once he'd finished, he sank onto his bedroll and bowed his head against his bent knees with a sigh dredged from the depths of his heart. *Giver, I don't know how much longer I can do this. Just help me get through tomorrow, will you?*

He'd have welcomed some sign or answer, even the faintest whisper in his own thoughts. Approval that he was doing the right thing, no matter how wrong it felt sometimes. Encouragement to keep on. Assurance that this would all end well—for the kingdom at least, if not for him. But no answer came. His mind and heart felt as empty and hungry as his belly had a while ago. And he had nothing to feed them.

Hearing the soft rustle of his tent flap and the sound of footsteps, he stifled another sigh. This time one of impatience. He might not know what he needed just then, but he knew what he did *not* need—another lecture from Idrygon. Reluctantly he raised his head and opened his eyes.

All at once, his hungry heart filled to bursting, for there stood Maura. Rumpled, travel-stained and exhausted, she was still a feast for his eyes.

She hung back a little as if uncertain what manner of welcome she would receive. Rath ached with regret that he had ever given her cause to question. A sob caught in his throat as he surged up from his bedroll and caught her in his arms. It took every morsel of restraint he could muster to keep from crushing her in his embrace of welcome.

"*Aira!*" His lips blundered over her face, eager to kiss every beloved feature. "*Aira, aira, aira!*"

He seemed to have forgotten every other word he'd ever known, but the lapse did not trouble him, for he recalled the most important one. The only one he needed at the moment.

She melted into his arms with a whimper of longing and love, both so intense they pained her. The weeks of their separation seemed like an eternity, and some long-slumbering part of him roused with ancient echoes of a reunion that even death and time had not been able to thwart.

How long they clung to one another, trading kisses and whispering garbled endearments, Rath could not tell. But when his surprise and joy tamed enough to think of anything beyond their passionate welcome, Maura felt larger in his arms than when he'd first embraced her.

"Come, *aira*." He drew her down to his bedroll. "You look weary and you must be starved. Let me call for food."

"In a moment." She smoothed back his hair in a tender, possessive caress. "Just now, I am only hungry to be near you."

Her gaze roved over his face, as if eager to satisfy herself he was not some elusive vision that might vanish the instant she looked away. When their eyes met and he looked deep into hers, Rath thought he glimpsed a shadow lingering there.

Perhaps it was the reflection of his own foolish worry that their reunion might be only a dream. Or did she fear that once the passing thrill of it had faded, the earlier strife between them might return to blight their marriage?

He would soon ease her mind on that score. "I feared I'd never see you again, *aira*. All these weeks I've longed to beg your forgiveness for how I behaved before we parted. I swear I did not lack faith in you, only in fate. I feared our love was too good to last. And I let that fear poison it."

Maura's arms went around his neck and she clung to him like a rock in a storm-tossed sea. "Is that truly all it was?"

"Is that not enough? What else could it be?" He held her close so she would not draw back, search his gaze and guess the truth if she had not already.

"Nothing." Her cheek nuzzled his shoulder as she shook her head. "It all seems so foolish now to have come between us when we ought to have savored our time together."

"The day you sailed, I came looking for you to ask your pardon. Grant it now, I beg you. I cannot bear another moment without it!"

"You have not been without it." She pulled away just far enough to cradle his face in her hands. "If there was anything to forgive, I did long ago. I was at least as much to blame."

"Never! You were being true to yourself and to our people."

His words did not seem to reassure her as he had hoped. "Even if you believe that, humor me with your pardon."

"To humor you and for no other reason." He wrapped his hands around hers and brought each to his lips in turn. "Now let us put that all behind us, except to take a warning never again to part in anger."

Like the soft, pink, magical petals of a queensbalm flower, her lips blossomed into a wondrous smile. "You have a bargain."

They sealed their pact with a kiss that made Rath ache with the memory of every night they'd been apart. Sensing his desire, Maura slid her hand beneath his robe to fondle him with a tempting touch that kindled fire in his flesh.

"Hold." He spoke the word almost in a groan. "You must have food and washing water to refresh yourself after your journey. My need can wait."

"Can it?" Maura planted a kiss at the base of his neck, then parted her lips to swipe her tongue over flesh that tingled with his barely curbed desire for her. "I fear mine cannot."

The whisper of her breath on skin moistened by her tongue gave him a ticklish chill. Though he tried to resist, his hand rose and cupped the gentle fullness of her breast through her clothes. Her nipple puckered at his touch.

With a wanton chuckle, Maura began to shed her traveling clothes. "Once quick and hot, to appease our appetites. After, I can eat and tell you of my mission."

Her mission, of course! Rath wanted to smack himself on the brow for not asking or even thinking of it. What kind of king let affairs of the heart distract him from such a vital matter?

"The staff—have you brought it?" Surely if she was here it must mean she and Delyon had succeeded in their quest.

"It was not in Venard. But we know where it is and hope to recover it soon." Her clothes shed, she untied his robe and slipped her arms into the now-loose sleeves with his. The soft fullness of her backside settled on his lap while her bosom nestled against his chest.

"Delyon is briefing his brother about everything that happened in Venard, as I will you…in due time." She raised her face to his, offering an invitation he could not resist a moment longer. "There is nothing we can do about it tonight, certainly not this very moment."

She kissed him on the chin. "If you resist much longer, I may think you are not as pleased to see me as you claim."

"That will never do, will it?" A husky chuckle rumbled deep in Rath's throat.

They both knew that was nonsense. But it gave him an excuse to surrender to his desire without feeling like an inattentive husband and an undutiful king.

"Very well." He eased her back onto his bedroll. "Let me show you how much pleasure I take in being with you again."

His mouth closed over hers, hot and eager. Into a single, deep kiss he distilled all the regret, worry and longing that had wrung his heart during the endless weeks they'd been apart. Then he sweetened it with the joy of reconciliation to create an intoxicating brew. "And let me show you how much pleasure I can *give,* now that we are together again."

"Together." Heat shimmered in Maura's gaze, like the air of the Waste in high summer. "Is there a lovelier word?"

"None that I know, *aira.*"

"So the Staff of Velorken was never in Venard at all?" Rath asked a while later as Maura consumed a tray of food he'd ordered for her. "Then your going there was all a great waste and put you in danger for nothing?"

He looked ready to throttle Delyon.

Maura shook her head and hurriedly swallowed the food in her mouth. "If we had not gone to Venard, I'd never have found out what the Han are planning. Then everything you have done might have been for naught."

Nor would she have discovered the distressing truth about her parentage. She had almost swooned with relief when Rath made it clear he suspected nothing. Now that the first blissful rush of reunion had ebbed a little, she wondered how and when she would tell him…and where she would find the courage.

"What are the Han planning that we cannot overcome?" Rath gave her hand a reassuring squeeze. "When we first landed on the Dusk Coast, I would not have wanted to meet even part of their army in open combat. But that was weeks ago. Every day more Umbrians join us. We are a great host now. I believe we can beat them, even without the Staff of Velorken."

His brow furrowed. "Which may be just as well, for I doubt I have the wisdom to use that kind of power."

"I trust that you do," said Maura. "And I fear we *will* need it, even with the army you have gathered."

She told him what she had overheard while hiding beneath the High Governor's council table—how Rath's army had been lured eastward to be crushed between a Hanish army from Westborne and another sent from Dun Derhan to help put down the rebellion.

"I don't understand." Rath flinched as if a hard blow had hit him from out of nowhere. "How do they know there *is* an uprising to put down?"

"One of the death-mages claimed to have mastered a spell for communicating with the Imperium." Maura described the underground chamber where she had found him with the large crystal. "It must tap some line of power that runs deep beneath the earth to carry thought messages."

While they were on the subject, her conscience urged her to tell Rath what else she had discovered that night. But where could she begin?

"Thank the Giver you have returned to me, *aira*." He raised his hand to graze her cheek with the backs of his fingers. "Even if you had not brought this news. Even if you had no idea where to find the Staff of Velorken. Without you, the burden of playing king grinds me down. But when I have you by my side, I feel I can do whatever I must."

Then perhaps she had better keep silent a little longer, if Rath needed her for support and to find the staff. After all, it was not as though discovering her parentage had altered her loyalty. Her blood might be some unfortunate mingling of two enemy races, but her heart was Umbrian. Nothing would change that.

"About the staff," said Rath. "How did you come to figure out its true hiding place?"

"Delyon deciphered an ancient scroll with a spell that helped me tap memories buried deep in my mind. The ones handed down from Abrielle through all her line to my mother and through Langbard to me."

Rath's eyes widened. "It is a good thing you insisted on observing the ritual of passing with Langbard the night he died. Or those memories might have been lost."

She had not thought of that. "It is a good thing you gave me time to do it rather than dragging me out of danger like you wanted to. It was the first kindness you ever did me."

"I thought it was the daftest thing I'd ever done." Rath rolled his eyes. "I'm glad it turned out well. So what was this memory Delyon's spell helped you uncover? Where did Queen Abrielle hide the staff if not in her castle?"

"She *did* hide it in her castle," said Maura between bites of food. "A different castle. An old castle that must have been very fine in Abrielle's day, and not yet hemmed in by forest."

"Aldwood, you mean? Vang's camp?"

Maura nodded. "If I had not been captured by his men, I might never have recognized it when I saw it in my memory vision." A shiver rippled through her. "It gives me the strangest feeling to look back and see how so much of what has happened to us, both good and bad, served this destiny of ours."

"It comforts me in a queer sort of way," said Rath after a thoughtful silence, "to think that if some ill befalls us, there may be a hidden purpose to it. One we may only fathom later."

"Highness!" called the guard outside Rath's tent. "Lord Idrygon craves an audience with you. May he enter?"

Rath exchanged a glance with Maura. "Do you mind?"

She tugged at the spare robe Rath had lent her to cover herself more modestly. It would be clear to anyone with eyes what they had been up to. If that came as any shock to Idrygon, too bad about him!

"Let him enter." She flashed Rath a mocking grin. "He has shown uncommon restraint waiting this long to barge in on us."

Rath chuckled and the tightness around his eyes eased. For

an instant he looked like the same impudent outlaw she had lugged back to Langbard's cottage last spring.

"Let Lord Idrygon come," he called back to the guard.

The words had scarcely left his lips when Idrygon strode in. He looked just as forceful as Maura remembered him from Margyle—though perhaps more in his natural element armed for battle. If he guessed what she and Rath had been doing only a short while ago, and if he disapproved, he did not show it.

"Highness." He snapped a crisp bow first to Rath, then to Maura. "I have been informed of the vital news you and my brother have brought."

"So have I." Rath motioned Idrygon to sit with them around the low table from which Maura had been eating. "A shame the coasts of Norest and Southmark do not have warding waters like the Islands."

"Aye, Highness." Idrygon looked grim. "I had hoped by the time the Imperium got wind of the rebellion, our forces would be in control of the kingdom and ready to repel any invaders."

"So had I." Rath picked up a thick slab of oatloaf and smeared it with fresh white butter. "I don't fancy being caught between two Hanish armies."

"There is only one thing to do," muttered Idrygon. "Make for this Aldwood place with all speed. The forest will provide our army with cover while Her Highness locates the staff."

Rath nodded as he chewed on the oatloaf. "Only one problem with that."

Idrygon raised one brow in an unspoken question.

"Vang Spear of Heaven." Rath's tongue lingered over the name with a kind of grudging fondness. "His band of outlaws hold the castle. He won't be fussy about handing it over to us."

Idrygon drummed his fingers on the tabletop, his frown deepening. "In that case, we will have to take it from him."

* * *

"Do you reckon he means it?" Maura asked later that night as she snuggled beside Rath on his bedroll. "About taking Aldwood from Vang?"

"He wasn't in jest." Rath yawned, anticipating his first truly restful night's sleep since leaving Margyle…and even before. "If there's one thing I've learned about Lord Idrygon, it's that the man hasn't a scrap of humor in him."

Maura's body vibrated with a silent chuckle. "It must run in the family."

"What? Are you saying Delyon has learning but no wit? I thought he was the living image of Langbard."

Hard as Rath tried to prevent it, an edge of his old foolish jealousy sharpened his tone. What had passed between Maura and Delyon during their dangerous quest? Had she ever turned to the handsome scholar for protection or comfort? Could that be the lingering wisp of shadow he'd glimpsed in her eyes?

Maura punctured his suspicions with a hoot of laughter. "Rath Talward! Don't tell me you fancied a rival in poor Delyon? Well, put your mind at ease. He's improved a good deal from when we started out, but I'd have given anything to have you as my traveling companion, instead. The trouble he got us into!"

As she told him how Delyon got them arrested by tearing down the Hanish sign, Rath longed to thrash the young fool for his heedlessness. Yet he could not stifle a contrary inkling of satisfaction that Maura had found Delyon more bothersome than attractive.

"You must have felt the same way about me when we were traveling together," said Maura, "and I kept landing us in trouble trying to help people all the time."

"Now and then." Rath ruffled her hair with his cheek. "Tricking the Han into giving you a ride to Venard—that was daring. I'm not sure I'd have had the nerve to risk it."

Even safe in the knowledge that it had all turned out well, the thought of her taking such a chance alarmed him. But that alarm was tempered with admiration for her quick thinking and courage.

"It's exactly the sort of thing you would have done! That is what gave me the idea. Anytime we found ourselves in a tight spot, I'd think, *What would Rath do if he were here?*"

"Soil my breeches, likely, if I'd been stuck under a table surrounded by Hanish officers and Echtroi!"

"You would not. Just think what you've accomplished since you landed at Duskport. Your name is on the lips of every Umbrian, and the Han are at their wits' end how to stop it. You've given people hope for the first time since the Conquest."

Much as he craved her approval, Rath could not claim the honor. "That was all Idrygon's doing. I'm just an overgrown puppet who puts on a show for the crowd and does what he's told whether he agrees with it or not."

"Like what, *aira*?"

He did not want to burden her with all his worries on their first night back together, but the open-armed warmth of her sympathy and support seduced him, just as her touch had seduced him earlier. Before he knew it, he was pouring out all his misgivings—about the butchery he'd witnessed in the Hitherland, and his continued pose as superhuman legend come to life.

"Now this business about seizing Aldwood from Vang. I am no great friend of his, but I hate the thought of using my army against our own countrymen. There must be some other way."

"To think I would hear you looking to solve a problem by means other than force." Maura's hair whispered against his shoulder as she shook her head. "Like it or not, you *are* more king than outlaw, now, *aira*. Idrygon may have given you the kernel of your fighting force to begin this rebellion, but the mainland folk who have since joined were drawn by you. Not by the trappings of the Waiting King legend, but by what it stands for. Something of King Elzaban lives on in you, and you must be true to it, Idrygon or no Idrygon."

Rath tightened his arms around her, silently vowing he would never push her away again. "It all makes so much more sense when I hear you say it than when all these daft thoughts are spinning around in my head. And Idrygon is so cursed persuasive. With your guidance, I will be able to make decisions I can live with and stick to them."

"Now that we are together again, we can support one another." Maura sounded weary but resolute. "Even against Lord Idrygon, if need be."

"Agreed." Rath pressed a kiss to her brow.

Though the Han were poised to sweep down from the mountains and in from the coast to crush his ragtag army, he had not felt so settled in his mind for a very long while.

Morning came far too early and with far too much noise. The beat of drums and the deep blast of horns roused the rebel army. Soon a rumble of voices filled the morning air along with the whinnies of horses. Maura clenched her eyes tight shut and burrowed deeper into Rath's embrace, wishing she could shut her ears, too.

Being back in Rath's arms gave her a deceptive sense of safety. But she knew it was only an illusion. The Han would soon be closing in from both sides and it would take the fight of their lives to liberate the kingdom.

Rath continued to snore softly. He seemed unaware of either the noise or the gathering danger. Maura wished she could let him sleep. But if she didn't wake him, someone else would.

"Time to get up, *aira*." She let her lips whisper over his cheek and ear as she called softly to him. "We have a busy day ahead of us."

"I'm afraid to open my eyes." Beneath the blanket, his hands roved over her body. "In case it turns out you're not really here, and last night was all a dream."

"Oh, I am here." Her lips sought his. "See if *this* convinces you."

She kissed him long and deeply, until her heart raced, her breath trembled and her head spun. Rath rewarded her effort by opening his eyes. He pretended astonishment to find her presence in his arms more than a dream.

He cast a resentful glance toward the entrance flap of his tent. "As sure as a cold winter, if I try to have my way with you now, Idrygon will show up demanding to see me."

No sooner had he muttered those words than the guard on duty called, "My Lord Idrygon wishes to speak with you, Highness."

"What did I tell you?" Rath whispered to Maura.

She choked back a bubble of laughter. "You weren't trying to have your way with me, though."

"No, but I wanted to." Rath flashed her a wry grin then raised his voice. "Let him enter."

Idrygon strode in, and started at the sight of Rath and Maura still lying together on the bedroll. "Your pardon, Highness. I thought you must be up and dressed by now."

He looked so flustered, Maura had to hide her face in Rath's shoulder to smother a fit of giggles.

"We were just about to rise for the day," Rath lied. "Now, what is so urgent that you needed to call on us at this hour?"

"Everything is urgent, Highness, as you must realize. It is imperative we make all haste to Aldwood. I reckon it will take us three days at a good hard march. With luck that will be time enough to—"

Before Idrygon could finish, sounds of a disturbance erupted outside the tent. Maura thought she recognized Delyon's voice.

"But my brother is in there and I must speak with him now!"

"I have my orders."

"Let him come!" cried Rath. To Maura he muttered, "We will end up with the whole camp in here, by and by."

Delyon stormed in, nearly bumping into his brother. He, too, started at the sight of Rath and Maura.

"Can this not wait?" snapped Idrygon. "I have important matters to discuss with the king!"

"More important than a life?" Delyon grabbed his brother by the arm. "How could you order her execution? Without Songrid, Maura and I might still be prisoners of the Han—dead even. And you would know nothing of the danger bearing down on you!"

"Songrid?" Maura sat up and reached for one of Rath's robes to cover herself.

"The Hanish woman is clearly a spy." Idrygon shook off his brother's grasp. "She used you to infiltrate our forces."

"Rubbish!" cried Delyon.

Maura had never heard him talk back to his brother that way. Had he forgotten how bitterly he'd mistrusted Songrid at first?

A glare from Idrygon cowed him a bit, for he continued in a less hostile tone. "The woman had no way of knowing who we were, I tell you. She helped us escape from that guard post and brought us through the mountains. Maura and I owe her our lives."

"Why would she turn her back on her own people," growled Idrygon, "to aid their enemies?"

While the brothers were too busy arguing to pay any heed, Rath and Maura slipped into robes. Then she surged to her feet and joined the fray on Songrid's behalf.

"Umbrians are not the only ones who have tasted Hanish oppression." She stood beside Delyon, facing his brother. "Besides, we promised to vouch for her and insure her safety. Put Songrid under guard if you feel she poses a threat, but do not kill her on account of your suspicions!"

Idrygon looked from his brother to Maura. The flesh above his lip trembled, as if he was struggling not to sneer at them both. Then he turned to Rath. "What do you say, Highness? Remember the slaughter we found at that mine? The Han showed those men no mercy. Why should we show any to one of them?"

What slaughter at what mine? Maura wondered as she watched Rath's expression turn grim.

"Please," she begged him. "I gave my word. Not all Han are bad any more than all Umbrians are good!"

Idrygon hammered his hand with his fist. "The woman is a threat, I tell you!"

"Enough!" Rath jammed his hands over his ears and glared at all three of them.

When they fell into shocked silence, he muttered, "That's better. Now, will someone explain to me what you are arguing about. Some Hanish woman, I gather."

When Idrygon opened his mouth, Rath pointed at Maura. "Let my wife speak first."

Fearing what might happen to Songrid while they argued over her fate, Maura explained the situation as quickly as she could. She wished she could be certain of Rath's decision. Only last night they had promised to support one another. But his frown deepened as she told him about the Hanish woman, and in his eyes she glimpsed a flicker of fear.

How could he believe they had anything to fear from one poor woman who was likely frightened out of her wits by now?

"If you could see what I saw in Venard," said Maura, "you would not doubt her. The most privileged women of the Han are as much oppressed in their way as any Umbrian except those who toil in the mines and the pleasure houses. They are little more than brood sows, and treated no better! If I had been in Songrid's place, I hope I would have had the courage to do what she did."

When Rath did not look properly sympathetic, Delyon added, "We should reward the woman, not kill her!"

"Idrygon," said Rath at last, "you believe this Hanish woman poses a threat?"

"Is it not evident, sire? No Han would act as this woman has, unless it was a plot of some kind. She probably means to reckon our numbers and eavesdrop on our plans, then sneak back to her own people with the information."

"Just as I did in Venard," said Maura.

That took Idrygon aback for a moment, then he nodded. "And if the Han had caught you, you would have counted yourself blessed to suffer a quick execution."

Maura could not dispute that. But neither could she betray the woman who had risked so much for her and Delyon.

"We are not Han." Rath's brow furrowed, as though he rued the decision he had felt compelled to reach. "You said that, Maura, remember, at Blen and Tesha's farm?"

She nodded. Having just mended the earlier breach between them, what would she do if Rath now made a decision *she* could not live with?

"We are not Han," he repeated, more to himself than to the others. "And we must not become Han."

"Of course not, Highness." Idrygon looked confident of winning his way, as usual. "We will drive those wicked unbelievers from our shores and wipe every foul trace of them from our land!"

Maura flinched as if he had struck her. What would Rath say if he knew she was a "foul trace" of the hated enemy?

"That is my hope, too." Rath kneaded his whisker-stubbled chin with one hand. "But what if, in our zeal to drive out the Han, we *become* the very thing we hate?"

A look of uncertainty flickered on Idrygon's face, but only for a moment. "Surely there is no danger of us becoming like them, Highness."

"There is more danger than you know." Rath shook his head slowly. "And if that is the price of victory, it may be too costly to bear."

"But what has this to do with the woman, Highness?"

"Everything." Suddenly Rath looked more sure of himself than Maura had seen him in a long time. "If the Han would show no mercy, then we must. I place this woman under royal protection."

Delyon and Maura each expelled a sigh of relief.

"Sire," cried Idrygon, "this is madness!"

"Watch yourself." Rath fixed him with a cold, level stare. "I know and value all you have done to bring us this far. But let us not forget who is king. Assign the woman a trustworthy guard to protect her from harm and to make certain she does not run off bearing tales. Mercy need not be foolhardy."

"Thank you, Highness!" Delyon made a deep bow. "I will make your orders in this matter known at once."

Idrygon shot his brother a glare of barely contained rage, then stalked from the tent after him. He did not spare either a look or word for Rath and Maura, perhaps fearing he might stray further into treason.

"Well done, *aira!*" Maura threw her arms around Rath's neck. "You spoke like a true king!"

"I hope I have made the right decision." He did not look fully convinced of it. "If this Songrid runs off to the Echtroi with information, I may have the shortest reign of any Umbrian king...not that I would find it a hardship to give up the crown."

"You can see for yourself." Maura bent to retrieve her clothes. "I can bring Songrid here to tell you her story. Once you have spoken with her, I know you will agree that—"

"No!" Rath strode to the opposite corner of the tent and knelt before a wondrously carved chest, which he opened. "There is no need for me to speak with her. If you vouch for her, that is enough to satisfy me."

"As you wish." Maura shivered as she slipped out of Rath's warm bulky robe that carried a comforting whiff of his scent.

His abruptness left her vaguely chilled, too. There must be more to his refusal to meet Songrid that he let on—but what?

From the chest, Rath took a cloth pouch like the kind Maura had used to store herbs and other magical matter in the peaceful days when she'd been nothing more than a wizard's apprentice.

The sight of it gave her an idea. "*Aira,* may I ask one more favor of you?"

"You may *ask* me anything." Rath measured a small quantity of fine dark powder from the bag into a flask. "Whether I can grant it is another matter, though I will try."

He called to the tent guard for hot water. This must be a morning ritual, for a small flagon was shoved in through the tent flap at once, wisps of steam rising from it. Rath scooped it up and poured some water into the vial.

"What will happen today?" asked Maura as she wriggled into her shift and gown. "Your men will march toward Aldwood?"

"Aye." Rath shook up the potion. "Today and tomorrow and the day after. And hope the Han do not catch us before we reach Aldwood. Why?"

"I was thinking…" Maura slung her sash over her shoulder. "I can do nothing about finding the Staff of Velorken until you have gained entrance to Aldwood Castle, one way or another."

"True." Rath softly chanted the growth spell then raised the vial to his lips and drained it in one great swig. "Pah, but that is vile stuff! I keep hoping I will grow used to the taste and not mind it so much. But I swear it gets worse every day."

"Must you still take it?" Forgetting her request, Maura flew to his side. "You have rallied the mainlanders as Idrygon wanted. I fear what effect it may have on you to drink such a potion so often."

"I'll be rid of it soon, one way or another." Rath's rugged features contorted in pain. "Idrygon says this is no time for the people to lose faith in me."

"Are you ill, *aira*?" With trembling fingers, Maura reached up to wipe away the fine drops of sweat that sprang out on his brow. "Was there something wrong with the potion?"

He gave a hoarse chuckle through clenched teeth. "Nothing that hasn't been wrong with it all along. Perhaps you had better go until it is finished working."

"I will *not*!" A spasm of shame writhed through her. "Was the potion doing this to you even before we left the Islands?"

His eyes squeezed shut and every muscle clenched tight to contain the pain, Rath jerked his head in a nod.

No wonder he'd been so ill tempered!

"Why did you not tell me, you great *lalump*?" she demanded, though she knew the answer.

He hadn't wanted to worry her, of course, over something she could not help. Perhaps he had not wanted to let her see him in a moment of weakness.

She grabbed the flagon of hot water. "Let me make you a brew to ease the pain, at least."

Rath shook his head. He'd sprouted almost a foot taller and had filled out until his robe strained at the seams.

"Any other potion," he gasped out the words, "would hinder...the power...of this one."

Maura cursed under her breath, torn between wanting to cradle this huge, fierce-looking man in her arms and a fierce urge to cram a dose of the bitter potion down Lord Idrygon's throat. Let him taste the agony he had forced upon Rath every day for weeks on end!

"There," grunted Rath at last. "The worst is over." He leaned forward, legs bent under the weight of his enlarged frame. "What was it you wanted again? Something about Aldwood?"

It took Maura a moment to collect herself after what she had just witnessed. "Oh, yes. I was thinking, I would be no help to you today, and Windleford is so nearby. With a swift horse, I could make a quick visit to Sorsha, then return by nightfall. Windleford is not still held by the Han, is it?"

"No." Rath lumbered over to the bedroll, sank down upon it and began pulling on his oversize clothes and armor. "Our scouts report the garrison pulled out several days ago, heading for the coast. We did not know what to make of it at the time, now it seems clear they've gone to meet up with the fleet from Dun Derhan."

Maura opened her mouth to take back her request. She had

just returned to Rath after a long, difficult separation. How could she leave him again so soon? In spite of his great size and power, it was clear he needed her as much as ever.

Before she could speak, Rath glanced up at her, his jaw still tensed from the pain. "I think it's a fine idea for you to visit Sorsha! I only wish I could go with you. Once this is all over, perhaps?"

"I will wait until we can go together and celebrate the liberation with Sorsha and Newlyn." Maura tried to sound certain of victory.

"Go now," said Rath. "A day's march is tiresome. It would do me good to think of you visiting with Sorsha, rather than plodding along on horseback, shepherding the army eastward."

The prospect did not sound very appealing, especially as the weather had grown cool. "Are you sure you don't mind?"

"Mind?" He gave a scoffing chuckle. "I insist you go, but on two conditions."

Maura moved toward him and wrapped her arms around his neck from behind, resting her chin on the crown of his head. "What might those be?"

"That you take a good escort with you, in case any stray Han are lingering in the area."

"Agreed." Though she had overcome the worst of her timidity since the night she'd left Windleford, she would never be reckless. "What else?"

Rath reached up to caress her face, his massive hand awkward yet strangely tender. "That you be back to me by the time this potion wears off tonight."

"Pity the fool who tries to stop me!"

A while later, Maura emerged from Rath's tent and began making her way through the ranks. "Your pardon. I'm looking for a man called Anulf. I have an assignment for him from the king."

Before she could locate anyone who knew this Anulf fellow, Maura caught sight of Idrygon marching about giving orders.

When he noticed her, she expected him to glare or scowl. But he strode toward her with a look of such good humor she wondered what had come over him. Once his temper cooled, had he realized he'd been too harsh and hasty in dealing with Songrid?

"Highness." He bowed. "A private word with you if I may?"

"Gladly, my lord. There is a matter I would like to bring to your attention." Perhaps Idrygon did not know the painful price Rath paid for taking the growth potion. He had successfully hidden it from *her*, after all.

She and Idrygon made their way to a spot where they would not be overheard by the men breaking camp.

Conscious of how precious time was to them all, Maura wasted none in sharing her concern about Rath and the growth potion. She was careful not to lay blame on Idrygon for the situation, assuming it would come as much of a shock to him as it had to her.

But his face betrayed no hint of surprise. "The pain passes, Highness, with no lasting damage. A small price, surely, for what it has gained us?"

"*A small price?*" cried Maura. Idrygon was lucky she did not have a weapon in her hand. "Perhaps if you were the one to pay it, you would think differently."

"Do you think I have not made sacrifices for our cause?" demanded Idrygon. "None of this would have been possible without the preparations I made over the years." His voice fell to a menacing hiss. "Yet all the credit goes to some unlettered outlaw posing as a legend! What is a few moments' discomfort a day compared with that?"

"Discomfort? Why, you vainglorious—" By a massive effort of will, Maura turned to walk away before she said things that would cause a breach the Umbrian alliance could ill afford.

She had barely taken a step when Idrygon caught her roughly by the arm. "You are a fine one to sling insults, *Highness*." The scorn in his voice cut like a switch. "I had hoped your coming might make your husband more tractable."

"If by that you mean I persuade him to abdicate leadership of our forces to you—" Maura jerked her arm free of his grasp "—you could not be more mistaken."

"Spoken like the spawn of a death-mage and a traitor!" Though Idrygon lowered his voice in a vicious whisper, his damning words thundered in Maura's ears.

The accusation wrapped around her throat and squeezed hard. And when she was certain it could not get any worse, she heard Rath's voice, coming closer with each word. "Maura, Idrygon, what is the trouble between you?"

20

As she watched Rath bearing down on her and Idrygon, Maura felt as if someone had shoved her over the edge of Raynor's Rift.

"What's all this about?" Rath wrapped one of his huge arms around Maura's shoulders and glared at Idrygon. "If you want to challenge my decision about the Hanish woman, take it up with *me*. I won't stand for you badgering my wife. Do you mark me?"

Maura braced herself for Idrygon to tell Rath what he had discovered. Meanwhile she cursed herself for confiding in Delyon. She hadn't expected him to keep her secret forever, but at least until the fate of Umbria was decided and she had a chance to break the news to Rath as gently as she could.

"On the contrary, Highness, I have reconciled myself to the presence of the *Hanish woman*." Idrygon's gaze bored into Maura's as one corner of his lips curled in mocking smirk. She knew he was not talking about Songrid. "Provided she poses no threat to our cause in the critical days to come, but proves herself helpful and agreeable, I see no reason to pursue the matter."

He addressed himself to Maura. "Do you believe the woman can be persuaded to cooperate, Highness?"

So that was what he wanted. She should have guessed. If his true aim had been to expose her, he would have gone to Rath at once, instead of seeking her out to reveal what he knew. She could buy Idrygon's silence in exchange for using her influence over Rath on his behalf.

Given only an instant to decide and reply, her mind buzzed with arguments for and against, while her heart felt as if it were being torn in two. Could she betray the promise she had just made Rath to stand by him in any disagreement with Idrygon? But what was the alternative—leave him bereft of her support and counsel altogether?

Besides, she might not approve of Idrygon's ambition or his methods, but she could not quarrel with his results. Without him, she and Rath could never have hoped to liberate the hated mines at last and purge the Han from great areas of the kingdom.

Maura met Idrygon's challenging stare. "Whatever her blood, the woman has already proven herself a friend to the Umbrian people. I am certain she would be willing to oblige any reasonable request for help."

In spite of all the worthy excuses she gave herself for what she was doing, Maura could not escape the feeling she had betrayed Rath and all her beliefs. Could it be her Hanish blood finally making its influence felt?

"Very well, then." Idrygon's dark eyes glittered with secret triumph. "If she continues to cooperate, nothing more need be said. If she proves intractable, however, I will be forced to raise the matter again with His Highness."

"If Maura feels we can trust this woman, that is good enough for me." Rath seemed unaware of the byplay going on in front of him. "Unless you have clear proof she poses a threat. Now, let us not fret so much about one Hanish woman that we forget the two armies of her countrymen closing in on us."

"On the contrary, Highness." Idrygon bowed. "I study to be vigilant of the Han in whatever form I encounter them."

He looked toward the swarming mass of mainlanders being

marshaled by his trained Vestan soldiers into something like orderly ranks. "I believe we are ready to march, sire. I must mount and lead them out. Will you join me?"

"I will catch up with you shortly."

Once Idrygon had departed, Rath turned Maura around to face him. "You see what I mean? He is a forceful character with ideas that don't bend easily."

Forceful and unscrupulous. Though he had gone, Maura fancied she could feel Idrygon's hands around her throat. If he believed she might pose a threat to the Umbrian alliance, he should have told Rath at once instead of using her secret to coerce her into helping him get his way.

"The trouble is, he's right nine times out of ten." Rath gave a rueful shrug. "That's what makes it so hard to oppose him the tenth time."

Maura could only nod in reply. If she tried to speak, she feared the truth would burst out of her.

"Any luck finding Anulf?" asked Rath. "I'll worry less about you visiting Windleford if I know he and the others are watching out for you."

"Not...yet." She forced the words out. "I was looking for him when I met up with Idrygon."

"Could you fetch Snake along with you, too?" asked Rath.

He'd told her how the beggar boy had crossed the mountains to bring word that she and Delyon had been captured. Though she wished Rath had been spared the worry, Maura was touched by what Snake had tried to do for her. It gave her hope that, if they could somehow defeat the Han, the ills that plagued her people might still be remedied.

"I tried to send him back to Boyd Tanner in Prum, but he wouldn't have any of it." Rath stared toward the columns of men on the march. "The young fool says he wants to fight the Han, but I cannot stand the thought of him coming to harm...or of turning a lad his age into a killer."

Maura guessed what he was thinking. "I'll try to leave him

with Sorsha and Newlyn. I reckon they could use his help around Hoghill."

More than ever, she longed to see Sorsha—to confide in her oldest friend and ask for her practical, caring advice.

"We'd better be quick about it before they all march away on us." Beckoning the nearest Vestan officer, Rath ordered him to find Anulf and Snake and arrange Maura's escort to Windleford.

Then he lifted her off the ground and wrapped her in a surprisingly gentle embrace. "Give Sorsha and Newlyn my greetings. Let them see I took better care of you than they expected when we left Hoghill in the spring."

Maura threw her arms around his neck and squeezed with all her might. "No one could have taken better care of me, *aira*! Do you reckon Idrygon would be scandalized if I kissed you now, in plain sight of your troops?"

When might she get another chance to kiss him? After their sudden separation when she'd been whisked away from the Islands, Maura had vowed to miss no opportunity to show Rath how much she loved him.

"Scandalized?" A deep chuckle rumbled through Rath's massive chest as he angled his lips toward hers. "I reckon he might be, but I don't care. This is one of those tenth times when clever Lord Idrygon would be dead wrong!"

"I can't get over it, mistress…that is…Highness," said Anulf a while later as he rode by Maura's side toward Windleford, with young Snake perched behind him. Three men had fanned out ahead to watch for trouble, while two more brought up the rear. "The last time I saw you, I wasn't certain you'd last another hour, let alone weeks and months."

For a moment Maura wasn't sure what he meant. Then it dawned on her. "At the mine, you mean? It was a very near thing. I almost didn't survive."

"I never saw the beat of it." Anulf shook his head. "A slip of a lass standing her ground against a death-mage and turning his power back on him. The air was fairly crackling with it. Why, the hairs on my arms stood straight up."

Snake stared at Maura with wide eyes.

"From that day on," said Anulf, "I never doubted but you was the Destined Queen, like Wolf claimed. So when I heard tell the Waiting King was on the march, I had to come join him. When the other lads from Beastmount got wind of it, naught would do but they must all come with me."

Maura's throat tightened. "You honor us with your service."

Anulf's face reddened. "If it ain't too forward to ask, Highness, whatever became of old Wolf? Last I saw, he was heading down the river with you in an ore barge. Half the reason me and the others joined the king's army was hoping we'd find him here. But we've seen no sign of him."

"Were you not told?" Maura wished she could share the truth with Rath's comrades, but she dared not antagonize Idrygon. "Your friend is very much alive. I saw and spoke with him not long ago."

She flashed Snake a look that bid him keep quiet about what he might know or guess.

"Did you?" cried Anulf. "It does me good to hear news of him. What is he up to that keeps him away from your lord's army? We could use a few more like him."

"He is doing his part for the liberation of Umbria, of that you may be sure," said Maura. "He is…carrying out a very important mission for the king."

It would do Rath good to see his old mates again. Especially now, with the pressure mounting. Was there some way she could arrange it without Idrygon being the wiser? Maura was mulling the problem over when one of the advance party came galloping back toward them.

He reined to a halt in front of Maura and Anulf. "The village is just beyond those trees, Highness. There's a crowd of folk holding the bridge. They don't look like Han—just villagers with hay forks and flails. Should we turn back or try to fight our way across?"

"No fighting," said Maura. "There has been too much blood shed in this land for too long. Bad enough we must battle the Han—I will not see Umbrians fighting one another."

"Go around then, my lady?" asked Anulf. "Look for a spot to ford the river?"

Maura shook her head. "It would take us too far out of our way. I promised we would rejoin the army by nightfall."

She thought for a moment, imagining herself still living in Langbard's little cottage on the edge of the village while the events of the past weeks played out. "If the garrison has left, the villagers may fear an attack by outlaws. Let me go and talk to them, show them we mean no harm."

"Are you sure, my lady?" Anulf looked doubtful. "If any ill befalls you on our watch, we might be sorry we weren't back in the mines."

"No harm will come to me. This is the village where I grew up. Just keep your men back until I have had a chance to speak with someone in charge."

Urging her mare forward, she called, "And while we are here, don't anyone call me *Highness!*"

She rode ahead, following the track through a bit of woodland. Her heart seemed to swell and grow heavy in her chest as she caught sight of Windleford Bridge for the first time in many months. During all the years she'd lived here, the village had never felt quite like home. But returning to it for the first time after a long absence, a warm sense of familiarity and belonging enfolded her.

Waving back two of the advance party, she slowed her mare to a walk and held her hands out to show that she came unarmed.

When she drew near enough that she could recognize several of the men guarding the bridge, she called out, "Master Starbow, how is business at your shop these days? Master Howen, did young Noll's hand heal from the burn of that pain spike?"

"Well, I'll be blessed!" The shopkeeper dropped the staff he'd been holding in a rather menacing posture. "Is that Mistress Woodbury who used to live with old Langbard?"

"It is." Maura pulled the hood back from her hair. "I've come to visit my friend Sorsha Swinley for the day, if you will give leave for me and my friends to pass. Has it been long since the garrison departed?"

"Five days, lass." Master Starbow stooped to retrieve his fallen staff. "At first everyone was so glad to be rid of them, we were beside ourselves. Then we got to thinking how the Han always kept order, at least. Before they pulled out, there was rumors going 'round of an outlaw uprising. Some of us reckoned that might be worse than what we had before."

"There *is* an uprising," said Maura, "led by the Waiting King as the legends have foretold. The Hitherland and the Long Vale are free of the Hanish yoke and the mines have been liberated. If this rebellion succeeds, you *will* be better off. When the cost of order is freedom, is that not too dear a price?"

Her question seemed to puzzle the villagers, for they grew quiet and thoughtful, muttering to one another. Then Noll Howen's father spoke up. "If you've only come for a visit, why have you brought all them men with you?"

Maura glanced back to see Anulf and the others clustered along the edge of the wood. One held a bow, ready to fire if she were attacked.

"Those men mean you no harm. They have only come to protect me on my visit. These are uncertain times and I feared there might be Han still lurking hereabouts. Now that you've assured me I will be safe in Windleford, I can bid my escort wait here until I return. If I do that, will you let me pass?"

The bridge defenders whispered among themselves and quickly came back with their answer, which the shopkeeper delivered. "You may come ahead, lass, and welcome home. If that young nephew of Langbard's is among your escort, you could bring him along, too."

For an instant, Maura puzzled what he meant, then she recalled Rath posing as Simple Ralf from Tarsh. "He…is not with me today, but he will be pleased to hear you remember him with trust. Give me a moment to tell my friends what I mean to do, then I will return."

Anulf shook his head when Maura informed him. "No, you don't, my lady. The river may keep trouble at bay on this side of town, but who's to know what might strike from out of the north? If aught happened while you were over there, and us cooling our heels on this side of the river, I'd have a Wolf hunting me the length of the kingdom."

Before she could protest, he handed his weapon and Snake off to one of the others then rode toward the bridge with his arms in the air.

After a brief exchange he returned, looking much better pleased. "They're willing to let four of us across with the lady provided the rest stay here and give no trouble." He nodded at the largest of his companions. "Odger, Tobryn, you and the lad are with us. The rest of you keep your eyes open and stay out of trouble till we get back."

As she rode across the bridge into Windleford, Maura called her thanks to Master Starbow and the others.

"This way." She pointed down a wide street that would take them through the village and out to Hoghill.

They rode slowly to avoid children and chickens scurrying about. An echo of her old dread seized Maura when they passed the garrison compound. Though the buildings were deserted, the place did not look as if any of the villagers had gone near it. Likely they feared the Han would return.

Maura's hand tightened around the reins. She must make certain that did not happen.

"Mistress Woodbury?" a young woman called from her doorway. "I heard you'd come back to town. Can you stop in later to take a look at my youngest? She had a cough that won't go away."

"I'll try," said Maura. She had nothing in her sash to help the child, but there might be some starslip growing untended in her old garden...if she could bring herself to go there.

As word spread of her return, more and more villagers turned out to greet her. Some came to ask her services as a healer, but more only wanted to wish her well. It moved her to see that they had appreciated all she'd done for them. Perhaps the people of Windleford had not realized how much they'd relied on her and Langbard until they were gone.

"Well, well!" Anulf chuckled. "A popular lass you are in these parts, High—er, mistress."

"Not always," Maura murmured. She longed to set her horse galloping to match her heart, bearing her that much quicker to Hoghill and Sorsha—the one friend who *had* stood by her always.

A few moments later, the beast had scarcely slowed when Maura scrambled from its back and ran into the Swinleys' house.

"Sorsha?" she called. But no one answered.

Maura ran from room to room in mounting alarm, but Hoghill appeared as deserted as the Hanish garrison. A cold knot of fear tightened in her belly. Then she spied Sorsha's egg basket sitting on the table, filled to the brim with fine brown eggs.

She sniffed the air. A thick mutton stew was bubbling in a kettle on the hearth, a low fire still burning beneath it.

Maura darted back outside. Cupping her hands around her mouth, she shouted, "Sorsha! It's all right. It's only me and some friends. You can come out!"

The barn door flew open and Sorsha raced toward her, ruddy brown curls rippling in the breeze. "Maura Woodbury," she gasped between bursts of frenzied laughter. "Don't you ever...give me...a turn like that again...you hear?"

Maura opened her arms and the two friends collided in a laughing, weeping, grappling rush of joy at being together again.

"I near swooned—" Sorsha wiped her warm hazel eyes with the corner of her apron "—when young Bard ran in saying he'd seen riders coming up the lane. I thought sure it must be the Han come back…as if they didn't take enough with them when they left."

"I'm sorry we gave you a fright." Maura introduced Anulf, Snake and the others. "I was so anxious to see you again, I didn't think."

A loud wailing erupted from the barn. "Is it all right, Ma?" Sorsha's oldest boy peeked out. "Can we come out now?"

"So you can, my good, clever boy," Sorsha beckoned him. "Bring the little ones, then go fetch Papa. Tell him Auntie Maura has come for a visit!"

"Look at them!" Maura hoisted three-year-old Lael into her arms while Sorsha took Baby Vela and jiggled her into a happier mood. "They've all grown so. Have I been away that long?"

"Half a year," said Sorsha. "Younglings can change a good deal in that time. Until now you've never gone more than a day or two without seeing them. This little one's walking, if you please. And Lael can talk up a storm once he gets over his shyness. You remember Auntie Maura, don't you, pet?"

The child gazed at Maura with a grave expression for his young years. His thick, dark brows, so much like his father's, knit together as he puzzled his mother's question. At last he replied with a silent but definite nod. How much longer could she have stayed away before the child forgot her altogether?

A tempting picture rose in Maura's mind of her and Rath living across the way in a cottage rebuilt on the foundation of Langbard's. Seeing Sorsha and the children every day as she'd once done. Providing healing for the village folk while Rath planted crops and raised a few animals.

It was no sense trying to fool herself that they could return to such a life if the rebellion failed. They would be lucky to escape with their lives back to the Islands. And if the rebellion succeeded, there would be no quiet life in Windleford for them, either. Rath would be a prisoner of his position, trapped in that elegant palace that held so many troubling memories for Maura.

And her? Maura dared not guess what the future held for her once her secret became known.

"How far have you ridden this morning?" asked Sorsha. "How long can you stay? Why don't you all come in and have something to eat."

Stirred from her haunted thoughts by her friend's practical, hospitable questions, Maura laughed. "Sorsha Swinley, you sound just like your mother—always wanting to feed folks. We only came from the other side of the river and we've all broken our fast. We will have to be on our way back before nightfall."

"So soon?" cried Sorsha. "We'll have to make the most of the time then, won't we?"

"Aye, mistress." Anulf turned toward the women. He had shown Snake how to make the baby chuckle by hiding his face behind his hands, then peeping out at her. "The pair of you go do as you please and don't fret about us. We'll just park ourselves out here and keep watch. If you need us to entertain the younglings while you visit, it would be more a treat than a chore."

Sorsha passed the baby to him before he had a chance to change his mind. "Could I bribe you to stay when Maura leaves?"

Anulf pulled some silly faces that made the baby crow with glee and even coaxed a smile from shy Lael. "If whatever I smell from your kitchen tastes half as good, mistress, you might be hard-pressed to get rid of me!"

"Does that mean I could coax you to take a honey biscuit and a cup of ice-mint tea?"

The men tried to decline politely, but Snake cried, "I'll have theirs, then. Have you got any cider?"

"Plenty." Sorsha laughed. "And there are biscuits enough for everyone. Come on, Maura. You and I always had our best talks over kitchen chores."

Leaving the children with Maura's escort, they went inside. Sorsha put water on to boil for tea then turned to her friend.

"Let me look you over proper. You're a bit thinner than when you left, but well enough apart from that."

Maura lifted the hem of her gown. "I still have the walking shoes you gave me. They've taken me many a mile since that night."

"Many a mile where, though?" Sorsha sat down in her accustomed place at the table opposite Maura. "A great many strange things have happened since you left. Did you have a hand in bringing them about?"

Maura nodded.

"I knew it!" Sorsha wagged her forefinger. "And what became of that Rath fellow you left here with? I had a few bad nights worrying about him, I can tell you."

"I can vouch for that." Newlyn Swinley appeared in the kitchen doorway, his dark rugged countenance alight with a welcoming smile. "I told her the fellow couldn't be any worse than me, but that didn't seem to ease her mind. Dunno why."

Maura chuckled. "Sorsha knew she could handle you, that's why!" She turned to her friend. "Now you know how I felt when you came home married to this mysterious stranger. But we both fretted ourselves for nothing. Remember at your wedding when you gave me your whole bride's wreath and told me you hoped I'd find a man who would make me as happy as Newlyn's made you?"

Sorsha looked dubious. "Rath the Wolf?"

Maura nodded. "We were married this summer on Galene."

"The island?" Sorsha motioned Newlyn to have a seat, then moved to the hearth to brew the tea. "How did the two of you end up there? And how did you end up wed? When you left here, you didn't look as if you trusted him much more than I did. What *have* you been doing since you left here?"

"Having the kinds of adventures you used to hanker after when we were young." Maura ticked some of them off on her fingers. "I was kidnapped by outlaws, then escaped and rode through the Long Vale on a stolen horse. I rescued an old woman from the Echtroi and found a hidden map to the Secret Glade. I was attacked by lankwolves in the Waste, chased by death-mage and crossed Raynor's Rift. I sailed to the Vestan Islands on a smuggler's ship, watched the Hanish Ore Fleet sink in the warding waters and met the Oracle of Margyle."

Sorsha's eyes grew wider and wider.

"Careful, love," said Newlyn, "the teapot's overflowing!"

Sorsha lowered the kettle back onto the hob in a daze. "By any chance did you find the Waiting King and wake him up?"

"It didn't happen *quite* that way," said Maura.

"Oh my!" Sorsha staggered back to the table and sank onto a chair her husband pulled out for her. "I said...didn't I say, Newlyn? I said all the upheaval in the kingdom lately must have something to do with you and Langbard and what went on here in the spring."

Newlyn nodded. "So she did. Almost as often as she said you'd come to a bad end on account of that Rath fellow."

Over many cups of ice-mint tea, Maura told them the whole story—or as much of it as she could bear to tell just then.

"Think of it," Sorsha murmured at last. "My timid little friend turned out to be the Destined... Oh my!"

She scrambled to her feet and made a curtsy so low, Maura feared her friend would topple onto the floor. "Highness!"

"Sorsha Swinley, don't talk nonsense!" Maura grabbed her friend by the arm and caught her in a swift, fierce embrace. "Part of why I came here today was to get away from folks calling me Highness. Now, I want to hear all about what's been happening in Windleford and Hoghill while I've been away."

"Near as nothing compared to all that's gone on with you," Sorsha insisted.

But once Maura asked about the children and one or two of the village folk, six months of family doings and local gossip soon came trickling out. Now and then as she sipped her tea, Maura could almost imagine the months turning back and her old, uneventful life within her grasp.

Newlyn had listened in deepening silence to Maura's account of her travels. Now he rose from the table. "I reckon the two of you have plenty to talk about that you don't want a man around to hear. Farm chores don't wait on quests or battles, so I'd best see to them."

"Tell those men we'll have dinner soon." Sorsha jumped up and gave the stew a stir.

Once Newlyn had left, she sat down again and refilled the teacups. "Now tell me whatever it was you didn't want to say in front of Newlyn."

"How could you tell?"

"Because I've known you so long, of course." Sorsha wrinkled her freckled nose. "Now, out with it!"

Maura blew over her tea to cool it. Though she hadn't meant to bring the matter up so soon, she should have known it would be hopeless trying to keep anything from Sorsha.

"There is something more. Something I found out while I was in Venard looking for the Staff of Velorken..." She hesitated, fearing what she was about to confess to Sorsha might somehow taint their friendship.

"Aye, go on."

"Remember how you once told me my parents must have been murdered by outlaws?"

Sorsha stared into the depths of her cup. "Do you reckon I should have told you the truth?"

"You knew?" Maura almost choked on a mouthful of tea.

"Just what I overheard Mam telling Pa once. About how she reckoned the shame of it killed your mother." Sorsha reached across the table and closed her hand over Maura's. "You felt like such an outsider in the village already, I didn't want to make it worse, so I thought up that outlaw story."

How had Sorsha's mother guessed what Langbard had never suspected? That didn't matter. A warm wave of gratitude for her kind neighbors engulfed Maura. In their friendship and tolerance, she had been richly blessed by the Giver. If they could continue to accept her, then perhaps others might when they learned the truth.

"We were only young then." She clung to Sorsha's hand. "Yet it never changed the way you acted toward me knowing my father was a death-mage."

"A death—?" If Maura had hurled the cup of scalding tea in her face, Sorsha could not have looked more horrified. "Oh, Maura, no! That can't be!"

21

Sorsha leaped from her seat and rounded the table to gather Maura in her arms. "What an awful thing to find out! You poor dear! Are you sure it's true?"

A bubble of laughter burst out of Maura, mingled with a sob. "I wish I could doubt it. But it is the only explanation that answers all the riddles of my past. Why did you sound so surprised? You said you knew…about my mother dying of the shame."

"The shame of bearing a fatherless babe." Sorsha shook her head. "Once I got old enough to understand, I thought it wasn't such a terrible thing to pine away over. This does make more sense, though I wish it didn't. How did you find out?"

Maura had barely choked out her story when a reproachful young voice called from the doorway, "Mam, are we *ever* going to get our dinner?"

"Of course, pet!" With a guilty start, Sorsha flew to the hearth. "Tell those nice men to bring the little ones in, and you go fetch Papa, like a good boy."

The two women quickly fell to the familiar, comforting lit-

tle tasks of getting a meal on the table. If they were both thoughtful and subdued while they ate, no one else seemed to notice.
Young Bard kept Snake and the men busy answering questions
about the far corners of the kingdom they had seen and the battles they had fought under the Waiting King's command.

The little boy's eyes shone with excitement, the way his
mother's used to whenever she'd heard some tale of adventure.
"It's like a story come true, isn't it, Mam?"

"Aye, pet." Sorsha helped the child to another slice of oatloaf. "But life doesn't always turn out like stories."

Anulf scraped his bowl clean. "I used to scoff at the old
stories, Mistress Swinley. Then I found myself in the middle
of one as outlandish as any I'd ever heard when I was the size
of your lad."

He told of how an argument in a tavern had led to him getting sent to the mines. "On the way there, I felt like I was as
good as dead already. Then this stranger began talking about
how he'd seen the Destined Queen with his own eyes, and how
she was on her way to wake the Waiting King. I thought he
must be daft, but the more he talked the more I found myself
wanting to believe him."

Maura listened, almost as entranced as young Bard. Rath had
only given her a brief account of the mine rebellion, downplay-
ing his own role. Now it thrilled her heart to hear the whole
daring, desperate story. The longer she listened, the more convinced she became that Idrygon was wrong—Rath did not need
the false trappings of a legend to inspire belief and courage in
others.

Newlyn Swinley scarcely seemed to heed their guest. Instead, he stared into his bowl and ladled Sorsha's mutton stew
into his mouth with dogged concentration. Perhaps he was trying to block out memories from his own time in the mines.

After the meal, Odger, Tobryn and Snake went off with Newlyn to dig rooties. Anulf offered to mind the children so the
women could take a walk over to Maura's old home.

On the way there, Maura told her friend the rest of what she'd been able to piece together about her past.

"What an awful shock it must have been to find out like that," murmured Sorsha. "It does explain a good deal about you that always puzzled me. Your poor mother! Do you reckon the death-mage forced himself on her? It chills my blood just to think of it."

"He said he'd loved her and kept talking about how she'd betrayed him." Maura glanced up, expecting to glimpse the thatched roof of Langbard's cottage even though she had seen it collapse in flames on the night she and Rath had fled Windleford. "I think she may have seduced him as a way of escaping."

"Oh my." Sorsha's eyes widened.

"If that *is* what she did—" Maura shook her head "—I cannot decide whether to admire her or despise her."

Sorsha stooped to pluck a stalk of laceweed. "Pity her, if she felt that was her only hope."

Maura replied with a nod and a sigh. She gazed around the tiny pocket of land where she'd lived for so many placid years, never guessing what her past or future held. Parts of the old place seemed so familiar, she fancied it might have the power to take her back to a time before any of this had happened. Yet when she glimpsed things that were changed or missing, her old life felt distant and lost beyond retrieving.

A strange air of peace hung about the place. Since the night of the fire, shrubs and flowers had grown up, spreading a mantle of soft, forgiving green over the blackened ruin of the cottage. Maura could picture Langbard sleeping peacefully beneath it.

But what of her mother? The body of Dareth Woodbury lay beneath this earth, too, laid there by Langbard's loving hands. Had her spirit found peace in the afterworld that had eluded her in this one?

Wandering over to her herb garden, Maura knelt and began

to harvest leaves from some plants, flowers and seeds from others. The familiar task brought her a measure of comfort and calm as she spoke of troubling matters.

"Does it truly make no difference in how you feel about me, Sorsha, to know I likely have Hanish blood?"

Sorsha sank onto a flat moss-covered rock on which she had often sat in the past for talks with her friend. "You didn't think it would, did you?"

Maura lifted a cluster of windwort blossoms to her nose and inhaled their wholesome scent. "I wouldn't have blamed you if it had. It changed the way I feel about myself."

"You mustn't let it do that. You're the same person you always were. The same person you'd have kept on being if you hadn't found out. This is not going to make a particle of difference to anyone who cares about you. What about your husband...have you told him?"

Maura shook her head. "It's one thing for you not to mind, Sorsha. You've known me all my life, and the Han have never done anything too awful to you. How do you reckon Newlyn would feel if you told him?"

When her friend did not reply right away, Maura glanced over to find Sorsha gnawing her lower lip, her brow rippled in anxious furrows. "I see what you mean. Perhaps you would be better off just to keep it quiet."

"That's the trouble." Maura tucked the sprig of windwort into an empty pocket of her sash. "I'm not sure I can."

As she continued to gather herbs, she poured out the whole story of Idrygon—how he had discovered her secret and was holding it over her.

"I don't like the sound of him." Sorsha's fists clenched. "I don't care if he tossed every Han out of Umbria with his own two hands. We wouldn't be any better off, would we?"

"You're wrong about that." Maura scrambled up from the ground. "I never much cared for him, even before this. But he's a man who knows how to get things done."

"Perhaps so." Sorsha didn't sound convinced. "What are *you* going to do?"

"I have to tell Rath, of course. In the end, everyone will have to know. I just want to wait and choose my time." She gazed around the garden. "I wish Langbard were here!"

"He is," said Sorsha. "In you. You observed the ritual of passing with him, and even if you hadn't, he spent all those years teaching and training you."

She rose from her sitting place with a sigh. "Now, I reckon you'll have to go see those folks in town with their aches and pains. While you're gone, I'll make supper so you can eat early and be on your way. I wish you could stay longer, though."

"So do I!" Maura wrapped an arm around her friend's shoulders and together they walked back through the fields to Hoghill. "This visit has been like a tonic to me. I will come again as soon as I can. I promise."

Maura spent a busy hour in Windleford doing her best to treat a number of folks who were ailing. She returned to Hoghill to find Sorsha red-eyed and worried, while a great string of sausages burned on the griddle.

"What's wrong?" Maura grabbed a fork and turned the sausages. "Nothing's happened to the children, has it?"

"Not yet." Sorsha gave a loud sniffle. "But it might if their father doesn't come to his senses!"

"Why? What's the matter with Newlyn?"

"A fit of daftness!" wailed Sorsha. "He just storms in from the barn and announces that he means to go fight against the Han. He'll not listen to a word I say!"

"I'm sorry, Sorsha." Newlyn stepped through the door that led to the bedchambers. He was dressed for traveling. "While there seemed no hope of getting rid of the Han, I was content to go about my business and stay out of their way. Now that there's a chance, I have to do my part to win our freedom."

"No, you don't!" Sorsha jumped up and grabbed a handful

of her husband's woolen vest. "The Waiting King has plenty enough men without you. Tell him, Maura."

Enough? Not against the combined ranks of two Hanish armies with their metal weapons and mortcraft. But if it came down to a fight like that, the presence of one Windleford farmer more or less would not matter. Except to be one less Umbrian dead in a noble but hopeless cause.

"There is a great host assembled, Newlyn. You would be one more or less among thousands. Sorsha and the children need you far more."

"I don't flatter myself that the Waiting King can not do without me." Newlyn looked torn yet determined. "But this is something I must do—for myself and for the younglings. I want them to grow up free, and to know I struck a blow so they could. Even if it is just one."

"I'd rather see them grow up unfree than fatherless!" Sorsha sounded angrier than Maura had ever heard her, but Maura knew that anger was only fear fueled by love. "And how am I to manage a place this size on my own with three little ones?"

"There's couple of lads from the village can come and tend the stock until I get back." Newlyn glanced over at Maura. "Win or lose, it'll all be over soon, won't it?"

Maura nodded, wishing she could think of something to say that might change his mind. "I was going to ask if Snake could stay here with you. He's had a hard life, but I think he has a good heart. I'm sure he would be glad to help out."

It might be easier to convince Snake to stay if she made it sound as if he would be doing the Swinleys a good turn.

Sorsha didn't seem to hear anything Maura had said.

"Please, Newlyn," she begged her husband. "After what we went through to be together, don't toss it all away!"

"All *you* went through, Sorsha!" He pulled his vest from her fierce grip. "It was you who hid me from the Han, kept me alive and gave me a reason to live. You brought me to Windleford and found a way for me to stay here. I've done nothing but run and hide since I stumbled out of that cursed mine. Now I need to stand up and fight."

Maura swung the griddle away from the fire and tiptoed out of the kitchen.

Not long after, Sorsha called everyone to supper, apologizing for the burnt sausages. Her eyes were still red and her voice sounded hoarse, but she had an air of peace about her.

When her boys demanded more stories from Anulf, she announced with a convincing pretense of enthusiasm, "Papa's going to go away with Master Anulf and Auntie Maura for a little while. I reckon he'll come back with stories to keep you entertained for a long time."

"Can I come with you, Papa?" asked Bard.

"Me, too!" Lael pounded on the table with his spoon.

"Next time." Newlyn winked at his sons.

Maura hoped there would be no *next time* like this in their lives.

"For now," said Newlyn, "I need you to help look after Hoghill and take care of Mam and Vela."

Bard looked disappointed, but replied with a grave nod. Lael followed his brother's example, though he looked a bit puzzled by what his father had said.

After supper, Newlyn went into the village to hire someone to tend the farm in his absence.

"I'm sorry." Maura watched as Sorsha packed a few supplies for her husband. "If I'd known this would happen, I never would have come today."

"Don't be daft. It was good to see you, and this business with Newlyn isn't your fault. It's just something he has to do. I reckon you understand that better than I do."

Maura nodded.

"He's been such a good husband. I couldn't have asked for better. It's as if the simplest meal I cook for him is always a feast and the most ordinary day a blessing."

"I reckon that's how the Giver would like us all to live," said

Maura. If more folk treasured the simple blessings of freedom once they had been won, then perhaps the dark years of oppression might have served some purpose, after all.

Sorsha dropped Newlyn's pack on the table and caught Maura's hand in a tight squeeze. "Find that Staff of Velorken quick as you can, to drive the Han away without too much bloodshed."

Newlyn's full weight seemed to settle on Maura's shoulders. "I will, Sorsha."

She must. With so many lives at stake, *try* would not be good enough.

"Any sign of them yet?" Rath tried to keep the edge of alarm from his voice.

"Not since the last time you asked, sire." The young Vestan soldier had no better luck concealing his impatience. "I promise I'll let Her Highness in the moment she arrives. Should I order a few men to go looking for her party?"

"No." Rath did not refuse the offer quite as quickly as he had the last two times. "I'm sure they'll be along soon."

If they weren't, he might ride out to look for them.

Hearing footsteps and the murmur of voices from outside, he leaped up and opened his arms to receive his wife. "Thank the Giver you're back. I was beginning to wor—"

He started when Idrygon stalked into the tent instead.

"Back? I didn't go anywhere." Idrygon looked around. "Where is Her Highness?"

"She'll be here any moment." Rath swung away.

"Where did she go?" Idrygon's tone suggested he not only had a right to know, but should have been informed of her going in the first place.

"Just for a quick visit to her old home in Windleford. There was nothing she could do on the march today. I made certain she had a reliable escort."

"How could you have let her go?" cried Idrygon. "We need her to find the staff!"

Rath spun about. He had chafed under Idrygon's tyranny for too many weeks. Swallowed too many orders he didn't agree with for the sake of a cause he'd been reluctant to lead in the first place. "If that precious staff of yours is there to be found, she will find it! And you know as well as I do, the Han have retreated from the Windle."

"The Han are not the only danger to be feared. What sort of lawlessness have they left behind?"

The question caught Rath like a surprise blow. In his eagerness to prove he had changed and would not hold Maura too tight, had he let her take too great a risk?

"I would not send my wife into danger! I told you, she took an able escort—several men I would trust with my life. And you are a fine one to talk. You sent her off into the heart of Hanish territory with only that feckless brother of yours for protection! It is a wonder he didn't get her killed or captured a dozen times over."

"Do not speak ill of my brother!" Idrygon's fists clenched at his sides, and he took a threatening step toward Rath. "Delyon returned safely from Westborne, with your wife and word of where to find the staff. Not to mention vital information about how the Han mean to press their attack against us."

"Information Maura gathered!" Rath shook his forefinger under Idrygon's nose. "She was the one who delivered *him* safely from Westborne, not the other way around. In the company of a few capable men, she could probably cut a swath through the High Governor's army."

Idrygon spun about on his heel. "I will send out a search party."

"You will not!" Rath grabbed him by the sleeve. "Maura said she would return tonight and she will. I do not want her thinking I doubted her."

"Keep your hands off me!" Idrygon batted away Rath's hold on him. "Fie, but I am sick of having to keep you in line!"

"No more than I am sick of being kept in line by you!" Rath

drew back his fist, ready to strike a blow that would make Idrygon's ears ring.

"Stop!" The urgency of Maura's voice stayed his hand. "What is going on here?"

Relief at seeing her safe made Rath forget his quarrel with Idrygon. *"Aira!"* He caught her in his arms and lifted her off her feet. "What kept you?"

Before she could answer, Idrygon spoke, his tone as overbearing and scornful as ever. "And what possessed you to sneak off like that in the first place?"

"She didn't *sneak* anywhere." Rath lowered her to the floor again, remembering some unfinished business. "She asked permission from me, her husband and her king. I agreed it would do her good to enjoy a day's peace with her friend after all she has been through these past weeks."

Ignoring Rath's quarrelsome tone, Idrygon directed his gaze and words at Maura instead. "I expected better of you. Think what might have happened if you'd run into a Hanish patrol. You wouldn't have wanted that…would you?"

Idrygon was in for it now! Rath stood back and crossed his arms, waiting for Maura to bite his head off.

But she did not. Instead, she hung *her* head and answered meekly. "You are right, my lord. I entreat your pardon."

"What are you saying, *aira*?" Rath wondered if his hearing had gone bad. "You cannot mean that."

"I do mean it." She turned to him with a look more troubled than this whole matter warranted. "With so much hanging in the balance, I should not have risked going to Windleford. I wanted so badly to see Sorsha again I did not think through what could have happened."

That made sense, though Rath did not want to make her feel worse, and he grudged admitting Idrygon might be right. "But nothing did happen. You saw Sorsha. You got back here a little late, but safe. You didn't meet up with any Han."

"No. We saw no Han." Maura's glance flitted sidelong to

Idrygon. In the flickering light of a single lantern her face looked pale.

Had something happened that she did not want to confess in Idrygon's presence?

She must confess the truth to Rath, Maura's conscience urged her as she lay awake beside him that night.

Both Sorsha and Delyon had claimed her parentage did not change who she was. Of course, Delyon had wasted no time sharing her sworn secret with his brother, so how far could she trust his word?

Besides, neither Sorsha nor Delyon had suffered as much from the Han as Rath had. Remembering his look of aversion when she'd mentioned introducing him to Songrid, Maura sensed his feelings for her could not help but be poisoned when he learned her true identity. *The by-blow of a death-mage and an Umbrian traitor.*

She fell into a fitful doze with those ugly words slithering in her mind. They spawned disturbing dreams in which she found herself back at Beastmount Mine, wearing the dark robes and mask of a death-mage and wielding a lethal gem wand. She felt herself being seduced by the tempting lure of power, unable to resist.

The din of horns and drums jolted her awake.

"By Bror!" Rath sat up and dragged a hand over his face. "Morning already?"

Idrygon strode into the tent.

"Do you mean to make a habit of this?" snapped Rath.

"Save your outrage! Make ready at once. We have just received word that the fleet from Dun Derhan has landed and the first of their troops are on the move. We must reach Aldwood and take up our position while there is still time."

"Curse them!" Rath was on his feet beginning to dress before Idrygon finished speaking. "Can we spare some men to divert them or slow them down?"

Their hostilities of the past evening forgotten, the two men quickly thrashed out a plan, which Idrygon marched off to set in motion. Once he had gone, Maura rose and began to dress.

When she saw Rath throw open the chest and take out the ingredients of the growth potion, she flew to his side. "Must you do this, *aira*? I heard how Anulf and the others spoke of your part in the mine uprising. You do not need these kinds of tricks to be a great leader."

She tapped her fingers against his chest. "It is in you—here. Not your size or the loudness of your voice that inspires people to follow you."

Part of him wanted to heed her, Maura could tell. He hesitated for a moment, perhaps remembering the pain that had not eased because it had become familiar.

Then he shook his head. "If we are to have any hope of defeating the Han, we will need every advantage we can muster on our side, however small. Now is not the time to shake the faith of our followers with a truth they are not ready to hear."

Maura winced in anticipation of the pain that would soon rack him. A pain she would be powerless to relieve.

"Don't fret, now." He pressed a kiss to her brow. "I will not have to do this much longer. Off you go. I'll come find you when it's over."

"You will not!" Maura clung to him. "If you have the fortitude to bear this, I will not run away and leave you to suffer it alone because I am too much a coward to watch."

"Very well." He mixed the potion. "I do not have time to argue with you, *aira*."

Rath's transformation wrenched her heart as fiercely as it wrenched his body. But she held him and caressed him, crooning every foolish endearment she would summon that might provide the tiniest scrap of comfort.

Once he had recovered, he gathered her in a brief, gentle embrace. "Thank you for staying, *aira*. It helped me remember why I am doing this."

"I just wish you did not have to," muttered Maura, still not convinced it was necessary.

As she helped Rath don his armor, they ate hurriedly from a tray of food that had been brought. Then they mounted their horses and rode out to rally their forces.

"Let every rider take a second man pillion!" Maura ordered. She sought out Songrid to ride with her as an example.

Word quickly spread through the ranks of the approaching Hanish force. The pace of the marchers satisfied even Idrygon, who sent a handpicked unit of Vestan archers off to slow the Hanish advance with strategic ambushes.

The rebels covered a good deal of ground that day. Not even stopping to eat or drink, the men took food while they marched from the wagons that moved through the ranks distributing bread, cheese and strips of dried spiced meat.

Even after the sun had set in fiery splendor behind the Blood Moon Mountains, Idrygon insisted they keep marching at least another hour before he let them stop and make camp. By the time Rath's tent had been erected and he took refuge inside for what was left of the night, Maura could see his armor hung upon his shrinking frame.

When she and Songrid dismounted, she heard Delyon call out to the Hanish woman. "There you are! I was beginning to worry when I couldn't find you."

He shrank back when Maura turned on him with a blistering glare. "I—I have been keeping guard on her."

"Have you, indeed?" Maura dropped her voice to a harsh whisper. "I hope you are better at it than you are at guarding your tongue! How could you, Delyon?"

"I'm sorry, Maura! I didn't mean to say anything, but when Idrygon ordered Songrid executed, I said something I shouldn't in the heat of the moment. There never was a secret my brother couldn't worm out of me if he tried. I still do not understand why it matters so much."

She had neither the time nor the energy to make him understand. The way he looked at Songrid, Maura suspected it would be a wasted effort. "I know you did not mean me harm, Delyon, but you have done me harm all the same."

A while later, she trudged into Rath's tent, eager to throw herself onto the bedroll and sleep. She barely stifled a groan when she found Idrygon already there engaged in a heated argument with Rath.

"Do the two of you do this every night?" She yawned. "Sorsha tells me her boys quarrel when they are tired. Why not wait and talk in the morning when you are in a better temper?"

"Perhaps you are right." Idrygon did not look tired as he turned to answer her. "A decent rest might make your pigheaded husband better able to see sense."

"I could sleep as long as King Elzaban," snapped Rath, "and it still would not change my mind. We have enough blood on our hands already. I will not fight our countrymen. There has to be another way!"

They must be talking about Aldwood, Maura realized, and how to deal with Vang.

"Countrymen?" Idrygon sneered. "They are nothing but common outlaws! Who cares whether they live or die?"

"The Giver cares." Rath's voice rang with certainty. "And so should we. I was a common outlaw, don't forget. I will ride ahead tomorrow and hold talks with Vang. I'm sure I can convince him to join with us. That will strengthen our numbers to fight the Han and spare any more damage to the old castle."

Maura slipped past Idrygon to stand beside Rath. Twining her fingers in his, she gave his hand a squeeze. She had never been prouder of him! He had truly learned to use his wits and his heart to solve problems instead of always relying on force. And he had made a good case for his decision, on grounds that should make sense even to a man like Idrygon. Now surely the argument would end and they could all get some sleep.

"Out of the question." Idrygon dashed her hopes. "You know this Vang creature, do you, from your outlaw days?"

"Aye. He is a hard man, but no fool. I had thought the same of you. Now I wonder. What harm can there be in sparing bloodshed?"

Idrygon paid no heed to Rath's insult. "If you hold talks with this brigand, you would surely be recognized and your identity exposed. We cannot afford that now."

He shifted his gaze to Maura. "Talk some sense into your husband, Highness."

She knew an order…and a threat when she heard one.

"Perhaps Lord Idrygon has a point, Rath." She could not bring herself to meet his gaze as she spoke.

"What point, *aira*? That it is a good idea to slaughter anyone who gets in our way?"

"No. Just that we do not have much time and…" She reminded herself how the bandit chief and his men had taken her hostage and what worse things they might have done if Rath had not rescued her. It was foolish weakness to risk her happiness on their account.

Weakness? The notion seethed in her mind. It was Hanish thinking to regard justice and compassion as a sign of weakness. If she believed that, then perhaps she was one of them, after all—deserving of Rath's suspicion and contempt.

"*Aira*, what is it?"

"There's something I should have told you…" She braced herself for the aversion she would see in his eyes when she finished speaking. "While I was in Venard I discovered…"

"Careful, Highness," warned Idrygon, but she refused to heed him.

"…that my father was Hanish. A death-mage."

"A what?" Rath's hand fell slack in hers.

Though Maura ached to take back her confession, her throat felt as if a noose had been loosened from around it.

22

Hanish—Maura?

Rath wondered if someone had blown a puff of madfern in his face. Or perhaps he was just so exhausted he was hearing things. What would make Maura blurt out something so unbelievable?

"H-how can that be?"

"Remember I told you about that chamber I discovered under the palace—the one with the crystal?" Maura's voice sounded so tight and plaintive. "What I didn't tell you was that a death-mage was there, as well, just when my invisibility was wearing off. When he saw me, he called me by my mother's name."

She choked out the rest of the story. Only after she had finished did Rath realize she'd been speaking in Hanish.

"*Aira!*" He began to laugh and couldn't stop. "This is the best news I have heard in weeks!"

He grabbed Maura about the waist and swung her around so hard, he almost knocked over one of the tent poles.

"*Good news?*" cried Idrygon. "Have you lost your wits?"

"Good news, indeed!" Rath set Maura on her feet and clung to her as his head spun.

It was a pleasant kind of dizziness, though. His hunger and weariness faded. Even Idrygon, for some of his wrongheaded ideas, didn't seem such a bad fellow suddenly.

"This makes everything all right, *aira.*" He cradled her face in his hands, stroking her cheek with one thumb. "You see, the Oracle of Margyle told me my heir would have Hanish blood. I thought that meant I would lose you, one way or another. That's why I was so set against your going to Westborne…with Delyon."

Maura looked deep into his eyes and seemed to read what had been in his heart. "You feared I would be killed or…"

That *or* seemed so daft now. "It was not you I mistrusted, *aira.* I just couldn't imagine another man *not* falling in love with you."

"You are daft, Rath Talward, to think you had anything to fear from Delyon." She glanced toward Idrygon. "In fact, it was he who betrayed me to his brother, though I doubt he meant to."

"Betrayed?" He did not like the sound of that.

"Highness—" Idrygon dropped into his tone of calm persuasion "—I can explain."

"*Highness* is it, now? A few moments ago it was *daft fool.* As for explaining, you will get your chance. First I will hear what my wife has to say."

She had looked as joyfully dazed by his response to her confession as he had been to hear it. But now her expression darkened. "When Lord Idrygon found out my secret, he threatened to tell you unless I helped convince you to go along with his wishes. Just now, for example, about attacking Aldwood rather than trying to persuade Vang to join us."

"I said no such thing!" cried Idrygon. "I swear it by all the ancient prophesies. I would swear it upon the Staff of Velorken itself!"

Those were solemn oaths, indeed. Rath doubted Idrygon would make them lightly. But why would Maura level such a serious charge if were not so?

"Perhaps he did not say it in quite those words. But his

meaning was clear enough. Remember this morning, when you caught us arguing?"

"Aye. About that Hanish woman…Songrid."

"About *this* Hanish woman." Maura tapped her chest with her fingers. "Idrygon said if she cooperated, there would be no need to press the matter further."

"That?" Idrygon shook his head. "I fear you misunderstood my meaning, Highness, and read more into my words than was ever intended."

"Liar!" Maura lunged toward him, but Rath caught her and held her back. "Your threat was plenty clear enough."

"Perhaps it is the way of your people to imagine threats where none exist."

"They are *not* my people!" Maura lifted her gaze to Rath. "You do not believe him, do you, *aira*?"

It was one thing to believe, but another to prove. "I only know what I heard. It could be that you mistook Lord Idrygon's meaning…"

"I did not!" Maura struggled against Rath's grasp. "He had said nothing about Songrid before you arrived. I know what he meant, whatever double-bladed words he used to mask his true intent."

She might hate him for what he was about to do, but Rath must risk it. "This is too important a matter to decide now when we are all weary and feeling the strain of what lies ahead. Let us sleep on it and ask the Giver's wisdom. We cannot afford to squander our energy squabbling among ourselves when we are facing the fight of our lives."

Some of the tension melted out of Maura as she pondered his words, but she refused to meet his gaze or Idrygon's.

"I would rather sleep than quarrel." She pulled away from Rath and sank onto his bedroll. "Right now, I would rather sleep than do anything."

"Wise advice, sire." Idrygon bowed and backed out to the tent. "I will leave you to your rest. I trust the truth will appear clearer in the morning."

Dragging a hand down his face, Rath muttered, "Sometimes the truth must be sacrificed for more important things."

"Spoken like a true king, Highness." Idrygon sounded pleasantly surprised as he disappeared into the night.

"A true king?" Rath glanced down at Maura. This time she did not look away. "I was afraid of that."

In between removing pieces of his armor, he wolfed down the cold supper that had been brought for him earlier. When he had stripped down to a light shirt, he felt Maura's arms slip around his chest from behind and her head press against his back. "You do believe me, don't you, *aira*?"

"Aye." He sighed. "But what am I to do? This army is a weapon of Idrygon's forging. I cannot wield it without him."

"I understand."

"If all goes well, I promise you Idrygon will be made to answer for his actions once this is over."

"And if all does not go well?"

"Put that from your mind, *aira*." Rath twisted around to take her in his arms. "After what I learned from you just now, I feel more hopeful than I ever have."

"Indeed, and why is that?"

"The Oracle of Margyle said my heir would have Hanish blood, which must mean you will bear me a child." He lowered his hand to rest on her belly. "Are you…yet?"

Maura replied with a slow, regretful shake of her head.

Rath refused to be discouraged. "Then that must mean we will both survive to breed our heir."

She seemed to savor the notion. "I reckon it must."

"And the child would not be much of an heir if it had nothing to inherit, would it?"

"I…reckon not. Does that mean we should trust in the Giver's providence?"

"I know it has asked a good deal of us." Rath tilted her chin for a kiss. "But it has not let us down yet."

"No, it hasn't. Do you suppose, if we ask nicely, it might show us a way to avoid a battle over Aldwood, without having to fight Lord Idrygon?"

Rath gave a hopeful shrug. "After tonight, I would not put anything past it."

A few hours later Delyon stared at the vial of growth potion in Maura's hand. "I'm not sure I can do this. If my brother finds out, he will have my head."

Rath looked equally doubtful, but Maura was convinced this would be their best chance to secure Aldwood without a bloody battle they could ill afford. The idea had come to her just before she drifted off to sleep—sent by the Giver, perhaps?

She thrust the vial toward Delyon. "Did you mean what you said? About making amends to me for telling Idrygon the secret you swore to keep?"

She had warned him the transformation would be painful, but he seemed more worried about incurring Idrygon's disapproval.

"I did." Delyon grimaced as he grabbed the vial and tipped it to his lips. He grimaced even worse when he had swallowed the contents. "Fie, that is foul!"

"So it is." Now that he had taken the potion, Maura could let herself feel a twinge of pity for him. "And Rath has had to drink it every morning for weeks. I doubt it will kill you to take it once."

"I'm not so sure." Delyon spoke through gritted teeth as his features clenched in a spasm of pain.

"It will pass, I promise you." Rath wrapped his arm around Delyon's shoulders. "Try to fix your mind on something else. One of your scrolls, perhaps."

The anxious set of his features told Maura he would rather swallow the horrible potion himself than watch helpless while someone else took it.

Delyon's gaze strayed to the corner of the tent where Songrid had put on Maura's gown.

The Hanish woman stared back at him with an anxious expression that bordered on panic. "My people are taught to hide their pain, for it is a sign of weakness."

"There is more than one kind of strength," said Maura.

Leaving Rath to distract Delyon with murmured words of encouragement, she tried to divert Songrid.

"Put this on." She handed the woman her cloak. "And make certain you keep the hood drawn over your hair. Now, do you remember everything else you must do?"

Songrid nodded as she pulled the cloak around her shoulders and tied it securely. "I must ride near Delyon. We must go where his brother can see us, but not too close. We must make him believe we are you."

"That's right." Maura gave her an encouraging smile.

"But what if he comes close?" Poor Songrid! She must wonder if she had traded one kind of trouble for another. "He will be angry if he finds out this trick. Again he may order me killed."

"After last night, Idrygon will want to keep his distance." Was she trying to convince Songrid and Delyon, Maura wondered, or herself? If Idrygon discovered their ruse, it would be just like him to take his anger out on the one person least able to defend herself.

"Do not fear, Songrid," said Delyon. His voice already sounded deeper and stronger. "I will not let *anyone* harm you."

Is that how it was between these two? Maura stifled a smile. And did either of them realize it yet?

When the worst of Delyon's pain had faded and he'd stretched a full foot taller, Rath helped him don the Waiting King's armor.

Then he grabbed Maura by the hand. "Now we must ride if your plan is to do any good."

They pulled up their hoods and kept their heads down as they left the tent. Rath saddled a swift horse. Then he hoisted Maura up behind him and they headed off toward Aldwood.

"Do you reckon this will work?" Maura asked when they had ridden well out of sight of the camp.

Rath nodded. "We will make it work!"

They rode as hard as they dared for several hours until at last they crested a bit of rising ground and found Aldwood spread before them. Several thin plumes of smoke rose from within the eaves of the ancient forest and a single tower jutted up through the lofty treetops. A chill of old fear slid through Maura as she remembered her previous visit to Aldwood.

Collecting the last scraps of *genow* scales she and Delyon had been able to forage from their sashes, Maura cast the invisibility spell upon herself.

Rath glanced back to make certain he could not see her. "I hope Vang Spear of Heaven will listen to reason."

He urged the horse toward Aldwood at an unthreatening pace. When a challenge rang out and several archers rose from behind a row of tall tree stumps aiming arrows at him, he reined to a halt and raised his arms in the air.

"Does Vang Spear of Heaven still hold this place?" he called.

Maura gave him a quick embrace, then slipped from the horse's back.

"Aye, who else?" came the reply to his question. "Who wants to know?"

"Rath the Wolf bids you thanks for your answer. I was a guest here in the spring and—"

"What, the one who fought Turgen, then disappeared?"

"The very one. Now I come with vital news for your leader. If he is still as canny as he once was, he will listen to me."

It seemed Vang was canny enough, for a short time later Rath stood before the bandit chief. Vang looked as menacing as ever with his scarred face and one empty eye socket. But his shaggy mane was thinning and going gray.

"Ye have gall, Wolf, I'll say that for ye—showing yer face back here after ye foxed me out of my prisoner and that fine sash. Not to mention lifting a purse and a good nag. Have ye come back to settle yer account after all this time?"

Rath pondered Vang's greeting for a moment then pulled a

wry face. "I reckon we parted with accounts even between us. Your nag and the coins for mine and our supplies. I did you a favor taking that rascal Turgen down a peg. I knew you would want to reward me, so I saved you the bother by collecting my own prize."

The hulking bandit chief leaned back in his great throne, hewn from a tree trunk. He tried to scowl, but one corner of his mouth arched up in a grudging grin. "That gall will land ye in trouble one day, Wolf. What brings ye back to Aldwood?News, I hear?"

Rath nodded. "News and an offer. The first you would be wise to heed and second you would be wise to accept."

"What is your news—that the Waiting King has chased the Han out of the Long Vale? That is an old tale now and of no great interest to me. Why should I care who sits in Venard collecting the taxes? In this little corner of the kingdom, I am lord and collect my own levy in my own way."

Rath shook his head and clucked his tongue as if disappointed in Vang's answer. "Your scouts must be cautious these days, not venturing far from home, or they would have brought you fresher news. The Waiting King's army is marching toward Aldwood, a few hours on my heels at most. They are many, they are desperate and they are led by a man every bit as ruthless as you. If you try to stand against them, I promise you a slaughter."

"A slaughter, is it?" Vang leaped up, shaking his great ham of a fist. "I will give them a slaughter if they come looking for one!" He hesitated, as if struck by a surprise blow from behind. "But what makes them desperate? Why should the Waiting King want a tumbledown castle on the edge of nowhere?"

"Because two Hanish armies are closing in on his force and this is the nearest spot he can hope to defend." Rath did not mention the Staff of Velorken. The less Vang knew about that, the better. "I reckon you might stave off the rebels for a while, but it would only leave you and them weakened for that horde of Han…just the way fighting me would have weakened you to fend off a challenge from Turgen. You chose the wise course once, Vang. Choose wisely again."

Men like Vang did not survive as long as he had if they showed fear. But Rath had lived this kind of life long enough that he could detect the most subtle signs. Vang was afraid, and a frightened beast could be dangerous when cornered.

The bandit chief bellowed. When a man came running, he ordered, "Send out three of our fastest riders. One to the north, one northeast and one northwest."

"With messages, Chief?"

Vang shook his head. "To scout. For armies on the march. As soon as they spot anything, they are to ride back at once with news."

The messenger headed off to carry out his chief's order.

"Haste!" Vang barked after him.

The man nearly tripped in his hurry to get out of sight.

"Now..." Vang turned his attention back to Rath. "If it is as you say, why should I throw in my lot with this Waiting King? I have done well enough under the Han."

"Until now," said Rath. "But your world is about to change one way or the other and you must decide how best to weather it. We both know the life of an outlaw is for young men. Your hold on power is only as strong as your ability to fight off the next challenge from some tough, ambitious young buck."

"I have plenty of good years in me." Vang flexed his muscles. "And woe to the fool who thinks he can take me down!"

"Woe to *you* if the Han put down this rebellion," said Rath. "For they will not rest until every ember of resistance has been crushed under their iron-toed boots. And with the new troops that have been sent to aid them, they will have the power to do it. Do you fancy ending your life in the bowels of the Blood Moon Mountains?"

Vang gnawed on Rath's words and appeared to find them

tough chewing. "Would I be any better off under this Waiting King? Will he not want to see his kingdom law-abiding and orderly? Would his prison be so much better than their mines?"

Rath glanced around at the tumbled-down castle. "His prison might well be better than this. And *anything* would be better than the mines. And who is to say you would be bound for prison? Umbria is a vast land. The Waiting King will need strong, shrewd men to help him rule it all."

"What daft talk are you spewing, Wolf?" Vang gave a hoot of scornful laughter. "You reckon the Waiting King is going to make me the lord of Norest?"

"Who better? Some *zikary* who has been licking up to the Han all these years, or a strong leader who has resisted Hanish oppression…in his own way?"

That notion struck Vang dumb for a moment. Rath used the time to hammer home another point. "Especially if that man came to the king's aid just when he needed it most? Think on it, Vang—in times of peace and order, a shrewd man can cling to power and a comfortable life on his wits alone. Even when the strength of his body fails."

The faraway gleam in Vang's one good eye told Rath he was tempted. But would that temptation prove potent enough to win his help? And would that help be enough to hold off the Han until Maura located the Staff of Velorken?

She must find the staff and she must find it quickly.

Maura made her way through the ruins of Aldwood Castle, trying to avoid drawing attention to her invisible passing. Meanwhile, she sifted through two sets of faint memories in an effort to find her way.

One was her recollections of Aldwood from her brief captivity in the spring. The other was the old memories passed down to her through a long line of Abrielle's descendants, of a time when this castle had been new and whole. If she could piece those memories together with what she now saw before her, she might be able to locate the long-hidden staff in time.

So far, she had not even managed to find her way underground. That burrow of passages, cells and storerooms where she'd once been held prisoner was where she believed the staff must lie hidden. If only she could reach one of the upper parts of the castle she remembered clearly, then she might find her way from there to the lower levels.

Ahead of her, three men lounged in a narrow doorway talking together in hushed tones. It sounded as though they were speculating about Rath's sudden arrival and what would come of it. Beyond them, Maura thought she spied a familiar courtyard. She stood for a moment, waiting for the men to disperse, but they did not. Instead, a fourth man arrived with word that Vang had ordered scouts sent out. This prompted still more talk.

Maura tried another way, but it led nowhere that she remembered and she feared getting lost in the maze of twisting passages and small chambers. So she turned around and headed back. The trio of outlaws had not budged in the meantime and did not look likely to any time soon. Maura could not afford to linger, for the invisibility spell might wear off at any moment.

Pitching her voice as deep as possible, she growled, "Have you lot nothing better to do than hang about gossiping?"

The outlaws all jumped and fled in different directions so quickly, the barred doorway seemed to empty by magic. Before any of them had a chance to turn and question where the voice had come from, Maura darted through it and found herself in the courtyard where Rath had fought the outlaw Turgen. From there, she was able to get her bearings and soon found her way underground to the cell where she'd been kept prisoner.

Today that small chamber stood empty, as did all the others, its door hanging slightly open. Maura paused for a moment, her eyes closed, trying to summon the faint, shadowy image of Abrielle bearing the Staff of Velorken through the twisting labyrinth of dim passageways.

The staff was there, though. She sensed its power in the same strange manner she'd often sensed the presence of mortcraft. Except the feelings it inspired were totally different. Mortcraft oppressed her spirit with its mixture of fear, doubt and despair. The nearness of the staff buoyed her with strength, courage and hope.

She had first felt it when she'd been Vang's prisoner, though she'd never guessed the source of the calm fortitude that had welled up within her then. Perhaps if she let it, the power of the staff would guide her now. She emptied her mind of all the fears that had swirled within it. Fears of what might happen if she did not find the staff in time. Different, but no less alarming, fears of what might happen when she did find it.

Then she eased her desperate grip upon the shrouded memory Delyon's spell had stirred in her only to discover it became clearer. Perhaps she did not need to search so hard, only stop struggling and let the enchantment of the staff draw her to it.

Giver, lead my steps. Maura repeated the words to herself over and over in a silent litany with the soothing rhythm of flowing water.

Then she began to flow with it—her feet moving without conscious effort. Down the passageway, through one open chamber, then another, down a long flight of stairs to a deeper level. In time she left behind the torchlit passages, slipping into shadows and finally into deep darkness. A notion flickered in her mind that perhaps she should strike a spark of greenfire to light her way, but the pull of the staff seemed to gain greater power over her when her other senses did not get in the way.

At last she felt herself in a larger chamber. A cool breath of air flickered from somewhere, whispering over her cheek. She halted—somehow certain her long search had come to an end. With trembling hands, she fumbled in her sash for a twig. Then she held it up, chanted the greenfire spell.

The familiar soft, verdent glow flared up, lighting a strange chamber, that also seemed oddly familiar. An array of sturdy pillars stood sentinel throughout the underground hall. Each looked like the trunk of a tree, complete with rough bark and roots sunk deep into the floor. Their stout upper branches fanned out to form a lattice of beams that supported the vast, high ceiling.

The place reminded Maura of the structure atop a Margylese hill where the Oracle liked to meditate—only on a much grander scale. By the dim greenfire light, she began to make her way through the room.

Her foot caught on something. She stumbled and almost fell.

Glancing down, she discovered the chamber floor was littered with great axes and other cutting tools, their blades gouged, dented and in some cases shattered. Clearly, many attempts had been made to cleave these underground tree pillars. Yet none of the trunks showed so much as a chip of its bark.

A paralysing chill of doubt slithered through Maura's belly. She had found the chamber, but where was the staff?

Hearing a sudden noise behind her, she quenched her greenfire and slipped behind one of the pillars.

Had their mission to Aldwood all been for nothing? Rath wondered as his talks with Vang dragged on and the bandit chief showed no sign of lending his support to the rebel alliance.

"Who are ye, Wolf, to offer me terms on behalf of this would-be king?" Vang fixed him with a one-eyed squint.

"I do not expect you to trust me." Rath could feel the edges of his temper fraying dangerously. "Only think on what I say and use your head. You will see there is only one choice ahead that will not lead you to disaster."

"That may be, or it may not," growled Vang. "I have yet to hear if ye spoke true about what is going on out there."

He waved one beefy hand toward the north in a dismissive gesture, as if nothing of any importance to him ever went on beyond the fringe of his forest.

At that moment, a lanky lad dashed in, gasping for breath

and clearly alarmed. "Armies, Chief—three at least—all heading straight for us! The two coming behind may catch the other, I reckon, before they reach here."

Rath cursed himself. He should never have left them to come on this fool's errand. What had made him think he could reason with Vang?

"You see?" he cried. "It is as I told you. War has come to your doorstep. Do not make the mistake of believing it will pass you by. Give me your answer, now! Will you take a risk for a better future or will you cling to what you have until it drags you down?"

Vang scowled over his choices, but when he opened his mouth to answer, Rath caught a glimmer of something that kindled his hopes.

"Chief!" A call from the back of the great hall interrupted Vang and made Rath spin around.

One of the outlaws strode toward them hauling Maura along, her wrists bound behind her. "I caught this one sneaking about down in the Deep Hall."

"You again!" Vang sprang up, glaring at Maura. Then he rounded on Rath. "What treachery is this, Wolf?"

Whatever hopeful sign Rath thought he'd sensed in Vang earlier had disappeared.

Newlyn Swinley sensed the noose of panic tightening around the throats of the Umbrian rebels. As he struggled up the steep, broken ground of the heath, he had to take care not to stumble over the gear that some of the men ahead of him had thrown aside in a desperate effort to make more haste.

Most of the men had little breath to spare for talk. Yet somehow word had spread that they were being pursued by not one but *two* Hanish armies, both of which were quickly gaining ground on them.

Another word on every rebel soldier's tongue or mind was *Aldwood*. If they could reach the ancient forest before they were overtaken, they might stand a chance against the Han. The Vestans would be able to fire their lethal arrows from behind cover against any Hanish charge. And if the battle went against them, the Umbrians could always flee deeper into the woodland where the Han would be loath to pursue them.

In the back of his mind, Newlyn fancied he could hear Sorsha begging him to do just that at the first sign of trouble.

But he was determined to get a few good licks in before taking to his heels. And that he would do only when all hope failed.

As he labored up the slope, he saw a man sitting stiff-backed on a dappled horse. An air of command hung about the officer, so intense it almost made Newlyn shrink back. He told himself not to be daft—this man was on *their* side.

Pausing at the top of the rise to catch his breath, Newlyn made the mistake of glancing behind him. What he saw made his nostrils flare and his heart hammer. The gap between the rebel stragglers and the vanguard of the Hanish force was closing fast. The vast size of that force sent a sickening chill through Newlyn and stirred dark memories of his time in the mines.

The man on the horse lowered the tube from his eye and stuffed it into a rounded scabbard.

"We must take the outlaw fortress," he cried. "And we must take it swiftly!" Wheeling his mount, he charged down the slope toward the forest, roaring orders and urging the front ranks of rebels to attack.

Newlyn had caught his breath by now. Turning his back on the pursuing Han, he ran down the broad slope toward the forest and its promise of refuge. If he had to fight the outlaws of Aldwood to get in, he would. He clutched a long, stout crook that had served him well as a walking stick on the march. Now he would wield it as a fighting staff. If he lost that, he had a hatchet looped in his belt and a long knife sheathed on the other side.

He would rather save them for the Han, but he might not have that choice. Any fool could see Aldwood was the rebels' only hope to avoid a slaughter. The men around him knew it, too, for they charged toward the ancient towering timbers with weapons drawn and war cries rolling from their throats.

The first hint of trouble struck Newlyn when one of the mounted rebel captains let out a scream of pain that pierced the rumbling thunder of running feet and pounding hooves. He glanced in the direction of the cry, expecting to see one or more arrow shafts bristling from the fellow's body.

The rider twitched and thrashed in his saddle, howling in agony until his terrified mount rose on its hindquarters and threw him to the ground. Only then did the screaming stop…for a moment. Then it rose from a different direction. From two different directions. What was going on?

The men around him must have wondered the same thing, for the pace of their advance on Aldwood slowed and their heads twisted this way and that, searching for the source of the assault against them.

"Over there!" a fellow running ahead of Newlyn cried, pointing westward as he veered to the east.

On instinct, Newlyn followed the other man, casting a glance westward. What he saw made his throat tighten and his bowels feel suddenly hollow. A troop of mounted Han must have separated from the main force and swung wide to the south. Now they galloped between the rebels and the shelter of trees.

At that moment a gust of wind blew aside a swath of cloud that had covered the sun. A sharp beam of light shot down to glare off the Hanish armor and glitter from the lethal gems atop the wands of several death-mages.

The Hanish riders galloped into the path of the oncoming rebels, pausing only to trade blows with a few mounted Vestans who rode out to engage them. But the rebel riders were far too few. Most had been assigned to the rear—carrying stragglers and harrying the front ranks of the Han.

Faced with a line of mounted Hanish soldiers and death-mages between them and the forest, the rebel advance stalled. It had been one thing to charge an outlaw stronghold, against a force that might be scattered, ill-equipped and taken by surprise. The Han were concentrated and well armed, with surprise firmly on their side. Not to mention the terrible power of the death-mages, which the rebels had not tasted until now.

A loud wail from nearby startled Newlyn and almost made him drop his crook. A tall man—from Southmark by the look of his headgear—jerked and quivered like one of the wooden dance-dolls Newlyn had carved for his sons. Blood seeped from his nostrils and the corners of his mouth as he screamed. Those nearest the suffering man moved away from him, in case the death-mage's wand should find a target in them.

Not knowing what else to do, Newlyn thrust out his crook and caught the man by one leg, pulling it out from under him so he fell. As soon as he went down, the screaming stopped...and another rebel's began.

Newlyn grabbed the Southmarker, who was still bleeding but alive, and propped him against an outcrop of rock where he was less likely to be trampled. Glancing up the ridge, Newlyn saw more and more rebels pouring over it, only to join a mass of seething, howling chaos on this side.

Then the horseman on the ridge cried again, "To Aldwood! Charge!"

Foolhardy as it seemed, when Newlyn heard the order, he knew it was their only hope. If they milled about trying to escape the bite of Hanish blade, arrow or wand, the enemy could pick them off a few at a time, at will. If they pressed the attack, he might not live to reach Aldwood, but those coming after him might.

This was what he'd told Sorsha he needed to do—not cower in the forest, but face the Han on a field of battle and wrest back what they had stripped from him on the day they'd branded him, given him a sniff of slag and thrust him into the mines.

"Charge!" Newlyn and a number of others took up the cry and sprang forward.

An arrow whistled past his ear and he heard a cry of pain behind him. But he did not look back. Instead, he dropped to a crouch and ran in a jagged shifting path that he hoped would make him harder to hit.

The sudden rebel surge seemed to catch the Han off

guard. When Newlyn broke through their line, he found himself between several men fending off sword blows from Hanish riders. One cried out and fell back, bleeding. Another went down under the flailing hooves of a horse when it reared.

While the Hanish soldier clung to the reins with one hand and lashed out with his sword, Newlyn caught him around the neck with his crook, pulling him half out of the saddle. Struggling to keep his seat, the Han dropped his blade. A young rebel picked it up and brandished it. Two others leaped up and hauled the Han down by his thick, golden white plume of hair.

Newlyn caught the Han's horse by the reins and vaulted into the saddle. He patted the creature's neck to calm it. "If we get out of this alive, I promise I'll ride you home and hitch you to a nice peaceful plow."

Perhaps it was the tone of his voice, or the reassurance of his touch. Or perhaps in some queer fashion the animal understood what he meant, for it grew less agitated and responded to his tug on the reins. Wheeling the beast, he rode it out of the fray. There he paused for a moment to get his bearings and see how he might make his best fight. Then, holding his crook like a short lance, he plunged back into battle again, knocking aside Hanish blades and unseating more riders.

His efforts seemed to hearten the other rebels. More and more threw themselves at the Hanish riders, who began to give ground, slowly retreating toward the edge of the forest. In some places, a trickle of rebels broke through their thinning ranks and ran into the shelter of trees.

"We might make it yet," Newlyn muttered, slamming his crook down on the blade hand of a Hanish rider.

Then a shattering spasm of pain ripped through him, worse than any he could remember. A cry broke from his throat. Like the pain, it seemed to go on and on. In his heart, Newlyn begged the horse to end his torment by tossing him and breaking his neck. It would not matter. All was lost. Out of Aldwood he could see a swarm of heavily armed outlaws emerging to bar the rebels' way.

Then, as quickly as it had struck, the pain released him from its crushing jaws. Newlyn had just enough strength to slump forward over the horse's neck, dodging the swing of a blade meant to take off his head. An instant before, he would have welcomed the blow. Now he clung to life.

For the outlaws of Aldwood had not barred the rebels way, after all. Instead, they had launched an attack upon the Hanish riders from behind. Lifted on a warm wave of hope, Newlyn pulled himself tall in the saddle again and gave a cheer.

"Onward!" he cried. "To Aldwood!"

Then another blade slashed out at him. This time, he was not able to dodge it.

"Onward to Aldwood!" From the edge of the forest Maura heard that hopeful call ring out above the din of battle.

Silently she blessed Rath or the Giver or whatever had overcome the bandit chief's suspicions and made him throw his men into the fray. When she'd been discovered and hauled into Vang's terrifying presence, she had pictured her worthy destiny crushed in his meaty fist.

While he had mulled over his decision, his rough features clenched in a dark scowl, hope had almost deserted her. Hearing his bellowed order for his outlaws to attack the Han, she had wondered if her ears were playing tricks on her.

"Come, witch." Vang hauled Maura along as he strode from the great hall. "We may need your powers in this fight."

Her gaze met Rath's as Vang marched them to the castle armory. She sensed what he wanted to know, but how could she convey such a complicated answer without words?

"Grab yourself a blade or two, Wolf." Vang gestured toward walls hung with a bristling array of weapons. He pulled down a massive sword that looked capable of slicing a man clean in two with a single stroke.

"Would you have a staff, by any chance?" Rath asked, directing a swift glance toward Maura before turning his attention to Vang's cache of weapons. "I've found they can come in handy during a fight."

Maura knew the question was meant for her rather than the bandit chief. Rath had learned something useful from Idrygon.

"A staff?" Vang gave a dismissive shrug. "Might be. Have a poke around."

"I will look while you choose a blade," said Maura. "It may be that I will spot one but find it out of my reach."

Would he understand what she meant—near enough at least?

"In that case," said Rath, "you may need some help to get at it." Lifting down a sturdy-looking blade, he tested the grip and balance of the weapon

Maura pretended to search for a staff, hoping Rath had some idea what she'd meant. As for his answer, did he mean they must find Delyon? With all his study of ancient writings, the young scholar might know how to retrieve the precious talisman that lay just beyond their grasp.

While Rath and Vang threw themselves into battle, Maura crouched behind the thick trunk of a long-needle pine, watching for a chance to use her skills to aid the rebels.

Overhead, thick banks of cloud raced across the sky. Behind them, the sun was sinking toward the Blood Moon Mountains. If only Rath's men could win their way through to the forest and hold off a Hanish attack until sunset, they might gain a reprieve long enough for her to find the staff.

From out of the battle, an Umbrian man came running straight toward Maura. He appeared to have lost whatever weapon he'd had. By the way he cradled one arm against his body she could tell he must be wounded. Before he could reach the shelter of the trees, a Hanish rider came galloping after him, blade raised to finish him off.

Maura had a wisp of spidersilk in her hand, but that would do no good. The Han would overtake the wounded man long before she could dart out and apply the spell. Almost before she realized what she was doing, she groped on the ground for a rock. Not too large a one, or she would never be able to throw it far enough. Not too small, or it would do no good, even if it hit the rider. Her hand closed over one that felt the right size for her purpose.

As she pulled back her arm to fling it, she whispered a plea in *twaran* that she had not even realized she knew. "Giver, guide my aim and strengthen my arm. I fight, not to take life, but to defend it."

A jolt of power surged through her. She hurled the stone with such intense force that she lost her balance and fell to her knees. When she picked herself up and checked to see if her effort had done any good, she saw that the Han had dropped his blade and his sword arm hung limp. His horse had swerved, now he brought it around and set off after his prey, determined to ride the man down before he reached safety.

Bursting out of the forest, Maura cried in Hanish, "Look out behind you!"

Unable to ignore the warning, perhaps because he'd heard it in his own tongue, the rider pulled his mount around to face whatever threat might be bearing down upon him. By the time he realized it had been a trick and turned back again, the injured rebel had staggered into the relative safety of the trees.

The Han yelled curses at Maura, then rode off. She paid him no mind, for something had caught her eye as she helped the wounded man to safety.

"Are you bleeding anywhere?" She lowered him to the ground between two large exposed roots.

Her sash bulged with the candleflax and laceweed she had harvested from her herb garden. How far away that peaceful spot seemed now, in time and distance!

The man shook his head, partly in answer to her question and partly in wonder. "Blood would have been pouring out of me if your aim hadn't been so good, mistress. I never saw a lass hurl a rock like that. I reckon I've broken a bone or two."

He grimaced as if remembering the injury that danger had driven from his mind.

Broken bones would take time and skill to set, but at least the man was in no immediate danger. Maura rummaged in her sash and pulled out a leaf of summerslip. "Chew on this. It should ease your pain. Once you've caught your breath, go take refuge in the old castle... I will look for you later to tend your hurts."

The man took the leaf with his good hand and stuffed it into his mouth with only an instant's hesitation. "Thankee for all, mistress. Or ought I say *Highness*? May ye be our queen?"

Maura patted his leg. "So I may."

Drawn by the kind of screams that had haunted her nightmares for many months, she scrambled up and headed back toward the battle. More men had managed to break through the line of Hanish riders and stagger into the shelter of the forest. Maura longed to stop and tend the wounded, but there was something she must do first, though she shrank from it.

She glimpsed a knot of death-mages clustered to guard each other's backs as they dealt pain and terror at will upon the rebels. One in particular drew Maura's gaze. She recognized his wand of the hard greenish metal called *strup,* and the menacing glitter of the poison gem imbedded in its tip.

She had no stolen wand to turn against him as she'd done twice before when confronting his kind. But she had a weapon that might prove even more potent. As she strode onto the field of battle, she reached back and plucked the cord that held her long, thick braid together. Then she fanned the hair out in loose ripples down her back and over her shoulders—the way she had seen her mother in her buried memories.

She wanted to protect Rath's men from the torment of those vile wands, and to do her part in snatching an easy victory from the Han. But there was more to what she was about to do than either of those. Maura needed the death-mage to know what she had found out about their shameful connection and she needed some acknowledgment from him. Preferably a hostile one, to confirm they were enemies even if she shared his blood.

For a wide area around the death-mages, the ground was empty. Having witnessed the torment they could deal out, the rebels would rather take their chances against the blades of ordinary Hanish soldiers. Those, at least, they could return in kind. And if they did take a blow from one, it might be a swift death. Merciful compared with mortcraft.

Maura marched as near as she dared to the path of the poison gem, then she advanced toward the death-mage who held it.

He paid her no heed at first. Perhaps he was concentrating too hard on the victim whose hoarse cries rang in her ears, urging her to end his pain even at the risk of suffering it for herself. Or perhaps he could not believe anyone would be daft enough to approach him when he had only to twitch his wand a few inches and make them bitterly regret their folly. Or was it possible he glimpsed her out of the corner of his eye but feared she might be another trick of his failing mind?

Closer and closer she drew to him, so he would be certain to hear her, even over the din of battle.

"Pravash!" she cried. In Hanish it meant *father.* Maura could not have addressed him by that name in Umbrian, even if he'd understood it. The Umbrian word for *father* would always make her think of Langbard.

"Look at me, Father! See what you begot with your conquest of Dareth Woodbury?"

The poison gem wand quivered and sank a little. The screams behind Maura stopped. The black-hooded head shook in denial. The hard, cruel mouth below the hood moved, but whatever words came out were too faint for Maura to hear. She could guess what the death-mage was saying, though, and to whom.

"If you are trying to dispel me, save your breath!" she cried.

"I am no delusion. But I am the cause of all you see around you and I will be the means of your undoing."

"It cannot be." In spite of his denial, the death-mage spoke loud enough for her to hear. "*You* cannot be."

"Why not?" With deliberate steps, Maura continued toward him. "When a man and woman lie together as lovers, is it not likely for a child to come of it? Even if that is not their intent? Even if they are bitterest foes? Even if their union makes traitors of them both?"

The death-mage shrank back, as if her words were as deadly as his wand. The two Echtroi on either side of him seemed to notice something amiss at last.

"What is the lowling wench blathering about?" demanded the one armed with an ice gem wand.

"Silence her!" ordered the one on the other side. "Then get back to work. These lowlings are putting up a vicious fight, curse them! If too many get in among the trees before the rest of our force comes, some may slip through our fingers."

The death-mage raised his wand and aimed. Maura braced for the pain to gnaw at her in its particular way. Having felt the torment of an ice gem and a shadow gem, she had hoped never to endure another. But if that was the price for this confrontation, she was willing to pay it.

The poison gem was pointed straight at her, yet Maura felt no pain. It must take an effort of will to trigger and channel that terrible power. It appeared the death-mage was unable to make that effort against his own flesh and blood. Perhaps she reminded him too much of the woman who had made him feel tenderness and passion, back when he still had a heart.

"You cannot do it, can you?" Maura challenged him. The last thing she wanted from him was leniency.

He shook the wand and glared at it, his mouth clenched in a rigid line. Still Maura felt nothing.

She raised her hand and held it out. "Give me that thing."

Now he glared at her. "You are immune to it, somehow."

"I am as vulnerable as anyone else." An unwelcome notion took stubborn root in her mind. "Perhaps you are, too."

She wanted to hate him for being who he was and doing the things he'd done to keep her people in fear and bondage. Most of all she wanted to hate him because he had tainted her and made her question everything she'd believed herself to be. That hate would be a measure of her identity as an Umbrian and her loyalty to her people.

Hate could be a potent and terrifying weapon. But suddenly Maura found herself disarmed, unable to summon its potency any more than her father could summon the power of the poison gem against her.

"Give me…" Her outstretched fingers began to tremble and her eyes prickled with tears she scorned to shed, for they would make her look weak.

Reeds bend before the mighty rage of the storm. Langbard's words welled up from the depths of her memory to remind her of a long-ago lesson. *Does that make them weak? When the storm passes, they rise again and flourish. Let your heart be supple as a reed, dear one, and as strong.*

"Give me…your hand."

She stood near enough, now, that if he leaned over the neck of his mount, he could do what she asked. But would he be able to bend so far?

Behind the black hood that hid his identity and humanity, his eyes glittered with what looked like terror. By refusing to bend, would he be broken by the tempest raging inside him?

The wand that was both his weapon and his shield lowered, and he swayed in his saddle—falling more than bending. Then his hand thrust out toward her, as if some potent force of restraint had suddenly snapped under pressure.

Maura lunged forward to catch his fingers in hers. But the tips no more than brushed when his jerked back and he let out a howl of pain that startled both Maura and his mount.

It stopped almost as quickly as it had begun and Maura

heard the death-mage beside him growl, "Don't be a fool! Give the little wretch what she deserves."

She had stumbled several steps backward when his horse reared. Now the pain she had invited moments ago engulfed and consumed her. Every fiber of her body seemed to burst into flame at once. She drew breath to scream, but before a sound could escape her lips, the fire in her flesh extinguished, leaving her limp and shaken. Another cry rang out, deep and rasping, with a shrill edge of shock and rage.

When her vision cleared, Maura could see her father and one of the other death-mages pointing their wands at each other. Having engaged in two such duels, she knew if it lasted very long there would be no victor.

"Stop!" She struggled up from the ground and moved toward her father.

She had taken only a single stumbling step when she heard the pounding of hooves behind her. A strong arm wrapped around her waist to pull her off the ground and onto Rath's horse. They galloped toward Aldwood.

"Don't scare me like that, *aira*! When I spied you walking toward that death-mage, I near spewed my guts right then. The Han I was fighting might have taken my head off if Tobryn hadn't jumped up and grabbed him by the hair."

"Please, Rath." Maura struggled in his arms. "I must go back to my father. He saved my life."

Unless she acted swiftly, he would pay for it with his own.

"Your who? He what?"

"The death-mage. My father." Maura grabbed the reins higher than where Rath held them and pulled to bring the horse about. "They told him to use his wand on me, but he couldn't. And when one of the others did, he…"

"I will do what I can." Rath wrested control of his horse back from Maura, then slowed the beast and eased her to the ground. "If you promise to stay in cover and see to the wounded. Will you?"

This dangerous task would require the horse's speed unencumbered by an extra passenger. It would also take a man's kind of strength and Rath's quick wits.

"I will." She nodded so hard, her whole body quivered. "I promise. Now go!"

There were no Han near by, but still she retreated behind the closest tree, in case a stray arrow flew her way or a mortcraft wand pointed at her. Peeking out from behind the broad trunk, she watched Rath speed back toward the death-mages.

But it was too late.

Some of the other rebel warriors had seen a chance to remove the greatest obstacle between their beleaguered army and the refuge of the forest. They fell on the dueling death-mages, hewing them down with quick strokes before taking advantage of the unguarded backs of the others.

Maura's legs felt like slender twigs, straining to hold her upright. And the great open space around her suddenly seemed lacking in air.

She told herself not to be foolish. Why should she care what became of a man she had wanted to hate until a few moments ago? Just because he'd resisted the urge to harm her, then come to her aid when someone else had tried?

Even that did not explain the sense of loss that engulfed her.

It was all over by the time he rode back.

Part of Rath rejoiced at the destruction of the death-mages. A vital path to Aldwood now lay open for his army. Besides that, he hoped the loss of so many Echtroi might make the Han hesitate before attacking Vang's stronghold, thus buying him some desperately needed time.

But his satisfaction was tainted with regret, as well. He had come to believe in the way of the Giver enough that he could not exult in the taking of life—not even of his worst enemies. Besides that, he felt a vague sense of waste. These had once been men of power and ability. What might they have accomplished in the service of some better cause? Now they would never have that chance.

"Gather up those wands!" he ordered the men who had done the grim deed. "Take them to Aldwood Castle for safe-keeping. I do not want them falling back into enemy hands."

Though these rebel fighters would not recognize him without his trappings of the Waiting King, they responded to his air of authority and quickly obeyed his orders.

Rath leaped from his saddle and knelt beside the death-mage whose gaunt hand still gripped the green wand with fierce will. Though he did not appear to be bleeding much, he had neither pulse nor breath. Rath pried the wand from his cold fingers, then closed his unseeing eyes with a gentle touch.

This man embodied all the cruel domination of his people…and yet… If not for him, Maura would never have been. Rath had neither the time nor the wisdom to cipher the complicated riddle of his feelings.

Hefting the body up, he found it surprisingly light for its size, as if it had never been a whole man at all, but only a hollow shell of one. He slung it over the back of his horse, which he towed back toward the spot where he'd left Maura. She darted out of the woods when she saw him coming.

"I'm sorry." Rath nodded toward the body. "I was too late. If you don't want to bother about him, I can—"

"No!" Maura's face betrayed some of the contrary feelings that battled within her. "I don't *want* to…but I owe him something."

"I know." Rath lifted the body off the horse's back to his own shoulder then set off into the woods.

Not far in, he found a flat grassy spot that was strangely quiet. There he laid down his burden.

"You'll need water." He handed Maura his drink skin.

Whether or not he agreed with what she was about to do, it would keep her off the battlefield. That might be the third best service this death-mage had ever done.

Rath gathered Maura into a swift embrace, pressing a kiss to her furrowed brow. "I'll come looking for you once we get our forces under cover. For now I must go find Delyon. If only I'd known…"

His voice trailed off, but she replied with a brief nod of understanding and reassurance. "Go. But be careful."

She glanced toward the long, black-robed form on the grass. "If I ever had to do this for you…"

The ache in her words brought a lump to Rath's throat. He'd

had to do this for her once, though the Giver had granted them another chance. There was a limit to how many such chances a body could hope for.

"Don't fret about me. I've spent my whole life wriggling out of tight spots." Still, it was not easy for him to let go of her, stride back through the trees and climb into his saddle to re-join the battle.

What he found there heartened him. The fall of the death-mages seemed to have inspired the rebels. Most of the Hanish riders had been taken down or driven off and the ragtag army now streamed toward the welcoming arms of Aldwood as night began to spread its protective cloak over them.

But far too many of his men staggered toward the forest, hauling wounded or slain comrades with them. Each one Rath passed gave his heart a pang. He wished he had Idrygon's de-tachment to think of them as nothing more than pieces to move in a game. But to him they were comrades who'd placed their faith in him—trusting him to make their blighted dream of freedom come true.

How would he live with himself if he let them down? Even if he died trying, he was not certain he would find peace in the afterworld if he failed his people.

"Wolf!" a familiar voice hailed him. "Leave it to you to show up when there's trouble afoot."

"Anulf!" Rath reined his horse to a halt and scrambled down. "I heard you were here making a nuisance of yourself. And Odger, too. The Han will be shaking in their iron boots!"

A chuckle caught in his throat when he spotted a wounded man slumped between them. "Theto?"

Anulf shook his head. "A farmer from a ways north. A good fellow, but he should never have got caught up in all this—him with a pretty wife and a fine family back home."

"Newlyn?" Rath fumbled at the farmer's throat for a pulse then let out a shaky sigh of relief when he found it.

"Aye, that's his name." Anulf pulled on Newlyn's arm to

bring it tighter around his shoulder. "Friend of the lady's. Shame she couldn't have talked some sense into him."

"Is he bad?"

"Not good. Lost some blood. I bound it the best I could, but…"

Then from up on the ridge Rath thought he heard someone call out, "The king!"

Oddly, he didn't feel strange that they meant someone other than him. But he didn't like the tone of the call—it sounded like trouble.

"Take Newlyn over that way." Rath pointed toward the western edge of the forest. "Maura's there. She will help him, if anyone can."

With that he remounted. "I must go to the king's aid."

"Watch your back, Wolf!" Anulf called after him. "I want a pint with you after all this ruckus settles down!"

"So do I!" In spite of all that weighed on his mind, Rath laughed. "If you're buying!"

He threaded his mount through the shadowy throng making their way toward the forest. Once he reached the edge of the crowd he was able to make better speed up the slope. What he saw when he reached the crest made him want to turn and race for Aldwood with the rest.

The setting sun had fallen below the barrier of clouds, but not yet disappeared behind the peaks of the Blood Moon Mountains. Now its dying rays reached out to glint off Hanish armor. Rank upon rank upon rank of it.

Rath hadn't thought there could be this many soldiers in the whole empire! In a massed battle, the rebels would be overrun and butchered. Given how fast the Han were coming, Umbrian stragglers were in danger of being overrun before they got up the hill, let alone down to Aldwood itself.

Rath rode up to a mounted Vestan soldier paused at the crest of the ridge. "The king—where is he?"

"There." The fellow pointed. "In a bit of trouble, I reckon.

I'd go to him but Lord Idrygon ordered me to stay here and keep these men moving."

Gazing into the distance, Rath squinted against the glare from the Hanish armor. He thought he could pick out one figure larger than the rest.

"Not that the likes of us would be much use to a great hero like him," said the Vestan.

"Oh, he needs us, all right." Rath gave his horse a nudge to head down the far slope. "Nobody's that great a hero."

His entrails tied themselves in knots as he rode toward the Han. He had told Delyon to keep as far away as possible from his brother. Clearly he should have told the young scholar to give the Han a wide berth, too.

The ragged rear of the rebel force seethed with chaos. Teams of riders grabbed the hindmost marchers and carried them farther up the slope before coming back for their next load. Vestan archers covered the disorderly retreat, firing arrows to discourage the boldest of the pursuing Han from drawing any closer. An answering hail of arrows fell like lethal rain upon the rebels, now and then finding a target. The heath was littered with bits of gear men had cast off to make better speed.

Here and there, parties of horsemen burst from the Hanish ranks to make swift, violent strikes against the fleeing Umbrians. Each time they were beaten back by rebel riders, including one giant warrior who scattered the Han with every plunge of his massive mount and every swipe of his huge sword. Rath hoped the enemy did not guess what he did—that Delyon was having trouble controlling both the beast and the blade.

A qualm of shame gripped him for having put the young scholar into a dangerous situation for which he was unprepared. He spurred his horse toward Delyon. The next while passed in a desperate, darkening blur as he helped fend off a series of attacks and herd the last remnant of his army toward the temporary safety of the forest.

By the time they reached sight of Aldwood, most of the

clouds had blown away and the moon had risen, nearly full. That silvery white moon was the rebels' heavenly ally, shining off the armored Han to make them easy targets for bow fire. Meanwhile, their shadowy leather-clad foes slipped with ease into the friendly darkness of the wood.

Rath feared the Han might pursue his men into Aldwood, in spite of the dark and their distaste for forests. To his vast relief, they stopped and withdrew out of bow range. Their commanders must have decided to wait until morning when they could see to attack and savor their victory.

Would the time that bought for the rebels be enough for them to recover the magical staff? And if it did, what manner of wish should Rath make with it to gain his people's freedom? After all, he would only get one chance.

Maura stared down at the still, silent figure shrouded in black that lay on the grass in that tiny glade. The drink skin in her hand felt as heavy as a brimming wooden bucket from the well behind Langbard's cottage. Could she bring herself to do what part of her felt she must?

To perform the ritual of passing on a man who had lived his whole life in opposition to the Precepts of the Giver seemed like a violation of those sacred teachings. And how could she stand to share the memories and experiences he had collected during his life? She would rather bathe in a festering bog or eat the contents of a hog troth! It felt obscene to undertake so intimate a connection with someone she had never known or wanted to know.

And yet…she could not deny the subtle tingle of curiosity to learn how he and her mother had come together and what had passed between them. Taken by itself, that would not have been enough to make her do this.

But her spirit had once been where his might be now. And if he had gone to that place of endless, crushing, suffocating darkness, it was because he had come to her aid. Besides that, no matter how much she might resist the idea, his blood flowed in her. If he remained forever a mystery to her, then part of her would be forever incomplete.

Maura knelt beside him and drew back the black hood that hid his humanity. She let out a gasp at the sight of his face— so gaunt and hairless. Even in death, his features did not look peaceful.

Taking the stopper from Rath's drink skin, she dabbed a little water on the death-mage's hands and lips and brow, all the while chanting the ritual words. Was there enough water in the whole Sea of Dawn to purify *his* thoughts, words and actions?

Reluctantly she let her spirit rove, searching for him. Calling. Would she be able to reach him? she wondered when she received no answer. Rath had almost not been able to find her when he'd tried.

Then she sensed a presence, the way she had sensed Langbard's during his passing ritual.

"Where are we?" he asked. "Why are you here?"

"I do not know what this place is." How could she explain to him, when she barely understood, herself? "But I may be able to put you on the path to the afterworld, if you are willing."

"The afterworld? Dareth told me about it and about your Giver. I doubt I would be welcome there."

Something about his apprehension stirred her sympathy a little, but she did not want to feel that for him. Curiosity and obligation were difficult enough.

"Would you rather stay here?"

"No," he replied at last, with an air of uncertainty that seemed foreign to him. "It feels too much like the life I left behind. I have left it behind, have I?"

"I reckon so."

"Then take me where you will. But first will you tell me one thing?"

"If I can."

"Were you in Venard a week ago? In the High Governor's palace?"

"Yes. That was me you saw. I followed you afterward and heard the things you said about my mother. That was how I guessed…"

Maura sensed his relief. Did it matter so much, now that he was dead, whether or not he had been going mad?

She sought to answer his unspoken bewilderment. "The spirit and the mind are not the same, you know. Langbard taught me that all ailments of mind and body stay behind when the spirit is freed of them."

"Langbard?"

"My guardian. The man my mother entrusted to raise me when she died."

"And when was that?"

"Before I was a year old." She was growing impatient with his interrogation. She could not afford to linger here for hours on end. "You said only one question."

"So I did." There was an air of apology in his reply, but he did not entreat her pardon. Perhaps it was something the Han considered a sign of the weakness they dreaded so much.

"Come, then." She had only to form the intent and she felt herself moving, drawing the death-mage with her.

As had happened during Langbard's ritual of passing, his memories cascaded through her mind.

She saw his childhood, different from other Hanish boys, for he had been raised by his own mother, a stern but doting widow. Because he was an only child and often ailing, she'd indulged and protected him, sometimes even seeking forbidden Umbrian remedies. Though not robust, the boy had been clever and strong-willed. When he was old enough, he'd been sent to train as a death-mage. He had thrived on the challenge of mastering the powerful dark forces of mortcraft, but he had also been clever enough to sometimes question the ways of his people. Those questions had never found satisfactory answers until one spring when he'd been sent to help put down a rebellion brewing on the northern isle of Tarsh. There he had captured Dareth Woodbury and she had captured his heart.

While taking her back to Venard as his prisoner, their party had been attacked by outlaws and they alone had escaped. Lost in the wild lands of the north, they reluctantly came to rely on one another. Reliance had blossomed into comradeship and she'd told him many things about her people and their ways. Things that intensified his questions and doubts about the way of the Han.

As summer ripened the wild beauty of the northlands, their comradeship had ripened into desire more potent and frightening than any feeling he'd ever known. The harder they had tried to resist it, the hotter and sweeter the flame had burned, until finally it had consumed them.

Hard as she tried, Maura could not remain aloof from the feelings that charged those memories. For she, too, had once burned with forbidden desire.

By the time the captor and prisoner had reached a more settled part of the country, they were both captives of their newfound passion—or so he'd thought. When she fled from him one summer night, the love he'd felt for her became a measure of his bitter betrayal. Certain she had willfully seduced him so she could escape, he had taken out his rage against Dareth on her people, especially those who wished to destroy his.

The next flood of memories left Maura shaken and revolted. She might have deserted him there, had she not sensed that every act of violence and torture he committed had rebounded to warp him in painful ways. Ambition, though a constant mistress, had also been a greedy and demanding one.

As his memories grew more recent, Maura saw his fellow Echtroi respond with derision to reports that some young woman in an obscure part of the country might pose a threat to their power. He alone had paid heed, for he remembered stories he'd once been told of the Destined Queen. And he knew the havoc one young woman had wreaked upon his life and his heart. His power grew as it became clear he'd been right to take the threat seriously. Yet the pressure upon him increased when Maura eluded his grasp and her threat to the Han continued to grow.

Then, at the summit of his power, he'd seen what he thought was a vision of Dareth Woodbury. His long-denied love and his long-buried doubts had risen to haunt him with the fear that he might be losing his mind. A lifetime of questioning and inner conflict had crystallized under the pressure of battle when he'd seen Maura and heard her call him father. When a fellow death-mage had turned his wand upon her, he had to intervene—even knowing what it might cost him.

After all she'd learned about her father, Maura had hoped it would help her make sense of her perplexing feelings for him. But it had only left her more confused.

"From here," she said, "you must continue alone. I have to go back."

A familiar, beloved voice replied, "Perhaps I can conduct him the rest of the way."

"Langbard!" Maura could not feel his arms physically about her, but comforting, cherished emotions embraced her. "I have missed you so!"

"And I you, dearest girl. It is one of the few clouds that shadows our contentment here—longing for those we have loved and left behind."

"There's so much I want to tell you." She clung to him even though she could feel him already slipping beyond her reach. "So much wise counsel I need from you."

"It is there within you, Maura. What could I tell you in a few moments that I did not show you during all the years we shared?"

Her old impatience with his riddling advice flickered once more. "You might tell me how to get the Staff of Velorken from its hiding place, for a start!"

Langbard chuckled. "But that would be a long story, I fear, and an old one. I have faith you will find the answer. Farewell, dearest child."

Her heart ached with an echo of the old bereft feelings that had overwhelmed her at the time of his passing.

"Now—" Langbard prompted his sworn foe in a tone of gentle impatience "—is there not something you wish to say before we take our leave?"

In the hesitation that followed, Maura sensed a fierce struggle, followed by a difficult but welcome surrender. "Farewell, dearest child."

Before she could reply, Maura felt herself slipping away from them. The last thing she heard—or perhaps she only imagined it—was Langbard's murmur, "Come along. There is someone waiting who is anxious to meet you again."

When she opened her eyes to find her wandering spirit returned to her body, night had wrapped around the tiny glade. Somehow, it softened the stark outline of the death-mage's robes, making him look less monstrous and more human.

Her obligation dispensed, if not her confusion, she rose to head for Aldwood Castle. She only got a few steps, when a bewildering compulsion overcame her. She turned back and pressed her lips to the death-mage's brow. "Farewell, Father."

When she rose to depart again, an elusive feeling of peace and renewed confidence stole over her.

As Rath led his horse through the trees toward Aldwood Castle, he could sense the contradictory mood of his army by the murmur of voices around him.

Some sounded jubilant—delighted and relieved to have reached the shelter of the forest and trusting in the Waiting King to bring them victory tomorrow.

Others were beginning to doubt.

For the first time since the Waiting King had landed at Duskport, his army had faced a true challenge. And they had been forced to flee in retreat. Friends and comrades had fallen in battle and all the magic of the Waiting King had not been able to prevent it. What awesome powers did he possess anyway, and when was he going to summon them to defeat the Han once and for all?

Their king could not help feeling greater respect and sympathy for the doubters.

"Rath!" Maura dived out of the crowd, almost bowling him over with the force of her greeting. "Thank the Giver you're all right!"

"And you, *aira*." He wrapped one arm around her shoulders. "After I left you, I worried you were too near the edge of the wood. You weren't bothered, were you?"

She shook her head. "Not in the way you mean."

"Did Anulf bring Newlyn to you?"

"Aye. I'm glad he found me. I dosed Newlyn well with summerslip and rebound his open wounds with a poultice." She glanced around at the men making their way toward the castle, their paths through the trees lit by a few torches and lanterns. "He should be all right."

Perhaps he would. Provided the Han did not overrun Aldwood tomorrow and cart him back to the mines he'd escaped once but could never hope to a second time.

Loud cheers rang out behind them, driving that woeful thought from Rath's mind. A crowd of faster-moving rebels surged forward, pushing aside everyone in their path. As they swept by, Rath saw a large figure in their midst, waving to acknowledge their cheers.

"All hail King Elzaban!"

"The Waiting King kept the Han from catching us!"

"He'll give them a taste of battle tomorrow!"

Hundreds of similar cries swelled into one loud, exultant chorus.

Maura glanced at Rath with a twinkle of mischief in her eyes. "Do you grudge Delyon getting the glory that is rightfully yours?"

He shook his head and meant it. Delyon deserved their cheers. The young scholar had done well to fill a difficult role never intended for him. Rath only wished *he* could have been an ordinary foot soldier—ready to take his part and follow orders, but not carry responsibility for the victory or defeat of their whole cause.

Ahead of them, Aldwood Castle loomed among the trees. Warm light spilled from its narrow windows and arrow slots. Its ancient stones echoing with the ring of more voices than had been heard within its walls for centuries. The crowd surrounding King Elzaban had disappeared through the front gate, taking its joyous din with it. Now the woodland beyond the castle walls seemed almost quiet, though many rebel warriors still moved beneath the trees and through the underbrush.

Maura glanced toward the night sky where a swath of stars twinkled through a gap in the foliage. "Praise the Giver night fell when it did, otherwise…"

Her words collided in Rath's mind with his recent glimpse of Delyon.

"Slag!" He slammed the horse's reins into her hand. "Find a place for him, will you? There's something I must do!"

He raced toward the castle, dodging men, pushing them out of the way. "Pardon! Let me by. Urgent matter for the king!"

He reached a large courtyard thronged with rebels. Their noise was nearly deafening as it echoed off the stone walls. At least it still sounded of good cheer—that was a blessing. If he could reach Delyon in time and drag him out of sight before the growth potion wore off…

Fie! Rath had waded through waist-deep snow with greater speed than he was able to make through this crowd. With each passing moment he grew more desperate and less restrained. He gouged with his elbows, trod on feet, growled blood-chilling threats—anything to bring him within reach of Delyon. He was almost there when the tenor of the crowd changed. Suddenly a hollow hush fell, followed by an ominous buzz.

As the men in front of Rath turned to whisper the news to those behind them, he was able to slip through. At last he reached Delyon, throwing himself in front of the young man in a vain effort to shield him from the horrified stares of the other rebels.

Within the massive armor of the Waiting King, Delyon had shrunk until it looked as if he might melt away altogether. A moment later, Idrygon strode through a nearby doorway.

"What is all this?" he cried, glaring at Rath and his brother.

Delyon pulled off his oversize helmet.

"Say," cried a man standing near, pointing at Delyon, "that fellow's never the Waiting King!" His accusing finger jabbed in Rath's direction. "He is…leastways he *was*."

At that moment, Rath would have given anything to be able to deny the charge.

"How could you jeopardize everything we have worked and fought for with a daft prank like this?" In a small inner chamber of Aldwood Castle, Idrygon glared at his brother and Rath. He'd hustled them there after Delyon's disguise had been exposed.

"It was no prank!" Rath stepped between the two brothers to bear the brunt of Idrygon's reproach. This had been his idea and Delyon a barely willing accomplice. "It was done to *preserve* what we have worked and fought for. You would not listen to reason, which left me no choice but to act in stealth. If I'd known the Han would come so close to catching us on the march to Aldwood, I might have done differently."

He considered for an instant. "On second thought, I would not. If Vang and his men had not come to our aid as they did, our cause would now lay dying out on the heath!"

"We are in a sorry pass if we need to call on allies of that sort." Idrygon shot a withering glance at Vang, who stood in the corner scowling at all of them.

Was the bandit chief having second thoughts about throwing his support to a doomed cause?

"Watch who you insult, fancy boy," he snarled. "You are a guest in my stronghold. And no more welcome than a musk-pig. Keep lipping off like that and I'll make the Han a present of your fine head."

"Try me, ox." Idrygon slid his blade a few inches out of its sheath. "When I'm done carving you up, you'll only be good for feeding our enemy's hounds. And even they might turn up their snouts at such foul meat."

Vang whipped out a long knife with extra blades bristling from the wrist guard. "We'll see which of us gets made into dog meat, islander!"

Rath feared it might be him, as he leaped between the two men. "Enough, you fools! Would you do the work of the Han for them? Bad as things may look now, they will only get worse if we lose either of you—or both."

Was this what it would mean to be king? he wondered. Spending all his time trying to keep hostile factions from each other's throats? Trying to forge a united kingdom from a handful of insular regions whose folk neither respected nor trusted one another—only to end up being resented by them all? It was not the way he wanted to spend his life.

But what other choice was there? Steal away and leave the Han to continue their brutal occupation? They would tighten their hold even worse in the wake of this uprising.

"Vang—" he pushed the bandit chief back toward the corner "—your choice to support the rebellion may have meant the difference between success and slaughter. I will not forget what I owe you and your men."

Though he shot Idrygon a menacing scowl over Rath's shoulder, Vang did back off. "*You* will not forget? Is this daft talk true, then? Have you been playing the king all this time?"

"Not playing." If only that's all it were. Suddenly Rath felt so tired he could sleep for a month. "By some ancient enchantment even I do not understand, I *am* the Waiting King."

He gestured toward Maura who stood quiet and thoughtful

in the opposite corner of the room. "And this is the Destined Queen who woke me. Together, I still believe we can liberate the kingdom as the old stories foretold—but we cannot do it alone. We have been blessed in our allies. Without Idrygon's foresight and planning, the rebellion would never have reached this point of open battle for our freedom. Without Vang's intervention at a key moment, all the effort that went before would have come to nothing."

Maura strode from her place in the corner to stand beside him. "Without Rath's leadership, the people of Umbria would never have risen to fight for their freedom. And without his persuasion, we would only have gained the refuge of the forest at a cost in blood we could ill afford. He needs your help now as much as he did on the battlefield. Will you come to his aid or will you betray him?"

"Treachery is not my way," growled Vang, who looked like an overgrown, disfigured child being unfairly scolded. "Any enemy of mine will know I am his enemy and expect no mercy. My sworn ally can count on my loyalty come what may." He thrust out his chin, directing a challenging look at Idrygon. "Can you make such a boast, my fine islander?"

"Do you question the honor of the House of Idrygon, filthy outlaw?"

"He does not!" cried Rath. "And neither should you question his. If I hear one more word of an insult from either of you, I will knock your heads together until your thick skulls soften enough to heed reason! Now, let us all put our minds to the problem before us."

"I hear men are deserting us in droves," said Idrygon, as if Rath's threat could not possibly apply to him. "They have seen the massed might of the Han and they have lost faith in the Waiting King. They are slipping off through the woods, looking for unguarded spots from which to make their way back home."

He gave Maura a look of grave mistrust. "Unless you have

taken possession of the talisman, we will be overrun whenever the Han choose to attack."

"The staff, you mean." Vang made a show of sheathing his knife.

"How does this scound—?" A warning glare from Rath tempered Idrygon's tone. "How does he know about the staff?"

Instead of trading more insults, Vang replied with a mysterious, insolent chuckle that left Idrygon sputtering with fury.

Suddenly, Maura surged up on her toes and whispered in Rath's ear. He listened, torn between a desperate need to hope and a fear of hoping too much.

When she finished speaking, Rath nodded, then glanced at Delyon, clad in an assortment of borrowed garments. "Go with her. If anyone can help her now, it is you."

"What was that about?" demanded Idrygon when his brother and Maura had departed.

"An answer to your question, of sorts," said Rath. "The staff is here, but protected by powerful enchantment. Maura will need all the time we can buy her, and even that may not be enough. We must prepare to repel an attack on Aldwood if necessary and hold out for as long as possible."

He turned to Vang. "Is there a high point in the castle where I might be seen and heard by the greatest number of my men?"

Vang thought for a moment. "The north tower has a balcony that looks out over the great courtyard."

"Good. Take me there."

"Not good." Vang shook his head. "Parts of that tower are ready to tumble down any moment. I've had more sense than ever to go up there."

Rath shrugged. "I am not asking *you* to go. And if that tower falls with me in it, you and Idrygon may battle one another to the death, with my blessing."

Vang looked as if he might relish that prospect. "It is your neck, Wolf. Never say I did not warn you. If you are fool enough to climb up that tottering pile of stones, I will show you where to find it."

"Lead on." Rath plucked a flaming brand from one of the wall sconces.

"What do you mean to do?" Idrygon did not appear disposed to approve whatever it might be.

But Rath was done with asking Idrygon's permission. If he was going to be king, it was long past time he started acting like one. "Something I should have done a while ago. If I had, we might not be in this pass now."

Before Idrygon could argue him out of his plan, Rath set off after the bandit chief.

By the time they jostled their way through the crowd to the base of the north tower, he had managed to seize a second torch. He wished he could get his hands on that potion of Dame Diotta's to make his voice carry, but there was no time to search the supply wagons now. He would just have to hope the tower's height and perhaps a little aid from the Giver might help his words reach the ears of as many rebels as possible.

Vang unbarred the door. "Watch yourself on those steps, and on that balcony. I wouldn't trust my weight on either, and it's a long way down."

Keeping Vang's warning in mind, Rath picked his way up the steep spiral stairs that wound their way up the inner wall of the tower. It would have been an easier climb if he were not toting a flaming torch in each hand, but there was no help for it. Once he reached the top, he needed to be seen by the men below.

Halfway up, part of the stair crumbled under his weight and he nearly lost his balance. Somehow, he managed to recover it without dropping either of the torches. The rest of the way up, he climbed even more slowly, testing each step with his foot before committing his full weight to it.

At last he reached the top of the tower. Part of the narrow balcony had crumbled away and the rest looked as if it would not be long to follow. There was a small blessing though—or rather two. On either side of the archway that opened onto the balcony were stone brackets in which Rath secured his torches.

Then he looked down into the courtyard below. A few faces were turned upward, their gazes drawn by the lights, no doubt. Most were paying him no heed, but talking among themselves in a steady rumble his voice alone could not hope to penetrate.

"Comrades!" he cried. The noise below did not lessen and no more faces turned toward him. In fact, some that had been now turned away.

Rath muttered a curse, then pulled his lips taut between his outstretched fingers and blew a long, loud, piercing whistle. A heavy hush fell over the crowd below. Rath sensed suspicion and hostility in that silence.

One voice rang out through the shadows. "Who's up there?"

While Rath searched for the right reply, someone else answered in a challenging tone, "Him what's been playing king all these weeks."

"The Waiting King!" shouted someone else. "Naught but sorcerers' tricks, that. He played us for fools and led us into a death trap!"

A grumble of agreement rippled through the crowd.

"Quit yammering!" ordered someone in a tone of harsh authority that sounded like Vang Spear of Heaven. "Let the fellow answer for himself."

Before he lost another opportunity, Rath sent a silent plea for inspiration winging to the Giver and began to speak.

"Comrades, I swear to you, I *am* the Waiting King, though there have been times I've doubted it as much as you do now."

Like a subtle shift in the wind, he felt the mood of the crowd alter, becoming a trifle more receptive. Suddenly, words welled up inside him and he knew he must seize his chance.

"I am not some drowsing king of old who knows nothing of your lives and troubles. I have delved in the mines. I have sweated and trembled for a sniff of slag. I have done a good many shameful things to keep myself alive. But I have also discovered the hero buried inside that outlaw. I believe there are sleeping heroes inside each one of you, no matter how you have lived before. The time has come to wake those heroes!"

A few shouts of agreement greeted his words. Rath thought he recognized the voices of Anulf and Odger among them.

"When dawn comes and the enemy attacks, will you stand and fight?" he challenged them. "Will you be heroes?"

A great surge of cheers and whistles burst on the night air.

Then, like an echo, a wave of noise answered from beyond the forest—the harsh jangle of metal blades beating against metal shields.

Delyon stared in horror at the metal axes, picks and saws rusting on the floor of the huge underground chamber in the skeletal grasp of long-dead hands. "It seems we are not the first who have tried to claim the staff. A dangerous business."

"So it is, gone about the wrong way." Maura hoped her guess was right. She did not want to end up as another pile of bones on this floor warning off future searchers.

Would another Destined Queen come here someday if she failed? Maura pushed the thought from her mind. She must not fail! Not after all she had gone through to reach this night and this place.

"When I was a child, Langbard told me all kinds of stories about Lord Velorken." She ran her hand over the rough, un-marked bark of the nearest tree-trunk pillar. "I recall one where Velorken was trapped in an enchanted forest. The harder he tried to cut down the trees that surrounded him, the denser they grew until his ax blunted."

"And he became weaker with each stroke." Delyon began to walk between the great pillars, taking care to avoid the piles of bones. "My grandmother told that old story to Idrygon and me when we were boys."

"Do you reckon it holds a clue to help us claim the staff?" asked Maura.

Delyon gave a slow nod. "It is as likely as anything. But I forget how Velorken escaped that forest prison."

Maura searched her memory. "Did he not climb the tallest tree, then crawl from branch to branch until he reached the edge of the wood?"

"That's right." Delyon's gaze traveled up the pillar beside him. "Idrygon always hated that story because force did not solve Velorken's problem."

Maura could believe that.

"But what are you suggesting?" Delyon shook his head. "That we climb one of these pillars? For all they look like tree trunks, they have no branches to provide hand- or footholds. And even if we climbed them to the top, it would only take us to the ceiling."

"True." Maura pulled off her walking boots and stockings. "But while you are thinking of a better plan, I mean to give this a try. We have nothing to lose. Come, give me a boost."

"Perhaps there is some incantation?" Delyon suggested as he came and stood behind her.

Maura kilted up her gown around her knees. "If you can think of one that might work, by all means start chanting."

In her own mind, a simple litany ran over and over—*Please, Giver, I need your help. Only show me what to do and I will do it.*

Delyon grasped her around the waist and lifted. Maura scrambled desperately for a hand or toehold in the rough bark, but found none. Perhaps Delyon was right—this was a daft idea.

"It will take you forever to reach the top at this rate." Delyon sounded breathless. "You're heavier than you look, lass. Can I let you down?"

"Aye." Maura tried not to think about all the rebels who might be buying her time to search for the staff at the price of their lives.

Delyon let go of her…but she did not sink back to the floor.

The tree bark that had blunted saws and axes somehow gave way to the gentle pressure of her fingers and toes, permitting her a fragile hold.

"How are you hanging on there?" asked Delyon.

"I'm not sure." Maura reached up with one hand and pressed it into the bark.

Slowly it shrank from the gentle, steady pressure of her fingers, forming a shallow cavity for her to grip. The same thing happened when she lifted her right foot and pressed her bare toes against the bark. She could not move quickly—only one arm or leg at a time—because she needed the other three to cling. But at least she could move. Moreover, the baffling enchantment that allowed her to climb was like a nod of approval from the Giver.

She made steady progress for some time, until she made the mistake of glancing down. Her head spun and her breath stuck in her throat. It was no Raynor's Rift, perhaps, but the hard floor of the chamber still seemed perilously far beneath her. Especially given her tenuous grip on the pillar. What was to stop the bark that had yielded to her touch from springing back out again, hurling her down?

For a moment she stopped, pressing her body to the pillar and squeezing her eyes as tight as they would shut. She struggled to slow her breathing. Then she opened her eyes, fixing them on bark in front of her, as if the force of her gaze might provide some extra grip. With grim resolve, she began to climb again.

A while later she startled and almost fell when Delyon gave a cry of alarm. "Please don't do that!" she called down to him. "What's the matter?"

"Y-your hand. It's disappeared into the ceiling!"

Maura glanced up. Sure enough, her arm looked as if it had been neatly severed just below the elbow. But she could feel her fingers burrowed into something above the solid-looking ceiling.

When she let go and lowered her arm, the rest of it appeared again, looking none the worse. "The ceiling must be an illusion."

A little more cautiously, now that she could see what she was doing, Maura thrust her hand back up and felt around for her grip. After bringing her feet each a step higher, she poked her head through the ceiling. A gentle breeze whispered through her hair and the high vault of the sky stretched above her, glowing with the soft pearly hue of dawn.

All around her, the tall trees that had grown from the floor of the chamber now stretched thick, leafy boughs that wove together, creating a lush green carpet. Grabbing one of the branches, she hauled herself up and gazed around in wonder.

"This isn't possible," she whispered. The chamber below was far underground. Even if she had climbed to ground level, she should be in some part of the castle. "But that doesn't matter, I suppose. As long as I find the staff."

No sooner had the thought formed in her mind than she could see a spot where some of the trees grew even taller than the others, creating an arbor like the Oracle of Margyle's.

Maura crawled toward it, groping to make certain her hands and knees had a solid spot to rest on before moving forward. She did not want to fall through the canopy onto one of those rusted ax heads. Somehow, the delicate weft of leaves and branches always felt solid beneath her.

Her need for haste overcame her caution. Staggering to her feet, she began walking toward the arbor. Her first few steps were hesitant, but soon she gained confidence. By the time she reached the arbor, she was beginning to wonder if she would be able to climb back down through the canopy again.

"Surely if the Giver has brought me this far," she whispered to herself, "I will be able to get the rest of the way."

This arbor was a little different than the Oracle's, Maura realized. Instead of being open at the sides, it had living draperies of vines falling from the roof to create walls. Gently pushing aside one bank of vines, she entered the structure.

In the center of it, resting on a low platform, lay the Staff of Velorken, just as she had seen it in her memory vision. Maura marveled at its beauty and at the aura of power and enchantment that surrounded it. Most of its length was a rich ruddy wood carved with long swirling tendrils of leaves. The top of the staff was a great hawk's head carved from dark ivory.

A pair of tawny gemstones gleamed as its eyes. The bird looked so real, Maura half expected it to open its beak and give a loud, shrill cry.

"I'm sorry to disturb you." She lifted the staff from its resting place, surprised to find it much lighter than she expected. "But our need is great."

She made her way back to the spot through which she had climbed. Holding tight to a branch, she dipped her head through the canopy and called Delyon. "Can you reach this if I pass it down to you?"

She began to lower the staff.

Delyon dashed to the base of the pillar and extended his arm. "I will try, Highness. If it is long enough."

Maura doubted it would reach all that distance, but before her fingers came in contact with the ivory hawk's head, she felt a tug at the bottom and heard Delyon say, "I've got it! I cannot believe this. I am touching the Staff of Velorken."

Her sense of urgency swamped her sense of wonder. Maura let the staff drop into Delyon's reverent hands, then she descended the pillar, half climbing, half sliding. Grabbing the staff back from him, she set off through the dim maze of passageways beneath the castle. Hope and confidence radiated through her with every breath and every pulse of her heart.

As she burst up to ground level, a ruddy glow in the east warned her dawn had come. A more ominous sound also heralded the sunrise. From beyond the edge of forest came the roar of combat.

Where was Rath? As Maura's gaze swept the courtyard, Songrid raced toward her.

Before the Hanish woman could speak, Maura asked, "How long has the battle been going on?"

"Not long. Just since first light."

"My husband—where can I find him?"

Songrid pointed toward the great hall. "That way. He and Lord Idrygon were—"

Maura did not stay to hear the rest. She raced to the great hall and found it deserted except for Rath and Idrygon.

"You see?" Idrygon cried when he saw the staff in her hand. "I told you not to risk joining in the fray while there was any hope of the staff coming to us."

Something compelled Maura to drop to one knee as she held out the staff to Rath. He stared at it with a look of aversion, as if she were offering him a death-mage's wand. After an instant's hesitation he reached out and took it from her.

"Quickly," urged Idrygon. "Make our wish. Wish death on the Han! Not only the ones on our shores, mind—*all* of them. That is the only way we can insure our freedom."

A cry of protest rose to Maura's lips, but Rath beat her to it. "Are you mad? How can I bring about the destruction of a whole race?"

"If it is your wife you are worried about," said Idrygon with the air of one granting a great concession, "then make it clear you wish death only on full-blooded Han."

Behind her, Maura heard Delyon cry, "What about Songrid and others like her?"

"Aye," said Rath. "Women, elders, infants? I cannot have that kind of slaughter on my conscience!"

"Weren't you once an outlaw?" Idrygon demanded. "Have you never had blood on your hands before?"

"Of course I have—too much of it."

"Surely this will be easier. You need not put your own life at risk. You need not watch them die. At this very moment, the Han are slaying our men. You *must* stop it!"

Rath shook his head. "Not that way."

For a moment, Idrygon looked as if he meant to fly at Rath in a rage. But he managed to control his temper before it burst out. When he spoke again, it was in a tone of persuasive reason. "Do this and I will grant *your* dearest wish, sire."

Rath gave a weary sigh. "Even if I would make such a bargain, you have no idea of my dearest wish."

"I have watched you close enough these past weeks to guess," said Idrygon. "Once this rebellion is over, you do not want the burden of ruling this troubled kingdom. You do not feel equal to the responsibility. You would rather settle down to a simple, peaceful life in some quiet village. Am I right?"

Rath did not answer. He did not need to. The longing in his eyes and the set of his rugged features ached with his true feelings.

"Rid our land of this menace," pleaded Idrygon, "and you need be king in name only. Sign a few documents, make the odd ceremonial appearance. For the rest, you may live as quietly as you please with your family, while I tend to the practical cares of running the kingdom on your behalf."

Rath's gaze sought Maura's. "*Aira,* convince me what I must do. I fear I have not the strength of will."

She knew how this offer must tempt him, for she felt the pull of it on her own will. Idrygon was a born leader, under whose rule the Vestan Islands were a haven of peace and prosperity. More than once since meeting him, Maura had wondered why destiny had not chosen *him* as the Waiting King.

But she had seen another side of Lord Idrygon, also—like the other face of this enticing bargain—ruthless and hungry for power.

"What do you expect her to say?" Idrygon's question crackled with scorn. "Do not forget, she is one of *them.*"

"Mind your tongue!" cried Rath, shaking the staff at him. "Do not goad me to waste my wish on you!"

Idrygon paled and jammed his lips shut, shooting a blistering glare at Maura.

What counsel could she give Rath? Maura asked herself. Idrygon's bargain tempted her as fiercely as it did him, yet the price of it chilled her heart. Her travels had taught her that many Han bore no guilt for the evil their leaders had inflicted upon her people. But if she urged Rath to show mercy, would it be a betrayal of her Umbrian heritage?

"Do not fear to embrace your destiny, *aira*." She ignored Idrygon's murderous scowl. "You may be a better king because of your flawed past. When I fought the Echtroi at Beastmount, I learned that I have the capacity to be a better queen because I do not crave power. I believe the same is true of you. The best leaders are those who would *serve* their people, not dominate them."

"Sire…" Idrygon protested.

"Silence!" cried Rath. "Let her speak."

Perhaps she'd already said too much. Too often since their destinies entwined she had compelled him to follow her lead. But this was no longer her destiny alone. She had no right to take the responsibility and freedom of decision from Rath. Even for the sake of all that hung in the balance, she could not deny him the choice and the chance to be a hero of his own making.

Her next words were some of the most difficult she had ever spoken to him. "The choice must be yours, *aira*. I have faith you will take the right course. Whatever you decide, I promise you my love and support."

"My lords!" One of Vang's men burst into the great hall. "I am bidden to fetch you, now. The Han are trying to set Aldwood ablaze!"

Maura's gaze flew to Rath. She saw his hand tighten around the staff, and she prayed the Giver would guide him.

Idrygon moved so fast, she was not even aware of it until he pulled her toward him, a short blade flashing in his hand. Clearly he did not trust the power of his bribe alone to sway Rath. He must add a threat, as well.

"Do not cross me, outlaw! Or you will be one king without a queen!"

Though Maura knew Idrygon was quite capable of doing what he threatened, a flare of righteous anger seared away her fear. Having struggled with her decision to give Rath a free choice, she would not let anyone take it from him.

Out of the corner of her eye, she saw Delyon rush forward. "Don't do this, brother!"

"Stay out of this, you pious fool!" cried Idrygon, his attention diverted for the instant Maura needed.

"I've made better men than you sorry they grabbed me." She leaped up, driving the crown of her head hard against Idrygon's chin.

He gave a muffled bellow of pain and his grip on her slackened. Maura spun out of his reach while Delyon knocked the blade from his brother's hand.

"Now, Rath!" Maura cried. "Use the staff!"

So much hung on his decision. So many lives on both sides. And he had run out of time to weigh his choice. The only thing Rath knew for certain was that he had neither the ability nor the right to wield such fearful power. Did any man?

Clutching the Staff of Velorken, he made the only wish he could trust, though he could not guess what would come of it. "Giver, let *your* will prevail. That is my wish."

Maura threw her arms around his neck. "I'm so glad I did not sway you. I would never have thought of that. But when I heard you speak, I knew it was right!"

If only he could feel so certain. If only he had felt *something*. A surge of magical power from the staff, perhaps, or some inkling of what his wish had wrought. But Rath knew nothing, felt nothing.

Had he wasted a wish that might have saved his people? Or had the Staff of Velorken been only a hollow myth, luring them to venture the impossible?

"Traitor!" cried Idrygon, diving to recover his fallen blade.

Rath thrust Maura behind him and raised the staff to defend them both.

The instant Idrygon grasped the knife, he let out a scream the likes of which Rath had only heard from victims of the death-mages. He had no time to puzzle what it meant.

He turned to Maura. "Go! As quickly as you can. Take Songrid and make your way out of the forest. Then go south to Prum. Folks there will take care of you."

One last time he kissed her. "I must go to my men and do what I can."

"So must I." Maura clung to his hand with a grip he had not the heart to break. "Let us not waste time arguing."

Fiercely as he yearned to protect her, Rath knew this choice must be *hers*. He acknowledged her words with a grim nod, then they ran from the hall together with Idrygon's howls and curses ringing in their ears.

A deafening chorus of such sounds greeted them when they reached the fringe of Aldwood. Vang Spear of Heaven came striding toward them with a dazed look, as if someone had hit him very hard on the head with something solid.

"What is all that?" Rath hollered to be heard above the din coming from beyond the forest.

"It's the Han." Vang shook his head. "They've all gone clean mad! We were in the midst of the battle when they all threw down their weapons and began stripping off their armor— howling like lankwolves at a full moon. Even the death-mages dropped their wands. No one knows what to make of it."

Rath turned to Maura, torn between contrary urges to laugh and weep. "Do you reckon this could be…"

"…the will of the Giver?" Maura's lips trembled as they curved into an astonished smile.

"One way to find out." Warily, Rath touched the tip of his finger to the hilt of his sheathed knife.

"Slag!" He pulled it back again, shaking it to ease the pain. "It feels like a red-hot coal! That must be why Idrygon dropped his dagger."

Maura rummaged in her sash. "I have some fresh merthorn leaves…"

"It can wait, *aira*. We must act now. Who knows how long this boon of the Giver's may last?"

Rath ran out onto the heath crying orders at the top of his lungs. "Do not touch anything metal! It will burn you. Archers, take to the field and surround the Han! Do not shoot unless they attack you! Bring rope to bind the prisoners!"

It took a moment for his meaning to sink in, then the men nearest him took up the cry, echoing his orders. Rebel archers burst from the cover of the forest, followed by men toting rope, strips of cloth, even bits of harness to secure their prisoners.

Rath and Maura followed. They had gone only a few steps, when a riderless horse trotted up to them and stopped.

"Look at the way it is staring at the staff." Maura ran her hand over the beast's smooth, muscular flank. "Do you reckon it's safe to ride?"

"Only one way to find out." Rath climbed into the saddle while the horse stood quiet. He patted it on the neck, then offered his hand to Maura, who scrambled up behind him.

She gazed over the battlefield where many other beasts were running free. "Why do you suppose the metal bits on their harnesses do not burn the horses?"

Rath shook his head. "I cannot guess, *aira*. Magic has always baffled me."

They rode around the battlefield, where Rath urged his men to show restraint toward the Han. "This is a boon from the Giver! Let us show ourselves worthy of it. Let us strive to live by the Precepts and honor life—even the lives of our enemies."

He glanced back when Maura tapped him on the shoulder.

"Stop and let me down," she bid him. "The herbs in my sash will not go far with such a horde, and they may refuse my help, thinking it weakness, but at least I can offer."

She was right. Most of the Hanish soldiers refused, cursing her, even as they writhed in pain. But shortly after the rebels had secured all their prisoners, a cool shower of rain fell, providing the Han with relief whether they wanted it or not. It also cooled the discarded weapons and armor until they were safe to touch and cart away.

That night, while Aldwood Castle echoed with songs of victory, Rath and Maura slipped away from the celebration to return the Staff of Velorken to its rightful place.

When she slipped down the pillar into his waiting arms, they indulged in a long, tender embrace in which exhaustion and wariness were tempered with profound relief and gratitude.

"What now, *aira*?" she whispered, resting her head against his chest.

Rath leaned back against the pillar. "We must march our prisoners to the coast and put them back on the ships that brought them here."

"Are you not worried they might return to attack us again?"

"Not right away. I doubt even they are warlike enough to mount an invasion without armor or weapons—which I plan to hurl down the deepest shafts of the Blood Moon Mines."

"What of the Han left behind in Westborne?"

"Aye, they must be dealt with, too." Rath looked weary but hopeful. "Without the Giver's help this time. I pray they will not put up too costly a fight."

Before she could ask, he added, "Then there is Idrygon. I do not know where he has disappeared to, or when he may return to plague us again. In truth, I am glad to be rid of him. It would tax my poor wisdom to decide a fitting punishment. We owe him a great debt for all he did to prepare for this rebellion, but that does not excuse other things he did…or tried to do."

Maura sensed there would be many problems in the years ahead to tax Rath's wisdom and his patience. "Are you sorry you did not make a different wish upon the Staff of Velorken, *aira*?"

Rath shook his head as he lifted his hand to stroke her hair. "I doubted I had it in me to be king. But I reckon as long as I strive to be worthy of a queen like you, I cannot go too far wrong."

Epilogue

Venard, one year later

The Council of Citizens listened with interest as Admiral Gull reported on a new fleet of ships under construction in Duskport.

"If the Imperium is daft enough to send troops against us again, they'll be in for a nasty surprise. Until then, and hoping that day never comes, our navy will be fitted for merchant duty between the mainland and the islands."

Gull passed around scrolls with drawings of ship designs and began to speak eagerly of materials, dimensions and rigging.

A warm sense of satisfaction stole over Rath as he listened to Gull and glanced around the chamber at so many familiar and trusted faces. This had been the secret to ease the burden of kingship and temper the unhealthy lure of power—letting his people govern themselves, with him as a kind of overseer and mediator. It was a role he could live with and in which he could find fulfillment.

Not that the past year had been without its challenges. There were still outlaws who would rather prey on others than earn their bread in the many kinds of lawful work opening up around the kingdom. Though Rath had done his best to encourage reconciliation, there had been reprisals against Hanish folk like Songrid who had chosen to remain in Umbria, as well as *zikary* who had collaborated with the Han. There were still folks who braved the dangers of the abandoned mines to harvest and sell slag. Those who were caught could expect no lenience from the king.

Progress was being made, too, Rath reminded himself. Under Maura's patronage, healers and teachers were being trained and equipped. The growing and gathering of herbs was being encouraged. Led by Delyon, a revival of the Elderways was gaining momentum. By the time one of his children was ready to take the throne and give him and Maura a well-deserved rest, Rath expected—

Interrupting that thought, a matron of the royal household slipped into the chamber quietly and whispered a few words in Rath's ear. Immediately he sprang to his feet and followed her out into the gallery.

"Rath!" Delyon slipped out behind them. "Is something wrong? My brother…?"

Rath shook his head. "Still no word of Idrygon. Do not take offense if I say I hope it stays that way. A masterful man, your brother. Not one I ever wanted for an enemy."

"I know. But if not Idrygon, what summons you away from the Council looking so anxious?"

Rath had kept walking as he talked, now his long stride picked up further speed. "One thing that frets me worse than Idrygon or even the Han—the baby is coming!"

"Is that all?" A look of relief spread over Delyon's features. "A joyful occasion, to be sure, the birth of an heir."

"Easy for you to say, my friend." Rath rubbed the damp palms of his hands on his tunic. "Wait until your turn comes!"

Waving farewell, he hurried off toward the family quarters with less than regal haste.

As he entered the birthing chamber, he heard Sorsha Swinley's voice, hearty and capable. "It won't be long now. A few more pangs and I reckon you'll be ready to squeeze that baby right out."

"Not long?" Striding to Maura's side, Rath grasped her hand and cast a reproachful look at Sorsha. "How long has she been laboring? Were you not told to summon me as soon as it started?"

"So you could do what, Highness?" The farm wife gave a vexingly unruffled chuckle. "Hang about and be as much nuisance as most men at a time like this? It has only been a few hours, and for a blessing, it should not go on much longer."

"Do not blame Sorsha," Maura bid Rath in a weary whisper. Her hair curled over the pillow in a damp, ruddy tangle. Her face glowed and so did her eyes. How could he deny her anything when she looked so beautiful, ripe with his child?

"I gave orders you were not to be called until my time was near. In this, a queen's commands overrule even a king's."

"But I wanted to be with you." He knew he could not have done much but worry, yet it seemed wrong that his child's birth should be so close and him not know.

"You are with me now." Maura's features began to tense. "You have a country to run, remember? And I have been in Sorsha's capable hands."

Her tired smile twisted into a grimace.

"Are you in much pain?" Rath nudged a moist curl off her brow.

Her lips were clenched too tight to reply, but she gave him her answer by nearly crushing the bones of his hand in her grip. Once the birth pang passed, she sank back onto the pillow and raised his throbbing fingers to her lips.

"When have you known me to let the fear of pain keep me from what I want?" Maura echoed the words she had spoken to him on the night he'd first claimed her for his own. That had been the happiest day of Rath's life…until now.

There was every bit as much pain in bearing a baby as there was pleasure in breeding it. The thought ran through Maura's mind as she clung to Rath's hand through several more pangs, each longer and harder than the last.

Then Sorsha bid her tuck up her knees and try to push, promising it would not last much longer. It still seemed like a long time to Maura until her baby came squirming and wriggling into the world.

"She looks more like an outlaw than a princess," Rath teased with a look of proud befuddlement on his face when he held his daughter for the first time.

The tiny creature seized his finger. "She has a grip like one, too!"

"Shall we still call her Abrielle, as we planned?" Maura chuckled. "Or would you prefer Ratha…or Vangette. Something with a fierce, outlaw ring?"

"Don't listen to your mother," Rath told the baby as if she could understand him. "Abrielle was a strong woman and clever and brave. It is a fit name for you."

The infant gave a lusty squall.

"I reckon your wee princess is hungry," said Sorsha, who was busy getting Maura clean and comfortable after the birth.

"What is that outlaw saying?" asked Maura as Rath settled her daughter in her arms. "About always eating and drinking when you have the chance?"

She lowered her shift and watched with contentment as the child rooted for her bosom and began to suckle.

A great rumble of noise sounded outside the window.

"What is that?" Maura asked.

"Why, the drums and horns announcing the birth of our heir." Rath pressed a tender kiss to her brow.

How would their subjects feel about the news? Maura wondered. She and Rath had revealed the truth of her parentage and been assured it would not stand in the way of her being queen. Still…a stubborn qualm of doubt lingered in her own mind.

As suddenly as they had begun, the clamor of the horns and drums stopped. Then, after an instant of silence, wave after wave of joyful cheering greeted the news.

"You hear that?" murmured Rath. "They love you both almost as much as I do."

Maura let a few tears fall as she heaved a sweet sigh of fulfillment. She thought back to her crowning ceremony and the sense she'd had that day of her and Rath being wed to their subjects. Now she was a mother, too. Not just of little Abrielle, but of a whole kingdom.

And any fear she might have felt at that great responsibility was swept away by a powerful wave of happiness.

Something is stirring again...

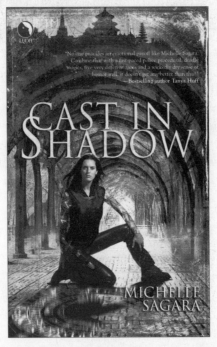

"No one provides an emotional payoff like Michelle Sagara. Combine that with a fast-paced police procedural, deadly magics, five very different races and a wickedly dry sense of humor, well, it doesn't get any better than this!"
—Bestselling author Tanya Huff

CAST IN SHADOW

MICHELLE SAGARA

Seven years ago Kaylin fled the crime-riddled streets of Nightshade, knowing that something was after her. Since then, she's learned to read, fight and has become one of the vaunted Hawks who patrol and police the City of Elantra. But children are once again dying, and a dark and familiar pattern is emerging. Kaylin is ordered back into Nightshade and tasked to find the killer and stop the murders. But can she survive the attentions of those who claim to be her allies along the way?

LUNA™

On sale August.

Visit your local bookseller.

Luna's Night Sky
© Amoreno 2005
www.DuirwaighGallery.com

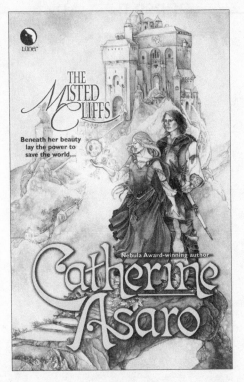

Wren and Sergei team up in the next Retrievers novel, CURSE THE DARK.

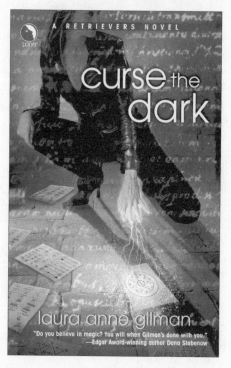

Their newest mission sends them to Italy in search of a possessed parchment (or maybe not possessed—all they know is that whoever reads it disappears). Compared to what's going on at home (lonejacks banding together, a jealous demon, tracking bugs needing fumigations, etc.) maybe disappearing won't be so bad…. As if!

On sale now.
Visit your local bookseller.